A SEASON IN MY LIFE

A Season in My Life

Richard Lawrence

To order additional copies of this book, contact:
Xlibris
1-888-795-4274
www.Xlibris.com
Orders@Xlibris.com
765222

I want to thank Xlibris for all the work they've done to get this book published.

I also want to thank Dayton Cook and all the folks at Inner Spark Creative LLC for their design of the book cover.

I want to thank my best friend Bill Ward and his wife Christina for always being there for me.

Three people no longer with me who were inspirations and pushed me to finish the book. Who preached never give up and left an undeniable mark on my life are: Ford MacElvain, Dorothy Mealy and Mike Dixon. I will never be able to repay their love and friendship.

I also need to thank all the hundreds of players I coached and met on the field. Friendships that I will always remember.

I also want to thank the readers since you're also a big part of the book!

"More spaghetti, Ben?"

"Donna, you know that I'm trying to lose some weight. I've got to whip myself into shape for the upcoming softball season."

"Ben, you're always on some kind of a diet, at least for a couple of days. Then boom, you're off on a candy-bar binge. Besides, you told me you're not going to play this year."

"I'm not! Well, unless someone gets hurt or gets thrown out of a game and we don't have anyone else to play. And if I ever do have to play, I don't want to make a fool out of myself. My plan is to only coach the team, but like the Boy Scouts motto, you have to be prepared."

"Didn't you get kicked out of the Boy Scouts?"

"No, it was the Cub Scouts, and it wasn't my fault."

"It never is!"

"That's a cheap shot! Besides, I want to look good in my uniform. Because you never know when some hot softball groupie might want her world rocked."

"Are you trying to make me jealous, Ben?"

"Am I?"

"Not in the least."

"Damn, I thought all you women were jealous at heart."

"Sorry to burst your bubble, mister. A smart woman knows she has the tool that makes men act like fools."

"There you go again, rhyming about pussies!"

"I prefer the word *vagina*!"

"Oh, I forgot. Ever since "The Vagina Monologues" became in vogue, women like to talk about their vaginas in the third person."

"What's wrong with that? You have a name for your dick, and you even talk to it!"

"I prefer the word *cock*! Dick is a man's name, and it's wrong to name your cock after a man unless it's a fictional character like Superman!"

"Well, Ben, it's no wonder then why you named yours Mr. Happy and not Superman."

I smile to myself, knowing she just won round 1. "Donna, don't you need to stuff some more food in that mouth of yours?"

"Yeah, Ben, I'll have some more."

"I'll serve you. After all, you're eating for two. And don't forget to take that folic acid crap."

Donna shakes her head and digs into her plate. "Ben, have you ever wondered about the meaning of life?"

"Damn, where did that come from, Donna?"

"Well, you know we're having a baby, and I do think of things other than sports and television, unlike you. You know there're other things out there!"

"Meaning of life? Like the 'why we're here' kind of thing?"

"Yeah, exactly."

"Well, Donna dear, you've come to the right place for your answer. The whole meaning of life is simple. We're here to learn. Pure and simple."

"Is that so, Einstein?"

"Sure, God is the divine teacher, and he grades us. Some tests we pass, others we fail."

"Are you passing, Ben?"

"Donna, I'm a fucking honor student."

"Yeah, and I'm Mother Teresa."

"Hey, those habits are sexy. Did I ever tell you I used to get a boner watching Sally Field in *The Flying Nun* when I was growing up?"

"Ben, you would get a boner watching *Leave It to Beaver*."

"Hey, Mrs. Cleaver was hot in that sexy little apron. You just know Ward couldn't wait to get home to get some of that. Do you know why the show centered on Wally and the Beaver?"

"No, but I'm sure you'll tell me."

"Because Ward and June were always fucking on those little twin beds."

"Ben, you always turn the subject to sex, regardless of what we're talking about."

"Donna, sex is the human condition."

"Where did you hear that?"

"I don't remember where, but I remember the quote. Isn't that enough?"

"For you, yes. But I still don't understand your obsession with sex."

"Well, my dear, it's quite simple. You're only here because Clair and Wayne did the nasty... well, at least once."

"Ben, they're my parents you're talking about."

"Donna, seriously, you think Wayne doesn't still give your mother the ole pickle tickle once in a while?"

"I really try not to think about it."

"Donna, we're programmed to have and, yes, to enjoy sex. God told Adam and Eve to go forth and multiply, which basically means to fuck, doesn't it? Truth be known, that's the real meaning of life."

"I thought you said it was to learn!"

"Yes."

"Let me see if I understand your devout wisdom. The meaning of life is to screw like rabbits."

"By George, you've got it! You get the golden penis."

"Well, you may not get it, mister. Talking about my parents screwing."

"Donna, I said they did the nasty. And for your information, I also find the word *screwing* tasteless. I much more prefer the word *fucking*."

"Well, FYI, I find the word *fucking* crude."

"Okay, then do you wanna make love then?" The phone rings. "I'll get it." *It must be another damn telemarketer*, I thought. *Who else would call at dinnertime during my verbal 'sexcapades'?* "Hello."

"Ben, this is Mark. I didn't take you away from anything, did I?"

"No, we just finished up dinner."

"Well, it's getting to be that time."

"Yeah, I was just thinking about that too!"

Even though it's cold as hell, at least for Alabama standards, it's time for us to start getting ready for the upcoming softball season.

Big Mark is the coach of ABM, the team we have merged with to form the Swinging Stixx. He also is one of the best home run hitters, not to mention one of the most intense guys on the field you'll ever meet. Off the field, he's really a pretty quiet guy.

"Have you told your guys about our plan?"

"Yeah, they seemed pretty pumped about it."

3

"They're tired of us beating each other up in league each year, and they're ready to kick some softball ass."

"Good," I said, "let's plan on starting practice next week."

We agreed on Tuesday, the fifteenth, the day after Valentine's Day. Okay, I have to admit something to you. Valentine's Day is my favorite holiday of the year. It's probably the only day of the year when you're guaranteed sex, unless you're married and it's your anniversary. But even on an anniversary, the guy has no leverage. I mean, the woman already has the ring and owns at least half of your shit unless you have a prenup.

But being single on Valentine's Day is a sure thing. Now I know that a lot of you ladies reading this may be offended or may be getting a little pissed from either the content or the language in this book. And you may even be thinking about taking this book back and trying to get a refund. Well, give it a few more pages, because you will learn more about men than you've ever learned from *Cosmopolitan*. You're also getting valuable insight on men straight from the horse's mouth. Sorry, back to Valentine's Day. Valentine's Day is a time for love. Yes, ladies, we do appreciate you. Maybe we don't say it enough, but it's tough sometimes for men to let you know how we truly feel.

But, ladies, if you want to know how to hold on to a guy, make him feel needed and, more importantly, wanted. You see, most men really just want to please their ladies. Really, we do! Now I have to admit I've read *Cosmo* from time to time. And to be honest, I really used to dig Helen Gurley Brown. Nothing is better than a woman who is both sexual and intelligent. However, this book isn't intended to be a relationship book. If you need a book on relationships, you may be a lost cause, because books on building a relationship will only fill your head with more useless bullshit than you can handle. People are making millions offering worthless advice. You want advice, watch *Talk Sex with Sue*. This book, however, is about me and my life, which, in its own right, is pretty fucked up most of the time. So, guys and gals, listen up. If you want a great relationship, learn to talk to each other. And more importantly, learn to listen. Finally, I just want to remind all of you about the song "Hold On Loosely." The chorus goes, "Hold on loosely, but don't let go. If you cling too tightly, you'll lose control." Ladies, remember that, and give your husband or boyfriend great sex, and they will worship you forever. Okay, so what the fuck, I may be offering a little advice after all.

And since I'm offering advice, there's just one other tidbit of knowledge I'd like to share.

Most women don't seem to realize how important things like fishing, softball, and drinking beer with your buddies are to a guy, especially for those of us who are ex-jocks. We need the guy time to bullshit and catch up with our buddies—in other words, to lie, drink, and talk about sex with our friends.

Donna, however, is an exception. She is unlike any woman I have ever met. She's funny, smart, and she loves animals.

And yes, she loves sex. She's a little tigress in bed. In fact, she's the best ever. And before you ask, yes, I do love her with all my heart. She is also four months pregnant with my child. Marriage? Maybe someday, but on our terms. I know, I know all the "it's a sin" bullshit; after all, I grew up in a church. My parents were Baptists and belonged to a small Baptist church. So I've heard all the "you'll burn in hell" stuff before. My father's favorite line was "If you're not Baptist, you're not shit!" That pretty much sums up religion in the South. One problem that I have with organized religion is that all the leaders, ministers, preachers, elders, etc. want to run your life. They want to tell you how and for whom to vote, what to think, what movies to watch, and what music to listen to. In other words, they try to brainwash you and run your life. In fact, the church leaders here in Alabama managed to get the state to vote no on the lottery, even though the money would have gone toward helping the schools. How stupid is that, especially when Alabama ranks near the bottom in national test scores for students? I think those religious zealots were more concerned that, had the lottery passed, it would have taken money out of their collection plates. They didn't care whether it would benefit the schools or not. And what makes it even worse is that people who want to buy lottery tickets will simply drive across the state line to Georgia.

Religion is a strange thing to me because I always thought of a church as God's house, a place to worship God. But in every church that I've even gone to, I find there's always some power play going on in the church.

Most of the time, it's behind closed doors. And speaking of politics, now the religious lobbyists are one of the strongest groups in Washington, DC. Don't get me wrong, I believe in God. After all, I'm a Republican. I just believe my God is about love and forgiveness, not dominating other people's lives. And there's always some idiot who wants to bring the Bible into an argument when they try to defend their position on a subject. The truth is, neither God nor Jesus wrote a single word of it. And who chose the books that are in the Bible? The church leaders? They chose what went in and what was left out. Honestly, the Bible is a great book. It has wonderful stories of love and wisdom and on how we should live our lives. But it is just a book. Reading it won't get you into heaven. Your deeds here on earth are what's important. I admit I'm no saint, but I don't need a preacher or religious head case to judge me or tell me how to live my life either. God can judge me someday. And I'll accept his verdict, but everyone else can kiss my ass.

Sorry about that. I tend to get on my soapbox from time to time, especially on the subjects of politics and religion.

Back to Valentine's Day. Valentine's Day is a time to spend the day with the one you love. Actually, it is a great holiday. I'm taking Donna out to eat. I've also bought her some candy and a Valentine's Day card. Actually, I've bought a box of cards. It's the kind first graders give. I chose the *Peanuts* characters. Yes, I can give her a fancy five-dollar card, but you must realize that in our relationship, we joke and kid around a lot. I know she'll love the cards because she loves the *Peanuts* cartoons as much as I do. In the Charlie Brown card, I've written a simple poem. I'm sure I'll write other poems or limericks throughout the book, so don't judge me harshly. What the hell, go ahead.

I know I'm no Maya Angelou.

> Roses are red,
> violets are blue.
> Enjoy the candy,
> since you're eating for two.

I know it's corny as hell, but she'll love it. Guys, remember this. Laughter is the fastest way to turn a woman on. And yes, we do laugh a lot. The other way to turn her on would be to buy her a new Lexus. Which one would you choose? I thought so. Besides, her card to me says:

> You talk a good game;
> you play one too.
> I really can't complain,
> since I know the real you.

If you must know, the game that night was a tightly contested, offensive-minded, high-scoring affair that went deep into overtime. The game ended up in a tie after both players were unable to answer the bell. The fifteenth rolls around, and it's D-day, the day of our first practice.

We all arrive at the complex about the same time. Practice starts at seven o'clock. It's fifteen, till my best friend David—we all call him Meat—rides with me to the complex. No, I don't know how he got the nickname, and no, I've never seen his dick.

When we get to the complex, Meat says, "Man, I'm so fucking pumped! I haven't swung a bat in three months."

Let me explain one thing about guys who play softball. I'm not talking about family reunions or after-church softball. I'm talking competitive tournament ball. It is almost an obsession. We eat, breathe, and live for it. We'd rather play ball than have sex.

Well, maybe not quite that much but close. Our main goal is winning championships: a state, a world, a national, or just a single tournament.

Like what Al Davis said, "Just win, baby." In the off-season, we train to stay in shape. We don't get paid to play, we do it simply for the love of the game.

After we get out of the car, Mark and his brother Ray walk over.

"How's it going, Meat? Glad to be playing with you instead of against you."

You must understand, guys who play softball know who all the good players are, names included. It's, after all, a form of respect.

Meat said, "Yeah, we should be loaded."

So far, so good, I think to myself.

Next up is Bryan; he played with Mark's team.

"How's it going, Coach Ben?"

Bryan is one of those "I've got more testosterone than sense" young guys, twenty-one years old and dumb as a stump. Kroy is his older brother, much quieter, with a dry sense of humor. Next up is Lewis. The best way to describe Lewis is, he is an honest-to-God geek. He reminds me of a cross between Beaver Cleaver and Ernest T. Bass. One of my players, Coy, comes up next. He's one of my original players. The best way to describe him is a fireplug.

He's probably all of five foot six and, to be nice, a little chunky. His nickname is Gimlet; actually, it's Short Fat Little Gimlet, but he's one hell of a pitcher. Next is Joey. He's the one guy who is hated more than Adolf

Hitler at the complex making his way over. You see, Joey talks trash, shit, and more trashy shit than anyone I've ever known. He makes Charles Barkley look like the pope on the field.

Joey says, "Ben, the man, what's up?"

I have to smile. I know he's going to be a handful to control, but damn, can he ever hit. Hal walks by without saying a word; in fact, he never says a word.

Dirk walks up and introduces himself. Dirk is one really nice guy, almost too nice to be playing with us. Calvin, one of my guys, walks over to the guys and says, "Word." I think that's Yankee ghetto for *hello*. Calvin is a black guy with a body that all men wish they had; I know I do. The closest thing to a washboard stomach I will ever get is if I buy a washboard. That leaves two: Todd and Stacey. Todd is about thirty-three, reminds me of a better-looking young Joe Namath. It must be the nose. Anyway, he has a great-looking wife, Holly. Big nose, great-looking wife—you know, he must be packing. Stacey is a student at Ashton, twenty-two, with a cannon for an arm. He is always out looking for trim... sex. Yeah, I know we sound crude, but it's because we are a bunch of hard-ass softball players. We are the Swinging Stixx. How did we come up with the name? Well, we've got game, and we have dicks and Stixx doesn't sound as crude as dicks. It really doesn't take a rocket scientist to figure that one out.

We start practice. Joey has to hit first. His reasoning is "I'm the best hitter, so I should hit first." Good enough for me. The first ball he hits sails over Stacey's head. Here he goes. "Stacey, don't fucking disrespect me. Watch me and maybe one day, you'll be a playa too." He hits shot after shot. Damn, he can hit.

Meat follows this could be interesting since Meat is one of my guys. His first swing of the year, he hits it out.

But as he hits it, he grunts like a constipated baboon, and of course, all the guys, in perfect harmony, grunt. "Uuh." Practice comes off without a hitch, no fights and no one cursing at one another. Damn, we may be on to something. And oh yes, everyone brought their own beer, except for Hal and Kroy, who don't drink. They must be Baptists or something.

On the way home, Meat asks, "What do you think?"

"I think we'll kick the shit out of a lot of teams. I just hope there not any distractions."

"Like what?"

"Hell, I don't know. Call me pessimistic. It just seems like something unexpected always comes up."

When I arrive home, there's a message from Donna.

"Ben, call me and let me know how practice went."

That's what I love about our relationship. Donna understands me. Not a lot of guys can say that about their wives or girlfriends. We live in separate houses and respect each other's space. She's also very independent. A lot of women would have pushed for marriage when they found out they were pregnant. Not Donna. I think she, like me, is afraid of the commitment. When she told me she was pregnant, we did talk about the options. Being a mother was not something she was ready for. And I wasn't ready to be a father either. In fact, I didn't want children at all. Not that I don't love kids; I do. But my parents fought a lot when I was growing up. And I always remember the old saying "The fruit doesn't fall far from the tree." However, I do understand that things can change.

But in my heart, I had hoped she wouldn't opt for an abortion. I guess my Baptist upbringing does play a part in making up my morals and values. While I do think abortion is morally wrong, I still think it's a woman's right to choose and that it should be kept legal because back-alley abortions have cost too many young women their lives. What is seldom talked about when abortion is brought up is the damage it can cause to the uterus of a woman. It can make having a child down the road much tougher.

Donna and I have talked openly about everything; we always do. But mostly, we talked about our fear of failure as parents. We ended up deciding to have the baby. For us, it was a clear choice.

Other decisions, like marriage, will be made later. The first poem I ever wrote was about my feelings at that time on abortion. This is it:

Abortion

A young girl walks in her appointments today;
to have an abortion is the choice she's made.
She knows not what she's about to do
or the painful death an innocent child will go through.
Listen, can you hear the silent screams,
the death of a child that's never seen?
Abortion is wrong, make no mistake.
It's not a choice you should easily make.

You see, God makes a child; it's not you and I.
But we make the decision if it lives or dies.
There are other choices such as adoption;
you see, abortion is not your only option.
Can you imagine what a baby must feel
when torn from its mother against its will?
Thousands of babies are aborted each day;
their mutilated bodies are simply thrown away.
So think about this before you go through,
Where would you be had your mother aborted you?

Sorry some of my poems are harsh. This was written in 1979 at the age of sixteen. I was dealing with the loss of my best friend from a car accident. I was looking for answers about life and why we make the decisions that we do. Abortion was one of the hot political topics then. I do feel that a woman has a right to do whatever she feels is right. To me, abortion is a moral issue and should not be a political one. We all have to make our own decisions in life. Someday, we may well have to answer for them.

I pick up the phone to call Donna.

"Hello, Ben."

"Hi, Donna, I got your message."

"How did practice go?"

"Well, no one got killed. So I guess it went pretty well."

"So everyone got along okay?"

"Actually, we did have one fight to break out. Nothing major. Only one police car showed up."

"A fight? You're kidding, right?"

I could tell she wasn't sure if I was joking or not.

"Yeah, dear, I'm kidding. I think we'll be pretty good though. Are we still on for dinner tomorrow night?"

"No, Ben, I have a date."

"What's her name?"

"Her? What makes you think it's a her?"

"Well, once you've had me, other men are out of the equation. So it has to be a woman."

"I've never said you were the best."

"You didn't need to. Your orgasms told me."

"You can be such a jerk sometimes, Ben."

"I love you too. See you at six."

Okay, it's a given that pregnant women eat—I mean, eat a lot, which is what they're supposed to do. But I'm still amazed at watching Donna put away food. We decide to eat at an all-you-can-eat buffet. That way, she can eat whatever she wants and how much she wants. And I can try to eat lightly. Yes, I did say *try*.

But when she grabs her plate and heads toward the food bar, it was like watching an old John Wayne war movie. You would have thought she was landing on Iwo Jima. She doesn't sit down till there are two plates filled with food and a cup of vegetable soup.

I couldn't resist, so I had to ask, "Can I get you anything else?"

"Yeah, I forgot to get a roll."

So you know what I did; I got up to get her a roll. I have to admit I have the utmost respect for women. Just the fact they give birth should get them some kind of medal for valor. I had a problem with a kidney stone once, and passing it was the worst pain I've ever felt. And considering I've torn tendons in my knee and ankle, not to mention a few broken bones, that says a lot. I say this because I was told that passing a kidney stone for a man is as painful as childbirth is for a woman. Whether that's true or not, I don't know. If it is and I were a woman, I would not have more than one child. That's for damn sure, because I never want another kidney stone.

Our next practice is scheduled for the following week. Well, an arctic blast comes down from the north. It's like thirty-four degrees, and these guys still want to practice. Well, our first tournament is in two weeks, so we go ahead with it. Meat arrives with a bottle of Jack Daniel's. God, what a friend. Just something to keep us warm, he says.

I decided to shag a few fly balls to stay warm but mostly to stay around Meat, who kept the Jack in his warm-ups. It was cold, so cold, in fact, I thought my testicles had crawled up inside me. I almost know now how it feels to have ovaries.

The funny thing about cold weather is, it pisses you off, and you can lose your temper easily. Some of the guys got a little hotheaded.

They were upset because they were cold.

I finally had heard enough bitching, and like all great leaders, I called for a summit at the local bar. Churchill had nothing on me.

It would really be interesting to know what would happen if all the world leaders got together and pulled a drunk—not just a little tipsy drunk, but "shitting in your pants" and "puking in the car" drunk. I'm serious! I believe the world would have no more wars, famine, or any other bullshit that is always in the news. I mean, think about it. When the president of the United States gets a blow job, he tries to cover his ass by lying about it. And what decent man wouldn't? I know I would, and I'm a Republican. The media covered it for months and ran the story in the ground. Then we had to endure the impeachment trial. I think the biggest problem with that was, those old farts in Washington were just mad that they weren't getting blown too. But what I don't understand is why a woman would keep a dress with semen on it and not wash it. However, she did sell it for some serious coin!

And honestly, if the president of the United States is in need of some poo nanny, you would think he'd at least be able to pull a good-looking actress or model. If you're going to fuck around, do it right. If anything, he should be impeached on bad taste in women. He was no Hugh Hefner where women were concerned. Jeez, guys, how great would it be to have had him for a father? "Dad, can I borrow Ms. March tonight?" Ben Hefner—that has a nice ring to it. Anyway, back to the news. My point is, the news media ran the story in the ground. That's why I hate nightly news; it's so damn depressing. Where are the fucking feel-good stories? Maybe I'm just sick and tired of watching the talking heads bash the war effort on terrorism, the economy, homeland security. Whatever! I may not agree with how the war is being run, but I sure as hell would rather be fighting the enemy in Iraq and Afghanistan than here in the United States.

But all that the news covers is some punk-ass congressperson bashing the president or some fucking Hollywood personality who doesn't know his or her ass from a hole in the ground spouting off while we have young men and women putting their lives on the line every goddamn day just so those fucking idiots can have freedom of speech. How would they feel if they had to worry about car bombs on Hollywood boulevard? But no, they run their fucking mouths, knowing that some waste-of-human-life newsman will put them on the newscast just because they're a celebrity. I guess you can tell that pisses me off. In a perfect world, television would be about sports, action movies, and *Sex and the City* reruns. Well, at least in my world anyway.

Okay, ladies and gentlemen, it's time to confess something to you. I'm really not a professional writer. Yeah, I know it's pretty fucking hard to believe, but it's true. I get carried away on a tangent. God, I hope I used that correctly. If not, it's because I don't know what the hell I'm doing. Outline? You've got to be kidding me. I'm doing this on the fly. Your guess is as good as mine how this book turns out. Hey, I never claimed to be a John Grisham or Tom Clancy. Those guys get paid a ton of money to write and are professionals.

I'm just... Well, I'm a wannabe. My point is this: I don't know where this book is going, but eventually, we'll get there. Just fasten your seat belt and hold on through the turns. And you might want to take a shit while you're at it. For some reason, writing this book has regulated my colon. I have had more bowel movements writing this book than a convent of nuns on ex-lax. And that's no shit!

Since I'm the coach and I don't have a regular nine-to-five job, I'm "self-employed." I get handed all the responsibility for ordering uniforms, bats, balls, etc.

I'll start with the uniforms. Deciding on the colors is always a pain in the ass. Everybody wants a different color scheme. I wanted white, gold, and green like the Oakland As. Vetoed. The colors come down to orange, blue, and white—the Ashton University colors—and teal, white, and purple. I decide that everyone should have a vote, just as long as I get my way. Fortunately, I save all my jerseys each year, and I have a teal-and-purple Nightmares jersey from 1998. It's purple with Nightmares in teal, outlined in white, and god, is it ever ugly. We meet at the bar to cast our votes; I wear the jersey in. I also make sure I'm the last one to arrive.

Bryan looks up to see me first and says, "Look, everyone. Barney, I mean, Coach Ben is here."

Reverse psychology really does work. Orange, blue, and white it is. Freud must be smiling somewhere out in the universe. And thanks, Mrs. Wilson; those psychology classes I bitched about having to take finally paid off. As fucked up as Freud was, he knew his shit!

I get home and call Donna. I guess I need to make sure she is okay.
"Hello."
"Hi, sexy lady! Just thought I'd check in to make sure you're okay."
"That's so sweet. You really are a nice guy, Ben."
"Of course, I am. I mean, you could have done a lot worse than me."
"Like who?"
Okay, I realize she is starting to play the game—our little game anyway. So to keep her in check, I decide to turn the tables on her.

"Well, tell me this, Donna, dear, who do you think would be better?"

"Well, Tom Cruise is pretty sexy. You know *Top Gun* is one of my favorite movies."

"No way you just said Tom frigging Cruise."

"Why? What's the matter with him? You said you would like him to play you if your book was ever made into a movie."

"I say a lot of things I don't mean. Tom Cruise has been through Nicole Kidman, Penelope Cruz, and then he jumps up and down on Oprah's couch like a madman because he was in love with Katie Holmes."

"I think that's sweet, Ben."

"Sweet my ass. If you ask me, his printer needs an ink cartridge refill." Donna laughs.

"Now, Ben, that was funny. Who would play you then?"

"Well, if I was casting me for a movie, I'd try to get Russell Crowe or George Clooney. But the perfect actor, if you could get him, would be Johnny Depp."

"Who would play me?"

"Maybe Ashley Judd or Jennifer Aniston."

"It depends on how the book turns out and if it's ever published. You mean, you don't know how it ends?"

"No! The book is about my life, becoming a father, my relationship with you, and yes, about guy things like softball, that take part over a six-month period of time. And to be honest, I don't know what's going to happen. Jeez, do I look like Edgar fucking Cayce to you? Hell, I can't even predict my bowel movements."

"Ben, you seem a little uptight. Are you worried it won't be accepted by the book companies?"

"No, I'm more concerned they'll like it for some unknown reason. I don't have a fear of failure. I have a fear of success."

"Why? You have patents and receive royalties from products you designed."

"Yes, dear, but the masses don't know that. I can go into a Wal-Mart and not be noticed. And I don't have to go on television for interviews now. I don't want to be a celebrity, not even a small one. I like being anonymous. Can you imagine Bill O'Reilly interviewing me? I'd probably piss my pants in fear."

"Then don't write it!"

"It's too strange to explain, but I have to write it."

"Ben, you're one big contradiction."

"And you're just figuring this out now? Here's the deal, Donna, I'm not a technical writer. I don't have any training except a creative writing class in high school. It's not a traditional book or even a concept. There's a lot of dialogue. There's no outline. It's like an X-rated Seinfeld episode on steroids. Of course, that's the beauty of it, at least in my mind. Plus, it's a mix of truth and fiction."

"In other words, much like your life."

"Exactly!"

"Well, just make sure I have a great figure with really big boobs in the book."

"Sorry, no can do. I don't like really big boobs unless they're real. Plus, yours are perfect. I'll give you a great figure before the pregnancy, but not big boobs."

"Okay, Ben, whatever. I'm going to turn in now. Love you! Good night."

"Love you too. Good night."

Morning comes much too fast. I really slept like shit. I guess I have too much on my mind. But I also have a lot to do concerning the team. Now I have to order bats. Softball bats are the most important things a player will use. The problem is, there are about fifteen different companies making them. Each company makes about five or six different models. So like any good coach, it's now time to do my homework. Every year, there are new bats each claiming to hit the ball farther and harder than their competition. Well, I've already received my annual catalogs from different mail-order companies, so I start my research.

I've found ten bats that I'd like more information on. So where do I turn? The internet. The internet is great! It's not just for pornography. Softball players can find out anything—and I do mean anything—about bats. The last few years, the price of bats has gone through the roof since bat technology has advanced. You used to be able to buy a bat from Wal-Mart and be okay. But not today. A good bat will cost a minimum of one hundred and fifty dollars and as much as five hundred. So you must invest wisely. And that's what it is, an investment. There is one bat every year that wins the bat wars competition. This year, it's an ugly wood color, perfect for our team. So I order one. I also decide to order the new and improved versions of the bats we used last year. The biggest problems with bats are cracking on composite bats and denting on aluminum bats. So I end up ordering a total of eight bats.

Next up is balls. I order my usual twelve dozen ASA (American Softball Association) balls and twelve dozen ISA (Independent Softball Association) balls. They are four different associations, and you have to hit their approved balls, and the only fucking difference is the colors of the stitches. It is like four competing gangs with four different-colored stitches. It's just another way to rip off the consumer. Where's Ralph Nader when you really need him?

The bats arrive in four days. We have a week before our first tournament, so we line up a batting practice, hitting with our new bats. A field test, you might say. I have to hit first since I am the coach and since I did all the fucking work. It's a warm day, about seventy-two degrees. Most bat companies won't honor a warranty if the bat is used in under, say, sixty degrees. I pull out Big Ugly, not the name of the bat, but I'm afraid that if I said the name, I would get sued or have a contract put out on me or something.

It's a composite bat that looks like wood and has a nice feel. First swing, smack hard line drive to the outfield. *Damn, this feels good.* Second, I take a hard swing and grunt like Meat, hard line drive into the gap in center field.

I hear Joey yell "P-rod!" which means you smoked it. I decide I'm going yard, home run. I take a big cut, and boom, it's over the fence; I'm starting to feel like Barry Bonds. Well, the next swing, my bubble bursts, or I should say the bat. I swing, and I hear a sickly crack. The ball dribbles back to the pitcher.

I look at the bat, and it has split open, yellow fiberglass material is sticking out.

I hear "What's the matter, Big Dog?"

I say, "This fucking piece of shit just broke, that what's the matter. Two hundred dollars for four swings. That's fifty dollars a swing."

That's what happens when you don't wait and let other teams waste their money first. I send it back to the company, and they send us a replacement, which also broke. It's now been six weeks, and the company hasn't answered my emails or phone calls or replaced the bat. I know we must learn from our mistakes. But at two hundred dollars a pop, it can get a bit pricey.

Well, after practice, we talk about our first tournament in Sheppard. Sheppard is a town northwest of Montgomery. It's about an hour and a half from Ashton. We decide to meet at the barbecue restaurant in Ashton at six thirty, Saturday morning. Now six thirty comes early for the college guys on the team, especially after a Friday night of partying, so we designate babysitters for Bryan, Stacey, and Joey.

Well, Saturday morning rolls around, and I jump up rushing around, trying to find my jock. A player needs a cup, even a coach that doesn't play like me. It gives you that bulge in the crotch, just in case some women are checking you out. I finally find it under the bed, half chewed up by Sparky. *Damn it, Sparky.* Sparky is one of my dogs, half poodle / shih tzu.

"Don't you have enough chew toys?"

Thank God Walmart is open twenty-four hours a day. I get there at exactly six thirty, and I'm the first one to show up.

The last one to arrive is Stacey at seven, still drunk from the night before. We all cuss him and then take off. We have an hour and a half to get to Sheppard. Well, after setting a land speed record, we get there in fifty-five minutes and without a single speeding ticket. I go to check us in, since I'm just about to piss in my pants, thanks to a big Diet Pepsi on the drive down. I pay our entry fee and make a beeline to the bathroom. I walk in, and this goddamn smell hits me.

"Jeez, Meat, is that you? You big stinking motherfucker."

I knew it was him because I could see his cleats under the stall and not too many people have white-and-orange cleats with the name Meat embroidered on the tongue of the shoe.

"Fuck you, Ben, you know I have to have my PGS [pregame shit]."

"But what the hell did you eat? So I'll be sure never to eat it."

"Julie and I ate sushi last night."

Julie is Meat's girlfriend. He is divorced. I should have known raw, dead fish shit coming out of a 270-pound man's ass. I shake Mr. Happy and get the hell out, don't even stop to wash my hands. Believe me, it was that bad. I wash my hands under the faucet next to the water fountain. I have to admit I had to see the expressions on the faces of the other guys coming out of the toilet. Like what the commercial says, priceless. I hurry to make out a lineup card, and we head to field 2. The team we're playing looks like they're out on weekend parole. Their name, I believe, is the Hitmen. They look like hit men anyway. Three of their players are wearing camouflaged pants; the rest are wearing cutoff gray warm-up pants. There is not one matching jersey in the bunch. In fact, I think only two guys have numbers on their backs that were probably state issued.

Here we are, in Sheppard Alabama, with new uniforms, looking like a million bucks, playing a bunch of convicts. *How the hell do we get out of here alive?* is my only thought.

I say to Joey, "Don't say shit during this game because if you do, one of those guys are liable to fuck you in the ass right on the field. Just remember in *Deliverance* that squeal-like-a-pig scene before you open your fucking mouth."

"Ben, I'm a grown fucking man. Don't worry, I'm cool, trust me."

"Trust me"—isn't that what General Custer told his troops before he got their asses killed at Little Bighorn?

"OK, Joey, we're cool. Just don't say shit!"

"Batter up!" calls the umpire. Here we go, the season is underway. Joey steps in the box, first pitch hits two feet in front of the plate, ball 1 is the call, the pitcher stares at the umpire till the umpire looks down. Next pitch, Joey hits a shot in the gap between the left and left center fielder.

"I see your number" comes out of Joey's mouth.

Oh no, here it comes.

"You're fixing to see my fucking foot up your candy ass, boy."

Joey shuts up. I think he figured out the rest of the story. Bryan's up next. He hits a single to score Joey. Big Mark hits a mammoth home run next. The Hitmen watch it as it lands in the top of an oak tree.

"Good shot, big 'un."

"Appreciate it, pitch," Mark says.

R-E-S-P-E-C-T—we have the Hitmen's respect. We go on to beat them 27–11. Hell, they even shake our hands after the game. We go to look at the bracket; we don't play till eleven o'clock. Time to walk around to check out the other teams here.

The only teams I know that are here are Gremlins, Dexter Associates, and FOF (Freaks on Fire). We play Dexter Associates next. We still have an hour and a half to kill. Oops, I shouldn't say *kill* in Sheppard.

Before we play again. So like most red-blooded softball players, we head to the trucks—I mean, coolers in the trucks.

We toss back a few cold ones, except Hal and Kroy. Kroy does break down and drink one of those fruit-flavored alcoholic drinks, something iced.

I've tasted it. It tastes like lemonade.

Hal breaks his silence. "Guys, don't drink too much. You won't be able to play."

Lewis speaks up, "Fuck you, Hal." Enough said.

"Swinging Stixx, report to field 1" comes out of the loudspeaker.

"OK, guys, let's do this."

Dexter Associates is a team of gnats. Their biggest guy is maybe five eight, a hundred and sixty-five pounds, but just like gnats, they're pests. They hustle entirely too much for a softball team. We win the flip and are the home team. Their leadoff batter is, I swear, four foot eleven. He slaps the ball to our third baseman. By the time Mark picks it up, the kid is standing on first base. Like I said, pests. And yes, they do suffer from short man's disease. They talk entirely too much for a team that I referred to as the Cashews. Cashews as in "hung like a cashew." Anyway, they score seven runs before we get the last out of the inning. Our team comes in the dugout with our heads hanging.

Like a great psychologist, I choose my words carefully. "Listen up, we are getting beat by a bunch of umpa-lumpas! God, I'm glad I saw Willy Wonka. Get your heads out of your asses and play ball!"

They laugh, but I can feel it gave them a lift. Softball is 20 percent physical, 80 percent mental; at least that's my theory. We end up coming back to win the game 19–12.

Our next game is at three. Time to find a place to eat.

Sheppard is not exactly Atlanta. I mean, there's no Hooters restaurant nearby. Hooters is the number one place to eat if you're a softball player.

They have good wings and, uhh, a good sports atmosphere. Yeah, that's it. Wait a minute, I'm not married. It's for the girls in tight orange shorts with nice tits. Where else can you get scenery and a salad? I'm sure the NOW woman will be on my ass if this book ever gets published.

Speaking of the NOW women, have you ever noticed... How can I say this nicely? Have you ever noticed that none of the NOW women would ever be mistaken for Pamela Anderson or Ashley Judd? There are no attractive members of that organization. At least none that I've seen on television. If I were stranded on a desert island with one of them and if my choice was to have sex with either one of them or a watermelon, I'd chose the watermelon. Okay, I plead the fifth on the watermelon. Well, with no Hooters around, we decide to eat at an Arby's. I order a giant roast-beef sandwich.

"Coach Ben, did I ever tell you about the Smoky Mountain Classic?"

"No, Bryan, you haven't."

"Well, a few years ago, we went to play in a tournament called the Smoky Mountain Classic. I was the youngest guy on the team. But, Coach Ben, I showed out, I killed the ball, the other guys just couldn't hang with me."

"Bryan, that sounds a little gay, don't you think? I mean, 'hang with me'?"

"Coach Ben, it's only gay if you're on bottom."

Everyone laughs. Then he goes on to one of the longest stories about pulling trim.

"Bryan," I say, using one of my favorite lines from a professional wrestler (I think it was Jimmy Garvin who said it), "when a girl has sex with you, she must think she's riding Space Mountain."

"You're right about that, Coach Ben."

"And when she's finished, she knows it's true, because everyone knows Space Mountain is the shortest ride in the park and when you're finished, you're sick at your stomach!"

That brings out the "ahhhs" from the guys. I have to admit being a latchkey kid isn't so bad. I watched so much television growing up. I'm sure it played a part in developing my philosophy on life. You may laugh at this, but it's true. I learned most of what I know about human relationships from watching TV. But most of that was just plain common sense. *The Andy Griffith Show*, *Father Knows Best*, *My Three Sons*, etc.—they all had a common denominator: you had one guy with some common sense, a few nuts, and a young boy or two. This is where I developed my coaching philosophy. I know it sounds strange, but just think about it. Andy had Opie's best interest in mind, and he knew when to give him a pat on the back or when to take him to the woodshed. Andy knew that Barney was an idiot; that's why he never let him carry a loaded gun. Andy also knew how to handle Otis, the town drunk. So as you can see, I'm Andy to a bunch of Otises, Barneys, and Opies, and I like to think I'm pretty damn good at it.

Well, we start toward the field. Our game time is in fifteen minutes. I hear someone say "I hope you guys bring your A game. You're going to need it."

Calvin, who only got about two hours sleep last night because he works part-time as a bouncer at a bar, chimes in, "Dude, our C game could beat you motherfuckers, you ain't shit."

Calvin's got balls. I'll have to give him that, I thought.

"We'll see, bro" is the reply.

Game time has arrived. The Freaks have won the coin toss and chosen to be the home team. Normally, I would want to be the home team just to have the last at bat. But in this game, I'm glad we're the visiting team. That way, we can make a statement.

Joey leads off with a single between third and short; Stacey follows it with a fly ball, which the outfielder drops. Runners and first and second for Calvin. As Calvin is getting ready to hit, someone yells, "Hit the ball, Uncle Tom!"

Calvin is the only black guy on the team. He calls for time from the umpire. The Freaks are an all-black guys from Westville. In fact, Calvin knows three or four of them. He steps back in the batter's box and hits three runs, home run. Dirk and Todd hit home runs that inning too. By the time the Freaks come to bat, it's 9 to zip.

"Good inning, guys," I tell them as they hit the field to play defense.

The first two batters hit shots at Coy, who makes great plays and throws them both out. Next guy lines out to short. Three up, three down. Nothing will shut up a team like good defense, and that's what we played. Final score, 24–3. That is an ass whipping in anybody's book.

The best and worst part of a tournament is breaks. When you're playing well, you just want to keep playing. Because if you sit around too long, you tend to get stiff, or you may drink too much, which is more likely to happen. A good coach may not be able to keep your muscles loosened up, but he sure as hell can make sure you don't get drunk. I am constantly saying, "Guys, that's enough." My catchphrase is "Quit or sit!" That usually works. The best part about sitting around is you get to know all the guys better, especially early in the year. Most of the guys that had played with Mark, I really didn't know much about personally. I found out Dirk and Hal were engaged—no, not to each other. I also didn't know that Hal, Kroy, and Joey played high school baseball with one another. That must have been a hell of a team. Hal's dad came to our tournament in Sheppard, and after every bat, Hal would walk outside to talk to him. If he made an out, his dad would tell him what he did wrong. I thought it was a little strange that a grown man would still be vying for his father's approval. Maybe that's why he never spoke to me.

I learned at a very early age that you have to do things for yourself. My father was always on the go, either to the family cabin in the mountains or fishing with his friends after work. That was okay by me. I mean, there was no added pressure to try to impress him, had he been in the stands. I think he came to three Little League games, two football games, and one high school game, that being my last one. Why I remember that, I don't really know. I guess, as we get older, we start to understand our parents better. We also realize that they aren't perfect. Hopefully, we understand that they did the best they could at that time. While my parents had their flaws, I've grown to understand them.

Well, game time is now at hand. We are to play X-Rated. They're out of Birmingham. Mark, who knows the tournament teams better than I do, lets me know that five of the team played with Caesars. They won the C class state championship last year. So it should be a tough game. A lot of players will play with other teams if their team is not playing that week and a team doesn't have enough players to play. They're called pickups. We win the flip and are the home team. X-Rated, like us, are well-dressed and are well equipped. Their uniforms are purple, gold, and gray. Their leadoff hitter smokes a ball past our pitcher's ear. There is an unwritten code about hitting the middle (at the pitcher). No team does it on purpose until the other team does it. Why? Because the pitcher is so close to the hitter, only about forty-five feet, and every year, a number of pitchers get hurt and some killed.

But when someone does it, it's called opening up the middle. You must protect your pitcher, so you hit at theirs. It can get ugly in a hurry. Well, Coy is pissed he missed the ball, not that he almost got killed. That is the mark of a true gamer. The next batter tries the same thing. He hits a one hopper smoked to Coy, who comes up clean with the ball and fires a strike to Kroy at second on to first a one-six-three double play. *Way to go, guys.* Their number 3 hitter hits a solo home run, and there are cleanup batter lines out to first.

Giving up only one run is good against a team like theirs. Joey steps up to hit, first pitch is outside, and he hits a shot up the middle.

"That's for you, Coy!" Joey may be a jerk sometimes, but he's a team player all the way. The pitcher stares at Joey, but you can tell he's a little shaken up. He walks Stacey and Kroy to load the bases. Meat's up and hits a deep fly ball that I thought was going out. The outfielder makes a nice running catch and fires toward second. It does score Joey, so we have a tie game with one out. Mark's up next and hits a shot at the third baseman, who catches the ball, but I can tell the infielder has really hurt his hand when he caught the ball because he caught it in his palm. When you catch a ball like that, it stings like hell, and no softball player will rub it. If you do, you're a pussy. Coy is the best player we have at hitting the middle. If you're a pitcher, you had better learn to hit it. I always put a star in the score book anytime one of my guys hits the opponent's pitcher, especially if they did it first. It's sort of the way football teams award stars if someone makes a good play. Well, Coy wants to make a statement. He steps in to hit. The first pitch is a ball inside. He wants a ball middle of the plate to outside. Second pitch is his. You hear a smack then a sickly crack. The pitcher falls down holding his shin. The ball rolls past the third baseman. Stacey and Kroy both score. The umpires call time, and everyone checks on the pitcher. I make a star in the score book and walk out of the dugout. His shin has a knot the size of a baseball on it; there's probably a fracture. X-Rated players are pissed and start trying to pick a fight. But the umpires cool things off before they get out of control. Todd hits a fly ball to end the inning. But after one inning, we're up three runs, one star to one run. The game does get a little nasty. Everyone is trying to hit Jay, which plays into our hands. We set our defense to cheat toward the middle. It takes them out of their game.

We do go on to win the game 18–14. We are in the championship game in the winners bracket, meaning a team has to beat us twice to take first place. If I do say so, we are sitting pretty good. X-Rated is beaten by FOF and put out of the tournament. They have never gotten over losing their pitcher.

We are at the trucks having our celebratory beers.

The finals of the losers bracket are FOF and Dobies' Construction are just getting started. We polish off a couple of more brewskis and decide to walk over to field 4 to watch the game. The game is in the fourth inning. Dobie's Construction is just a bunch of rednecks. Why do I call them rednecks? Well, three guys are wearing T-shirts, the kind that is given away in a cigarette carton. The women cheering for them are cursing at the officials, and I bet not one of them weighs less than two hundred pounds. The children running around these women are filthy, and not one kid is wearing a pair of shoes.

I make a joke to Calvin. "I bet the only reason they're playing ball this week is so they can fog their trailers for roaches."

Calvin laughs and says, "Ben, that's sick!"

The Freaks are looking pretty good. It looks like we will probably be playing them again. Najuan, a guy Calvin knows from the bar, is the first batter. He hits a slow roller to the third baseman, who can't make a play. Runner at first, no outs. Next guy up looks like the rapper Snoop Dogg. He hits a roller to the shortstop, who runs over to second to turn a double play, but Najuan slides in and takes him out. The throw sails over the first baseman's head. The shortstop starts jawing with Najuan, who pushes him out of the way. The redneck sucker punches him, and both benches clear. Actually, I should say *erupt*. All of us head for the trucks, because you never know when some idiot may pull out a gun. I've been playing softball over twenty years and never seen a fight like this one—fists are flying everywhere; even the wives are fighting.

Ten minutes later, when Sheppard's finest arrive, blue lights flashing, the fields clear. Everyone starts running. After the arrests are made, the complex director comes over and hands me the first-place tournament trophy. After all, we have no one to play now in the finals. We decide to get the hell out of town while the getting was good. On the way out, I call Donna.

"Hello."

"Donna, we're on our way home."

"How'd you do?"

"Not bad. We won the tournament."

"Not bad? Shouldn't you say *great*?"

"No, we won by default. We never got to play the championship game."

"Why?"

"A little fight between the two teams in the finals of the losing bracket."

"You weren't involved, I hope."

"Hell no, I'm a lover, not a fighter. How do you feel?"

"I feel fine."

"No morning sickness?"

"Ben, it's six p.m."

"Are you up for some company?"

"Are you?"

"I'm up now. My cup is about to strangle Mr. Happy."

She laughs, and there are chuckles from the back seat.

"Are you still in uniform? You know I like a man in uniform."

"Yeah, I'm a bit sweaty and dirty, but nothing a little Irish Spring can't fix."

"I'll see you when you get here."

Houston, we have liftoff. The police have started to search cars. And inside one of the Freaks' cars, they have found a loaf-bread sack of weed. Talk about having a bad day. The police are still picking up teeth off the infield as we drive off. First tournament, first win of the season. A pretty fucking good start. Our drive home is uneventful except for the fact Joey rode back with us. It is my first time to really have a conversation with him. Coy and Calvin also are in the truck. I ask Joey why he had to be so loud on the field. He says that was just a way to pump himself up. Softball players do it for the love of competition. Most of us grew up playing baseball, and it's a way to continue that. But I think the main reason is, we need the challenge of competing.

When you play, you form a bond, a friendship not only with your teammates but also with players from other teams. I don't think most women really understand that.

Whether it's softball, bowling, or horseshoes, men need to prove that they are worthy. It's the same way in nature. Two male deer will lock horns for a doe. I've even seen male bass protecting the bed where the female lays. Most of the wives seldom come to games. Holly is an exception, and she is there almost every weekend. She really is an attractive woman, and I think she enjoys the games. There's so much testosterone in the air; plus, she gets a lot of attention from the guys. Julie, Meat's girlfriend, comes every once in a while. And sometimes Lacy, who's Bill's daughter, comes although she is only four.

The ride back to Ashton is much more relaxed than the ride down. We don't break the speed limit for once. We even stop at Krystal and buy two sackfuls. We listen to a CD I had burned. It was titled "Slow Jams." We all sing along to Meat Loaf's "Two out of Three Ain't Bad" and Dobie Gray's "Drift Away." As much as I want to make us out to be a bunch of bad asses, I really can't. I mean, we're just normal, everyday guys who love to compete.

I get to Donna's and walk in. She's eating Cap'n Crunch cereal out of the box on the sofa. Her dog, Scruffy, is at her feet. I give her a kiss.

"Ben, you've been eating at Krystal's."

"Yeah, we stopped and bought a couple of sackfuls."

Nothing wrong with her taste buds, I thought.

"Well, thanks for thinking about me."

"I brought you something even better."

"And what's that?"

"Come take a shower with me and I'll show you."

As we get undressed, I have to smile at Donna. She is starting to show just a little. But she is still as beautiful as ever. Maybe even more so. Maybe it's the pregnancy glow you always hear being talked about. Mr. Happy is excited anyway.

I think Steve Martin was the first person that I heard of who named his dick. His was Mr. Happy. So I named mine Mr. Happy too. Stupid? Yeah, a little. Original? No, but Burger King might have sued me if I called my dick the Whopper or McDonald's had I named it the Big Mac. Sometimes I refer to mine as Happy Herman. Yeah, I know that's pretty juvenile. But hey, it is funny!

There is something so incredibly erotic and very sensual about taking a shower with someone you love. It's a great start to foreplay. Warm water washes over our bodies as we lather each other up. It is stimulating, to say the least. Lately, though, there's one thing I worry about when we make love. And that is if Junior will come out with an indention in his head. I know that sounds crazy, but when I'm inside Donna, things do feel a little different. The doctors assured us it was okay. In fact, the semen is supposed to help induce labor when it's time. Granted, this could all be in my head. It's just that I just don't want to be inside his. Donna has a bar of soap in her hand and starts lathering me up. I look down at her belly and say out loud, "Well, Junior, you may end up being a special education child after all." We toweled each other off and walk hand in hand to the bed. There I give her a soft kiss. Our lips barely touch.

But then our hands begin to explore each other's bodies. There is something to be said about soft, sensual love. Sorry to break the mood, but I have to admit something. I love to give Donna oral sex. You've probably expected me to say I love to eat her pussy. Hey, even I think that sounds crude. Cunnilingus? Hell, I couldn't spell it without spell-check, much less pronounce it. And honestly, ladies, how would you like to hear "I want to give you cunnilingus, baby!" That'll fuck the mood up in a heartbeat. So I usually just say "I want to kiss it." I have to be honest, the vagina has to be the greatest engineering feat God ever accomplished. It's absolutely perfect. Hell, it can even multitask. Yeah, sorry, I know it broke the mood. Maybe next time! Afterward, as she lies in my arms, we talk.

Guys, remember, you should always talk to your lady, especially after she's given you her love. I know we guys just want to go to sleep, but it is important to women to talk. It also lays the foundation for your next romantic encounter.

"That was great, Ben."

"Yes, it was. We do make pretty good music together, don't you think?"

She smiles and says, "Yeah, we do."

We tease each other a lot, but she knows down deep how much I care.

I look at her and say, "You know, Donna, sex is like painting a picture."

"Why do you say that?"

"Well, anyone can put paint on a canvas, but few can paint a masterpiece."

She smiles and says, "Well, it was better than a black *Velvet Elvis*! You know, Ben, I have an ultrasound appointment next Wednesday. We may know Junior's sex then."

I haven't given much thought about the sex of our child. I guess I hope it's a boy, but honestly, it doesn't matter as long it is healthy. We cuddle up then drift off to sleep.

It's Monday afternoon and the first night of league softball. We have two teams that play league on that night but in different divisions. Both teams play under the name Nightmares. We own the league. We have our tournament team in the four-to-six home run league, and a couple of guys Calvin and Coy play with, the one-to-three home run team. I want them to help teach the game to the younger guys. Meat always rides to the games with me, and usually, he will get to my house an hour early to drink beer, shoot pool, or watch porn. Sometimes all three. Well, I've just bought three new pornos, so we decide to watch one. Meat has stopped at the barbecue restaurant and brought some sandwiches. Barbecue, beer, and porn—no better way to get ready for a ball game. Ladies, you must remember there's nothing wrong with guys watching porn. We learn a lot from it. Think of it as sex education for guys. Really, we do learn from it. I actually learned how to give cunnilingus to a woman from watching a girl-on-girl scene. Who better to watch than a woman? I mean, they know what they like, right?

We load the DVD up. The name is *The President's Hoes*. I guess they wanted to take advantage of President Clinton's fuckups. Why men are attracted to pornography is a tough thing to put into words, especially for me. I love to see a woman naked. It is truly a glorious sight. I actually find looking at a *Playboy* magazine more erotic than watching porn on a video. The pictures are more sensual, and in my case, I feel the ladies aren't exploited well, not as much as they are in a video. When I was in my teens and my best friend found his father's eight-millimeter porn movies, we would rush to his house after school to watch them. We were all horny, inexperienced young men. So in a sense, we found the movies educational since we didn't know anything about sex. So it did fulfill our need for knowledge. If I watch a movie today, it does nothing for me. It may be, in part, because I feel sorry for the actors. Yes, I will talk about sex, masturbation, and even porn throughout this book because all three are parts of our everyday life. And I happen to find sex an interesting topic. Human sexual behavior is one of the most fascinating subjects around. Donna and I have had great conversations on the subject. She finds movies more distasteful than I do, and I can understand her point. Women are portrayed as sluts and are used as a semen target. The women often have more than one partner at a time in the scene. They're forced to talk graphically, and at the end of each scene, the men ejaculate either on their faces, in their mouths, and on their breasts. And the men in the pornos are treated like a piece of meat because that's what they are. They usually have big cocks and can cum on cue. Donna and I differ on one thing, however, and this is it: the men and women who make adult videos choose to do it. Yes, they make pretty good money, at least more than they could by working at a fast-food restaurant.

So they choose that life. I'm sure they know all about AIDS and the dangers of unprotected sex. I've seen quite a few documentaries on the porn industry. So I know that a lot of the actors have drug habits to support. Some actors may just be too lazy to get real jobs. I've heard the actors get paid anywhere from a thousand to five thousand dollars per scene. They make more in one day than a welder makes in a week. Granted, they are taking a greater chance with their lives too. My point is that it is their choice to make.

Donna is more sympathetic about the exploitation of the actors, especially the women. She believes a lot of the women porn stars may have children to support. Or maybe they are even runaways that need the money to survive. That may be true. But it is still my belief that both the men and women who make adult movies have a choice. You will probably hear me say that throughout the book.

Life is about learning. It's about making decisions. It really is! Look, I love watching movies. I also enjoy making love. But I would never make love on camera. If Donna wanted to make love on camera just for our enjoyment, I wouldn't do it. Some things are sacred to me. That doesn't mean people who do it are wrong. It just means that's the choice they've made. So when I watch a porn movie, I see it for what it is—fucking on film—because the actors don't make love on camera. There's really nothing sensual in the movie because the actors rarely kiss and there's never any foreplay either. It's my belief that if someone would make a sweet, romantic movie with a tender yet explicit love scene, they would make a fortune because it would be believable and women may even want to watch it.

Time to leave for the game. Later that night, when I get home, I call Donna to check in just to make sure she's feeling okay. Our conversation turns into why married couples get divorced. We really do have some intellectual conversations from time to time. There are many reasons that couples divorce. Money is one of the big reasons. I have some friends who spend more money than they can afford.

Far too many couples try to have everything early in a marriage instead of saving for it. You learn to appreciate things more if you have to save to get them. Credit card debt will put a huge strain on, if not outright kill, a marriage. Arguments over children can strain a marriage because children learn at an early age how to play parents against each other. And it's up to the parents to be unified and not let that happen. Religious differences—I know a couple who were happily married, till the wife became a Jehovah's Witness. Her newfound beliefs such as not celebrating Christmas and birthdays, as well as not accepting blood transfusions, caused their breakup. Infidelity, I think, is the second-biggest reason for divorce. I think a couple who're thinking about getting married should have to live together for at least a year before they can apply to get a marriage license. Why? To make sure they're compatible, especially sexually compatible. Some people have different sexual libidos. It's my belief that sex actually gets better the longer you're with someone. Why? You become more comfortable with each other. You can discuss your likes and dislikes honestly without hurting each other's feelings.

But we have decided the number one reason for divorce was partners lying to each other. Trust is something that is earned. Once it is lost, there's little hope of getting it back. Yes, sometimes it may be easier to lie than to be honest, but lies tend to pile up, and then you end up living that lie. Then you have to try to keep up with all the lies you've told. Then at some point, you get caught in one. Donna and I both agree marriage is tough enough and you really have to work to make a go of it. And if you can't trust your partner, it's impossible.

Our conversation then turns to baby names. Naming a child really is a big deal. The child will have to live with it the rest of their life—or at least until they're old enough to have it changed. I have to admit I like the traditional names, not names that become a fad. My favorite name for a girl would be Reagan. Yeah, after the president. But hey, I'm a Republican. And it is a pretty name. I also don't believe a child should ever be named after a family member either. I think each child deserves their own identity and to not have to live in the shadow of someone else.

"Ben, what names for a boy do you like?" Donna asks.

I think for a minute before answering. "Well, I like Ethan a lot. I also like Nathaniel, Brian, and Alexander."

"Those are good, Ben. But I like the names Cody, Tyler, and Gabe."

"Those are good," I say, knowing there's not a snowball's chance in hell they would be used if it was a boy. Those names are too eighties. But since I do not want to cause an argument, I agree.

"What about names for girls?"

That's a tough one, I think.

"Well, Reagan is my favorite, but I sort of like Monica and Phoebe."

"Ben, those are characters on *Friends*."

"Yes, but they're still girls' names. Have you ever seen an ugly Monica or Phoebe?"

"No."

"Well then, I rest my case."

"Well, I like Erica and Ashley if it's a girl."

"Those are good names. I could live with either of them."

"Great," she says.

With that, we say good night.

Well, it's Wednesday and yet another night of softball. We have a Nightmare team and a Swinging Stixx team in this league. And yes, they do have to play each other. It's all ISA, which is different from the other leagues. In ISA, you are allowed to steal bases, and if you hit more home runs than you're allowed, it ends the inning. I sponsor all four teams, so I have guys on all the teams play tournaments with us if we need them. Wednesday night is the only time my teams play against each other. The

Swinging Stixx team is a little more hard-core. I mean, they play a little harder and want to win a little more.

The Nightmare team just wants to have fun, drink beer. Generally, they don't give a shit. This is the first season that I'm not coaching the Nightmare team. I think the guys are a little upset with me although I tried to explain the reasons why. Since the Swinging Stixx are the tournament team, I feel obligated to be with them. I have three pretty good friends on that team: Tom Whatley, Steve Wilson, and Maurice Paglamano, or Pags. Now Whatley is the more vocal of the guys. He can hit, and he knows it. He'll tell you "Damn, I can hit" as he rounds the bases. He can't field a lick, but damn, can he hit. He's a lot like Joey, but not quite as annoying. He's played long enough that people don't take him seriously. Steve can also hit it with the best, and he and Whatley will bet each other on who'll get the most hits, RBIs, anything.

Pags, well, Pags is also a great ballplayer. But like Tom and Steve, he won't slide or get dirty because it is a game and he doesn't want to get hurt and miss work. But Pags is a great team chemistry guy. He's also an engineer, and what makes him the most appealing is, he's fun to fuck with. He can take it and dish it out as well.

I hate to admit this, but the Nightmare team this season is not going to be very good, at least not up to our normal standards. We have lost some players and cannot keep the talent level up. Well, tonight, the Stixx play the Nightmares in the first game. Joey leads off the game, he hits a ball to third, which Pags pounces on, and he throws him out.

Whatley says, "I thought you could hit."

Kroy and Todd follow him with back-to-back singles. Mark comes up and hits a double down the right field line to score them both. Runner on second, still one out. Meat comes up next. Meat doesn't like to wear softball pants during league; he likes to wear shorts. Tonight, he's wearing these metallic-gold shorts. We've all given him hell about it. Meat and Whatley go way back to Little League, and they're constantly fucking with each other. Whatley, for some reason, hasn't said anything about the shorts. Huh. Meat unloads, he hits a towering home run to left. As he rounds the bases, the first baseman, Rex Fulson, says, "Good hit, big 'un."

Whatley, who plays second, says to Meat, "Is that all you got?"

Meat grabs his crotch. Meat is almost walking around the bases. Whatley starts to follow him. I'm wondering what's up. As he touches home plate, Whatley jerks his shorts down to his ankles, and Meat trips and falls—funniest thing I've seen in years. Meat gets his shorts back up and starts to chase him around the field. Of course, he can't catch him. He looks like a bull chasing a deer. Hal and Dirk hit fly balls to end the inning. Well, Whatley is the leadoff hitter. He puts his batting glove on and then gets a drink of water, getting ready to hit. He steps in the batter's box. Meat tells him how low he is. First pitch, he hits a single between first and second. He doesn't run right away; he turns to Meat and spits ice water on him and runs down to first.

"Damn, I can hit and spit."

Meat says, "That's your ass, Whatley. Paybacks are hell."

Men will be boys if given half a chance. Well, the Stixx win the game 18–13. Since we only have one game tonight, because there are an odd number of teams in the league, we go up on the hill to the parking lot to have a beer. The Nightmares has a second game against the Fire Department. We're sitting on the tailgate of my truck when Meat gets up and walks over to Whatley's truck. He reaches in his cooler and pulls out a bottle of beer. Now we have a cooler full of beer, so I'm not sure what the big bastard has up his sleeve. He pops the tops and shotguns the beer down his throat. He is, after all, a professional. He walks with bottle in hand between two cars, and yes, he did fill it up with piss. Well, Todd, Stacey, and I just stare as he puts the cap back on the bottle and puts it back in the cooler.

"Don't say a fucking word."

When someone as big as Meat says "Don't say a fucking word," well, you don't say a fucking word. After all, Whatley has started all this shit. Well, games are played with an hour time limit or with a run rule in effect. The Nightmares game takes the full hour with them winning 19–12. But that's not what matters.

The guys make their way up on the hill—Whatley, Wilson, Pags, the whole team.

Whatley walks past Meat and says, "You know I was just showing you some love."

Meat says, "Oh yeah, you really got me, it was really fucking funny."

Whatley knows then something was up. He walks around his truck to see if his tires were flat. They were okay. He looks to see if Meat had pissed on his truck. That was okay too. *Hmm!* Meat has put the bottle of piss on the bottom of the cooler to cool it off.

"Hey, Ben, any of you need a beer?"

———

"Sure, I'll have one," I say.

Todd and I walk over and get the two beers on top. Whatley only has four beers to begin with since he drank two before the game.

We pop the tops and start drinking. "Ahhh."

There are two beers left—a fifty-fifty chance. He pops the top and starts drinking. Damn, he got the good beer. He walks over and starts picking at Meat.

"Meat, I love you, man, but you should know by now that I'm the master. I fuck with people for a living!"

Meat says, "You're right... You're the fucking man."

There's an unwritten code among softball players: "Don't fuck with a man's beer." It's almost as bad as fucking his wife. Whatley walks over, gets his last beer, and walks back over to the truck. Guys start to part, sort of like the Red Sea in the Bible. No one wants to be in front of him when he drinks it. He turns it up, and piss goes flying everywhere.

"Goddamn it, Meat, you big bastard!"

He chases Meat between cars, trying to throw it on him, and we are laughing our asses off. About that time, a Ashton police cruiser pulls into the parking lot. Now technically, it's against the law to drink beer on city property. He sees the beer in Whatley's hand and calls him over to the car.

"What's going on here, son?"

Whatley says, "Officer, that big bastard over there pissed in my fucking beer. That's what's going on. And I want to press charges." Then Whatley says something we can't hear.

The officer steps out and says, "Big guy, you're under arrest for unlawful urination."

Now that's a law I have never heard of, but he puts the handcuffs on Meat and puts him in the back seat of the car.

"Ben, call Julie and tell her to come post my bail."

He drives off. I ask someone to borrow their cell phone.

"You don't need to call her! He'll be back in five minutes. That was my cousin!"

Whatley cranks his truck and aims it toward the exit, leaving it running. Next, he fills a cup up with his piss and tops it off with what was left in the bottle. Sure enough, the cruiser pulls back in. The door opens, and Meat steps out, still in handcuffs. When he steps far enough away from the car, *splash!* Piss all over his chest. Whatley runs like hell to his truck, hops in, and leaves.

By the time the cop gets the handcuffs off, Whatley is pulling away. He rolls down his window and yells, "Don't fuck with the master!"

Meat is pissed, in more ways than one. We're trying hard not to laugh.

"Ben, take me home."

"Okay, but your stinking ass is riding in the back of the truck."

The moral to this story: don't fuck with a man's beer unless you're ready to pay the ultimate price. Just another night playin' ball.

Thursday morning, I receive a call from Mark.

"Ben, we've decided to go to Dothan to play this weekend."

"Okay! But I have got to go to Atlanta. I haven't been up there in a while to see my mother, and she's starting to make me feel guilty. But I'll tell Calvin, Meat, and Coy. What time are you leaving?"

"Six a.m. We play at ten."

I give all my guys a call. They all can go except for Meat. He's in a band, and they're playing on Friday and Saturday night at one of the local clubs. Meat plays the bass guitar, and actually, he's not bad. He even sings a few songs in the band. Their band is good, at least for local standards. I just wish they had a decent group name. Their band name is Fourth and Four. I thought up several names that I thought were better. But they didn't like them. My favorite was the name Third Wish. Think about it. You open up a bottle, and a genie pops out. She says you can have three wishes. What would you wish for? First, I would want good health. Second, I would want to be wealthy. But what would you wish for on the third wish? It's your last one. World peace? Nah, even a magical genie couldn't make that shit happen. No more famine? No, that's God's way of controlling the world's population. End global warming? I'm not really sure it exists, and besides, Al Gore wouldn't have anything else to run his piehole about. A bigger dick? No, I can live with what I have. I guess I'd wish to be abducted by aliens. Why? Hell, I feel left out. I've never even seen a UFO, much less an alien. I think they must have something against abducting fat people. I mean, think about it. You never ever hear a fat person say they were abducted by aliens. Either the aliens are prejudiced against fat people or that beam of light you always hear about has a weight limit. Aliens must also be prejudiced against IQ too. You never hear about a rocket scientist, doctor, or lawyer being abducted either. But wouldn't it be great if they abducted lawyers and dropped them off on another planet like, say, Pluto? Wait, Pluto isn't even a planet anymore. But I'm sure if you filled it with lawyers, they'd sue to have it reinstated. But if all the aliens want us for is our sperm, then hey, I'm their hookup. I have a lot they can have. And if they hand me a cup and some alien porn, I'd fill it up for them. Experiments? Hell, they can do whatever they want to, except stick an anal probe up my ass. Yeah, that episode of Cartman getting an anal probe on *South Park* still bothers me.

Okay, so I'm fascinated by the paranormal: UFOs, ghosts, ESP, and other weird shit. It is truly fascinating. And while I'm on this subject, I have to admit that I've seen a ghost too. I'm not shitting you about this either. Way back in 1987, in my parents' basement. And I am man enough to tell you that I ran up the stairs like a scared child. I was playing with a Ouija board at the time it occurred and challenged it to give me a sign. It did, and I've never used one since. And no, I wasn't smoking anything either. The ghost was that of a man, and I could tell he was an evil spirit. How did I know? By the look he had in his eyes. But what was so scary about it was, he just appeared about five feet in front of me. Before it happened, I felt this terrible cold sensation around me, the kind that makes the hair stand on the back of your neck. Then boom, I looked up, and there he was, looking right through me. I couldn't scream. Hell, I couldn't move for what felt like an hour. When I finally got my shit together, that was when I ran like hell upstairs. I actually think I only touched two of the thirteen steps. Of course, no one upstairs would believe me. And they still don't to this day.

Sorry about that, I got offtrack a little. I will do that a lot in this book, so get used to it. And I'm not going to apologize about it anymore! But I still think that Third Wish is a great name for a rock band. I wrote a song that I'm trying to get the guys to record. Just for fun, of course. It's too trashy to get any airplay, but it is funny as hell. One of the guys in the band has a small recording studio at his house. That's where they record all their demo tapes. I'd like them to record my song just so I could send a copy to Howard Stern. Why Howard? Because he's the only one I know that might appreciate it. And now that he's on Sirius Satellite, he could play it without getting fined. Plus, I've always been a fan of his. We couldn't get him in our market when he was on regular radio. But what do you expect? This is Alabama and the Bible belt. But I did watch his show on E! I also read his books and own the DVD *Private Parts*. What I respect about Howard is that he refused to cave in to station directors when they tried to change his show or to get him to tone it down. Honestly, that really takes some balls. I think I'm a little that way too. But I'm sure if this book ever gets published, an editor will tone it down. Since I don't have Howard's clout, I'm sure I'll have to go along with it. Right now, Howard is a have, and I'm a have-not. Anyway, the song really is pretty funny, but you'll have to read the lyrics. It's called "If My Hand Had Titties and My Dog Could Dance."

> If my hand had titties and my dog could dance,
> I wouldn't need your loving, wouldn't need your romance.
> I could save all my money and buy a brand-new truck.
> Don't need your pussy; I've got my own hand to fuck.
> No need to buy a diamond or a fancy string of pearls.
> No need to wear a condom; I'm through fucking girls.
> 'Cause my hand's always beside me; it's there through thick and thin.
> And when I get horny, it's raring to go again.
> My hand doesn't get a headache like my girlfriend did.
> It doesn't get pissed if I forget to close the toilet lid.
> I don't have to go downtown and buy it maxipads.
> It doesn't turn into Satan once a month, and I'm so damn glad.
> My dog, I know she loves me 'cause of all the things she'll do.
> She brings me my paper; she'll even bring me a brew.
> But my dog cannot two-step out on the dance room floor,
> and she'll shit in my bedroom if I forget to close the door.
> You see, women have the pussy, and as men, well, we're all fucked,
> so we tell 'em that we love 'em and hope with just a little luck
> maybe they'll let us inside or our dicks might get sucked,
> but call the Chevrolet dealer and cancel that brand-new truck.

Okay, what did you expect? I never claimed to be Paul Simon.

Well, while the team gets ready for the Dothan tournament, I get ready for Atlanta. Saturday rolls around. I call Mark and wish them good luck. I'm off to Atlanta to visit my mother. The tournament is a big one. The winning team gets twelve bats; second place, twelve gloves; and third place, twelve bat bags. So the best teams will all be there. Mark promises to call me at Mother's on my cell phone when they finish.

Speaking of my mother, we talk often on the phone, and when we do me, she always makes me feel guilty about not coming home enough to see her. But what does she do the whole time that I'm up there? She stays on the phone. I usually end up watching the Braves and a lot of ESPN when I visit. Now I go home about once a month. It's about a two-hour drive from Olive Grove to Linwood, Georgia. Not a bad drive, but there's a lot of traffic in Atlanta that I hate to deal with.

When I arrive at my mother's, she is on the phone. In fact, she talks the first forty-five minutes I'm there. Well, when Mother finally gets off the phone, we talk.

"Benny ever since your father passed away, I just feel so alone. I just don't hear from anyone."

"Mother, I'm sorry Dad died, but you knew it was coming for the last four years he was alive."

My father had been bedridden from a series of strokes. He couldn't eat, talk, or anything else. He was on a damn feeding tube.

"At least you know now that he's better off."

"Yes, but I still miss him. That's something you'll understand better when you get married. Benny, when are you going to get married? You're forty now, and you need to settle down."

"Mother, I will get married if and when I want to. And at the moment, I don't want to."

"Well, you know I would like to have a grandchild from you before I die."

"Well..." I thought for a minute. "You may be in luck there."

"What do you mean?"

"Well, Donna's pregnant. She's due in July."

"Who is this Donna?"

"The woman I've been seeing."

I remember that Mother hasn't been down to visit in over six years. That was a couple of years before my father's last stroke.

"I told you about her."

"When are you getting married?"

"We're not, at least not yet."

"You mean the baby will be a bastard?"

Well, I'm starting to get pissed. But I do realize she is my mother and she was brought up in a different time. Not to mention, she's hard-core Baptist.

"Mother, children are not referred to as bastards today."

"Well, I want to meet this Donna."

"You will, I promise."

The conversation with my mother reminds me of my high school days. My mother never liked one girl I brought home. Not one. One weekend, when she and my father went to the cabin for the weekend and weren't due back in till Sunday, I had a date with... I'll call her Marla since I don't want to be sued. Saturday night after dinner and a movie, I took her back to the house to prolong our date. Just as soon as I got Marla's clothes off and was about to play gynecologist, the kitchen door opened up and in stormed my parents. Evidently, they had a fight and cut short their trip. We tried to grab our clothes, but to no avail. My mother screamed. Then she started yelling, "What the hell are you doing on my couch? That's the couch I sit on and you're... Get this bitch out of my house!"

Needless to say, after that, my mother has never thought much of the woman I date. My father's only comment when we were alone was "How was it?" It was a shame I never got to find out.

The phone rings.

I answer, "Hello."

"Is Georgia in?"

"It's for you, Mother." I hand her the phone.

"Hi, Dave. No, I haven't heard. So there's a new update. I'll look at it."

I knew right then it was another multilevel/pyramid patsy like my mother. I love my mother, but she is a sucker for these multilevel/pyramid schemes, always has been. She has been waiting on these things to pay off millions for years. But they keep stringing her along with other elderly folks and other people who fall prey to their schemes. There is no telling how much money these things bilk out of people like my mother. I know she's put in over twenty thousand dollars, but she'll never admit it. She always says it's her money. I just wish the government could do something about them. But she won't tell me the names of the people running them because she knows I'll report them. She hangs up the phone. My cell phone rings. It's Mark.

"Ben, we ended up fifth."

"That's not too bad," I say, trying to get a feeling how he felt.

"No, we just came up a little short, but everyone played hard."

If I had a dollar for every time I'd heard that... I thought, *No, my penis is not small!*

"Well, Mark, thanks for letting me know. I guess I'll see you Monday night at the park."

Well, it's back to the Braves game. God, I can't wait to get home. I miss my dogs Sparky, Skipper, and Dusty. I have a friend taking care of them. His name is Ford. He is the reason I moved to Olive Grove in 1989 from north Georgia. I took a job working for his company. When he retired in the early nineties, so did I, although I do still have some projects that I work on the side from time to time.

And I even started this book. *Boy, do I have to fill Donna in about my mother when I get home,* I think. Mother goes to the computer to check her email update.

Sunday finally arrives, and I'm getting ready to make the drive back to Olive Grove. I stop by Best Buy to pick up a new CD to listen to on the drive back. I decide on Van Halen's *Best of Volume I*. God, Van Halen kicked ass when David Lee Roth was with them. I mean, Sammy Hagar was good, but he was no Diamond Dave. "And the Cradle Will Rock" kicks in. I crank it up.

Funny how loud music can relax us. Plus, you need it to get through the traffic in Atlanta. The Atlanta traffic is the reason I got rid of my Corvette and bought a truck, because some idiot cut in front of me and almost got me killed two years ago. Plus, being forty, I thought it was time to drive something a little more mature. So I bought a large truck. That's not to say that if this book sells, I wouldn't consider buying a convertible Jag. But the truck is more practical and has more metal for protection. When I was a teenager, I never had any thoughts about death, till my best friend in high school was killed in an automobile accident at the age of sixteen. That's when I started writing poetry. It wasn't very good poetry, but it helped me deal with his loss. Today, however, I know there's something to live for: Donna and Junior.

Since I have two hours to kill, maybe I should tell you a little about myself. I was born on July 7 I know that makes me a Cancer. And I fit the typical Cancer traits to a tee. If you haven't guessed it yet, I have a problem with commitment. I will explain the reasons why throughout the book. The fact is, I've started writing several books. Some were scrapped like the fictional book about killers who met their victims online through one of the dating services. I heard that may have actually happened. And I didn't want to give anyone ideas. The other was one based on a dream I had. It was about a guy from Atlanta who wakes up alone in Phoenix. But he was all alone. No one could be found. The streets were empty, but all the buildings were still intact. The television only showed reruns of shows from the fifties and sixties. It was like an episode out of the *Twilight Zone*. Eventually, he did meet some people like him. I won't go into further detail because I may actually one day get back on it. So as you can see, I have a wild imagination. But then again, you probably already know that since I admitted I've seen a ghost.

The drive home is uneventful, except I saw a number of deer grazing on the side of the expressway. They are beautiful animals but do cause a number of deaths each year when they run in front of someone's automobile. So I always approach them cautiously. As I pull into the garage, I hear "Woof, woof, woof!" Here they come.

Ford asks, "How was your trip?"

"Same ole shit! How were the dogs?"

"Pretty shitty! Sparky ate shit the whole time you were gone."

Ah, home sweet home.

Sunday night, it's HBO night. My all-time favorite shows on there are *The Sopranos, Sex and the City, The Larry Sanders Show*, and *Dream On*. God, I love HBO. They have their shit together when it comes to television series.

I now own all the *Sex and the City* shows on DVD. I just wish Carrie had told Big how she felt. And god, what I wouldn't like to do to Samantha. I only wish I could have written the scripts.

Oz was also a great show. But *Oz* was just so intense. I think I would kill myself before I ever went to prison. If misguided kids in trouble were forced to watch just one episode of *Oz*, especially one where some young man gets raped, it would scare the shit out of them. I remember watching the documentary *Scared Straight* when I was in school. It scared the shit out of me. And I was straight.

I decide to call Donna to let her know I'm back home.

"Hello, Ben."

Damn, caller ID. I wanted to surprise her.

"How's the hottest woman this side of Halle Berry doing?"

"I'm fine. How's my little semistud short of being Brad Pitt?"

God, she's good at this game, I thought.

"How was your mother?"

"She was her typical self, as crazy as a rabid dog on Viagra."

"You shouldn't say that about your mother. She, after all, gave birth to you."

"I know, I know, and she never lets me forget it either. I did tell her about you and the baby."

"How did she take it?"

"The way I thought she would. She called you a slut and wanted to know when the wedding was."

"Well, you can't blame her. You dropped a bombshell on her."

I thought, *God, women always stick fucking together.*

"You're not pissed about being called a slut?"

"No, my parents have referred to you as a no-good sack of poop. I just put things in context."

"A sack of poop? They don't know me that well, and they could at least say *shit*. *Poop* is so juvenile! Besides, how can they judge me? I've only been with them on a couple of occasions."

"Exactly my point, Ben. They don't know you. They just know you got their little girl knocked up. That's why we're having dinner with them next week. Is Tuesday good for you?"

I pause long enough to get my shit together. I know I have to agree to dinner. I just don't want to look like I've caved in.

"How about Thursday? It would work better for me."

Now, guys, you have to realize that actually, Tuesday would have been better for me since I have a full schedule on Thursday and I'll have to change some business appointments. But at least it gives the appearance of not caving in; plus, it puts me in control. You see, I know she already has cleared this with her parents, and maybe Thursday will be a bad day for them. Guys, this is what is known as being on top of your game. And I am in the zone.

"Actually, Ben, Thursday works better because my father has a union meeting on Tuesday. I just thought you had a busy day on Thursday. That's why I set it up for Tuesday."

"No, Thursday is good. How about six thirty?" I say.

"That'll work."

With that, we say good night.

Okay, I know. I know she got the best of me again. But see, she doesn't know that. So I'm still in control, although I did agree to have dinner with her folks. Damn, I just realized that if her father is having a union meeting, he probably is a Democrat. Damn, it's going to be a long fucking night.

Well, it's Monday, getting ready for tonight's games. Both Nightmare teams have fairly easy games. There's just one small problem: weather.

There's a 70 percent chance of rain. All day long, it looks like it is going to rain. I walk outside, and my glasses fog up.

Damn, it's humid.

Meat calls at five o'clock.

"How's the weather look?"

"Looks like the games are still on, Meat."

"Well, it's starting to rain up here."

"Just bring your ass on. You know how the weather works. If we get rained out, we'll go get some wings and beer."

"Damn, Ben, I hope we get rained out now. Just mention wings and beer to a softball player and you've got them in the palm of your hand."

Most guys would rather eat wings and drink beer than go out with Sarah Jessica Parker. Notice I said *most*, not *me*. God, I've got to stop watching *Sex and the City*. I'm sorry, but women talking about sex just does it for me. And the truth is, we men know they all do it. I would just like to be a fly on the wall when Donna and her friends are talking sex in the break room at work.

"Ben, it's like the movie *Gandhi*. It's a four-hour show, worthy of an Oscar, and you fall asleep exhausted after it's over."

Okay, so I made that up. Meat shows up at five thirty, and we hit the road. We always have to get our game face on, and to do that, you guessed it—rock music. Tonight we're in an old Southern rock mood: Blackfoot, Mother's Finest, and Molly Hatchet. Since Meat's not writing this, I'll say it for him: "That's fucking music!" I'm traveling down the road, and I'm flirting with disaster comes blaring out the speakers. We're getting ready now. We always end up playing Blackfoot's "Highway Song" last. It's the greatest Southern rock song of all time, at least in my book. And this is my book. Sorry, Skynyrd fans, "Free Bird" is second.

Well, when we get to the complex, it's looking bad. We get our gear out and make our way to the fields. Most of the guys are already there.

"Coach Ben, what do you think? Think we'll play?" Bryan says.

"What do I look like? The fucking weather channel? I don't know. We'll either play or drink beer."

About that time, the bottom falls out. It takes them all of five minutes to call off the games. I tell Todd to make sure Bryan and Lewis put their floaties on. I'd hate to see them drown. I heard "Kiss my ass, Ben." I don't know which one said it, but it was one of the two.

Holly says, "What about me?"

"Holly, Todd paid enough for those puppies. I'm sure they'll keep you afloat."

"They're real, Ben."

"And so is the hair on my head."

She pulls off my cap.

"It looks real."

"It should. I pay enough to keep the bald spot covered."

"Ben wears a rug, Ben wears a rug!"

"Goddamn it, Holly, if I wanted the whole town to know, I'd have taken out a fucking full-page ad in the *OA News*. And besides, it's not a toupee, it's a hair replacement system."

"What's the difference?" Holly says.

"About four thousand dollars a year."

"Ben, you should just shave your head. Michael Jordan does, and he's sexy."

"Holly, Michael Jordan is a gazillionaire, and he's known all over the world. He can get away with shaving his head. I can't."

"Jeez, you guys are so vain."

"Todd, will you please get your wife off my back? She's killing me."

I will admit my bald spot is a touchy issue with me, and yes, I am a little vain. Admitting you're bald is like admitting you take Viagra or you shave your testicles. Some things are better not said. No, I'm not telling you about any of the above.

———

We decide to go to Buffalo Connection to eat. They have the best wings and five different beers on tap. We spend the rest of the night talking about my hair replacement system and, oh yeah, the next tournament.

It's about ten o'clock when I get home. I decide to call Donna since she had taken a couple of days off from work. She had a doctor's appointment and was going to visit her parents, probably to give them the lowdown on me. You know, what to say, what to ask. So I call her up.

"Hello."

"Donna, how did the visit go with your parents?"

"It went well. I hooked their computer to the internet and showed them how to use it."

"I bet your dad has already got an adult ID pass so he can look at porn."

"He's Methodist! Methodist men don't look at porn."

I thought, *Bull-fucking-shit.* "And I'm Mel Gibson too."

"No, Ben, you're more like Mel Brooks."

"That hurt. Anyway, Donna, the reason I'm calling is—"

"Phone sex."

"No, but we can work that in. It's my mother. I guess you'll have to meet her soon."

"Wow! That sounds serious. I really am looking forward to meeting her. She can't be as bad as you say."

"What have I told you about her?"

"Only that she hated all your old girlfriends and that she looked a little like Shirley Jones."

"Well, picture Shirley Jones possessed by Satan on a bad PMS day."

"She can't be that bad."

"Well, when I told her you're pregnant, she insisted on meeting you. She's going to push marriage down your throat, and she may even call you a slut. After all, she is Baptist."

"Ah, I can handle her. Besides, you know my parents think you're a piece of poo redneck."

"I really wish you would stop saying that. Besides, I thought it was a 'sack of poop.' And for your information, I don't have a rebel flag on my truck or a bumper sticker that says Shit Happens, nor do I have a gun rack behind the seat. So I'm not a freaking redneck. I can't help that I have superhuman sperm and that the pill didn't work."

"Well, you could have gotten a vasectomy. I mean, you didn't want children anyway."

I couldn't believe what I just heard. A man has a special bond with his penis. I mean, we even give it a name and talk to it. Well, at least I do. Hell, I even have a Christmas stocking for mine. The thought of a vasectomy—well, like Dr. Smith said to Will Robinson on *Lost in Space*: "The pain, the pain."

"Ben, it's just a little snip, snip."

"Okay, Donna, that's enough." I say that to get her off the subject. The boys were now officially on strike, so I might as well forget about the phone sex.

"Ben, I do have some interesting news. They did an ultrasound today, and they're pretty sure the baby is a boy."

Wow! That is unexpected. I am speechless. I guess I had hoped it would be a boy. "Ben, are you okay?"

"Yes, I just wasn't expecting that."

"Well, it could have been a shadow, but it looked like a little ding-a-ling. They're going to do another in a few weeks."

With that, we hang up.

I decide to watch a movie so I won't have nightmares of the grim reaper trying to cut my balls off.

I decide to watch *A Fish Called Wanda*. It's one of my favorite movies of all time; plus, Jamie Lee Curtis is so hot in it. I had almost put *On Golden Pond* in the DVD player, but it almost makes me cry. Okay, okay, I admit I've cried watching two movies. And, guys, it's okay to cry if the movie has a sports theme in it. The movies were *Something for Joey* and *Brian's Song*. I always lose it when Gale Sayers says "Brian Piccolo is my friend." In real life, they must have had a great friendship. If you've never seen either movie, I suggest you watch them. In fact, watch them with your lady. She'll think you're such a sensitive guy.

And women just love sensitive guys. And you know where that could lead!

Damn, this book is informative! Dr. Phil, eat your heart out.

Well, it's Thursday morning. I awake with a call from Donna.

"Hello."

"Ben, remember, tonight we're having dinner with my parents."

"I know. I haven't forgotten."

"Well, be nice. Use that 'I'll charm the pants right off' side of your personality."

"Okay, but if your mother gets naked, it's not my fault."

"Ben... I..."

"What now?"

"I'm serious."

"Donna, I promise to play nice. Jeez!"

"Okay, see you at six."

I could tell by the tone in her voice she has her apprehensions. Well, I do too. Clair and Wayne are a bit rigid for me. I feel like they looked down their noses to me the first time I met them. Knowing they think I'm a sack of poop doesn't help the matter.

I bet neither one of them has ever had so much as one alcoholic drink, much less ever been drunk. Not that I advocate that. I don't. They're just a little too tightly wound for me. A drink might loosen them up, but I doubt it.

I rush around like crazy and try to get everything done. By the time I walk in the house, it's 5:05 p.m. I let the dogs out in the backyard and start to get undressed. By the time I hit the shower, it's 5:15 p.m. It's a ten-minute drive to Donna's house, so I know I have time. In twenty minutes, I manage to shower, shave, shit, get dressed, and feed the dogs. I walk out my door at a quarter till. Life is all about timing.

I arrive at Donna's a few minutes early. I'm greeted at the door by Scruffy. His name says it all. He's a mixed dog that Donna found along the interstate.

"Donna, are you ready?"

No answer, but I could hear the hair dryer in the bathroom. I walk in.

"Oh, Ben, you startled me."

"Sorry, Donna! But you need to get the lead out or we'll be late."

"I'm hurrying as fast as I can. Look on my bed and pick out which dress I should wear."

While she puts on the finishing touches to her makeup, I look over the dresses. Guys, women always like for men to tell them what they should wear but never take our advice. Knowing this, I'll pick the worst of the three. She has a light-pastel-blue dress, a peach-colored dress, and a red dress on the bed. My favorite is the peach.

She walks out and says, "What do you think?"

I notice she has sort of pink eye makeup on. "I like the red one!" I say, knowing immediately that it would be eliminated.

"Well, I think I'm going to wear this one," she says, picking up the peach-colored dress.

I smile, knowing my reverse psychology has once again paid off. Who cares if only I know it.

She gets dressed in a hurry. "Zip me up, Ben?" With that, it's off to the races.

"Are we still going to Red Lobster, Donna?"

"No, there's been a change of plans. Daddy doesn't like seafood. He wants to go to the Outback, if that's okay?"

Damn! He already has a leg up, I think. "Yeah, it's okay."

Looks like it's going to be a long tricking night.

We pull up to the Outback just as Wayne is getting out of their automobile. Timing... At least they are punctual. We get out of the car, and Donna runs to greet them.

Clair is a nice-looking, very classy lady. She is fifty-four years old. She dresses very conservatively, but she does have a nice rack. I know you shouldn't look at the chest of your girlfriend's mother. But that may be what your lady looks like in twenty-plus years. So it's okay.

Wayne has a medium build, a little belly, with white hair and a pencil-thin mustache. He looks like a banker, kind of like Milburn Drysdale on *Beverly Hillbillies*. He is a supervisor at the automobile plant in town. I believe he is fifty-six years old. I extend my hand.

"Nice to see you again, Mr. Davis, Mrs. Davis."

"Ben, you should just call us Clair and Wayne," says Mrs. Davis.

"Okay... Clair, Wayne, how have you been?"

"Fine" comes from Wayne's lips.

"Okay, what do you say we try to find a table before the crowds get here?"

With that, we walk in. I'm going over all the news in my head, trying to find a subject on which I'll agree with them, sort of news light.

"How many in your party?" asks the hostess.

"Four for nonsmoking."

"Please follow me."

We're seated, and the waiter comes right over. I know him from softball. He plays on a local league team.

"How do you do, Mr. Thompson?"

"Fine, John, how are you?"

I always believe you should treat your waiter with respect. And I always overtip. Most of them are in college and need the money. Plus, you don't want to piss them off or they may spit in your food. We place our drink and food orders. Time for small talk. Fuck!

"Wayne, what do you think of the Braves and all those young guys they have? They're playing pretty good, aren't they?"

"I don't keep up with baseball much. I'm waiting for football season to start!" he says.

Okay, I think, *then I'll talk football.*

"How do you think Auburn will do this year?"

"They should be good enough to win the SEC West."

We chat about football a few minutes till it plays out.

Wayne looks at me and asks, "What do you think about this Middle East mess?" By that, he means the war on terror.

I try to couch my words so as not to upset him but also try to be honest. "Well... to be honest, we have made some mistakes."

"Like putting troops on the ground and endless search for weapons of mass destruction?" Wayne says.

"No, while I think our intelligence was wrong about what Saddam had, and I don't think the strategy was the best, I think it was a good idea because I'd rather fight the terrorists there than here in the US."

"Well, I hope those idiots who voted for Bush enjoyed all the body bags and injuries of our boys that came home."

"I really think that's not an—"

"Ben." Donna steps in. "Will you go to the car and get my handbag?" she says.

She gives me one of those "cool it" looks. Knowing that she is correct, I do so. I need some air anyway. Walking across the parking lot, I think to myself what a fucking piece of shit Wayne is. I go back into the restaurant with Donna's bag.

"Ben, I'm sorry, I should not have brought up the war," Wayne says.

Hmm, Donna or Clair must have chewed him out good. "Well... Wayne, it's a touchy subject. To be honest, I don't like it either. I just don't have the solutions to the problem."

With that, we enjoy our meal. When the check comes, Wayne and I both reach for the check.

"Boys," Clair says, "this one's on me. I don't want you guys arm wrestling for it."

I look at Donna, and she nods in approval. We walk to the car and say our good nights.

Donna and I get in the car.

"Ben, Daddy was just testing you. He loves the Braves. He has a den full of memorabilia just like you."

"Why did he... Never mind."

We get back to her house and say good night. She gives me a soft kiss and says, "I love you!"

"I love you too, Donna!"

On my drive home, I tell myself it wasn't that bad. I guess I can understand his position. If my daughter were pregnant and not married, I would be upset.

You don't know if the father will take care of his child. There are too many deadbeat dads out there. If you can make them, you should be able to provide for them. So I guess I understand Wayne's position. I'll just have to prove him wrong. Maybe what we all should do is try to put ourselves in their shoes. That really applies to everything in life. There are always two sides to a subject, and maybe if we look at both, we might understand the other person's view. If you want to know the truth, I'm not fond of the Republicans or the Democrats. The problem is, there's just no middle-of-the-road party. Neither party really gives a shit about us or our problems. They may say that they do so you'll vote for them. But their main goal is reelection. You have to remember, all politicians are ego driven. And most are lawyers, which says it all. I believe the lawyers who turn to politics are just too lazy to chase ambulances. It's much easier for them to get paid off by lobbyists than to go to court. When I go to vote, I just always try to vote for the lesser of two evils. It used to mean a Republican; now I don't know.

Our next tournament is in Penson, Alabama, in Meat's part of the woods. Penson is on the state line about eighteen miles north of Olive Grove and just across the Chattahoochee River from Georgia. The tournament is an invitational, meaning anyone can play no matter what class they are in. We play at nine, Saturday morning. We arrive at the softball complex, which really is a nice complex, maybe only a year or two old. We're playing a local team. They really aren't that good, but they just enjoy playing ball. Well, we struggle early, but we finally get the bats going and beat them in five innings by the ten-run rule.

Our next game is at one o'clock. We have time to kill. Meat invites us to go to his house and take a dip in the pool. We stop by a Wal-Mart to buy swimming trunks and towels. David "Meat" has a nice house, and his pool is new. It even has a nice diving hit board. All the guys jump in the water to cool off. When I was growing up, we had a public pool across the street from my parents' house, so I learned to swim and dive at an early age. Five or six of the guys decide to have a diving contest. Holly, Todd, and I are the judges. Joey does a flip, followed by Bryan trying to do a swan dive, which looked more like a dying duck.

"Bryan, that looked like shit."

"Coach Ben, if you can do any better, bring it on!" he replies.

"Be careful what you wish for, Opie."

Okay, so I wanted to show the boys up a little. I pull off my jersey and go inside the house to put on my trunks. I come out with my Jimmy Buffett trunks on. The guys all start making fun of them. That didn't last long though. I tell Dirk to get off the board and let a pro show them how to do it. I walk to the end of board and take a couple of springs. Damn, the diving board is pretty good; it has lots of spring. "Guys, I'm going to do just one dive unless any of you can do it." I run toward the end of board, take two springs, and do a one and a half with a full twist and hit it perfectly.

I come up to the surface, and all the guys' mouths are still open. They just couldn't believe a semifat forty-year-old could pull that off. To be honest, neither could I since it had been years since I was dumb enough to try it. I get out of the water and get a hug from Holly.

"Ben, I'm so impressed, and your hair system stayed on!" she says.

"Holly, I'm good at a lot of things and great at others." Then I give her a wink.

We have about thirty minutes till game time, so everyone gets out to dry off.

And it's back to the fields. The team we play is AFS; no, I don't know what that stands for. But I do know they wore yellow jerseys. A men's softball team should never wear yellow or pink. It just isn't right. You might as well have a sign on your back that says "I'm a pussy."

They are the visiting team, so they bat first. I've never seen them play before, so we don't know much about them. They score four runs in the top of the first. We come to bat, and it's time to answer. And boy, do we. We end up scoring eleven runs. After one inning, it's 11–4. They have never gotten over that inning; plus, our guys have started picking on them about the yellow jerseys. We win the game 21–15.

Our next game is at four o'clock, against Powerhouse Softball. We go to the trucks for refreshments. Some of the guys throw horseshoes. Mark and I talk.

I ask Mark why he is so intense.

"Ben, when I first started playing, I was horrible, and everyone made fun of me. I remember everything everybody ever said. It made me bust my ass to get better to prove them wrong."

Mark is correct; he was absolutely terrible. I remember him well. I must admit that I have tremendous respect for him now. A lot of people would have quit, but not Mark. It drove him to improve himself, and he did. He is now one of the best, if not the best, home run hitters around this area. I like guys who don't make excuses or blame everyone or everything for any problems they have. If you have the will to succeed, you will.

Donna told me I should include this story, so I am going to talk about it just a little. When I was nine years old, I fell out of my tree house. My head busted open like a cracked egg. I almost died. Truthfully, I think I did as I had an NDE (near-death experience). When I came to, I couldn't talk; I had suffered brain damage. I finally got so I could talk, but I had this terrible speech impediment. I stuttered. Kids at school made fun of me. I would go home crying. My mother set up speech therapy classes, and my father told me to beat the shit out of the next kid who made fun of me. The advice and therapy eventually worked. I no longer sounded like Mel Tillis, and no one else fucked with me. It did require me to work my ass off. I had to learn to speak all over again. One good thing, however, came out of it. It made me more confident in my ability to overcome any problems in my life. And like Mark, it made me appreciate the things that I have to work for.

It's getting close to game time, and we make our way to the field. Powerhouse is a great offensive team but a little weak defensively. I change my lineup to have more left-handed batters at the top of the lineup. Joey leads off with a deep fly ball that the right fielder could not get to. He ends up on third. Bryan follows him with a single to right, to score Joey. Todd hitting third hits a shot that hits the third-base bag and kicks toward the dugout. Dirk hits a three-run shot: "Home run!" Mark and Meat hit back-to-back doubles to score one more. Kroy hits a single to score Meat. We end up scoring six runs in the top of the first. Powerhouse comes in to bat and scores five runs. So it's 6–5 after one inning. It was a seesaw game back and forth. We take the lead in the top of the seventh inning on a three-run homer by Hal.

"Good hit, Hal," I say.

"Thanks," he replies.

Damn, he talked to me.

I decide it was time to make a pitching change. Coy is a good pitcher, but this is slow-pitch softball. I decide to let Bryan pitch. He has a little knuckleball; it doesn't move around much, but it does mess with the hitters' heads.

When you can see the laces of the ball, it tends to mesmerize you. Bryan works his magic. Powerhouse goes three up, three down.

We win; we're in the finals. There are still two games to be played to see who meets us for the championship. We head toward the truck. Powerhouse will play the winner of Roscoe's and Riverview Auto. Dirk's wife volunteers to go pick us up something to eat. She's a sweet girl. She comes back with a shitload of burgers from Mickey D's. Nothing tastes as good as a Big Mac when you're starving, well except maybe two. And I need to say this about McDonald's: Why in the hell does our justice system allow a couple of fat girls and their parents to sue them? I mean, McDonald's didn't shove the burgers down their throats, neither did they give them the food for free. The girls' parents are the ones who should be responsible for letting them become obese. McDonald's has never claimed to be a health food chain.

Back in the eighties, D'Lites opened up. Their claim was lower-fat burgers, healthier fast food. What happened to them? They went out of business. My point is this: America, open up your eyes; if little Joey is fat as hell, take responsibility. As a parent, it's up to you, and you have to take the lead even if it means pissing him off. Take away his video games, make him play outside or ride his bike. Stop letting him eat burgers and candy at will. And stop lawyers from these damn frivolous lawsuits. They overload our judicial system and make lawyers rich, thereby creating more fucking lawyers, like we don't have enough as it is. Just my opinion, and now I'll probably get sued.

Our game time is seven o'clock. Roscoe's beats Riverview Auto. I don't remember the score. I'll just say it was a lot to a little. Sorry, I had a few too many beers. Howard Roscoe sponsors Roscoe's. This guy is the Donald Trump of Rockville. He owns chicken plants and hardware stores, and he has an ego the size of his bank account. Softball is just an advertisement for his ego. He buys and sells players like stock options. Roscoe's beat Powerhouse easily. Bryan, Kroy, and Joey know some of the players on the team. I think they went to school with them. Since we're in the winners bracket, they would have to beat us twice to win the tournament.

The game starts off with us scoring three runs in the first; they come in to hit and score five. Roscoe is screaming and yelling at his players and the umpires all game long. He reminds me of Billy Martin in a road rage. No matter what we do, we can't seem to catch up. We end up losing the first game 31–26. Rarely in softball does a team get double dipped. "Lose two games back-to-back for a championship." So I tell the guys I have confidence in them. After all, we're a damn good team. We're the home team for the next game, so they bat first. They start the game by hitting shot after shot up the middle. Bryan gets his glove on a few. It's enough to slow them down, but not enough to get an out. Now I don't get pissed off often.

But when the batters would hit the ball at Bryan, they would say "Sorry, Bryan." They knew what the fuck they were doing. Bryan comes in the dugout after the first inning; his hand is swelling up.

"Bryan," I said, "I'm putting Coy in to pitch. You may have broken bone in your hand."

"Coach Ben, I'm okay. I can't back down. They'll think I'm weak."

As a coach, you have to do what is best for the team. You have to leave personal feelings out of the decision-making process. Sometimes, though, emotion gets the better of you. Bryan is a trooper, and he's a good kid with a lot of heart, so I decide to let him stay in. Well, we start to get taken out of our game. Instead of trying to get hits, we want blood.

We try our best to knock their pitcher out of the game. A little redemption for Bryan. Well, the bottom of the seventh rolls around. We're down by nine runs. Now it's not about winning; it's personal. Bryan can't hold on to a bat, so we have to pinch-hit for him.

Fuck winning!

I tell the guys, "Let's get some payback."

Coy hits for Bryan. First pitch, he hits a shot at the pitcher's shin.

"Bingo, payback motherfucker!" comes out of Calvin's mouth.

The pitcher gets up and gets ready to pitch. Mark's up and hits a shot over the pitcher's head for a single. Meat's up next. He grunts and smacks a hard one hopper that bounces up and drills their pitcher in the ribs. Bases are loaded. Their pitcher motions over to their dugout; he's hurt. Roscoe comes running out of the dugout and mouths off to me, something about bush league bullshit.

"Fuck you, you piece of shit!" I respond.

"Do you know who I am?" Roscoe replies.

Mark chimes in with "You're fixing to be a motherfucker taking an ass whipping if you say another goddamn word."

We finally make the third out to end the game. We lost 28–26. But in my heart, I honestly feel like we won, maybe not the game. But we have come together as a team, and that's the main thing.

Monday morning rolls around, and I decide it's time to start getting the swimming pool ready. I take off the leaf cover. What a pain in the ass. The water is green and looks like a cesspool. David's pool is already nice, clean, and swimmable. I have to admit I hate this time of year. There's so much yard work to do to get everything ready for summer. Mark calls me on my cell phone.

I hate cell phones too. I said I'd never own one. But with my mother's health, I thought it would be wise to have one. I think cell phones are a threat to our sovereignty as a nation.

Why? Because we let them run our lives so much. Not a day goes by that you don't hear about an automobile accident caused by some idiot driving and talking on the phone at the same time. I've stopped going to the movie theater because someone's cell phone would ring or they would call someone on their phone. And worst of all, I hate them in the dugout at softball games. I hate sitting in the dugout when, in someone's bag, a phone starts to ring. It really pisses me off.

"What's up, Mark?" I say.

"Ben, I think we'll take this weekend off. I've got to go out of town on business. And three of the guys have a wedding to go to."

"That's cool, Mark. It will do me good. I've been wanting to do some fishing anyway. See you tonight, big guy."

Meat shows up at the house at five thirty, ready to go play league ball.

"Ben, where are we playing this weekend?"

"We are taking it off. I was thinking about going fishing. Do you want to go?"

"Ben, do you really need me to answer that?"

Meat loves to fish, and he's damn good at it. We have permission to fish a local doctor's pond. It's a great pond that we stocked four years ago for him. There are already bass up to about seven pounds in it.

We grab a few beers and head for the softball complex. When we arrive at the complex, a couple of players from Lee County Holding Co. come up and ask how we did in the Penson tournament, knowing full well that we had been double dipped. It is their way of rubbing it in. I tell them we had been double dipped. Hell, I can't lie about it.

"I heard you guys went two and cue."

Going two and a cue is losing two games and going home to barbecue. It's my little way of getting back at them. Yeah, we sucked, but we didn't have all our players—which we all know is just an excuse. But the truth is, their team really does suck.

Tonight, we have Moon's Real Estate. They're a good team. We sometimes have problems with Wild and Wet Water Park. They may be the worst team I have ever seen outside a team called the Tree Huggers.

Bryan shows up and tells me he can't play. I look at his hand, and it's still badly swollen.

"Damn, Bryan, did you have x-rays made?"

"Yeah, Coach Ben, they told me it was just a bad bone bruise."

I make out our lineup card, and we head over to field 5. We have Wild and Wet first. It was no contest; we scored twenty-two runs in the first inning. We beat them 35–1 in three innings. Moon's is up next. Their team has a lot of new faces in it. They give us a better game, but we beat them in five innings 19–8. Mark and I inform all the players that we're not going to be playing this weekend. Those who want to play can pick up and play with other teams. Calvin walks over and tells me he wants to talk to me.

"What's up, Calvin?"

"Ben, I'm going to have to give up weekend ball."

"Is anything the matter?"

"No, it's just that by working at the bar, I don't get enough sleep. I feel like shit on Saturday, and I'm not helping the team. Plus, my wife is bitching that I don't have enough time for her."

Ah, the truth finally comes out. Women don't understand why we need to play ball. Sure, we're grown men in our twenties, thirties, and even forties, like me. Even men in their fifties, sixties, and seventies are still out there playing. Wives are jealous when it comes to guys playing softball.

Girlfriends are jealous too. Problem is, they have nothing to hang over our heads. They can't divorce us and take half our shit like a wife can. Girlfriends come to watch the games. They will cheer their asses off till the player/boyfriend is dumb enough to get married, then the shit hits the fan. I've seen it many times: "You don't spend enough time with me." How many times do we men hear that, guys?

"Well, Calvin, I don't know what to say. I mean, it's your decision. Do you want some time to think about it?"

"No, Ben, but I still want to play league on Mondays, if that's okay with you."

"Sure, Calvin. But you know we'll miss you on the weekends."

"Word." With that, Calvin leaves.

I call Mark and tell him what happened. Both Mark and Meat went through divorces recently, so they can understand. Mark, however, has remarried, a wonderful woman named Rusti, while Meat is still dating. Julie is his latest girlfriend.

"Mark, do you know anyone whom we can pick up to take Calvin's spot?"

"Actually, Ben, I do. You'll like this kid. He's twenty-two years old. His name is Terry James. TJ had played with Penson Merchants. They just broke up."

"Is he any good?"

"Yeah, he can play, but he is a little cocky."

"Great. Give him a call."

Calvin meant a lot to the team not just as a player but also as a leader. And he is one of my best friends. I know he's not dead, yet I used the past tense. But who's writing this? You or me? Okay then.

Sure, I'll see him on Mondays, but still let me mourn just a little bit.

TJ shows up to play on our Wednesday night Swinging Stixx team. He introduces himself to everyone. He's a likable kid, but does he have game? More importantly, can he tolerate all our bullshit? So I thought I would test him. I don't think he could hold his own with the master. Fact is, very few can.

"TJ, I'm Ben. I'm the coach. I heard you were a pretty good player."

"Actually, Coach Ben, I've got more game than a PlayStation."

Damn, I like him already. A quick-on-the-draw smart-ass. "TJ, have you got a problem playing for a coach who was fucking before you were born?"

"Ben, I can respect the fact that you have been fucking longer than me. But on the other hand, Coach B, I don't need Viagra to keep my dick hard."

"I don't either, TJ."

"That's not what I heard, Coach B."

That son of a bitch.

"Meat, you overstuffed sack of shit, you know I don't always take Viagra. Why did you give a rookie dirt on me?"

"To level the playing field."

"OK then, I'm going to tell him the Buck Rogers story."

"You do that and everyone will know the 'big toe in the hot tub' story."

Damn, the problem with having a best friend whom you drink with is that he knows all about your PAST (plenty about your sexual tastes).

"Meat, you bastard. Someday, someday, you'll get yours."

"Yeah, yeah."

The best way to describe TJ is a likable Joey. TJ isn't the ballplayer Joey is now, but he could be down the road. He doesn't seem to rub people the wrong way like Joey can. Well, we win both our games, and TJ goes six for eight in his debut with two home runs, and yes, the kid fits in well. He's got game, and he can talk smack with the best of them.

Well, Kroy informs me that he, Joey, and Bryan were asked to play for Roscoe's this coming weekend. I can't believe Bryan is going to play with those bastards, especially after what they did to his hand. But that's his decision; he's a grown man.

Throughout our lives, we're forced to make decisions. Some are easy to make; others are much tougher: what car to buy, what college to attend, who we want to spend the rest of our lives with. We have to hope we choose the right ones. Sometimes you can correct a poor decision. Other times, you can't. I guess the best examples I can think of are these: Marry the wrong woman; you can always get a divorce. It'll cost you a lot, but you can change it. Have sex with the wrong person; you can get herpes or, worse, AIDS. You can't change that. Without thinking about it, each day we make many decisions.

You want to know my worst decision? Not going to medical school. I always wanted to be a doctor. I've always had an interest in anatomy. In fact, it was my favorite class in high school. While I didn't want to be a surgeon, I knew I had to get a medical degree to be what I wanted. And that was to be a psychologist and help those in need of counseling. I realize I get to do it anyway, at least to a degree. But I may always regret that choice. Some may say you could go back to school and realize that dream. But I've gotten lazy as I've gotten older, and no way would I or could I handle the class load. Cop out? You bet! I did write this little poem years ago; it's called "Choices."

In life we have to make decisions
in which we can win or lose.
It's tough to change or make revisions,
so be careful what you choose.
A conflict between the brain and heart
may confuse you down this road.
It's not important where you start,
only if you're able to carry your load.
We cannot see what lies ahead
or erase our own past.
Have faith in the path you're led,
for there your fate shall be cast.

Yes, it may seem a little dark. It is! My point is and has always been "Don't blame other people for your problems." We make choices every day that could affect us our whole lives. There are thousands of men and women in prison who made bad decisions. There are young men and women who become parents far too early because of bad decisions. Don't blame society for your ills; just look into the mirror. And take responsibility for yourself and your actions.

Well, the weather is starting to warm up now. But that's what you expect in late April in the South. The azaleas and dogwoods are in full bloom. The bass are moving up into shallow water to spawn. God did do an incredible job creating the world. It's a shame we are the ones who fuck it up so badly. If I ever do get to heaven, and I hope I do, I have a few questions for God. What's the reason for armadillos? I can't think of any good thing about them. They have torn up my yard for the past few years, and I actually found one drowned in my swimming last year. They can carry disease, and jeez, do they ever smell. But if I could ask God only one question, it would be, why are there so many wars and so much hatred based on religious beliefs? I thought religion was supposed to teach us about God's love. Not to hate a group of people who don't share the same religious beliefs you do. Most of the wars throughout history have been fought over different religious beliefs. World War II was fought over Germany and Hitler's hatred for the Jews. People were burned to death because they were thought to be witches by the church, just because they were different. Let us not forget the Catholics and the Inquisition.

I just don't understand it. I realize God isn't to blame; we are.

Even today, we still have racism in this country and throughout the world, people hating another group because their skin is a different color. And instead of trying to understand the cultural differences we may have, we hate. Maybe because it's the easy way out. The same thing is true with sexual orientation. When we see two men or women together, we wince. We don't try to accept them for who they are. We label them for what we think they are, which is wrong. Humans, by nature, are judgmental. Why do we do this? I can't say. Even the Bible says "Judge ye not. And he who is without sin cast the first stone." But then we still do. That's pretty screwed up.

Yeah, I know I'm getting away from softball, but after what happened in 9/11, I admit there's so much I don't understand. I still can't believe anyone could fly planes into buildings killing so many innocent people. That video clip is still etched into my memory. It will always be. It took me days to get over the shock and put into words how I felt. I wrote this. It is called "American Pride."

You can destroy all our buildings,
taking thousands of innocent lives.
One thing that you'll never kill
is our American pride.
You see, in a time of crisis,
Americans pull together,
helping those with their every need
through the roughest weather.
You can never take away
our love for this nation.
And soon our wounds will heal
from this deep laceration.
When the Trade Center fell,
as a nation we all cried.
But we shall prevail
because America is still alive.

As much as I bitch about politicians, I will always remember President Bush standing on the pile of rubble and declaring we were down but not out. I also remember all the volunteer work that many Americans made during the 9/11 cleanup and even the volunteers who helped out when hurricane Katrina hit New Orleans. Yes, we have made mistakes before, but we always prevail. The speeches that President Bush gave after 9/11 were the best I ever heard. And those lives lost that day will never be forgotten. Time after time, we have shown what we Americans can do when we're unified. I just hope it always stays that way.

Saturday finally rolls around, and Meat shows up. Time to go fishing. Now let me explain something. As much as we enjoy softball, we are fishing fiends. I have three boats. One is for big lakes, one is for river fishing, and one is for small ponds. I told you, I take it seriously. My barn is full of fishing tackle. I have seventeen rods and reels. And I'm not talking about cheap shit either. It's the best equipment money can buy. I have twenty-six plastic boxes of assorted worms and lures. When it comes to fishing tackle, I'm second to none. Now I have met rock stars, famous celebrities, and politicians. The only time I have ever been in awe is when I met Roland Martin. I was tongue-tied. Now if you don't know who Roland Martin is, well, he is a fishing legend. I watched his show religiously. He is the freaking man! He even gave me some fishing tips once. It would be a tough choice as to who I'd rather have for a father: Hugh Hefner or Roland Martin. I'd probably still choose Hugh Hefner for one reason and one reason only: you can't fuck a fish. You see, people, this book is full of intellectual knowledge.

But I bet somewhere out there, someone has tried to screw a bass.

Meat shows up at 6:00 a.m. "Ben, I think we're going to kick some major bass ass today."

"True dat"—to borrow one of Calvin's lines.

We load up everything and hit the road.

"Meat, let's stop and get some breakfast."

"Already taken care of that." He reaches in the back seat and hands me a large paper bag.

I open up the bag, and inside are six biscuits, two bags of pork skins, soda crackers, two cans of sardines, and a bag of Oreo cookies.

"Who's the man?"

"Well, what about the beer, Meat?"

"I got a case iced down in the cooler."

"Meat, you are the motherfucking man."

If you knew us, you would know that's the highest compliment we give out. We get to Dr. Frank's pond thirty minutes later. It is truly a beautiful sight. It's about a nine-acre pond. Easy to fish it in a day or however long the beer lasts. We get in the boat, look at each other, and in perfect harmony, say "Mass bass carnage." It doesn't take long to catch our first fish. Meat catches it on a spinner bait over some brush tops. It weighs about three and a half pounds. I'm throwing a soft bait called a superfluke. I throw it up around a stump and let it sink a bit. Bam, big boy hits it. Oh yeah, he's a big one. My drag takes off, and I let him run with it. I fight him about two minutes and finally manage to get him in the boat.

"Meat, whatcha think it weighs?"

"Nice fish, probably three pounds."

"Bullshit. He's every bit seven pounds," I say.

He doesn't know it, but I bought this new digital scale yesterday. I break the scale out. Six pounds, nine ounces is the reading.

"Ben, I see you pulling down on it to make it heavier."

"What? You're accusing me of cheating. You wrote the book on cheating, you bastard."

I release the fish back into the water to catch another day.

"How 'bout a beer, bro?" Meat throws me a beer.

Like the commercial says, it doesn't get any better than this. We throw down the sardines and Oreos and wash it all down with beer. We end up catching twenty-three fish. Meat catches the most with fourteen; I catch nine. But I had caught the biggest fish, so everything evened out.

It starts to look like it might start raining. There's thunder coming from the west, so we pack things up. Fishing is like softball; it's a way we men bond. Meat is like the little brother I never had. So what if he's three inches taller and about fifty pounds heavier? He's still my brother.

On the drive home, our conversation turns to softball.

"Ben, do you think TJ can fill Calvin's shoes?"

"No one can take Calvin's place, but I think he's a good guy. I just hope that all the guys can keep their egos in check."

Ego is the one thing that can destroy a softball team, especially a good one. Sometimes a guy will whine about where he hits in the lineup. A good tournament team has to have good hitters throughout the lineup. You can't afford to have any weak hitters or you'll get beaten. There are times when a player goes through a slump, but if the guys pick him up, he'll snap out of it. And he'll even carry them at some point in the season. The one thing I don't tolerate is guys cutting down one of their own teammates. You should never kick a player when they're down. Even if we are men, we still have feelings.

We get to the house and unload everything. Meat calls Julie on his cell phone.

"Baby, where do you want to go eat supper? Okay, I'll be home in fifteen minutes."

"Bro, where are you going?" I ask.

"Where do you think? Red Lobster."

I laugh. "Figures."

Monday arrives, and I have a busy day ahead. I have to take Donna to the gynecologist for another checkup. She goes to a clinic run by two brothers. One is a gynecologist, and the other is a urologist. How would you like to be a fly on the wall at that family reunion? On the way to the clinic, she starts to nag at me.

"Ben, now that you're forty, you need to get a complete checkup."

"Donna, I had my blood pressure checked three weeks ago."

"I'm talking about your prostate, and while you're at it, maybe have a colonoscopy."

Why is it women want us to be with them for strength when they're undergoing tests? But then all of a sudden, they want us to have something tested. Is it to even things out? I'm not Bill Clinton. I don't want to feel your pain. I'm sorry. I don't want a doctor sticking his finger, much less a camera, up my ass either. We arrive at the doctor's office, and she goes in.

Forty-five minutes later, a nurse comes into the waiting room. "The doctor would like to see you, Mr. Thompson."

All kinds of scary shit start going through my head. *Did they find something wrong?*

The doctor walks in. "I'm Dr. Tate. Are you Ben?"

"Uh, yes, I am."

"Ben, Donna tells me that you've never had a prostate exam, and she would like you to have a complete physical as well."

"Doc, I'm okay, really. I don't think I need anything right now except maybe to lose a little weight."

"Well, Ben, you would be surprised how many men your age get cancer of the prostate."

Damn, he just went and used the *C* word. Since cancer runs in the family, it is a little unnerving.

"Okay, okay, I'll call and set up an appointment," I say.

"That won't be necessary. Donna set up your appointment already, in two weeks."

That damn woman, I think. "Doc, how did Donna's tests go?"

"She and the baby seem to be in perfect health. Everything looked fine. She won't be able to have sex, though, for a few days."

That's right; you guessed it—fucked again.

When I get Donna in the car, I let her have it.

"What's up with that, Florence Nightingale? I didn't deserve to be put on the spot like that."

"Yes, you did. You would never go to the doctor without being pushed. And besides, you're going to be a father, and our child is going to need someone to play catch with. So your health is important to us just as much as it is to you."

Damn, I hate it when she's right. Now I can't wait to play ball tonight.

Meat shows up at five thirty on the nose.

"Ready to play some ball, dawg?"

"Yeah, I guess."

"All right, tell your bro what's the matter."

"Fucking Donna goes to get a checkup, and the next thing I know, she's made arrangements for me to get a camera and a hand shoved up my ass."

Meat says, "Well, you know I work in the health field, and there's not much to it."

That is good news, I think.

Now maybe I can relax. Meat wouldn't lie, or would he? Hmm.

We arrive at the complex. Tonight, we have Handy Rental and Billy Bob's. Neither team is really that good, but they slip up on you. Everyone is there, so I make up the lineup. We win the coin toss and elect to take home, so we take the field. Handy's leadoff hitter pulls a ball down the line. As he rounds the bag to go to second, his foot slips off the bag and catches the ground behind him. He goes down like he were shot, clutching his knee. Damn, I bet he blew out his ACL. We all run out to see if we can help. The supervisor calls for an ambulance. Time is called, and the game clock is stopped. Anytime a player is hurt, we all have to put ourselves in their place. Does he have a family? Does he have insurance? I know I've had knee surgery, shoulder surgery, and ankle surgery. That's why I don't play much anymore and I just coach. The ambulance arrives in about seven minutes. They load him up and cart him away. There is sort of a shadow hanging over the rest of the game. We actually took it easy on them; we won 13–8. Billy Bob's is a local chicken finger restaurant. I got sick from eating there once, and we were running a little late from the injury break we took in the first game.

"Guys, let's blow these guys out. If we end it in three innings, I'll buy the beer."

Three innings later, it is over 25–2. I start loading up the bats as the guys exit the dugout.

"Tell him," Kroy says.

"Tell me what, Kroy?"

"Bryan has something to tell you."

"All right, Kroy, leave us alone."

Bryan, who I've said was the chosen one, because he reminds me of myself.

"Bryan, what's wrong?" I think he was mad I batted him eighth.

"Coach Ben, you have been better to me than anyone, you're the best coach I've ever had."

"What is it then?"

"You know I'm friends with a lot of the guys on Roscoe's. Well, Mr. Roscoe asked me to play ball with them."

Boom, I wasn't expecting that. I try to stay calm.

"So what did you decide?"

"I guess I want to give it a try, Coach Ben."

"Well, Bryan, if that's what you really want to do, then you should do it. But just remember that I'll have to get someone to take your place and you won't be able to come back."

I try to make it easy on him even though I knew he was making a big mistake. It's like the song says: "Another one bites the dust." I just hope Bryan learns from this, that the grass is not always greener on the other side. I know he won't make it with Roscoe's, but I can't stop him. Nor will I try. I think we all need to grow, and sometimes that means to learn from our mistakes. I knew he was making one, but at least it wasn't life-and-death.

I wish him well and shake his hand as he turn in his uniform.

Meat and I get to the parking lot, and Mark and Joey are still hanging around.

"Coach Ben, I started a message board for us. Swinging Stixx softball."

"We can post game info and goof on one another on it," Joey says.

"Mark, Bryan just told me that he was leaving to play with Roscoe's."

"Yeah, I know. Kroy told me that earlier. I just thought Bryan should be the one to tell you."

"Well, we need another ballplayer."

"I think Roscoe's is fixing to cut Donte loose. Let's wait and see. I know if they do, we can pick him up."

A few days later, we have Donte Grant. Donte is a strong big guy, probably voted "most likely to commit homicide" by his senior class. I know he'll be the enforcer on the team. I get home from the game and check out the team message board. Joey, Mark, and Lewis already have posts up. I think something simple would do. I put "Stixx no. 49" where name was required. Subject: Todd's and TJ's noses.

> Guys, I know the name of a good plastic surgeon that could remove the five unsightly pounds of fat you call a nose.

That should do it, I think.
I hit Submit.

Later that night, I check the message board, and TJ has responded.

> This is for Ben:
> Roses are red; violets are blue. Our noses are big; our dicks are too.

Well, that's not too bad for an amateur, I think. I've decided to show them why I was the teacher's pet in Mrs. Hopkins's creative writing class. It was the one class in high school that I was not a pain in the teacher's ass. So I type "the nose poem" in the subject box and begin.

> The Nose Poem
>
> Nothing smells as sweet as a freshly cut rose;
> nothing quite as scary as a big fucking nose.
> Tea is not sweet without some sugar,
> but nothing as ugly as a big nose with a booger.
> If a woman has a big nose, well then, I'm no fan.
> She can ever forget about me being her man.
> But on TJ and Todd, the big nose is jolly,
> because without the honker, Todd wouldn't have Holly.

Stupid, I know, but you'll get used to it. But at least it rhymes. I have read some poems lately by some so-called famous poets. Hell, their poems don't even rhyme. What's up with that shit? I will have to say, the guys got a laugh out of it. Holly even thought it was great. I didn't realize at that time there are a lot of people that read the message boards. Guys I didn't know from other teams are even chiming in. And the poem isn't even good. When I was growing up, I liked to read Lewis Grizzard's columns in the Atlanta newspaper. He was a gifted storyteller. And his books were great. He had a down-home, commonsense way of expressing himself. Some might say it was his writing style; I think he was just being himself. That's who I am. On the field or off, I'm just Ben. I guess that's what bothers me about Bryan leaving the team. I don't think he knows who he is or what he really wants.

Tuesday morning, I have a hair appointment. I go to Atlanta to have the bald spot taken care of every month. It would be nice if they could invent a pill you take once that would give you a full head of hair. I tried minoxidil. It grew fine little hairs that never grew into big hairs, except on my ears. After four months of using it, I stopped. My ears began to look like a werewolf's, no shit. Donna suggested once that I put a little wax on them. I had helped her do her legs once, and it worked out well. She said it didn't hurt much at all. I told her that before I put it on my earlobes, I would have to try it somewhere else.

"What about your arms, Ben?"

"No way," I say. "Someone would think I was shaving them. It will have to be where no one could see it."

She says, "Your ass! You have a hairy ass, and no one would see it."

I agreed. Now I have to admit there's something erotic about lying on your stomach and having a girl spread this goo on with a paddle. Or maybe it's the attention she is giving my ass. Anyway I had a hard-on that won't quit. She put these strips of cloth or something on my waxed cheeks. When the time came to take them off, *rip!* "Jesus!" I almost blacked out from the fucking pain. The blood in my hard-on said, "Fuck it, I'm outta here."

"Donna, that's it, no more. I'll go wash the other one off."

Before I got the sentence out of my mouth, *rip.* Now you're not going to believe this, but just like the movie *The Sixth Sense*, I saw dead people. My life passed before my very eyes. In fact, when I came to, I saw a bright light with a shadowy figure in it. "Ben."

Oh my god, it's the voice of Satan. I done went straight to hell.
Smack!

"Get your ass up, Ben."

And just like a doctor spanking a newborn baby's ass, I was back.

"Donna, that was erotic. Spank me again!"

"Ben, you're sick" was her reply. "Ready for your ears now?"

"Not no, but fuck no, you are not touching me with that shit ever again. I'll pluck the damn hairs out."

I went to the bathroom and picked up the tweezers. It hurt like hell, but when I had finished, I had bald ears again. Since I'm getting older, I've noticed the hair on my ears and my eyebrows grow like I've fertilized them. But my bald spot keeps getting bigger. Getting old sucks, but I guess it beats the alternative.

The moral of this story, if there is one, is this: When a woman says it doesn't hurt much, remember, to women, giving birth is painful, but to men, a hangnail is. If a woman can live through her vagina bursting open and a baby squirting out, waxing body hair isn't shit. Men never listen to women when it comes to your body.

I arrive for my hair appointment. My usual stylist is out sick, so I have a substitute stylist. It is a man. I tell them at the front desk I would prefer a woman. I'm sorry I feel nervous having a man run his hands through my hair. They send in Elaine. She's nice enough, but she smells like an ashtray. I don't smoke, and I have sinus problems, and this is all I frigging need. She washes and dries my hair. She then begins the process of reattaching my unit, gluing hair down. I have to pull my shirt up over my nose to filter the smell.

She notices this and asks, "What's the matter?"

"Elaine, to be honest, I detest the smell of cigarettes."

"I'm not smoking here!"

"No, but it's in your clothing. That's what I smell."

"Excuse me for living."

"Keep on smoking and you won't be living long."

If you hadn't guessed, we didn't speak anymore. When she finishes, I give her a twenty-dollar tip.

"Here, put this towards the purchase of those nicotine patches."

I start my drive back home. I start to plan for our softball tournament in Panama City. The tournament is the largest one in the southeast. I've got to find out who can't go and make the hotel reservations. A coach's work is never done. I get home and decide to check out the Alabama message boards. "The Stixx Suck" was the title. *Let's check this out.*

The Stixx are the most overrated team in the state. They've never won anything or beaten us.

They signed it Cock-a-Doodle-Do. Damn, I have to reply to this.

Re: The Stixx Suck.
Since you didn't say who *us* is, it leads me to believe you are a spineless piece of shit. You probably still live at home with your mama. In fact, she probably still wipes your candy ass. We will be playing in Ashton this weekend, so bring your cock-a-doodle-poodle-noodle to Ashton, if your mama will drive you there.

I sign it Coach *Big* Stick. *That'll stir some shit up*, I think.

Wednesday morning rolls around, and I don't have anything to do. I'm sitting at the table, eating my cereal, and the phone rings.

"Mr. Thompson, I'm Betty Taylor, a nurse for Dr. Tate. You have an appointment in twelve days, but we have a cancellation and would like to know if you can come in today for your prostate exam."

"Uh," I say, "this is short notice and I, uh—"

"Good, we'll see you at two o'clock."

"Wait!"

Click.

If you're a man, you know we need time to prepare ourselves for these things. Damn, my hands start to sweat. I've lost my appetite. I'm a shaking German shepherd in an electrical storm. I turn on CNN. Today's topic: why people are dying from simple medical procedures. This, to me, is an omen, I think. Now I don't care that they were talking about knee surgeries. My prostate is attached to my ass, which is attached to my leg, where the knee is located. Logical? Well, it is to me.

I arrive at the doctor's office and sign in and take a seat in the waiting room. Why is it that when you're waiting in a doctor's office, you always feel the need to take a shit?

Maybe it was my poor sphincter muscle's way of sending out an SOS. I get up to go to the bathroom.

"Mr. Thompson, will you come on back?"

Oh shit, I think.

The nurse says to follow her. "Take your clothes off and put on this gown."

"Nurse, I really need to take a BM first."

"That's a normal reaction for men. You'll be fine."

"For men"? What did she mean by that?

In walks Dr. Tate, a.k.a. Mr. Hand. Damn, he had some massive hands. Yes, I fucking notice his hands because he is about to shove one up my ass.

"Ben, how are we doing?"

"Doc, I'm sure you're doing fine, but I'm about to have a hand shoved up my ass." I start to think about all those rape scenes on *Oz*.

"Actually, it'll just be a finger or two, well, yeah, maybe the whole hand."

The bastard is trying to be funny. Of all the doctors in the world, I get someone who thinks he's Buddy Hackett.

"Stand up, now bend over." The moment of truth has arrived. He puts on rubber gloves, squirts some shit on them. "Just relax."

"Doc, I have to tell you, my ass is a virgin!"

"I've popped a lot of cherries, son. Damn, Ben, that's a nice shave job. But you really didn't have to shave it, you know."

I feel my face becoming flushed. He inserts his finger up my ass. *Ouch, that stings!* Let me tell you, the pain is not as bad as the humiliation. I try to joke about it.

"Doc, do you realize, in some states, we just consummated marriage?"

"Ha, that's a good one." He takes off his gloves.

"Well, Doc, how is it?"

"Well, it was good for me. Was it good for you?"

"Just a little advice, Doc. Don't give up your day job for stand-up comedy!"

"It appears to be normal, Ben. It's not enlarged."

I knew it—all this shit for nothing. I've often wondered what makes someone want to specialize in certain medical fields, especially urologists and proctologists. Checking people's urinary tracts and asses would not be for me.

Softball—thank God for softball. I decide tonight I'm going to play. I have to hit something; it might as well be a softball. I don't play much anymore. Usually, when I do, we're short a player. I've had far too many injuries, but I want to let out a little frustration.

Meat arrives at five thirty. I haven't started to get dressed yet.
"You going tonight, bro?"
"Yeah, we've got time. Let me check the Alabama board out first."
Cock-a-Doodle-Do had answered my reply.

> Stixx no. 49, we will be in Ashton this weekend too.
> We will be your worst nightmair.

This is too good to pass up.
"Meat, look at this. Didn't he spell *nightmare* wrong?"
"Yes, he did."
I just have to respond.

> Re: Stixx No. 49
> Jethro, I know you graduated the sixth grade and all, but maybe, just maybe, you should let your mama check your spelling just so you don't look like a complete idiot. You would only be my nightmare—notice the correct spelling if I had to teach you in grade school. Now go back to the television and finish watching *Romper Room*, Poodle Noodle.
> Stixx no. 49

I get dressed for the game. We grab a few beers and head to the complex. Tonight we have BTB (Big-Time Bailers) and the Crew. I make out the lineup. Pretty much the same lineup, except batting eleventh B. Thompson.
"You gonna hit tonight, Ben?" Kroy says.
"No, Kroy, I just like how my name looks. Of course, I'm going to hit."

Ten years ago, I was one of the better players around. But Father Time and injuries have taken their toll on this forty-year-old body. BTB is a decent team. They're mostly students at the university. We hit first, Joey leads off with a single, Kroy and Todd follow him, scoring Joey. Mark hits a long home run. We're really cooking. Meat doubles to right, and Dirk singles him home.

Hal singles up the middle. Coy grounds into a fielder's choice for the first out. Ray hits a fly ball, which the left fielder drops. Lewis gets a walk. The moment of truth has arrived. Richard, the man, is up with bases loaded. If I said I wasn't thinking about hitting a grand slam, I would be lying. I step into the batter's box. I call time and take a deep breath. First pitch is short ball 1. Next pitch. *Crack!* A deep bail. It's got the distance. Damn, foul ball. I heard "Straighten it out, dawg" from the dugout. Next pitch. *Crack!* I watch the ball a minute at home. Looks like it's gone, then it hits the fence. Damn, I start running. I make it to second without having to slide.

"Coach Ben, you should be standing on third."

The bench starts giving me hell about not hustling.

"I'm old. It takes me a while to get started."

"Yeah, that's what Donna told us too" comes from Meat.

I feel all the weight lift off my shoulders. We go on to win the game 31–8 and win the next game 19–7. Scores really are not important. What is? Being with friends, experiencing that rush of adrenaline just one more time, at least for this *old* man.

Now in my forties, I can honestly say, looking back at my life, I wouldn't change a thing. Sure, I've made many mistakes, but I have learned so much from them.

These guys will learn from their mistakes as well. Life is about learning. We only stop learning when we die. I sometimes think I'm too old to be a father. Some guys I went to high school with are already grandfathers.

I guess Donna is right; I do have to take care of myself better if I plan on being there for Junior.

"Good game, guys. I need to know who can and cannot go to Panama City. The tournament is in three weeks. We've got a lot of work to do to get ready for it."

Meat says he can't go because the band is playing that weekend. The rest are a go.

"What are we doing this weekend, Coach Ben?"

"We will be playing here in Ashton. It's an ISA qualifier. In fact, the next two weekends are qualifiers."

"Ben, I can play this weekend, but next weekend, I told Roscoe I would play with them in Florida," says Joey.

"Joey, we will need you. We have ASA District then."

"Ben, I gave him my word."

"You'll have to call him and let him know that we are playing in the district that weekend."

That's the problem with pickup players; their loyalty gets split.

On the way to the car, I stop to talk to Mark.

"What's up with Joey? Did you know about this?"

"No, it's the first I've heard about it. But Joey will be with us. He just wants to be stroked a little."

"So he needs to be told how much we need him?"

"That sums it up pretty good."

"Okay, I'll make reservation in the morning for fourteen of us. Seven rooms."

"I think Holly is going down with Todd. They'll get their own room, Ben."

Well, I'll still get seven. I have my own one then, just in case someone else goes.

Meat and I start the drive home.

"Meat, can you believe Joey told Roscoe that he would play with them without checking with me or Mark?"

"Ben, Joey is not a team player. He is very good, don't get me wrong, but it's all about him."

Like I said before, ego will destroy team chemistry. And Joey has one as big as a 747.

I get home and walk in the door. Donna is here.

"How did it go?"

"It went well. The old man even showed the boys he could still play."

"You played? On those bad knees and ankle?"

"Donna, you sound like I'm on my deathbed. Give me a break."

"Ben, I just don't want you to get hurt."

"I'm okay. My back is just a little sore."

Then like any good man would, I try to make her feel guilty.

"Oh, by the way, I went to the doctor today for my prostate exam."

"What did he do?"

"What didn't he do? He just about stuck his whole damn hand up my ass. At least that's what it felt like."

"Did he find anything?"

"He found a couple of kernels of corn and a Snickers bar."

"Damn it, Ben, what did he say?"

"He said I had a nicely shaved ass. Seriously, that's what he said. He also said my prostate was normal and he would see me next week for the colonoscopy."

"What can I do to make you feel better?"

Guys, you know where this is going. If you don't, then you're dumb as a stump.

"Let me grab a shower, and I'll let you give me a massage."

"Okay!"

I took a nice, hot shower, shampooed, and shaved. Yes, down there too. When I came out of the bathroom, Donna was lying on the bed—as Ray Stevens would say—naked as a jaybird. I look down at Mr. Happy. Houston, prepare to launch. I walk over to the bed and stare at her, admiring her body.

"What are you doing, Ben?"

"Just realizing how lucky I am." I lie down beside her, and I brush her hair back and give her a sweet, tender kiss. I pull away for a moment. "Thanks."

"Thanks for what, Ben?"

"For caring about me enough to be a pain in my ass."

"Ben, I don't just care, I really do love you."

"I really love you too."

I've said those words to a lot of women. But I think this is the first time I truly meant it. And for the next two hours, we make slow, passionate love. Women truly are wonderful. And just think, guys, God made Eve from just one of Adam's ribs. Just think what he could have made with two.

I'm still amazed at how much women change after they've had an orgasm. They're so relaxed, mellow. They're not bitchy or bossy. Life would be so much better if women would only give men more sex. But they won't. Want to know why? I'll tell you why. A lot of women are taught early on in childhood that sex is wrong and that they shouldn't enjoy it. And that's all the boys want. OK, that part may be true. And I understand parents looking out for their daughters. They don't want any unwanted pregnancies or diseases for them. I understand this. But some girls are taught to use sex for what they want. Sex is their ace in the hole. No pun intended. They hold it over our heads. They know we're addicted to it. And the truth is, most women want it as bad as we do. I have a friend in Atlanta who was getting married. On his wedding night, when his bride came out of the bathroom, what did he do? I'll tell you. He got out of bed with his hard dick in hand and masturbated in front of her. Then he told her "Don't ever try to use your pussy to control me. I don't need it."

Now I realize that was dumb as hell to do. But you know what? She never used sex to control him. Of course, she left him two months later. But that's another story. The moral to this story, if there is one, is this: *Before* you get married, make sure you are compatible. I said it earlier, but it bears repeating. I really think couples should live together for a year before they get married. It should be mandatory. That way, they would know if they are compatible. Sex is one issue, but like the old saying goes, you never know someone till you live with them.

Although Donna and I don't live 24-7 together, we are together enough to know each other's faults. And believe me, not a lot of women could handle my little quirks. And she is no saint either. She is a total neat freak. Everything is in its place. But our sex life is great. And that can make up for a hell of a lot.

It's Thursday morning, I decide to check out the message board. Our board is full of guys bragging. Stacey is talking about pimpin' hoes at the bar. I've never asked him exactly what *pimpin' hoes* meant. In the seventies, it was a prostitute's boss. Today I think it means picking up girls. I guess I should stay updated on my slang terminology. Stacey, to be in his twenties, looks about sixteen. I remember when I was his age, I was young, dumb, and full of cum. Today I'm older, smarter and just wish it would get harder. Actually, I have no problem with the last one—thanks to Viagra on some special occasions. If Bob Dole, a war hero, and some of the professional athletes can admit using it, so can I. I don't use it all the time, just when I get the chance to have sex twice in one day or want it to last longer than an hour.

When a young man is in his teens, through his early twenties, his dick will get hard when the wind blows. I remember when I was in the eighth grade, I would wait for everyone to leave the classroom before I would get up. I could not control my erections. Of course, it could've been Ms. Clayton. Damn, I wanted her. Didn't know what I wanted. All I knew was, my dick would get hard when she was around. Hell, it's getting hard thinking about her now. She was about five foot four, probably a hundred and five pounds. She had the best legs and ass of any teacher I ever had. She played tennis in college and played twice a week with Ms. Blackmon. I think she was twenty-eight years old.

I knew nothing about sex although I had seen a girl's vagina before. I used to play doctor with my neighbor. I knew at the age of five that she had an "inny" to my "outy." But in class, I would fantasize about Ms. Clayton taking my virginity.

I truly believe young boys should have sex education with a sex surrogate teacher their first time. Why? Hell, we didn't know how to please women. We got used to jerking off at such an early age. And most of the time, we did it as fast as we could to keep from getting caught. And we thought we were fooling our parents going into the bathroom so much, like we have seven bowel movements a day. I remember my mother asking me once if I had been using her hand cream. I told her some lame excuse about using it on my baseball glove. It sounded good at that time. But I think they realized I was jerking off; at least my father did. I'm sure they heard the whimpers coming from the bathroom from time to time. One day, I decided to use something different, and it was the biggest mistake of my life. I decided to use Vicks VapoRub. Needless to say, I thought my penis was on fire. I must have yelled out loud because my father walked in to check on me and saw me splashing cold water on my dick.

He said, "You used VapoRub, didn't you?"

"Yeah!"

"Well then, you might want to use some soap on that!"

My mother asked him what the matter was.

"The boy is just constipated."

We men program ourselves to get the job done quickly and to get out of the bathroom so no one will notice.

And that causes a lot of men to become premature ejaculators when it comes time to be with a girl. We're actually probably lucky not to cum in our pants. I lost my virginity at the age of fifteen. The girl was seventeen.

It took me five minutes to figure out how to get it in and thirty seconds to finish. I know I didn't do her any good. My point is, if boys have an older woman to show them how and what to do, they would be better lovers today.

I know I was probably a lousy lover till I met Lydia. I was twenty-one; she was forty-three. We met at a bar. She had just been divorced, and I was horny—a lethal mixture, at least at that time. She taught me more in six months than I learned in twelve years of school and four years of college. I will always be grateful, and the women in my life since should be grateful to her. She taught me how to pace myself and, more importantly, how and where to touch the buttons, where to kiss and lick—you get the idea.

But I still have this image of Ms. Clayton in those terry cloth shorts and shirt playing tennis. How I can imagine taking her sweaty body to bed. It's like the Rolling Stones song "You Can't Always Get What You Want." But if you try, sometimes you just might find you get what you need.

When Donna and I make love, it's like time stands still. Yeah, that sounds stupid, but there is a special chemistry, a bond that I can't explain. I've heard the term *soul mates* used often when describing a relationship. I don't know if that is possible. But I do feel like I've known her for an eternity. It's like the Billy Joel song. It goes something like "She's got a way about her. / Don't know what it is, / but I know that I can't live without her." I hope I got the lyrics right; if not, sorry, Billy. It is a beautiful song. In fact, when we get married, I want it played at the wedding. Yes, I said *when*. I'm not completely stupid. I mean, I'm not letting her get away. We just have so many things to do and work out first before we take that final step. I admit the thought of marriage scares me to death. But I also know I would die if I lost her.

Okay, so you're scratching your head now. Not sure if you like me or hate me. I understand that. I am a little strange at times, although most women find me quite entertaining. Hey, I said I have quirks that I'm completely honest about.

Back to the board. I check on the Alabama softball message board. Another response from Poodle Noodle, my name for him anyway. His message is short: "I'll see your ass in Northbell." I thought about answering it, but I've realized I pissed him off enough. Who knows, this idiot may show up with a gun or something. I admit I like to yank people's chains. And I have always been competitive in anything I do. I'm sure it stems from my tree house fall and having to prove myself. But I do hate to lose too. You see, I know myself well; I do a lot of reflection. I know at times I have this childish alter ego that I can turn on at will. And when I'm with the boys, it's on.

In all reality, I'm quite boring. I don't like to go out a lot, especially to large parties. I prefer much-smaller groups of people. I used to love parties, but then again, I loved bars too. Now I'm more of a homebody. I love a quiet life in the country, not the fast-paced city life. I have few wants and really no needs that haven't been met. I hate to travel, especially by plane. I've traveled by air twenty-seven times. And I will die stuck on that number. The last two flights were horrible. I thought the plane was going to crash. I promised God that if he let me live, I'd never fly again. And I won't. If I have to go somewhere, it will be by car, bus, or train from here on. I don't fear death. I fear only fear. The thirty seconds to a minute that a plane falls from the sky has to be the most frightening time for the passengers, of which I'll never be one again.

Some people may think I'm deep or maybe aloof. But in reality, that's far from the truth. In many ways, I'm still that scared little boy who fell from the tree house, A kid who wanted attention but didn't know what to do once he had it. You may feel sorry for me. Don't I love my world. Yes, I allow folks into it. I also care greatly about others and what goes on outside my world in the real one. All the hatred, pollution, fighting, and cruelty bother me. But I can't make idiots see things as I do. So sometimes I block it out and slip back to where I'm comfortable. With Donna and now Junior, my world is perfect, while the real world is in turmoil.

I often play the what-if game in my head. What if I were president? Since you may be curious, I'll tell you. If I were president, I would call every head of every country and offer to meet with them personally to try to smooth differences that we may have with them, because honestly, America is perceived as arrogant fucks in much of the world. We think we're hot shit, and we turn away from things that aren't in our national interest. The truth is, to be a world leader, you have to lead by example and by taking the lead, by talking to not just your allies but your enemies as well. If I were president, I'd take off the embargo of goods. I would call the leaders of Iran, North Korea, Syria and say "Let's straighten things out." Man to man, I'd meet with them to talk and try to understand their points of view instead of talking about them on the news sound bites and in speeches and instead of talking down to them and threatening them with sanctions. Our fight shouldn't be with them. Our fight is with terrorists, those who hate because they know nothing else. You can't rationalize and talk to them. Evil has no conscience. While I'm at it, I would tell the UN to go fuck themselves. They're all a bunch of spineless, good-for-nothing pieces of shit anyway. They only worry about themselves and the countries they represent. If I were president, I'd tell our leaders to get off their worthless asses and do something. The Congress, the Senate—all they want is to make life hell for whichever party is in control and, of course, be reelected. Instead of working with one another for the betterment of our country, I'd tell them to stop with the pork barrel spending. I'd call out individuals and embarrass them in public to let the people know what their representatives are doing. Their job isn't just to bring home the pork to the areas they represent; it's to do what's right for the entire country. Of course, I'm not president, nor will I ever be. But I can hope that someday, someone will see the light before it is too late. Hopefully, President Trump is just the right man at the right time! And I believe that will happen. Sorry I digress. Back to the book.

This weekend, we are playing in an ISA qualifier. To me, ISA is the most fun of the softball associations. You are allowed to steal. In fact, you're allowed to have a designated base burglar. A base burglar is allowed to run for anyone in the lineup. He can only be used once an inning. He comes in handy if you have a slow runner or someone who's a little banged up. Also, in ISA, you're allowed to bat up to twelve batters, whereas in the other associations, you're allowed a maximum of eleven batters. What is the most interesting is, the home run rules. In our class, we're allowed four home runs. In ISA, the fifth home run ends the inning, whether there's one, two, or no one out. So if my leadoff batter leads off an inning with a home run with none left, it ends the inning. It would be a triple play. What it does is, it makes you keep the ball down and save the home runs for when two or more guys are on base. It really is a lot of fun. We actually play better in ISA.

Saturday morning, Meat shows up raring to go.
"Ready to go bring a little man home, Ben?"
"A little man" is a first-place trophy, by the way. That's the kind of attitude you like your players to have.
"You know I'm all about bringing some hardware home."

The weather today is perfect softball weather. The highs are supposed to reach a high of eighty-three or so. There is no rain in sight. Our first game is at nine. We play a team called Red Hot.

I see Mark getting out of his truck in the parking lot. I pull up behind him.

"What's up, Crusher?" I don't know where that name came from, somewhere out of my gray matter. Anyway, he liked it.

"Crusher—that's pretty good, Ben."

"Well, you do crush the fucking ball. It only seemed fitting. Mark, what do you know about Red Hot?"

"I only know they're out of Newnan, Georgia."

Just as we were talking about them, an SUV pulls up. Out step six guys. I will try to describe them. They have on red shirts, red pants, red caps, and red socks and shoes. One of the guys is really fat. He looks just like a big damn tomato.

I turn my head to keep from laughing.

"Excuse me," one of the tomatoes says. "Where do we check in?"

Mark says, "There's a table near the concession stand."

"Holy V8 Batman. Do you believe that shit, Mark?"

"Ben, I've seen some ugly shit, but that tops it."

"Mark, you mean that tops the salad."

We laugh as we walk into the complex.

Now if you wear uniforms as ugly as these, you either (A) have no sense of fashion, (B) are color-blind, (C) are good as hell, or (D) are downright stupid.

"Coach Ben, it's a pretty bad example you're setting when we get here before our coach."

"Look, guys, I had to stop and get beer and gas. Plus, this morning Mr. Happy needed some exercise, so I had to bust a nut before I left."

"Ben, you know you never have sex before a game."

"Mark, that rule only applies to players. Coaches are exempt."

Mark and I make out the lineup as the guys are warming up. We decide to sit Hal since he has played every game this season and because we have thirteen players and can only bat twelve.

"Swing Stixx, report to field 1" comes from the loudspeaker.

Game time. We post the lineup and tell Hal that we'll try to get him into the game. He doesn't say a word but goes to the end of the bench to sit.

I think he is pouting. We win the coin toss and elect to take home. Number 13 for the Red Hots leads off. He hits an opposite field shot down the first baseline. Ray, our first baseman, never moves. It goes past him so fast.

Their second hitter steps in the batter's box. He's a little left-handed hitter. He slaps the ball to Mark, who guns him out at first. It was a close play, but he was out. He is pissed.

"Blue, that's the worst fucking call I've ever seen."

The umpire, whom I know (his name is Tim Rammell, and I know him from the message board), is pissed. First rule in softball: don't show up or piss off umpires. Second rule: never use profanity.

The umpire walks over to him and says, "One more word and you're gone. Ejected."

"Dodo!"

"Number 23, you're gone!"

Their coach says, "Blue, you can't do that."

"I think I just did. Want to join him?"

"No."

"Then get back in your dugout."

I look at the guys in the dugout.

"Don't say a fucking word to the umpires."

Softball is so much a mental game. We have the umpires on our side as long as we keep our mouths shut. The Hots are pissed off and hit four consecutive home runs. Now that is a good thing because even though we're down five to nothing, they have used up all their home runs in one inning. The next one ends the inning. The next batter tries to hit the ball up the middle. Coy throws him out at first. They end the inning by popping up to Ray at first.

"All right, guys, let's play our game and hit it in the face," I tell the guys that as they come off the field.

"Joey, Kroy, Dirk, Mark, sounds like four runs right there."

Joey leads off with a ball hit to the third baseman, who bobbles it for a moment then throws to first.

"Safe!" says the umpire.

It was a bang-bang play.

Actually, I thought Joey was out, but like rule number 1, don't show up the umpire.

"Blue, you've got to call it both ways" comes from their dugout.

I was right; the umpires were on our side.

"This is your warning, Coach" comes from the umpire to the Red Hots coach.

Kroy then hits a double in the gap. Dirk then hits a single to score Joey.

"Way to hit the ball, D," I say.

Mark's up, and we all are making a bet how far the home run will go. He swings. There's a drive. Damn, the outfielder is under it. It was deep enough to score Kroy.

"That's the way to get the run in, big Mark."

Meat steps to the plate and hits a shot up the middle. First and third with one out. Todd steps into the batter's box.

TJ says, "Hit one for Holly or I will."

Todd looks at TJ, who is coaching third base. *Crack!* A three-run homer. Coy grounds out, and TJ flies out to end the inning. But the score is tied 5–5. The good part is that we still have three home runs left and the Red Hots have none left. Their first batter leads off with a fly ball, which TJ misplays and drops. The runner reaches second base. Hal is furious. He slaps the bench with his hand and walks out of the dugout.

"Shake it off, TJ," I say.

The next batter hits a fly ball that I thought was going to stay in play but manages to barely clear the fence for an inning ending out. In ISA, it's a triple play. There is absolutely nothing that will take a team mentally out of a ball game like a three-out inning ending homer.

"That's the way to throw the leather, guys," I say it loud enough to rub it in the Red Hots' faces. They've just shot themselves in the foot. The best time to kick a team in the mouth is when they're down. "Guys, let's go ahead and put a fork in them. They're done."

That's just what we did. We end the game 23–6. I actually feel sorry for the Red Hots, but they did it to themselves. First, they break rule number one, then they wear the worst colored uniforms you can wear. Anything, and I do mean anything, red automatically makes you a target. A matador has a red cape to piss off the bulls. If I'm passed on the highway by a red sports car, I will speed up because they will attract the heat of the police. If a cop is out there, he will stop them. Why? Because red is so easy to see and they know the driver is probably cocky.

Well, the Red Hots have just pissed the bulls off. I look at the bracket, and we have a two-hour break till our next game. You've guessed it; the guys head to the trucks. Now since it's only ten o'clock in the morning, it's a little early for drinking beer. So I wonder about the complex. I have to admit I know a lot of the guys from other teams. I've met most through the AlabamaSoftball.com. The site is owned and run by McCray. McCray is a great guy. He was also the ISA commissioner. And he has done a lot for the sport over the years. The site is where I met Baxtey. We pick at each other often on it because he is a Georgia Bulldogs guy and I'm a Georgia Tech guy. But it's all in fun. There are several guys who post often on the message board.

I make my rounds talking to the guys and head toward the trucks. I can't drink beer this early at a softball tournament. If it were fishing, it would be a different story; you can drink beer all day long because the only thing strenuous you have to do is load up the boat. You don't tend to get dehydrated fishing like you can by playing ball. Playing softball makes you sweat like a sinner in church. So early on, you need to drink water and Gatorade.

The guys start talking about women, one of our favorite subjects, especially since there are no women around. When you start talking about women, whether it's a girlfriend, a wife, or a one-nighter, the subject of sex always comes up. All men claim they never get enough, which always leads us to the subject of pornography.

First thing we have to settle is, who is or was the best porn queen? This is a tricky question because you have to consider their acting ability. Granted, they aren't a hell of a lot of lines to remember, but it is a consideration. Second, you have to debate performance. The worst thing a porn actress can do is to keep looking into the camera. It is just not professional. How they give a blow job is probably the most important thing they're judged by. That actually accounts for two-thirds of their grade. Do they use too much hand? Do they slobber too much? And most importantly, how far down do they go? There are probably more things to grade an actress's performance in porn than there are in a Hollywood production. How they look is also a must. You see a lot of porn stars with C-section scars. That is a turnoff; you get low marks for that. In the last seven or eight years, there has been a push to have the women completely shaved on their private parts. I have to admit I like it shaved; it doesn't have to be completely bald though.

One thing that does turn me off are tattoos and body piercing. If a woman has her ears pierced, fine, but not her tongue, eyebrow, or anything else. That is just trashy. I wouldn't want a woman with a pierced tongue anywhere near Mr. Happy even though it's supposed to feel great. There's too great a chance to do Happy harm. Also, I have to admit I'm not into tattoos, especially those people who cover their bodies in them. I once saw one of my father's friends who was in his late seventies at that time. He had a tattoo of a topless hula dancer. The tattoo was wrinkled; age spots covered it. It had aged just as he had. Plus, I'm also scared to death of needles and getting hepatitis or AIDS. And to be honest, tattoo artists don't look very sanitary.

Our porn-queen vote is for Tori Welles as the queen of porn. The subject then turns to what our porn names would be.

"Guys, what would your porn name be if you did a porno?"

Meat says, "I would be Sweet Meat!"

"Todd, how 'bout you?"

"Easy. I would be Rodd Jammer."

"Mark?"

"Woody Reamer, Coach Ben."

"TJ, how 'bout you?"

"I would have to be Willie Packer, and yes, I can."

Lewis chimes in to say, "I would be Dick Long."

I laugh. "Shit, Lewis, you would have to be Dick Hand, 'cause that's when your dick stays—in your hand."

"Well, Coach Ben, what would your name be?" Lewis says.

"Easy. I've thought about this before. I'd call myself Buster Nutt."

"Coach Ben, you have too much time on your hands," Dirk says.

Meat chimes in, "Hell, it stays in his hand."

Game time is fast approaching. Our next game is against the Thunder Stixx.

"Swinging Stixx, report to field 4."

We head to field 4. The Thunder Stixx are a new team. I've seen them at a few of the tournaments, but we haven't played them yet. All I know about them is that they have the best-looking uniforms I've ever seen on a softball team. While the Red Hots are the ugliest, these are the nicest. I guess I was a little jealous. They are white, dark green, and metallic gold. They look like the Fighting Irish of Notre Dame. Their sponsor is a car dealership. The son of the owner plays and coaches the team. The Stixx win the coin toss and elect to be the home team. That would be all they would win. They have quite a few supporters in the stands; they must have had thirty people cheering for them.

"Let's go, Stixx! Let's go!" It sounds like a college football crowd.

The game is uneventful. We beat them to death 28–2. After games, teams always shake hands and say "good game." It's that sportsmanship thing to do. I am last in line to shake hands.

"Good game. Enjoyed it. Good luck next game."

Now it is my turn. I get to the coach/sponsor. "Coach, those are the best-damn-looking uniforms I've ever seen in my life."

His eyes light up like a little boy on Christmas morning. "I had them custom-made."

"Well, they look great." I could have told him "good game," but we both know it wasn't, but at least it ended on a positive note.

We decide to head to the truck for a beer. When you can stay in the winners bracket, it doesn't hurt to have a few beers. You have longer breaks between games, so you're not playing continuously. You shouldn't get dehydrated.

We get to the truck. The guys have brought a tent canopy for some shade from the sun. They begin to put it together. I pull out my chair. I think, *I'm just going to listen to these guys.* I have always been fascinated with human behavior. Sociology/psychology is one field of work I wish I had pursued. I remember watching *The Bob Newhart Show* growing up, the one where he plays Bob Hartley, the psychiatrist. It's hard for me to understand why so many people need to have someone else help them solve their problems. I know I'm not the sharpest tack in the intellectual pack, but I have something far more important: common sense.

The Bible often talks about gifts from God. And my gift, if I have one, is understanding people. I swear I can look into someone's eyes and know what they're feeling. That's why I'm a great softball coach. You have to understand the players and how what goes on and off the field can translate into what they do on it. I realize I'm getting away from softball a bit. Hell, I do that a lot. But I want you to understand exactly who I am and where I'm coming from. Few people know the real me or can see behind the walls I place around myself for protection. I let people see what I want them to see. I think Donna and Meat may be the only people who really know me, the real me.

I'm often amazed how many people don't want to take responsibility for their actions. They want to blame God. I know because I have. They blame their parents or the government for all their problems. Life may have dealt them a shitty hand. But we all have to play the cards we're dealt. If you play them long enough and play them well, you can win, regardless of where you're from. I guess you could say life is like a game of gin rummy. What you pick up and what you lay down determines if you win.

I understand there are some people who need a doctor's help, who are in need of counseling. And a lot of the times, they are very successful people. They turn to a psychologist/psychiatrist for help. Some are with PhDs, doctors, lawyers who can't solve their own problems. I'm just thankful that I'm able to think things through for myself. The answers to our questions are easily found if we understand ourselves and use common sense to help us rationalize them.

I know by now you're saying "This guy is crazy." No, I'm really not! You see, I understand the many facets of my personality. I can be the writer of a trashy song or a patriotic poem. I can talk about sex and porn or even what blessings God has bestowed on me. Why? Because I understand myself. It took me a long time to do that. And you know what? I like who I am. My belief is that God made me who I am.

There's a song by Aaron Neville called "To Make Me Who I Am." In it there's a line that says "I've broken bread with the devil, fallen on my knees to God." It's all about learning from our mistakes. My job here on earth is to learn and to help others if I can. And I've made mistakes that I've learned from too. I've also learned from my accomplishments. Donna says that I am simplistically complex. I thinks she means I am a deeply complex person who uses simple common sense and logic to work through things. I hope that's what she means.

I really didn't intend for this book to be about me. It was supposed to be about men's softball and why we play. I didn't intend it to be so much about my philosophy on life. But it has. This book has turned into a release for me—a release for the things I've kept inside. I doubt that it will ever get published, and to be honest, I don't care if it does. Should it and you hate it, then maybe you can sell it on eBay. My real hope, though, is that maybe, just maybe, you can (if you haven't already) learn to love and accept yourselves.

Back on the hill, the guys' conversation turns to deer hunting, how many deer they have killed, which hunting rifle they use, where they hunt. I don't say anything to them, but I don't even hunt Easter eggs. It's not that I don't believe that hunting is needed. There is already an overpopulation of deer here in Alabama. And we do need to keep the population thinned, but I just simply cannot kill anything. To me, there's no satisfaction in killing something, no joy. If I had to hunt or starve to death, I'd hunt. But as long as there's a grocery store nearby, I'll shop for food. Maybe my reason for not hunting is, I watched *Bambi* as a child. Maybe it's just that I have a soft spot in my heart for animals. I get upset when I hear about animals being abused. Dogfights and cockfights make me sick to my stomach. Those people who attend and sponsor those should rot in jail. Bullfights too. I'm not ashamed to say that when I hear about a matador getting gored, I'm not bothered by it. When anyone mistreats an animal, they deserve to burn in hell. I know some of you will be furious about these comments. If so, you can kiss my ass because I don't give a fuck. You may think roping a calf or stabbing a bull is sport, but I personally think you're the lowest forms on earth. The only things I have ever killed are poisonous snakes. I know snakes are not necessarily bad. But those snakes got in my swimming pool and goldfish pond, and they had to go. The biggest problem I have with deer hunters is the joy they express in killing these animals, like there is some challenge in shooting something from a tree wearing camo while wearing the scent of a doe in heat, often hunting over a planted green patch or corn. Yeah, that takes a big man. Hell, I feel bad if I run over a squirrel or if a baby bird falls from the nest. That may not be the macho thing to say, but it's true.

Game time is getting here fast.

"Okay, guys, let's hit it. Enough about killing deer. Let's kill some softballs."

We play Players. They're a good team out of Columbus, Georgia. We win the coin toss, the home team.

"Home team, hit the field" comes out of the umpire's mouth.

The guys are a bit slow getting to their positions.

"Come on, guys, show a little hustle out there. They aren't going to lay down and give us the game."

Hal is the last one to get in position.

"Play ball," says the umpire.

I'm already feeling uneasy. When two teams are pretty much equal play, the game usually comes down to who wants it the most and who hustles the most. Their leadoff hitter hits a ground ball to Kroy at shortstop. He fields it cleanly and throws him out. Okay! Maybe I overreacted. Their number 2 hitter hits a grounder to Lewis at second, who boots it, but instead of staying with the play and trying to get the runner out, he gives up on it.

"Come on, Lewis, stay in the game, shake it off!"

When a player takes a playoff, it can cause a negative effect on the team. Calvin used to make sure everyone stayed mentally in the game, but he's not here. Their number 3 batter hits a line drive for a base hit to Hal, who takes his time getting to the ball. The batter gets to second base on what should be a single. So instead of a runner on first and with two out, it's second and third with one out. I know that doesn't sound like a huge difference, but it is. It takes away the chance for a double play but also the force out at second. Not to mention the fact you have two men who can score on a single base hit.

"Okay, guys, show a little life out there." I can tell we're as flat as a pancake. I can tell Hal's mind isn't on the game.

The cleanup hitter who is built like a beer truck is up next. He hits a shot up the middle. Todd hustles to the ball, but he has no play at home, so he throws the ball to the cutoff man. Runner at first, still one out. The next batter hits a one hopper to Mark, who throws to second for an out. Runner at first two out. Their number 6 hitter hits a line drive to the gap between Stacey and Hal. Stacey dives for the ball, but it just tips his glove and goes to the fence. Hal, whose job it is to back up the play, is standing in left field, playing pocket pool, doing nothing.

"Will somebody make me a play?" I say.

Seventh hitter hits a two-run homer. Finally, the number 8 hitter hits a fly ball to Joey for the third out. It seems that in slow-pitch softball, there are a lot of five-run innings. Down five normally doesn't bother me, but there is something wrong; I just can't put my finger on it. Joey leads off with a single to start the bottom of the first.

"Hit with me, guys."

Joey always does his job. Kroy lines out to the left center fielder. Both guys have hit the ball hard. Sometimes when a team is flat, scoring runs will kick them in gear. Dirk steps into the batter's box. On the second pitch, he sends a drive halfway up the bank behind the fence for a two-run homer.

"Way to hit the ball, D."

Mark and Meat hit the ball hard for outs. But at least we scratched for a couple.

"Let's flash some leather."

Unfortunately, it seems we can't get our heads out of our asses in the game. We end up getting thumped 23–8.

Guys like to throw things when they lose, especially when they know they didn't play like they can. There are gloves, batting gloves flying. There are people cussing up a storm. I wait for everyone to pack up their gear and to leave the dugout before I say anything.

"Guys, meet me over by the water fountain."

I could handle my speech two different ways: one, I could give them the old "it's a double elimination, we're still in it" speech, or I can take them to the woodshed. I think Andy would probably take Opie to the woodshed.

"Guys, that was the worst excuse for a game I've seen this year. There's no way we should have been beaten that badly. Some of you busted your ass, and some of you acted like you were in *The Twilight Zone*. Now if someone has a problem with me, let me know, because if someone doesn't hustle this game, I will pull your ass out of the game just to embarrass and disrespect you like you've done not only to yourself but to the team. I could be out fucking fishing. I really don't need this shit."

No one says a word. I start my walk up to the parking lot. When I get to the truck and open up a beer, Whatley walks over.

"Damn, Ben, did you check for polyps while you were in their asses? Because you got up in there deep. I could hear you up here."

Whatley has a way with words; I couldn't help but smile.

"Did you see our game? We were flat as hell."

"I watched some of it. You weren't just flat, you just fucking sucked."

It's hard to argue with the truth, and Whatley is right.

All my guys avoid me like I had the plague. They know I am pissed. I used to hate it when our high school coach would crawl our asses, so I know how they felt. If someone didn't hustle, our coach would take it out on the whole team. Why? Because if you singled out a player or two, they're liable to quit, or the rest of the team will get on them.

"Whatley, how's your team doing?"

"How do you think we're doing? We just got our asses beaten. We suck, but at least we hustled."

Whatley, like me, has been playing softball for quite a while. I think he is about thirty-five, which is old to be out here with these twenty-two-year-old kids. But Whatley still enjoys showing these kids how to hit. Attitude has changed over the years with players. When I played ball in school and early on with my softball career, we had respect for our teammates and the coaches and, yes, even the umpires. Today kids are always saying "Don't dis me, disrespect me."

I think it all started when some of the pro players all started talking trash, getting tattoos, and wearing earrings. To me, that's disrespectful.

"Swinging Stixx, I need a lineup."

Well, game time is here. I walk over to Mark.

"Mark, go ahead and make the lineup out. I'm going to stay up here."

"Ben, are you okay?"

"Yeah, I just want to prove a point."

"You're not mad at me, are you?"

"Hell no, you're a gamer, you left nothing on the field."

"With ASA state qualifiers next week, I want guys to pick up their game."

"Okay, if you think that's best."

Whatley walks over. "What the hell was that?"

"Psychology."

The Stixx take the field. Some of the guys look up toward the hill. I just raise up my beer. They're getting ready to play A-One fence.

A-One is a good team. I think they're from somewhere south of Montgomery. A-One leadoff hitter hits a shot off Kroy's chest. Kroy picks up the ball and throws to first for the out.

"So, Whatley, how does it feel to be an icon?"

"What are you talking about, Ben?"

"You're TJ's hero. He told me so."

"Bullshit."

"No, I'm dead serious."

Home run, A-One; Stixx, down two to nothing.

"Well, TJ's dad was sorta a hero of mine. He was all everything in school."

Whatley and I continue to talk. The game seems to be flying by. The Stixx are down 15–9. Lewis and Ray hit back-to-back singles to start the inning.

"Whatley, here's your boy. What do you think he'll do?"

Whatley yells, "Hit it to your daddy!"

TJ calls for time, steps out of the batter's box, points the bat up to Whatley like Babe Ruth did. *Crack!* The ball comes flying off the bat, clears the fence by forty feet. Whatley looks over and smiles.

"Maybe you're right."

"You know what? We could use a player like you on the Stixx. Think about it."

The Swinging Stixx fight hard all game long but end up getting beaten 17–15 and put out of the tournament. I walk down to tell them I was proud of the way they fought all game long.

I say, "Keep your heads up, because next week is the state qualifier." But I remember something this weekend I had forgotten."

Being a coach is more than filling out lineup cards or coaching bases. It's being a leader. I try to lead by example. When I was growing up, there were a lot of older men who took the time to answer questions I had. My father guided me early on, but there comes a time, for whatever reason, when we can't talk to someone that close to us. The transition from boy to teenager to man seems like it happens overnight. I look back at my transition and the men and women who guided me. When I was eighteen, I thought I was a man. I had lost my virginity at fifteen, I had to register for the draft, and I could vote at eighteen. But one thing that I wasn't was responsible. The drinking age at that time was eighteen, and I started going to bars. Like most young guys, I wanted to hook up—you know, to pick up women.

College was months away, and I had a summer job at a state park. I thought I had it made. My boss at the state park in the summer of '80 was this crusty old fart named Phil. I remember my first day at work; I was hungover from the graduation party and really didn't want to do much. The job at that time was picking up trash and cleaning up pavilions. I was told when I took the job that I would be moved to the beach once if opened. And this was all that was available for the time being. The beach opening was only a couple of weeks away. And I could handle this shit for a week or two. At least none of the girls I knew would see me. But on that first day, Phil busted my balls. He stayed on me the whole day. I really don't know why; maybe he realized I was hungover and he wanted to make a point. Maybe he wanted to show his authority. If a trash can had maggots in it, I had to change it. I had made up my mind I wasn't going to come back for this shit tomorrow. *Flipping burgers would be better than taking this shit*, I thought.

At the end of the day, he said, "I guess you're going to quit, aren't you?"

Now picking up trash, to me, was demeaning as hell for me. And for this eighteen-year-old, I had all I was going to take. Try to imagine picking up shitty diapers and changing trash bags with rotting food and maggots.

Hell, I had just graduated from high school for this shit! The world was my fucking oyster. I'll be damned if I was going to take shit from some old man picking up trash. I was only being paid four dollars and ten cents an hour, which was minimum wage at that time. Hell, I could live with the pay if I was on the beach with the good-looking women around, but not to pick up fucking trash and having an old man with a god complex crawl up my ass.

"What makes you think that?" I said.

"I know your type," he said. "You've been spoiled your whole life, and you think this is beneath you. I bet you're still sucking on your mama's tit."

I couldn't believe he just said that. I wanted to punch him in the mouth. But I thought an arrest wouldn't look good on my college transcripts, though now I realize he was correct about being spoiled, at least to a degree. It pissed me off then. Now Phil was a retired military man, so he didn't mince his words. I had never been called spoiled—arrogant, yes; a jerk, lots of times; but spoiled? Never.

"Let me tell you something. I have never been spoiled, I've worked for everything I ever got."

"So I guess you'll be here at six thirty in the morning."

"Yes, I will."

I have never backed down from a challenge, and Phil just threw one out. I realized later that he knew more about psychology than I ever will. Why I let this cranky old man get to me, I don't know, but he did. Most people that do this type work for a living, you would expect them to be high school dropouts. He seemed far too intelligent for the job.

Well, the next day, I was the first one in the parking lot. It was Sunday morning. *I'll show him*, I thought. *Spoiled my ass!*

That morning, he took only me out to help him. We had to have three pavilions cleaned up by ten. That was when the groups that rent them start to show up. We emptied trash cans full of spoiled food and washed off picnic tables. That day was a start of a friendship that I'll never forget. We busted our asses to finish up what we had to do before lunch. So we had an hour or two to kill. We sat on a picnic table under one of the pavilions and talked. I learned that he had quit school when he was sixteen to join the military. This was during World War II. His brother had been killed, and he wanted to serve his country. How many people today would make that sacrifice? He told me that the greatest thing he could do was fight for his country. If it meant dying, so be it. How many people today feel that way?

The story of Pat Tillman and his brother came to mind. Pat Tillman, as most of you know, had a great professional football career but gave it up after 9/11 to join the military. He didn't have to; he wanted to. He gave his life for this country, so if you want a hero, look toward him. He is an American hero.

Phil and I would talk about life, father-and-son relationships, everything. I guess that at that point in my life, I needed a reality check. And he gave me one. The day that the beach opened up, I was offered my transfer, but I didn't take it. I chose to stay on the cleanup crew for the rest of the summer. That was the best decision I've ever made. Phil became a mentor, a close friend. Actually, he was the father I wished I had. He was tough but fair. He offered me advice when I asked for it and even when I didn't. And I think I helped him somehow understand his sons better. I would go to his house after work to have a drink and to talk but mostly to listen.

That summer, the summer of 1980, I not only understood what it meant to be a man. I became one. From '80 to '84, I worked part-time. In '85, after college, I went to work full-time in a different department. I would still see him. Around that time, I began to see little changes in him. He would stutter and forget little things. He also started to have headaches. I suggested he see a doctor. My fear was that he might have a brain tumor or something like an aneurysm. He did go, with his wife's prodding. In April of 1985, he was diagnosed with Alzheimer's disease in the early stages. The day he told me about it was one of the hardest days of my life. He got the news over the phone at work. When he told me later that day after work, he hadn't even told his wife or children. He didn't feel sorry for himself like I would have, and he wasn't even angry. He only felt bad for his wife and children, about the pain his ordeal would have on them. In 1986, he was forced to retire at the age of fifty-eight—much too early for a man with so much to give. I would stop by his house at least three times a week to visit. In 1989, when I moved down here to Alabama, I would call at least once a week. And when I went home to visit my parents, I would stop by to visit.

The last time I saw him when he was still fairly clearheaded, he told me, "Benny, I may or may not know you the next time I see you, but I want you to know that I'm proud that you've turned into such a fine young man. My life as I know it is ending, but yours is just beginning. Benny, you can make a difference. So make that difference."

He had often said that. I guess that was his philosophy. But I knew I had to say something. "Phil, you taught me so much over the years. If I could be only half the man you are, my life would be a success. I can't put into words all that you've done for me. It's a debt that I can never repay. I will always owe you. I guess what I'm trying to say is, I love you, and it may be wrong to say this, but I wish you had been my father." I saw a tear well up in his eye.

"Benny, I would have been proud of you had you been my son, and in many ways, you are. But you have a long life to achieve the things I couldn't. So make the most of it. Make me proud."

We hugged each other, and I drove away. After pulling out of sight, I pulled over on the shoulder of the road. I began to cry. It was one time in my life that I lost complete control.

In 1991, he passed away not from the Alzheimer's that was eating away at his brain but of cancer.

At his funeral, I was asked to give a eulogy. My first words were "Phil was not a saint or a millionaire. He was something far greater. He was what all of us should try to be—a man who was respected and loved by all who knew him, someone who made a difference, at least in my life."

I think everyone in the chapel agreed with me. The last thing he ever said to me before he got too ill was when I told him thanks for helping me become a man. His response was "It was in you all the time." That was Phil never taking credit.

Alzheimer's is a horrible disease. When President Reagan admitted to the country he had it, I felt a tremendous sorrow for Nancy and the children. It is horrible watching someone you love die slowly. The worst part is, you're helpless to do anything about it. I only hope President Bush changes his mind and allows stem cell research. It's the only hope we have to combat this disease.

I admit I can see a little of myself in some of the young guys on the team. I try to remember how I was at their age. I try to listen to them. I laugh at some of the stupid things they do. But maybe, just maybe, I can give them some advice that will help them down the road. Nothing in life is guaranteed, and I hope these guys make the most out of their chances. Softball is, after all, only a game; it's not our life, certainly not mine.

The guys pack up their gear and head to the cars.

"We play Monday night at eight thirty and nine thirty!" I shout out.

Mark is looking a little down.

"Mark can't win them all."

"No, but we can try, and today we didn't."

Mark doesn't take losing well, and he shouldn't. But I learned a long time ago that you can get ulcers worrying about things that are out of your control.

Meat and I pack up and drive out of the parking lot.

"Whatcha thinking about, Meat?"

"I'm just a little bummed out about the game."

"Hell, that's over and done with. We can't do anything about it now," I say.

"I just get pissed when guys don't hustle."

"Well, next week, we'll talk to everybody before the game."

We pull into the drive, and Meat loads his gear into the Caddy.

"You still look like Big Daddy Pimp driving that thing."

He laughs. "Yeah, I hear that from the doctors all the time. They drive sports cars, and I have a Caddy. But women think I have money."

"I thought it was because you need the extra headroom for that pumpkin head of yours."

"No, I need the extra space for my big dick."

"Yeah right. Whatever you have to tell yourself to boost your ego."

With that, we leave the park. I drove alone home.

When I arrive and walk in the door, I am greeted by my dogs. It's amazing how dogs can lift our spirits when we are down. Skipper jumps up on the back of the sofa with this "pick me up so I can lick your face" look in his eyes. I do. A dog's love is unconditional. It has to be. When I took the dogs to be neutered, it was one of the hardest things I ever did. Being a man, I can't imagine letting a doctor cut my balls off for any reason. If a doctor told me "Mr. Thompson, you have testicular cancer, and we have to cut your balls off," I would tell him "Like hell I'm dying with these boys hanging. I came into this world with and going out with them."

Well, when I went to pick up the dogs the next day, those little guys were all over me. They didn't blame me at all for their surgery, but I still felt guilty about it.

"Who needs to go pee, pee?"

They rush to the door. I let them out to do their business.

Since I haven't been home this early from a tournament all year, there is a lot of daylight left. I could do some yard work. No married men do that on Saturdays.

I decide to watch a little television. I haven't seen my new *Barney Miller* videos that just came in. I've joined one of those videotape clubs when *Barney Miller* became available. The show really was ahead of its time. It's one of my all-time favorite shows. Like I said before, so many shows have its leader, usually the star. In this case, Barney is the leader. That's funny to me only because the idiot deputy on *The Andy Griffith Show* was named Barney. And here Barney was the leader. And just like Andy Griffith did, he used common sense and psychology to lead his men. The characters on *Barney Miller* were incredible. You had Wojo, Fish, Yemana, Harris, Dietrich, and Levitt. All the characters were so different, but together on-screen, they had such incredible chemistry. It's the same way on the softball team. If you have good chemistry, it makes everything work more smoothly. If you don't, you are fighting an uphill battle like today.

The first episode I watch is where Harris is trying to get his book published. You guess it. That's when I decided to write this book. Now I realize everybody and their brother think they can be the next John Grisham. Not me. If this never gets published, I'm okay with it, really. There are thousands of would-be authors out there who are a hell of a lot better than me. This is a challenge only to myself. It's also an outlet. Maybe what I actually should be writing is a script; it would make a hell of an HBO series or movie.

Anyway, the second episode of *Barney Miller* is just finishing when one of the dogs farts. Now I could say it stank, but that would be an understatement. Just like how combat veterans have flashbacks, I have one: back to Bellsouth and Meat in the bathroom.

"Jeez, you little stinking bastards."

I look over the three dogs and realize it was Sparky. How did I know it was him? ESP!

Well, he eats shit, and his poop stinks worse than the others, as do his farts. ESP = extra stinking poop. Sparky is the cutest dog I have ever seen. If this book gets published, he'll be on the cover. I've talked to my vet about his eating shit. In fact, he gave me this food additive that is supposed to break the habit. It was supposed to make his shit taste bad. I know you're thinking what I thought. How could anything make shit taste worse? Not that I've ever tasted shit. Well, it did work. He no longer ate his shit. He would eat Skipper's, Dusty's, squirrel, deer, or even armadillo shit. Finally, I just said "Fuck it." I thought if he was going to eat shit, it might as well be his own. However, I do try to keep him from eating it. If I'm outside, I watch him like a hawk. And if he even thinks about it, I yell at him. That usually works.

But speaking of my dogs, I have to admit they are all spoiled. I feed them the most expensive food money can buy. Four ounces cost seventy-four cents a can. I could feed them chicken and save money, and this cute little dog wants to eat shit. What is up with that?

"Let's go for a walk, boys."

I take the dogs out, and sure enough, Sparky takes a dump. I'm at least fifty feet away, and I start gagging. Just as he finishes, he turns around to inspect it. I know what he's thinking. He's thinking, *Can I eat this shit before I get swatted by the dickhead?*

"Don't even think about it, Sparky. I'll kick your fucking ass."

Sparky gives me one of those "you win this battle, but I'll win the war" looks. I just get the dogs back in the house when I see a black sedan pull up in the driveway.

My house is a good quarter of a mile back off the main road. In fact, you can't see it from the road. All my friends know to call me before they come out just to make sure I have the dogs inside. My dogs love to ride in cars, and if they see one, they run right toward it, thinking they're going to go for a ride. Yeah, I know they're not very smart. I have a sign up as you enter my driveway: "Run over my dogs and die." So I get a little pissed when people show up unannounced.

Out of the car step two men. They look like Will Smith and Tommy Lee Jones from *MIB*. Since I know there are no aliens here, although sometimes I think Sparky is from another planet. I think they could be undercover cops or, damn, even worse—Jehovah's Witnesses. I see *The Watchtower* and *Awake!* in their hands. I should've known. Don't get me wrong, I don't care what someone's religious beliefs are; just don't come knocking on my door on a Saturday afternoon. They walk up to me.

"You're a long way away from Area 51, aren't you?" I say, trying to be cute. But evidently, they didn't get it.

"I'm Ray, and this is Charles. Have you got a few moments?"

I think, *Ray Charles—I wonder if they can sing "Georgia on My Mind."* I say, "Look, guys, I know what you're selling, and I'm not buying, okay?"

"We just want to share—"

I cut them off. "Gentlemen, I was brought up a Baptist. My father was a deacon at Lebanon Baptist Church, since I can tell you're not Baptists, because a good Baptist would never wear polyester suit on Saturday in the summer."

"Can we just leave this with you to read?"

"No, I really don't want to read any of your religious propaganda."

"Have you ever read one?"

"Yes, and it pissed me off. It told young boys that masturbation was a sin. Every time I jerk off now, I wonder if God is watching, but I still do it because it feels good, and I realize if God didn't want me to do it, he wouldn't have given me this hand."

They look down at their hands.

"Yes, that's right! I use the same hand to jerk off with what I use to shake hands. As a matter of fact, I just jerked off ten minutes ago. Now if you don't mind, would you please leave?"

Jeez, I sometimes have to wonder if these religious bounty hunters get some kind of reward for every person they bring into the faith, like the Boy Scouts getting badges. This is not my first run-in with them, nor will it probably be my last. I wonder if they make a spray than can to keep Jehovah's Witnesses at bay like they do for mosquitoes.

Monday rolls around, and I have a dental appointment. I don't get too hyper for just a cleaning. Plus, I have a very attractive hygienist. She's very gentle, and there's just something erotic about having a strange woman putting her fingers in your mouth, unless you start thinking about her having sex the night before. Damn, she could have had her hands around another man's cock or, God forbid, massaged her boyfriend's prostate. Fortunately, I'm convinced mine is a lesbian; at least that's what I keep telling myself. I get called back and take a seat in the chair. I'm wearing an old Nightmare jersey.

"Do you play softball?"

"As a matter of fact, I do," I say.

"My boyfriend just started playing this season."

Damn, she's not a lesbian, and she has a boyfriend. I know girls who have boyfriends will do anything, and I mean anything. After all, they're vying for the grand prize: a wedding ring. Now I am glad that they have to wear rubber gloves.

She finishes up without any problems. "We'll see you in six months."

It's funny how your mouth feels like a virgin after a cleaning. You almost don't want to eat anything for a while. I said *almost*. I decide to stop by Wendy's to rebuild the plaque and tartar I just lost. My teeth feels so naked.

After I polish off my triple with cheese, I decide to stop by a tackle store a friend owns. Tray, the man who owns the bait-and-tackle shop, is an interesting guy. He's an engineer by trade but gave it up to open up a tackle store and marina. He actually is doing quite well with it.

One story I have about him is one day me and another regular of the store; his name is Coach. Actually, it's Tony, but everyone calls him Coach because, well, he coaches high school football. Anyway, Coach and I decided to go see Tray, who had opened a booth in a flea market. It was to sell the shit he couldn't sell in his shop. Well, we got there a few minutes before closing. Tray asked us to hang around till he shut down and then to go with him to have a beer afterward. Well, he didn't have to ask us twice.

We decided to go to this bar called the Blue Barn. None of us had ever been there before. But names don't matter; as long as the beer is cold, I can go anywhere. Well, at least that's what I thought. We walked in, and Coach and I were wearing old T-shirts, so we sort of fit in with the crowd. Tray, on the other hand, was wearing a fancy shirt with pearl buttons and flaps on the shoulders fastened with buttons, looking sort of general-esque. We walked up to the bar and had a seat. I was on the end near the pool table. Well, up walked this dude who would make Charles Manson look like Jerry Falwell. Now God has blessed me with the ability to tell when someone's monitor is missing a few pixels and I don't get scared often, but I was drinking this beer as fast as I can and was doing the best I can to keep Coach in a conversation. I was hoping that he, Charlie, just gets his beer and goes back to whatever hole he had crawled out of.

Well, just my luck. Charlie asked, "Where you fellas from?"

I looked over at him because I sure as hell didn't want to piss him off by ignoring him. I was thinking about what I'm going to say. When it comes to survival, I can think pretty quickly, so I said to him, "Howdy, my name is Jesse, and this is my brother Billy Bob." I pointed at Coach. "We're from a small town near the Everglades called Deadwood." That was the only name that popped into my head as I was thinking about the HBO series by the same name.

"Who's that pretty boy with that fancy shirt on? Is he with the CIA?" Charlie, of course, was talking about Tray.

"No, he's our cousin Lester. He lives up this way, and that shirt he's wearing, he won at a turkey shoot."

"Well, he looks a little shifty to me."

"Ah, he's okay, really." Now Tray does have a temper, and I could tell he was getting pissed off. I heard Coach telling him to be cool.

Then Charlie looked over at Coach again. Coach, who lost part of one arm in an accident when he was a child, had his sleeve hanging down over the stump. And Charlie noticed this. "Is he packing?"

I looked over at Coach to see what Charlie was talking about.

"No, no, no. He lost his arm when he was a young boy."

Coach leaned in and told Charlie his story. "When we were boys, Jesse and I fished in the Everglades almost daily. One day, I caught this big ole bass, and as I reached down to pick up the fish out of the water, a gator jumped up out of the water and bit my arm off. All I have left is this stump." He pulled his shirt up to show Charlie his stump.

Charlie jumped back like it still had the gator attached. "Son of a bitch! I thought you were shitting me." After that, Charlie started telling us about his life. He did have a pretty fucked-up life.

But I also knew we needed to leave before he hit us up for money. I looked at Coach and asked him if he was ready. He was. We bought Charlie a beer and backed our way out of the bar.

Once outside, Tray looked at us and said, "I was about to kick his ass."

Coach's reply was "He would have killed you."

The experience did give us one more thing to talk about at the tackle store. The tackle shop always is good for a story or two. If we're not talking about fishing, we're talking about women.

And of course, Tray always has an update on what the bass are hitting and where they're biting from every lake in Alabama. He's like a walking encyclopedia where fishing is concerned. The guys who hang out in tackle shops come up with some of the greatest lines about women I've ever heard.

One guy was on a cell phone talking to his wife in the store one day, and when he hung up, he said, "Would starve to fucking death." Now that didn't make sense, so naturally, I asked what he meant.

"If women didn't have a pussy, they would starve to fucking death."

Now I didn't know his wife. So I wasn't about to defend her honor. Plus, he was one of the biggest rednecks I've ever seen. He came complete with the gun rack in his truck; not to mention he was wearing a shirt that had a rebel flag on it. So I said what every other man would have said in that situation: "True." Not that I agreed with him, but I wasn't about to take an ass whipping from him either. I learned a long time ago to never fuck with a man who has a rebel flag on either his shirt or his truck and never ever take a child trick-or-treating in a yard that flies a rebel flag. I took my niece and nephew trick-or-treating once, and a man answered the door in full KKK garb. Talk about scared shitless.

See, if you keep reading this book, you'll find some valuable insights you can use later in your life. Well, it's time to go home and to get ready for tonight's game. It will be interesting to see if our team responds after what happened to us this past weekend.

Meat shows up on time as usual.

"Bro, I've got our pregame fix." He shows me a gallon cooler.

"What's in that?"

"Margaritas. I was getting tired of beer anyway."

"Cool," I say.

So we decide to call Buenos Nachos and place an order for cheese nachos and extra jalapeño peppers. Damn, my diet is shot to hell, but we might as well do this right. Our friendship is much like the president and vice president's; we always vote the same way on issues. Of course, I'm the president.

We show up at the park forty-five minutes before game time. Pags' calls on the cell phone.

"What are y'all doing?"

"We're throwing down nachos and drinking margaritas in the parking lot."

"Save me some, assholes. I'll be there in ten minutes."

He joins us just as we're finishing off the last nacho.

"Damn, y'all didn't save me any."

"You snooze, you lose, Pags'"

We did pour him a margarita out of guilt.

"You nacho-eating bastards, I hope it burns a hole in your ass tomorrow."

Speaking of which, it is funny how jalapeño peppers hurt worse coming out your ass than going down your throat.

"Who do we have tonight?" Pags' asks.

"Just a couple of scrub teams," Meat says.

Mark pulls up in the parking lot.

"What's up, Mark?"

"Not much. Did you hear from Hal?"

"No. Why should I?"

"Well, he did give Kroy his uniform and said he quit."

"Well, that doesn't surprise me any, Mark. I say good riddance."

"Yeah, he said he was too good to sit the bench."

"Hell, he only sat one game. I think everybody else has sat at least one game."

Mark says, "Actually, I'm glad. He was sort of a baby."

"Well, Mark, I know a guy who wants to play with us. His name is Ryan Williams."

"Yeah, I know him. He's damn good."

"I'll give him a call."

We make that long walk down the steps to the complex. Our first game is against Loser's Inc. It's not their real name, but it should be. They have some players that aren't fit to carry a water bottle, much less play in a game. Remember the movie *Revenge of the Nerds*? Imagine them trying to play softball. I just wish we had better teams to play tonight; it would help us prepare to play the ASA District this weekend. I make out our lineup. I decide to have some fun with the lineup. Since this team couldn't beat us even if we blindfolded ourselves, I bat the guys in reverse order. Instead of Joey leading off, I bat him last and Coy first.

Loser's bat first. I have my outfielders play in shallow, like you would if you played Wiffle ball. Well, the game doesn't last long. We score twenty-two runs in the first inning. After that, everyone bats opposite-handed. We still score nine more runs. We win thirty-one to zip.

Our second game is against Not Worth a Crap—also not their real name. They aren't the worst team in the league; they did beat Loser's Inc. in a close game.

The same thing happens. We drill them twenty-four to zip. I think we played a total of forty-five minutes, and that was us doing most of the batting.

After the game, I call the guys together to find out if anybody won't be here this weekend.

Joey speaks up and says, "You know I'll be playing with Roscoe's this weekend."

"Joey, like I told you, we expect you to play with us this weekend. You have to make a decision: who do you want to play for?"

I thought in my heart of hearts he would make the right decision.

"Let me know Wednesday what you decide to do."

Joey has been playing ball with Mark, Dirk, and Kroy ever since I can remember. I didn't expect him to necessarily have loyalty for me, but I didn't expect him to turn his back on the other guys.

Walking out to the parking lot, I ask Mark, "What do you think Joey will do?"

"Ben, I honestly don't know. I've talked to him till I'm blue in the face."

"Well, Mark, if he doesn't play with us, we will have to turn him loose."

I hate the idea of cutting someone from the team, but in softball, you're either with us or against us. If we let him play with Roscoe's and then allow him to come back and play with us in Panama City, we would have a major chemistry problem. What I can't understand is, we're going to Florida the following week to play. Why can't he wait a week?

When I get home, I decide to call Donna. It would be nice to hear her voice. Plus, she has just gotten home from visiting a sick aunt. Since I know how my visits go with my family, I can only imagine she is happy to be home. I dial her number.

"Hello."

"How's my little oversexed honeybun doing?"

"Is this Ben?"

Oh shit, I thought. It's Clair.

"Yes. I'm sorry, Mrs. Davis. I thought you were Donna."

"I'm sure you did. I'll get her." I could hear her laughing as she called for Donna to pick up the phone.

Donna picks up. "Ben, did you just hit on my mother?"

Not knowing what to say, I do what most guys would do: lie. "No, of course not. I knew it wasn't you. I thought it was Jan, and I was just going to mess with her. But I do have to say, your mother sounded pretty hot on the phone."

"Well, I'm going to tell her."

I hear her say "Ben said you sounded hot on the phone." I hear her mother say "Well, I am." I decide to speak up to change the subject.

"Donna, I was just calling to see how you were doing and to see if you want to go out tomorrow to eat maybe and maybe a movie?"

"That actually sounds great. Do you want me to ask my hot mother to come along too?"

"Sure, I've always had this fantasy about a mother and daughter together."

"Ben, I'm going to shoot you."

"I'm sorry I was just playing. Tell your mother I'm sorry too. I hope I didn't offend her." I can hear Donna telling her mother what I said.

"Ben, she said she was offended that you apologized."

With that, we hang up. *Women*, I think.

I decide to check out the message board. I go in and turn the computer on and click on the message board. I couldn't believe what I was reading. It seems everyone was trashing the Stixx.

> The Swinging Stixx are the most hyped team in the state.
> Stixx suck.
> Swinging Stixx could only finish in the top ten if it were a dishwashing contest.
> Nice uniforms, shitty team.

Damn, what's up with this? If I respond to it, it would only make things worse. I switch over to our message board. Teams are trashing us there too. There are some posts from some of my guys calling Joey out. They had heard our conversation and were pissed that he would turn his back on them. One player called him a traitor. One said he was only out for himself. One player said to go ahead and quit and that we didn't need him, and that is by his best friend on the team. This is not good. I don't know if they were trying to use psychology or not, but they were pushing him in a corner. At that moment, I know he couldn't come back. I call him and try to explain that the guys were hurt and that they felt he had turned his back on them and tell him not to take it seriously. But the damage to his ego was done. Joey has decided to play with Roscoe's. And Joey is, without a doubt, the best hitter we had on the team. You just can't lose a player like that without missing his bat in the lineup. But he has done this to himself.

I call Mark.

"Mark, I just talked to Joey. He's leaving. We have another big void to fill."

"Well, Ben, we can see if Parker will play."

Parker is a player who used to play shortstop for ABM.

"I guess we could move Kroy to second and use Lewis in the outfield."

Every year, teams always have a turnover. The good teams can pick up and go on without missing a beat. I just hope we can. I notice TJ has a post: "Ode to Ben." I click on it.

Well, TJ has more talent than sense, I think. Granted, his poem didn't take much talent, but then again, he has no sense. Whether he realizes it or not, he is creating a happy distraction to everything that's going on. I am glad to see he's trying to get our players' minds off the turmoil that's surrounding our team and back on having fun.

If we can overcome these last few days, we may be able to survive these blows we're taking. In my heart, I know it's going to take time to jell with the new players we're getting. But I also fear that more guys will jump ship. If that was to happen, then I think we'd sink like the *Titanic*. To be honest, I'm also questioning how much of this mess is my fault. I know, in some ways, I can't relate to players of today; I guess time will tell.

For now, I will put TJ in his place.

I am glad to see TJ trying to loosen the team up. He might not have known what he was doing, but it seemed to work. Well, everything has gotten back to normal, except we don't have a leadoff hitter. Players from all over the state have started to read our board. We may not win every tournament, but we sure as hell are entertaining. We have even heard from Cock-a-Doodle-Do. It turns out he was the Red Hots player that got tossed out of the game against us. There are a lot of responses to him.

> It seems our team chemistry is still pretty good. When you have girlfriends and wives defending you, what can be wrong with that? I think we'll be a closer-knit group without Joey. Time will tell.

It's Tuesday morning. I'm awakened by the dogs barking. Those little guys are better than an alarm clock. Every morning at seven o'clock, they all have to go empty their bladders. I think it's called synchronized pissing. If only it were an Olympic sport, I would have had three medalists. We all go outside to piss on a tree. I have been going out with them to piss in the mornings since they were tiny puppies. That's how I trained them to be semihousebroken. I put on a robe if it's cold, or sometimes I just go out buck naked. That's the good thing about living so far back in the woods. You're free to pee on any tree.

Today is the day I start back on my diet—again. When I get on the scales, I weigh 230 pounds. Damn, I've put on so much weight since my last knee surgery. Drinking beer with Meat and the guys sure hasn't helped either. A couple of years ago, I was at 185 pounds; that's forty-five pounds of fat. It's my fault. I have to take responsibility. My name is Ben, and I'm a fat fucking slob. There, I said it! Just like an addict, I admit I need help. First thing I do is make a sign to hang on the refrigerator: "You're a fat fucking slob!" That should do it. Next thing is to throw out the junk food, ice cream, cookies, potato chips. I feel like I'm saying goodbye to someone I love. I also have the urge to play Elton John's "Funeral for a Friend." So far, so good. Now I need to find a diet center to join. I realize I can't do this shit alone. I start my search through the phone book. What I'm looking for is a place that will kick my ass if I cheat, sort of a sadistic Weight Watchers, maybe with a motto: "You cheat, we beat!" or "You gain, your pain."

Well, I have no luck. I make a few phone calls. Everyone I talk to is too damn nice. Finally, I find one whose plan includes giving diet shots. I think they're a combination of B complex and B_{12}. Their claim is, they help speed up the fat burning. Good, I hate needles worse than having a doctor sticking a finger up my ass. I call and set up an appointment. It's in an hour. That way, I can't chicken out. I shower and get dressed.

I'm starting to get a little queasy feeling like I had on my first date. I decide to try to find some music that is fitting for the drive over to Northbell, something fat. There are a lot of songs about fat women: "Baby Got Back," "Ain't Gonna Bump No More (with a Big Fat Woman)," "Fat Bottomed Girls." Why aren't there songs about fat men? That is something those NOW women should look into.

I decide to call Donna to tell her the news.

"Hello, Ben."

"Hi, pumpkin. I just thought I'd call and tell you I've got an appointment at the diet center."

"You do?"

"Yeah, I've got to get some help if I'm going to lose any weight."

"Well, I'll help any way that I can."

I know she would, but I also know she would be eating like a Saint Bernard in front of me. After all, she is eating for two. *This won't be easy,* I think.

"Ben, I'll call you tonight to find out how it went. I'm showing a house in a few minutes."

"Good luck," I say. With that, I start the truck. Off to the Diet Center.

Anyway, I arrive at the diet center. I was lucky to call when I did; every two weeks, they have their new members show up for this orientation. That's just another name for diet boot camp. Well, today is that day. I walk in the door. Inside is the waiting room, and it is pretty crowded. I have to say I didn't feel that bad at all. Although I've realized I had put on weight, these people are just freaking huge. One poor woman must have weighed four hundred pounds. She has taken up two seats. I also notice that I am the only man in the room. Compared to the women in the room, I look like Arnold Schwarzenegger. *How can anyone let themselves get so big?* I think. I know people get depressed; I know about chemical imbalances. But all those things are just excuses, especially since we all have friends and families. Hopefully, they would tell us the truth. I admit my weight gain was because I got lazy. And now it is time to pay the price.

"Mr. Thompson, come on back."

I walk toward the back of the building.

"Please step on the scales."

The moment of truth has arrived: 232 pounds. To hide my shame, I look around. I notice that all the nurses are petite, little things. This one little blond is fine as hell. There's something erotic about nurses. It may be that they're all dressed in white. They look like virgins. Maybe it's the cute little hat. I could see that one of them has a tattoo under her white stockings. She has just lost some points in my score book.

Now it is my time to see the doctor. She is dressed the same way. She is slightly pale, with blond hair. I could see her as a dominatrix. She is, however, very pleasant and encouraging.

I get my next appointment set up and buy my shot card. I also get my first injection. *Ouch, that hurt.* I get it in my left hip. Now it is up to me to win the battle of the bulge. I'll keep you posted throughout the book.

I leave there and go straight to the grocery store. I buy fruits, veggies, and those low-calorie, frozen dinners. I know this won't be easy, but I can do it.

107

When I get home, there's a message from Dr. Tate's nurse: "Mr. Thompson, you need to stop by the office and pick up your precolonoscopy kit. Your appointment has been moved to this Thursday. Give us a call if you can't make it."

Shit, I've forgotten about that damn appointment. I call the doctor's office. "This is Ben Thompson. I'm returning a call."

"Yes, Mr. Thompson, you need to pick up your kit and start tomorrow so you'll be cleaned out by Thursday morning."

Now I remember when my father had his colonoscopy and had to drink that shit. And that's exactly what makes you do shit and shit some more.

"Okay, I'll be right over."

I arrive and get my gallon of gunk. They give me instruction, which is basically to drink all this shit.

Now I'm really depressed. I could use a Whopper and a beer. Did I? No, I went home and had a Weight Watchers dinner and a Diet Pepsi.

Wednesday mornings, I usually start getting ready for the game. Today all I can think about is having a camera shoved up my ass. A finger was bad enough, but a camera? Okay, I admit it: I'm a wimp. So what? You want to take my place? I didn't think so.

I decide to get on the internet to find out more about the procedure. They showed pictures of the colon from the inside. It showed pictures with polyps, pictures with cancer, and pictures of a colon with a side order of fries. Actually, it was picture of shit. Evidently, this person didn't get cleaned out well enough and was forced to have an enema. That would not be me. I start on my gunk. *Gunk* sort of describes the taste; it reminds me how the ocean tastes, but not as good.

Meat calls me at noon.

"Are you getting your game face on?"

"No, I'm waiting to shit. You'll have to go to the game without me."

"What's going on, Ben?"

"My colonoscopy is tomorrow morning."

"Damn, sorry to hear that, bro."

"Just let the guys know I won't be there."

"Okay, big dog. I'm heading home. I'll post it on the message board."

"Meat, just don't tell them about the colonoscopy. Tell them I'm out on business."

"I'll take care of that. Just relax and take it easy."

"Thanks, Meat. Talk to you tomorrow night."

Meat really is the best friend I've ever had. The phone rings again. This time, it's Donna.

"Ben, remember, your appointment is tomorrow."

"I know. Are you going with me? I think they may have to put me under."

"Well, I do have a hair appointment. Can you get someone else?"

"Yeah, I will."

I hang up the phone. *Women!* I think. I'll never take her ass anywhere else. I wouldn't be in this mess if I hadn't taken her in for checkup. It's true, no good deed goes unpunished. And you wonder why we're not married.

Well, the gunk is starting to work. I rush to the bathroom. God, the cramps are killing me. I can feel it coming on. *Wwwhhhifissshhhh.* Oh god. In all my life, I have never had shit coming out of my ass at the speed of light. It is like warp-speed travel on *Star Trek.* I swear, it created a black hole somewhere in the universe. It at least created a vacuum in the toilet; I could feel my ass being pulled into the bowl. The rest of that afternoon, I shit, reshit, and shit some more. Yeah, laugh now; it may be your ass later.

Finally, at about ten o'clock, it has let up. I've just had some gas. I decide to post a message on the board. I click on our board. There's Meat's post:

Ben won't be there tonight.

There are already about seven responses.

Damn, the boys must've missed me, I think. I click on Meat's.

Ben will not be at the game tonight. He is making a
gay porno where he takes a camera up his ass. It's called
"Ben's CANdid a Camera."

That motherfucker, I think. I will get him now. Now I'm glad Whatley threw the piss all over him. I click on Lewis's reply:

Ben, maybe they'll find Jimmy Hoffa up there.

I couldn't read anymore. *Paybacks are hell,* I think. I start to plan my revenge.

I toss and turn all night. Every time I have to fart, I get up and go to the bathroom. I have this fear of shitting between the sheets. I just can't wait for this shit to be over. No pun intended. Well, maybe just a little.

D-day is here. I get up, let the dogs out, and grab a shower. I'm off to the hospital. When I arrive, there are so many damn papers to sign. Finally, they take me to an area to undress and put on one of those little paper gowns. Then a nurse starts an IV. All I can think about is food. They cart me in a room, and the doctor speaks to me.

"Yeah, yeah, I know just what you have to do," I say.

When I come to, I am in the recovery room, nauseated as hell. They give me a Sprite to settle my stomach. Finally, my shit—uh, bad choice of words—my senses start to come back to me.

The doctor arrives after what seemed like an eternity.

"Ben, we found a polyp. We removed it. I don't think it's anything serious, but they can turn into cancer. It's a good thing you had the colonoscopy."

Donna walks in. "Ben, they said you can go home after you can urinate."

I have to admit I was glad to see her.

She must have changed her hair appointment.

After about forty-five minutes, I am able to piss, and she then takes me home.

"Thanks, Donna! If you hadn't been such a bitch, I may have developed cancer."

"You're welcome, I think. Was that a compliment?"

"No, this is a compliment." I bend over to kiss her.

"Ben, your breath is bad. Wait till we get home and you can brush your teeth."

It appears that everything is back to normal. When I get home, I grab a quick bite to eat then grab a shower. Then this tired puppy is off to bed.

I awake the next morning to sunbeams coming through the blinds. Although I still feel a little weak, still I feel like a weight had been lifted off my chest. Today I have to prepare for the tournament. So many things to do and to check. First thing is to wash out the watercooler—check. Make sure there are enough softballs in the bag—check. Wash my uniforms—check. Everything seems to be in place. Wait, make sure Sparky hasn't chewed up my cup—check. It's a go.

The rest of the day is mine. I'm not going to do anything except watch a few movies and regain my strength. I picked up *K-PAX* a week or so ago. Any movie that deals with UFOs or aliens always interests me, as you well know by now.

I once had a dream about being abducted by aliens. It was after watching *Close Encounters of the Third Kind*. The dream that I had was actually pretty funny. In it, a UFO landed out by my pond. I decided to take a closer look. So I walked out of the house down to it, taking with me a camera, because I figured I can make some serious jack from *World Weekly News* if I get some photos and an interview. About that time, a little gray guy came out in a flying saucer and zapped me with some kind of stun gun, kind of like in the cartoons. The aliens then took me into their ship and them zoomed up into outer space.

Damn, the earth looks pretty cool from up here.

I knew the aliens were smarter than me. After all, they came from millions of light-years away. I decided I would try to make a deal with them. The conversation went something like this:

"Excuse me, Captain, I didn't catch your name."

Since they spoke telepathically to me in the dream, I'll interpret for you.

"I am Ooga Mooga from Zulakasrar."

"Look, Ooga, I'm not going to bullshit you. I know you're smarter than me."

"True, earthling."

"So let's make a deal."

"Curtain number 3."

"No, not the game show, Moogie! I'm offering to be your sperm hookup, bro. All I want is some of your vast knowledge."

"What do you seek, earth boy?"

I'm thought, *What can I make the most money with? A cure for cancer? A cure for baldness? To be able to read people's minds?*

"What do you seek, earthling?"

"Oogie, I want to know how a man can permanently enlarge his penis."

Now you may laugh at that, but just remember, ninety-five out of a hundred men wish they had a bigger dick. I could make billions. I could make Bill Gates look like a busboy. I notice that Oogie and the other little guys seem to be laughing.

"Aetu, aetu."

111

"Whatcha say, Oogie?"

Oogie dropped his space suit.

"Oh my god." His dick was the size of a jelly bean.

"Earthling, why do you think we seek human sperm?"

"Oogie, you should try some of those enlargement pills."

"They don't work, earthling! We've tried them."

"Well, Oogie, how is it you can travel through space and time and still be hung like a gnat?" Uh-oh, I think I pissed him off. Aliens must be sensitive about penis size too. Maybe he'd heard that before from Mrs. Mooga.

"Off my ship, Jethro."

No!

I woke up on the floor. I haven't drunk tequila since that day. I told you, it was a weird dream. Time for the movie.

Saturday morning arrives, T-day. The weather couldn't be better; I couldn't be better. Well, maybe I could. I haven't had sex in seven days, but who's counting? The dogs start barking. I look out the window and don't see anything. Wait, there comes Meat over the top of the hill, radio blasting. I couldn't tell for sure, but I think he was listening to "Play that Funky Music." He seems a little too happy for seven o'clock in the morning.

"Ben, I'm ready to kick some ass and bring home a little man."

Right then, I knew.

"You had sex this morning, on fucking game day, didn't you? You won't be worth a shit!"

"If it wasn't sex to Bill Clinton, it's not sex to me."

Hell, that made sense to me. Off to the complex we go.

We're the first ones to arrive. I am glad about that since I caught hell last week. Everybody starts showing up about the same time. No one seems too hungover. You can always tell who's been drinking on Friday night because they show up on Saturday morning wearing sunglasses with their heads hanging. I like playing ASA ball because a home run for an out only counts as an out. It doesn't end an inning like in ISA. Our new guys, Parker and Ryan, show up. I know Parker from playing against the old ABM team. He's a damn good shortstop, and he may be the funniest guy I've ever met. Ryan used to play for an A-class team. He also played college ball with Joey. I know that he's a stud.

Our first game is against the Storm. They're a pretty good team, a hitting team, but inconsistent on defense. They look like the Oakland As: gray pants with yellow-and-green stripes and three different jerseys. They're wearing green jerseys with "Storm" across the front in yellow and white. Pretty sharp uniforms. I hate to admit this, but I'm more nervous than usual. A softball team is like a jigsaw puzzle; if the pieces fit, it's easy to solve. But if you're missing a piece or two, it'll never look right. Since we're a long way from completion, I hope we can find the missing pieces.

We win the coin flip and choose home. The Storm's leadoff hitter hits a line drive to left for a single. The number 2 hitter then hits a shot up the middle. Parker dives and knocks it down, flips to Kroy at second for a force out.

"That's what I'm talking about," I say.

That play seems to pick up the team. It has helped loosen things up.

The Storm's number 3 hitter is an animal. His name is Ricardo. He's called Bulldog by his teammates. He hits the ball as hard as anyone I've ever seen. Somehow Kroy manages to catch it and throw it back to first for the double play.

"Kroy, that was a hell of a play!"

"Ben, I never saw it till it hit my glove."

"Sometimes it's better to be lucky than good," I say.

We were both that day. We didn't win the tournament, but we finished second to the Tornados. But we played about as well as we could, considering it was the new guys' first tournament with us. And we qualified for state. Meat had his best day as a Swinging Stixx. He and Mark tied for runs batted in, and he hit five home runs.

Looking at our team while it's good, I still think there are a few pieces missing to the puzzle. I hope we can find them before the state tournaments start. After the game in which we lost to the Tornados 22–20, I get everyone together.

"First, guys, I want to say I think we played a great tournament. Next, I need to know who can't go to Panama City next weekend for the Southeastern."

Everyone can make it. At least we'll have our full team. I still feel we're missing something. It's hard to put my finger on it. I know the team could use another power hitter. But what we need most is a team leader, someone that can step into Calvin's shoes. Mark and Meat are respected by everyone, but Meat is fairly new to the team, and Mark is a little too intense at times. What I need is Whatley. He would help keep the team loose, and he is respected by everyone. The only problem is, he plays tournaments with someone else. I'll have to work on him. The power hitter I want is Jerry Reynolds. I'll have to call him too.

Getting ready for tournaments that are out of state is a pain in the ass. First, we have to find out what wives and girlfriends are going so we can make hotel reservations. We have to determine who will share rooms. Next, we have to decide who is going to drive and who needs a ride. I know I will probably drive down. That way, I'll be free to go wherever I wish.

Donna hasn't said what she wants to do yet. It would mean for her to take a day off since we have to leave out on Friday morning. She seems a little reluctant. I guess it's because she will take maternity leave in a few months. We'll have to have a sit-down. Tonight we're supposed to go out for dinner. I'll press her to make a decision.

I arrive at Donna's at five thirty on the nose. One thing I learned from Phil was to always be punctual. I hate having to wait on people to show up. It's so inconsiderate. So I make it a point to always be on time. Since Donna and I have our own houses, we each have a key to the other one's home. I let myself in.

"Donna, I'm here."

I'm greeted by Scruffy. Scruffy is her dog. I'm not sure exactly what he is. He was dumped out on the road, and she took him in. He really is a sweet little dog, so ugly he's cute, but he's also sweet. People who dump animals out on the road are worthless pieces of shit. I personally think they should have their asses beaten. If you can't take care of an animal, you should not have one. I know I may sound like Bob Barker, but it's true. Pets require a lot of work, love, and attention, almost as much as a child. If you don't want to take responsibility for your pet, don't have one. Or find an old pet rock. A pet is an animal, and if a female is in heat, horny males will follow. The next thing you know, you have a litter of kittens or puppies. It's not the animal's fault; it's yours. So unless you're a breeder, your animal should be spayed or neutered. And if I ever catch you dumping an animal out on the road, I will chase you down and beat your ass. Got it?

"Ben, I'll be ready in a minute."

How many times have we heard that?

She comes in the living room.

"How do I look?"

Men, this is a loaded question. If I say fine, she will take it as "You could look better." Remember, in dealing with women, proper use of adjectives is the key. *Great* is "good"; *awesome* is "better."

"Wow! Donna, you look great."

And she did. Notice the use of *wow* and *great* in the same sentence? Use both and you get double coupons.

"What about my hair?"

"It's fine."

"What's the matter with it?"

Uh-oh. Think. Always answer a question with a question.

"What did you say, Donna?"

"What's the matter with my hair? You said it was fine."

"Donna, your hair is beautiful. I was mesmerized with your dress. Is it new?"

"Yes, I'm surprised you noticed." I could hear a change in her voice. *Whew, I saved my ass*, I think.

We leave for the restaurant. I have made a new CD.

It is for moments like this. It's all love songs, but all the songs are sung by female artists. It has my favorite songs, seventeen in all. It starts out with "Love Takes Time" and ends with "I've Got Love on My Mind." And yes, I do have it on my mind—all the time.

We pull up to the Red Lobster. We choose it because Donna's craving seafood and I didn't get to eat there the night we went out with her parents, because Wayne doesn't like seafood. That still pisses me the fuck off. Also, it wouldn't be too bad for my diet. I can get the grilled catch of the day and the veggies. We place our orders, and I start the conversation.

"Donna, honey, I need to know if you're going to go to Panama City with me? I need to get hotel reservations, and I need to let one of the guys know if I'm going to need a roommate."

"Are any of the other wives or girlfriends going?"

"Well, I know Holly and Darla are, and I think Laura is."

"Ben, is Julie going?"

"I don't know. David is supposed to find out tonight. If you and her decide not to go, David and I will room together."

"Would you like me to go?"

Damn, another loaded question. *Think, Ben, think.* I actually would prefer her not to go, only because it limits what I could and couldn't do with the boys.

"Of course, I would like you to go. I just realize that driving down to watch eight to ten softball games isn't your cup of tea."

"You're right. I think I'll stay here. If Julie stays, we can go to see a movie or do some shopping."

I excuse myself to go to the bathroom. Inside the bathroom, I call Meat.

"Hey, bro, Donna just told me she's not going. Tell Julie that if she stays, then she and Donna can go to a movie or shopping. And maybe she'll stay."

"Okay, Ben, I'll call you back later."

I get back to the table. Our food has just been brought out. So far, so good.

"Ben, since I'm not going, what will you guys be doing by yourselves?"

"Well, Donna, we will be playing ball most of the day and into the night. After we finish, we'll probably just go out to eat," I say.

I know where this conversation is leading.

"You won't go out to bars with the boys if they go?"

"Donna, if the boys go out, Meat, Mark, and I will have to go to babysit, to make sure they don't get drunk. I'm not going to be out looking to pick up women, you know that. I may be a lot of things, but when I told you when we first got together I would never cheat, I meant it. And I do."

"I know you do, Ben."

I remember once while talking to Phil, I asked him if he had ever been unfaithful in his marriage. No, he said. He told me he had been propositioned many times and that he might have been tempted a time or two. But to him, the greatest thing a man could do is to honor his word. He told me that when he said his wedding vows, he meant them. I wonder how many men and women, for that matter, actually take them seriously. I know of men who left their wives while they were battling cancer or women who left men when they had financial problems. "For better or worse, in sickness and health, from this day forward till death do us part, so help me, God"—that statement is easy to say for most. But how many couples actually keep it? I know Phil did. And so would I.

While Donna and I are not married yet, I did promise her that I would be completely monogamous. And at this stage in my life, it isn't that hard to do. I have known a lot of women over the years, and I have learned that when you find something good to keep it, cherish it and enjoy it. Like I told Bryan, the grass isn't always greener on the other side. A relationship is just like the song "Love Takes Time" says. And it takes time for a man and a woman or, for that matter, any relationship to grow, with sex just being part of that equation. It really does takes time for a man and a woman to learn what the other's likes and dislikes are, to discover that special sexual chemistry. I know I've said it before, but it's something we all need to be reminded of daily. You have to be open and communicate with each other. Tell each other what you really want. And to do that, you have to trust each other completely. I, for one, actually believe sex gets better each and every time. Sure, it may be the same woman or man, but the longer you're together, the more relaxed you feel. And the greater freedom allows you to express yourself to your partner. I think that with women, it takes much longer to open up than it does for a man.

Donna and I know each other well enough now, and we talk freely about our sexual desires and fantasies. Besides, there are only so many positions of the *Kama Sutra* that aren't painful. To me, there are actually only about five or six positions that are comfortable for both partners anyway. I mean, I don't think standing on my head with a leg wrapped around her and the other wrapped around my balls is going to give either one of us greater satisfaction. I may be wrong.

We finish dinner, and it's home for dessert. At least, I hope it is. As we pull into the driveway, my cell phone rings.

"Hello."

"Ben, Julie said that she is staying here too. It's just you and me in PC."

"Well, that's great. I'll tell Donna. Donna, David said Julie is going to stay here too."

"All right, Meat. I'll call you tomorrow."

Everything is falling into place, now with just a little luck. We walk into the house. Donna walks over toward the phone to check her messages. I walk up behind her and put my arms around her waist.

There's one message: "Hello, I'm Bill, and I would like to talk about how you can rid yourself of credit card debt. Call me at 8-0-0 H-E-L-P-M-E-2, extension 1-0-2-6."

"New boyfriend, Donna?" I laugh.

"Yeah, he has a big cock too."

I take her hand and put it up to my crotch. By this time, I have a nice erection.

"One this big?" I ask.

She smiles and says, "Let's take a shower."

We go to the bedroom and undress. We take turns undressing each other slowly in a teasing manner. Finally, we are down to just our underwear.

She removes her bra slowly, almost in a teasing fashion, then her sexy little red panties. The she helps me carefully slide my shorts over my erect penis. God, she is beautiful. I must admit I always get this nervous feeling inside before we make love. I guess that's called anticipation.

I turn the water on, and we climb in. We don't really shower so much as we begin foreplay. We take turns soaping each other up. First, I soap up her breasts. Softly, slowly, I slide my hands with the soap down her body till I get to her most sacred areas. She trembles as my hand rubs over her vagina then her buttocks. She then washes my penis and, in a playful gesture, strokes up and down. Even though we have done this before, it is still the most intense and passionate moment of my life. We share a very soft kiss, with our lips barely touching under the flowing water. As the last bit of soap is rinsed from our bodies, we reach for the towels to dry off.

"Ben, you always try to act so macho, but I know what you are inside."

"What's that, Donna?"

"You're a sensitive, caring, loving man. You're a—"

"I think the word you're looking for is *pussy*."

"No, I wasn't going to say that. I was going to say 'a hopeless romantic.'"

"No, but I did. You know they say you are what you eat."

She laughs out loud, which excites me more.

We walk toward the bed hand in hand. I lie down beside her and slowly move my hand from her breasts down her body. I can't help but notice the little hump around her belly. I stop.

"Donna, Junior is starting to grow," I say excitedly.

She says, "I know. I'm afraid you may not want me anymore."

"Darling, that's not true. And I hope you know that by now. I realize that sooner or later, we'll have to stop having sex for a while. I mean, I wouldn't want to give Junior a concussion or brain damage."

"What about now?"

"I want you more than ever before, and if Junior has brain damage, I promise we'll get him enrolled in the best special education school around."

If one word could describe that night, it would have to be *magic*.

I awake at six thirty. Well, it's time to go home to the boys. I give Donna a sweet kiss goodbye, and I'm on my way. I just hope Ford hadn't forgot to stop by to let the dogs out. Nothing like going home to a kennel. I open the door up; no unusual aromas floating around. Then I hear the pitter-patter of puppy dog feet.

"How's it going, fellas? Tell me all about it. Who needs to do their business?"

I walk outside with the dogs to make sure Sparky doesn't eat any shit and to check the bird feeder.

I don't plan on going out looking for a woman, but I do plan on going to a strip club. I know what you're thinking. No, Donna wouldn't care. She just wouldn't go. That's the problem; I would feel guilty and not go. Some of the wives will go to the club, however. At least, I heard they went last year. Nudity is not a bad thing. I know some people think it's a sin. That's their problem, not mine. I mean, if God can create the universe then create this little planet we call earth and fill it with plants and animals then create man and woman, surely he wouldn't forget to tell them "By the way, Adam, you and Eve need to put some clothes on. You know it's a sin." I think God only told them to go forth and multiply. The only thing he said not to do was eat the forbidden fruit. "Go forth and multiply" implied either "Go make love" or "Work on your math skills." Since there were no teachers in the Garden of Eden, I think he meant to make love. Writing this down makes me think about one more thing: have you ever wondered who the first lawyer was? Here's a hint:

> "Psst, Eve, come here. Do you know half of this garden belongs to you? That's right. This fruit tree, it belongs to you. Take a bite."
>
> "But God said not to."
>
> "God and Adam can't tell you what to do. It's a violation of your civil rights. If they don't like it, we'll take their asses to court and sue."

That's right; the serpent was the first known lawyer. If you've ever wondered why a lawyer is sometimes referred to as a snake in the grass, now you know. Is that on time or what? See, this book is filled with interesting tidbits of knowledge. That only I know or can make up at the drop of a hat.

I now turn my focus on getting Jerry and Whatley on board. I decide to start with Jerry. Jerry was a great football player at Northbell. After he graduated, he started playing softball. He can absolutely crush the ball. He got married a couple of years ago and now is a father. He has gotten away from tournament ball. But maybe, just maybe, he's ready to make a comeback. I have one thing in my favor: he plays league ball with us on Mondays. I'll give him a call.

"You have reached the Reynolds at the tone. Please leave a message."

"Jerry, this is Ben. I want you to think about coming out of tournament-ball retirement. I really need another big bat in the lineup, and yours is as big as it gets. Let me know as soon as possible."

I thought acknowledging the fact he's a great hitter might sway his decision in my favor. Now to Whatley. I can't use psychology on Whatley. He knows he can hit. I'll have to use another tactic. I'll call him on his cell phone. I dial his number.

"What's up, Ben?"

"Whatley? Have you got caller ID on your cell phone?"

"Ben, this is 2014. You mean you don't?"

"Whatley? I've got a proposition for you."

"Ben, I'm not into guys. I'm married."

"Fuck you, you sack of shit. I'm talking softball."

"Oh, my bad."

"Whatley, you're thirty-five years old, and you're a superstar on a shitty team."

"And your point is?"

"My point is, I could use your sorry ass on the team."

I could tell he was intrigued.

"Why me?"

OK, time to close the deal.

"First of all, I need someone to help lighten things up. The guys are too intense."

"That's for damn sure."

"Second, TJ and Stacey idolize you. Why? I don't know."

"It's because they know greatness when they see it."

Damn, he's in his MFICH character. That means "Motherfucker, I can hit." He coined the phrase. Now I'll probably owe him a royalty.

"Third and most importantly, you bring your own beer."

"What does Meat have to say about it?"

"Hell, he'd love to have your sorry ass on the team."

"He isn't still mad off about the piss bath?"

"No, if he were, he'd have killed you already. I just wouldn't bring the subject up to him."

"All right, count me in."

"I'll talk to you later. What, oh, by the way, we're going to the Southeastern in Panama City next weekend. Let me know if you and Denise can go."

"Will do, Ben."

Damn, that was too easy. I'm sure you already know this: I spend entirely too much time on the phone.

I think I'll go make a post on the message board welcoming Whatley to the team. But first, I'll call Mark and Meat.

"Hello."

"Mark, I picked up Whatley for the tournament team, and I think JR may also be in."

"Damn, that sounds good. Two more big bats in the lineup."

"Yeah, and it also gives us a bench so we can rest, guys."

"Sounds good to me. What does Meat think?"

"I'm calling him next."

"Well, give me a shout back later."

"Will do."

One down, one to go. I actually should have talked to Meat before I picked Whatley up. But I'll ask him what he thinks before I tell him I'd already picked him up. I dial Meat's cell phone number.

"Hello."

"Meat, you overgrown sack of shit, I need to get your input on a couple of things."

"Like what?"

"I'm thinking about picking Jerry and Whatley up for the tournament team. And I wanted to know what you think about it."

After a long pause, Meat says, "Hell, I think it's great. Do you think they'll play?"

"I've already talked to Whatley. He's in. I left a message for Jerry, but I think he'll also play."

"Then why the hell did you ask me what I thought when you already made the decision to pick them up?"

"It was an afterthought."

"Fuck you then."

"Kiss my ass, you big bastard."

"Damn, Ben, we'll be loaded."

"True, in more ways than one."

Meat says, "Fucking Whatley and the Meatster on the same team. That could be the seventh sign. Now I'm really pumped."

"Meat, I've gotta run. I'll give you a shout later."

I thought that went pretty well. Didn't you? Talking on the phone just wears me out. I just don't know how my mother does it. Time to go make my post.

I click on our board.

Subject: Welcome Whatley?

Message: Guys, I just want to inform you we picked up Tom "MFICH" Whatley today. He will either make us a great team or drive us to drink. Since most of us drink already, I think it'll make us great. Whatley told me he planned to take TJ and Stacey under his wing. I know that's a scary thought, but I think we should make him feel at home anyway.

Ben

Well, all this work on softball has made me tired, so I guess I should do some real work. I realize all of you know little about my employment. All you know is, I'm self-employed. But what you probably want to know is what it is I do. No, I'm not a gigolo, although I'd probably be great at it. Getting paid to give women orgasms would be like taking candy from a baby. Here's what I really do. A few years ago, I invented a piece of equipment that Ford's company manufactures. I receive monthly royalty payments. To say I'm blessed would be an understatement. I am currently working on a product that, if all goes well, will be aimed at the pet consumers. I won't say anything more about it because there would be no way of protecting it. So you see, I'm not really a bum. Among softball, my project, and this book, I have little free time. I'm not looking for sympathy, just understanding. OK, maybe a little sympathy. Hell! I can tell you're still curious about my project, right? Okay, it's a tick remover. It's for people who don't like removing ticks from Fifi. It runs on a watch battery with a small circuit attached. It looks like tweezers with a little trigger. You squeeze the tweezers together, and a contact sends a small electrical impulse into the tick, causing it to let go. Nothing fancy, although I'm having a problem with the circuit. I'm really not too concerned that you know about it because if this book is published, I will have either finished it or scrapped it.

Now you'll be able to sleep tonight. I won't mention the project anymore in the book; it's pretty boring. I just didn't want to give a bad impression. I am a Republican after all. And impressions mean a lot.

I finish up my work in the shop and decide to call it a day. I'll call Donna, eat a Healthy Choice dinner, and turn on the tube. Damn, I live such an exciting life. I go inside to call Donna. I see I have a message: "Ben, this is Jerry. I can play, but I can only play two, maybe three tournaments a month. Let me know if you still want me."

Great, I think. I call him back and get his machine.

"Jerry, whenever you can play is fine with me."

Then I call Donna. After listening to Donna tell me all about her day (she has sold a house today, yada yada...), I eat my supper then turn on the TV and the computer. I surf the net for a while. I have my own routine. I check out ESPN, Drudge Report, and a professional wrestling site. Damn, where would we be, where would I be without the World Wide Web? What the hell did people do before internet? I'd personally like to thank Al Gore for inventing it. Finally, I decide to see if anyone has made a reply to my post on the message board before I settle in for the night. TJ has already made a poem welcoming Whatley.

Okay, TJ will never be remembered for his writing skills. And I'll never be known as a great author either. But hey, we try. Like what Tom Cruise said in *Risky Business*: "Sometimes you just have to say 'what the fuck.'" I see that Meat, Mark, Lewis, and just about everyone on the team have left posts welcoming him. I really feel better now about the team. We may not win a state championship, but we'll have a lot of fun trying. Time to hit the sack.

Wednesday morning, it's rise and shine. I've got to make hotel reservations. And tonight, we have league games. But first, I'll go for a swim. Off to the pool. Since I don't have neighbors, I never wear swimming trunks when I'm alone. I put my towel on the table and dive in. I'm in the water ten minutes when this minivan pulls up. Two nicely dressed women get out. I figure they have the wrong address.

From the pool, I ask, "May I help you?"

"Yes, we would like to leave you some literature to read."

"Are you Jehovah's Witnesses?" I ask.

"Yes, we are."

"Ladies, you would have a better chance selling me Avon than your religious propaganda."

Did they take the hint? Can a fish fuck an elephant? Hell no, they walk down toward the pool.

OK, I don't have swimming trunks on, and the towel is on the table. What do I do? I think.

I give Mr. Happy a couple of tugs and step out of the water, butt-ass naked.

"Ladies, I'm—read my lips—not interested."

They stand there dumbfounded, staring at my cock.

"The water's cold, okay!"

They turn and walk away like two zombies.

I feel a little guilty, but I just get so damn tired of people bothering me at home. The Jehovah's Witnesses must have me on their "Ten Most Wanted" list because they keep sending these bounty hunters over. What pisses me off most is, they just have no consideration for the people they solicit. In their own minds, they're doing God's work, but in my mind, they're just a pain in the ass like telemarketers. I hate them too. I think it was Garbo who said "I want to be alone."

Everyone on the team will make their own reservations. We all have agreed to stay within a block or so to one another. I finally get through to a Fairfield Inn. I get my usual no-smoking room. I hate going into a room if it smells like an ashtray. It's bad enough sleeping on a strange bed that you know strangers have fucked on. But to have to breathe stale cigarette air is too fucking much to bear. No air freshener can cover up the smell of cigarette smoke. It's a smell that penetrates everything.

That was easy enough. My day is starting out well. Even the Jehovah's Witnesses couldn't rain on my parade. I wonder if the ladies got excited seeing Mr. Happy. I bet it was a first for them anyway. Once they tell their Witness master or whatever the leader is called, I'm sure they'll get a medal of some kind. It's like the military giving out a Purple Heart for those injured in battle; maybe they'll get a Purple Penis medal. I can hear it now: "Sister Lewis and Sister Lee, I want to award you the Purple Penis medal for going above and beyond in the line of duty. I hereby award you the Purple Penis medal for your courage of staring Satan and his penis in the face and not backing down."

I get dressed and ready to go to town. The phone rings; it's Donna.

"Ben, are you going to be home for a while?"

"Well, I was getting ready to go into town."

"Can you postpone it for a few minutes? I need to talk to you."

"OK, I'll wait."

We hang up the phone.

Damn, she seemed serious, I think.

Donna pulls up to the carport. When she gets out of the car, I can tell she's been crying.

"Donna, honey, what's the matter?"

"I don't know where to start."

I'm thinking, *Is she breaking up with me? Is there something wrong with the baby?* "Donna, start from the beginning."

She takes a deep breath. "Ben, I'm afraid. I'm afraid I won't be a good mother. I didn't want to get pregnant. And now that I am, I'm scared. I don't want to grow to resent my own child, and I'm afraid I'll lose you too."

I think back to a conversation I had with Phil. We were talking about this same subject and why some men don't take responsibility for their actions. He told me, and I remember it well: "Benny, being able to put your penis inside a woman doesn't make you a man. Any man can do that. Any man can father a child, but not every man can or will be a father, especially a good one. Some men don't want to take responsibility for their actions. That's why so many children are raised outside of marriage. That's why so many women are on welfare raising children alone. Benny, you're like a son to me. And in you, I saw a willingness to prove others wrong, to stand on your own two feet. That's why I've pushed you so hard. And if you only remember one thing I say to you, remember this. Always take responsibility for your actions. Don't be just a man, be an example for other men."

I think a moment about what I should say.

"Donna, I love you and our baby. At first, no, I didn't want to be a father. I didn't think I could be a good one because a child is such a huge responsibility. But we are in this together and for the long haul. I realized the last time when we made love how much I want you, how much I love you, but more importantly, how much I need you. When you drove up crying, I thought you wanted to break up. I don't know what I can say to relax your mind, except something I was going to do after I got back from Panama City."

"What is that, Ben?"

"Donna, will you marry me? I'm sorry I don't have a ring yet, but you can pick out whatever you want. I just want to spend the rest of my life with you and our child."

"Ben, I don't want to trap you into marriage."

"Donna, you're too late. You trapped me the first day we met. I didn't know it then, but I know it now. I want us to be together, forever. So what do you say, Mrs. Thompson?"

She throws her arms around me. "Yes, yes, I'll marry you."

If I said I wasn't scared, I would be lying. All my life, I've only had to take care of myself. Now there'll be a wife and a child to take care of. I just wish Phil were here to talk to. But I know what he'd say: "You're doing the right thing." Marriage scares the hell out of me because so many fail. And there are some couples that stay together for one reason or another that should divorce—like my parents. I love both my parents, though, and after I matured enough to realize they did the very best that they could do in raising me, I've always thought they should have gotten divorced. Growing up, I always knew they loved me. But there were times that I wasn't sure if they loved each other. They fought a lot. My mother, in fact, filed for two divorces while I was in elementary school. My parents were like oil and vinegar. You could shake them up, but soon, they separate. I used to think they stayed together for my sake. But as I grew older, I realized they needed each other. Their problem was, they didn't know how to communicate with each other. Neither took criticism well, nor did they know how to talk to each other. Calling someone a drunk or a fucking bitch might grab their attention, but it was no way to solve a problem or issue. My father did drink too much. But he was never physically abusive to my mother, only verbally, which can be as bad, if not worse. Both leave scars that saying "I'm sorry" can't erase. My mother, who was a bit hyper anyway, would get agitated with my father easily, and after that, an argument would ensue. After years of analyzing their relationship, I came to the conclusion that they loved each other but just didn't know how to show it or say it.

Growing up, I think it was watching their relationship that made me scared of a committed relationship of my own. I'm not blaming them. I just don't want to end up like them. The tragic part of it all came after my father became incapacitated after a series of strokes. My mother stayed by his side for four years, taking care of him. If that isn't love, I don't know what is. It's just a shame it took them so long to realize how much they loved and needed each other.

While I don't want to spend my life living a mistake, I don't want to think about what might have been either. I could never turn my back on Donna or my child. Like Phil said, take responsibility, but is that really enough? Though I love Donna, will our marriage last? I guess there's only one way to find out, since nothing in life is a sure bet. Only time will tell.

Well, tonight is league night. Time to get ready.

Meat arrives at five thirty on the nose, with a six-pack in hand.

He heads straight for the bathroom. Well, he stops just long enough to pick up the new *Penthouse*.

"Taking an early PGS, are you?" I say.

"Got to! My colon is on overtime. I feel like Mount St. Meat is about to erupt."

"Well, turn the damn vent on this time. That orange spray alone can't cover the smell of your shit."

"Picky, picky."

Well, at least it's taking my mind off things. Meat turns on the vent.

After about five minutes, Meat comes out of the bathroom.

"That may have been the mother of all shits."

"Meat, you're one sick bastard."

"True, but I did bring beer."

"I'm not drinking that beer! You took it in the bathroom with you. It has your shit vapors all over it."

"Suit yourself. What have you been doing all day besides jerking off?"

Meat takes a drink of beer.

"Donna and I are getting married!"

"Pssst." He spits beer all over himself. "What did you just say?"

"I said Donna and I are getting married."

"I thought that's what you said. Damn, bro, that's all of a sudden."

"Well, she's scared."

"Of what?"

"She's afraid I'll leave or something. This will let her know I'm in this with her."

"Well, thanks, asshole. I now owe Julie five hundred dollars."

"For what?"

"She said you and Donna would get married before the baby came."

"Meat, you don't suppose they... No, they wouldn't do that, would they?"

"I don't know, but they are women."

"True enough!"

Meat laughs. "Well, you know I'm here for you."

"Yeah, just like you were with the colonoscopy. I still remember the post 'Ben's Can Did a Camera.'"

"You have to admit that shit was pretty funny."

"Yeah, with friends like you, who needs friends?"

"That hurts."

"It was supposed to. Let's go."

The drive down to the complex is uneventful.

"David." I always call Meat David when I'm serious. "Don't say anything about this. I'm serious."

"I promise, dog, not a word."

We pull into the parking lot, and Todd and Holly, along with TJ and Mark, are there. They come over to the car.

Todd says, "Congratulations, Ben."

"On what?"

"On getting married."

Holly says, "Donna called me a little while ago and told me."

"Who else knows about it?"

"The whole team," Holly says.

I think, *That's all I need.* I look over at TJ. "Do you have something to say?"

"Will you adopt me now so Donna can be my mommy?"

Everyone laughs.

I guess I'm glad everyone knows now and I don't have to try to hide anything. I probably couldn't had I tried.

The games that night are a blur. I do remember Meat hit a home run. When he comes into the dugout, he gives me a hug.

"That's for my godchild."

"Who said you would be the godfather?"

"I made you Lacy's godfather, so either I'll be the baby's godfather or I'll kick your ass."

"Okay, consider it done."

I have to admit I was honored when David and his ex-wife asked me to be Lacy's godfather. She is such a sweet little girl. I just hope she grows up to look like her mother.

After the game, we get together to talk about the tournament in Panama City. We will leave out at three o'clock on Friday. It's a good five-hour drive, and we have to play at ten. Some of the guys will have to leave work early so they can make it. But it appears that everyone is still going. I still plan on going, but my mind will be here at home.

Thursday morning is a mad scramble for me. I just have so much to do. I have to wash clothes then start packing for the tournament and wash my truck. Ford plans on staying with the dogs. I just hate the idea of putting those little guys in the kennel. The only time any of them have stayed overnight in the kennel is after they had surgery.

On the way into town, I decide to take my truck by Truitt Radio to have a satellite radio installed. Having over a hundred digital stations is hard to pass up; plus, there are no commercial interruptions. It would also be good for the trip too. It's a pain in the ass searching for stations while you're driving. While I'm waiting to have my satellite radio installed, I call Donna.

"Hello."

"Donna, I want you to come over tonight and plan on spending the night."

Donna has never stayed the entire night at my house. She always goes home so she can let Scruffy out.

"And you might as well bring Scruffy with you. I won't take no for an answer."

"All right, Ben, I'll come over about six."

I decide I would cook dinner. I make out my grocery list while I wait.

My friends in high school used to give me a hard time because I took home economics. What those idiots didn't understand is, I was the only male in the class with twenty-four girls. And if that wasn't enough, I got to bake and eat cookies. So unlike our former First Lady / Senator and Secretary of State Hillary Clinton, I baked and ate cookies. I can also cook just about anything with a little help from Betty Crocker. I decide on having a couple of nice fillets with a salad and scalloped potatoes. My diet will be shot to hell, but maybe with a little luck, I will be able to burn off those calories later on tonight. That's what separates winners from losers. A good game plan.

"Mr. Thompson, your truck is ready."

Well, by the time I get home, it's four o'clock. I have to start rushing around.

The first item is to get the potatoes ready for the oven, marinate the steaks, and toss the salad. Everything is ready to go. Only one more thing to do: get myself cleaned up. Donna arrives on time. I put the potatoes in the oven and preheat the grill. Donna and I sit down.

"Donna, you know I believe everything happens for a reason. Call it God's master plan or whatever you want to. While I never thought I'd want to be a father, the idea of a child excites me in a challenging way. I can try to be the father that I wish I had."

"Ben, what would that be?"

"I don't know. I guess part my father, part Phil, and maybe part Jim Anderson."

"Who's Jim Anderson?"

"Donna, you didn't watch much TV growing up, did you? He was the father on *Father Knows Best*."

"Okay! But, Ben, why don't you just be yourself?"

I hear a beep. That means the Foreman Grill is ready. Time to put the steaks on.

We sit down to dinner. At first, it's a little quiet. The conversation is pretty much about how great a cook I am, which is true. Then Donna asks me questions about my religious beliefs.

"Ben, you said everything happens for a reason, that it was God's master plan. What did you mean? What are your religious beliefs?"

I swallow my piece of steak and try to put into words what I believe.

"Donna, I really do believe in God. I believe that Jesus is the son of God and that he died for our sins. I've accepted that. But I do have some problems with organized religion. I can't take everything a preacher says as divine fact. I have my own beliefs. I guess I believe much like Sylvia Browne does."

"Who is she?"

"She is a psychic who says that before we are born, we chart our lives out with God."

"What about the Bible?"

"Donna, the Bible is missing books. It was put together by men who chose what to include and what to exclude. Don't get me wrong, it has some wonderful wisdom in it. The Ten Commandments should be used as an example to live our lives. But some of the stories are hard to believe."

"Like what?"

"Let me go back to being brought up a Baptist. We were told that if we sin and didn't repent, we would burn in hell. We were also told that God knows everything. If God knows everything, then why did he save Lot and his family from Sodom and Gomorrah?"

"Why?"

"I'm asking you that."

"I don't know, Ben. I guess he thought they were the only ones worthy."

"Okay then, do you know what happened?"

"Yeah, Lot's wife was turned into a pillar of salt when she disobeyed God's word and turned to look back at the city."

"Okay, that is true. But the rest of the story is that Lot's daughters got him drunk and had sex with him and bore his children. Lot had an incestuous relationship with his daughters. He also would probably be considered a pedophile today. The story sort of ends there."

"Is that true?"

"Yes, look it up! I guess that if I put my beliefs in words, it would be this. We live in a sinners' world. We are faced with temptations of this world as a test. We pass some, and yes, some we fail. We are born to learn, to be tested so that eventually we will be able to better serve God. Sex, drugs, money, power—they're here to tempt us, to test us. For instance, the Bible doesn't say being rich is bad. It says the love of money is bad. I think it says that it is easier for a camel to go through the eye of a needle than for a rich man to reach the kingdom of God. Something like that anyway. I believe that the men who wrote the Bible did so to put fear into the followers. Preachers preach on eternal damnation just about every week. And I cannot buy into that. I think God knows we will fail sometimes and that we will sin. I think that in a way, that's the only way to learn—from our mistakes. Donna, just look back into history. How many women were burned at the stake by the Catholic Church as witches. They did this to control the masses. It's in all religions, not just the Christian faith. It's not God's fault, it's man's. Religious zealots are to blame. The only problem I have with God is, why good men have to suffer. But that's a whole different story."

"Ben, you do have issues!"

"Of course, I do. When a preacher says vote against a lottery because it's morally wrong. I have an issue when I know the money would go for education."

"Well, I voted for it."

"I know you did, dear, but that's because you can think for yourself. A lot of people take their minister's word as divine fact. Look at Jim Jones and the Peoples Temple. How many idiots drank the Kool-Aid? Same with David Koresh. Those guys were crazy too, yet people followed them. Why? Because people want someone to lead them to God instead of searching on their own. You see, God knows we are going to sin. It's what we learn from it that matters."

"Ben, what about rape and murder? What do people who commit those learn?"

"Hopefully, what it feels like to be put to death by paying for your sins. I do like the Bible's quote—'an eye for an eye'—on that subject. Remember, we still have free will and we are subject to laws that govern the land."

"Ben, you seem to know a lot about religion. Why don't you go—"

"To church? Because most people who go are snobs. They go because it's the socially accepted thing to do. I also don't go because churches are so political. There are more power plays in church than in a hockey game. People give money to a church so they can have a say in how it's run. I've seen great ministers run off because the nephew of one of the big contributors has graduated from the seminary. It happened at my old church before I moved here."

"Wow! I didn't know, Ben."

"Donna, I talk to God daily, usually before I go to sleep at night. I don't think he listens, but I talk."

"I'm sure he listens to you. After all, you are hard to ignore."

The subject of religion is something I try to stay away from in conversation. People are worse about their religious beliefs than political ones.

It's ironic how many people die in the name of their faith, how many wars are based on religious hatred, intolerance. There are extremes on every side. It's also an argument you can't ever win. All you can do is piss people off. Somehow, though, I don't think the hijackers on 9/11 got their thirteen virgins or how many they were promised when they met Allah. Hopefully, he sent them straight to hell. And hopefully, it is the Baptist hell with the fire and brimstone. To me, hell would mean being forced to listen to polka music. Yikes!

Donna looks up to me and says, "Well, what do you think of Joshua for a boy's name?"

Women, I thought. I smile and say, "Too biblical."

We laugh and finish our meal.

Donna has rented a movie she wants to watch—*Bridget Jones's Diary* or something like that. So we put it in and cuddle up on the sofa. Okay, guys, I admit *Bridget Jones* is not my cup of tea. But sometimes you have to watch a chick flick or at least pretend you're watching it. I find that it is easy to daydream during the movie. After the movie, we turn in. And to answer your question, no, we didn't.

Friday Morning, rise and shine. Panama City, here we come. Ford is going to stay here and take care of the dogs. I've said all my goodbyes; now all that is left is to wait for the Meatster. I can hear him driving in. He pulls over and parks out of the way, and as he steps out, he lets a "Wooo! PC, here we come." I can tell he is really pumped up. I don't have quite that much excitement at the moment, but I'm sure it'll come.

"Someone took their happy pills this morning."

"Ben, I'm always happy to go kick some team's ass, drink some beer, and look at some of the finest ass Florida has to offer."

Okay, Julie, if you're reading this book, he really didn't say that. I'm just trying to induce more book sales. It's all made-up. You know Meat would never ever look at another woman. God, I hope she believes that. He throws his shit in the back of the truck, and we're off.

Panama City is about three-and-a-half-hour drive from Opelika—I should say, *normally* a three-and-a-half-hour drive. Meat has a bladder of a two-year-old, so about every twenty or thirty miles, he has to stop to take a whiz. That's a piss for those of you who don't know. I guess the fact that he was pounding down beers in front of me didn't help his bladder any either. After all, I am the designated driver and couldn't drink anything except Diet Pepsi. And of course, he is constantly telling me how good the beers tasted. What a friend, right? Well, ladies (if any of you readers are ladies), you know by now guys talk about sex, sports, women, and sex. Pretty much in that order.

Since Meat had been through a pregnancy before, I have questions.

"Meat, when Candy was pregnant, did you notice and feel different when you would make love?"

"Of course, you do. You'll have to learn different positions, and probably at some point, you may have to stop. Sometimes it may be painful. Is Donna having any trouble?"

"No, actually, after the early bouts of morning sickness, she has got so she wants it all the time."

"You lucky bastard."

"Really, the only thing that's a little sensitive is her nipples. It's just that when I'm inside her, it feels like an earthquake has shifted things around."

"Does it feel bad?"

"No, but—"

"Then stop fucking complaining."

"Well, I guess I'm afraid of giving the little guy a concussion or something."

"You don't have to be worried about hurting him. There are muscles that'll protect him. Plus, you're probably not big enough to get close to him."

"Fuck you."

"Did I hit a little nerve? Wait, did you say little guy?"

"Yeah, the ultrasound showed what appeared to be a weiner."

"Hell, that's great. I get to teach him how to spit and grab his crotch. Women hate that shit."

"Well, you'll have to put up with Donna bitching then."

"Hell, I can handle her."

"Yeah, brave words from the biggest pussy-whipped guy I know."

"That's just wrong!"

"What's wrong?"

"Calling me pussy whipped."

"It's true, isn't it?"

"Yeah, but it's still wrong. You're supposed to be on my side."

"Sorry, dude!"

"You're forgiven. Now just stop at the next station. I have to piss."

We finally arrive at the condo where the couples will be staying. Coy and his wife, Darla, are already there.

"What's up, you gimlet little bastard?"

Jay looks over at me and says, "Meat's already toasted, isn't he?"

"Yeah, he drank all the way down."

"Hell, Coy, if Ben would learn to drive the speed limit, we would've been here two hours ago."

"You asshole, if you didn't have to piss every twenty minutes, we would've been here two hours ago."

"I can't help it. I have a weak bladder."

"Why don't you guys get married? You argue like an old married couple" comes from Coy.

"Fuck you, you little pissant." I look over the place and ask, "Hey, Coy, whatcha got to drink? I need to catch up."

Coy walks over to a cabinet showing about fifteen bottles of booze.

"Whatever you want, big daddy."

"Damn, Coy, I take back anything I ever said that was bad about you. One thing I do know is, we may not be the best softball team, but there aren't many teams that will outdrink us."

Meat, in his stupor, says, "Word."

I fix a gin and tonic and kick back. We sit around the living room and talk softball. A couple of hours later, there's a knock at the door. The next group of guys and their ladies show up. It's Whatley and his wife, Denise, and Mark and his wife, Rusti. Meat wakes up from his nap.

"Damn, Ben, you didn't tell me the strippers were here. Hi, Rusti. Hi, Denise."

They just look at him and realize he is "kazoobered" out, a.k.a. shit-faced.

"Hi, Meat," Rusti finally says reluctantly.

Both Whatley and Mark are in the Overachievers Club too. In fact, everyone on the team is. The Overachievers Club simply means that their wives look way too good for them. Trust me. They'll admit it. The guys, I mean. About an hour later, Todd and Holly arrive. By seven o'clock, everyone has made it down. We all decide to go to Shuckums to eat. It's an oyster bar. The entire team joins us. We all know that this may be our last good meal before the tournament.

The Southeastern is played around the clock. You may have a 6:00 a.m. game or a 3:00 a.m. game. What you want to do more than anything is not fall into the losers' bracket. That's when you have no control what time you play. You may not even get to sleep at all. Of course, the wives couldn't care less because they'll be lying on the beach, looking at guys, and working on a tan the whole time.

After we finish eating, I excuse myself and step outside to call Donna. I get her voice mail.

"Donna, I was just checking in and wanted to see how you were doing. Call me later." I go back inside.

"Ben, we're going to a strip club. Are you in?"

Honestly, I don't want to go, but I don't want to appear to be a party pooper. God, I can't believe I just wrote "party pooper" in this book. My mother will be shocked.

We all load up, and it's off to the Golden Nugget. Okay, I admit the name isn't the best. It makes me think about a golden turd. But it is a nice club if you're into strippers. There was a time in my life that I loved strip clubs. Now I have to admit I find it tasteless. You may think I'm bullshitting you, but it is true. I really do feel sorry for strippers and prostitutes. I've seen too many programs on them. Most of the girls are single mothers, runaways, or worse, drug addicts. I try to be a good sport though, and we pay the cover.

As we walk in, the song "Baby Got Back" is playing. That's the one song that Coy can dance to. I look over, and he is bobbing his head to the beat.

Meat says, "That's an omen, dog."

We go inside and find a series of tables. That way, we can all sit together. Strip clubs have some strange rules. One is, you cannot go in wearing a T-shirt. Here it is: you have to wear a shirt with a collar, and the girls are buck naked. It doesn't make too much sense. I'm not sure why a shirt with a collar is so important anyway, unless it's to give the bouncers something to grab when they need to throw someone out. It's not like you can't find your billfold wearing a T-shirt.

Friday night, and the place is rocking. I'm sure the girls make a lot of money on Friday and Saturday night. I can't help but wonder what the bank thinks of these women on Monday when they show up to make a deposit into their checking account. "I want to deposit this"—handing the teller six grand all in one-dollar bills. That must be funny. There must be at least thirty strippers working tonight. Some are onstage; others are working the floor, doing private table dances. The waitress comes buy to take our drink orders. I notice a few of the guys are focused on the ladies. I think that this may be the first time they've been into a gentlemen's club. They walk up to the stage and insert a dollar or two inside the ladies' garter. I walk up to the stage and point to our group and tell five of the ladies that we would like a private table dance.

I think, *What the hell, I should buy some of the young guys a dance.* TJ, Stacey, and Lewis, among others, should have a little fun.

When the song is finished, the ladies make their way over. I point out who the dances are for. To be honest, I was a bit hesitant to bring the wives and girlfriends.

But I think they enjoyed the club as much, if not more than the guys. Maybe they realize they would get the benefit of their guys' excitement. It's hard! Oops, bad choice of words. Let me rephrase that.

Being in the club, I start to look at things a little differently than when I was younger. It used to be about seeing the women. I guess if that's the reason for going, you're pretty much a loser. It's not like you're going to bang any of the strippers. Now I look at this as a study in human behavior. You're probably saying to yourself, "Bullshit! He's looking at all the naked women. Here it is. Donna is pregnant at home, and he's out with the boys, looking at titties. What a fucking jerk." At least that's what the female reader is saying. A male reader would say, "You're the man, dude." Seriously, though, if you're ever in a strip club, look around at the customers. It's interesting as hell. I sit and try to figure out what they do for a living. Some are obvious. The four guys with flattops and that are acting cocky are probably stationed at a local army base. The group of older guys wearing business suits are probably in town for a convention. The guy sitting by himself in the corner with the crazed look in his eye is probably a serial killer. Hopefully not. I look down at the guys getting their table/lap dance. I can tell they're having a good time. Meat seems to be having a good time too. Of course, I do notice the ladies. You can't help not to. Most are attractive.

I do notice several C-section scars, so they must be mothers, probably single moms. About 90 percent of the strippers have breast implants. And some of the boob jobs are much better than others. A lot of the time, you can notice the scars around the nipples. Sometimes if they went through the armpit or navel, they get pointed in opposite directions. Of course, there are some good ones too. I think I said this before to you, but I'm not really into big boobs. And I don't like implants at all. They really do look fake. Don't get me wrong, if a woman wants them, then she should get them. It's just that I prefer a natural look. I would be against Donna ever getting them. It's also my experience that women who think they have small breasts are great lovers. I think they try to make up for their lack of breast size. That's my observation anyway. I'm sure, however, that big boobs do make the strippers a lot more money. So I can see the economics of having them.

The dance is over, and I stand up to pay the ladies for their dance for the boys. I have to admit I look each lady in the eyes as I pay them. And to be honest, not one has a twinkle in them. I'm sure in everyday life, they are unhappy. They walk off to the next table, and I decide to take a leak.

I go into the bathroom, and some of the guys who I'm sure are at a convention are talking. They have arranged through an escort service to have some women sent to their hotel room. I could tell both are married by the rings on their fingers. Yes, ladies, I feel sorry for their wives. Cheating is wrong. I guess they didn't take their wedding vows very seriously. Seeing them gives me this sudden urge to call Donna. I walk to the door and get my hand stamped so I won't have to pay to reenter.

It's ten forty-five. I hope she's not asleep. I guess I'm a little worried too since she hasn't called me back. I dial her number again. This time, there's an answer.

"Hello, Ben."

"Well, you are home. Has the boyfriend left yet?"

"Yes, and I'm just sitting here, reading a book with Scruffy."

I could tell she isn't in a great mood. She seems a little down.

"How's it going with the boys?"

"Okay, I guess. I just missed you and thought I should call. You seem a little down. Is everything okay?"

"Yeah, I guess I'm just think about everything."

By that, she means the baby, I'm sure. I start to think back to the guys in the restroom. God, I hope I never become one of them. I decide then and there I needed to be at home.

"Donna, I'm going to come home. I'll be leaving in an hour or so."

"Why would you do that? The guys need you."

I think, *Not as much as you do.* "Donna, I want us to get married this weekend, even if it means going to Vegas. We can always have that church wedding you want after the baby is born. Donna, this is something that I really need to do."

"What's gotten into you, Ben?"

I am not sure how to answer her because I am not sure myself.

"Donna, it's just something I need... something I want to do. Mark can handle the team."

"We don't have rings yet!"

"We'll get them tomorrow," I say.

"I'll see if the minister can do a service after church Sunday. I really don't feel up to going to Vegas."

I could tell there's a little excitement along with a little apprehension in her voice.

"Okay then, I'll see you around 10:00 a.m. I love you, Donna."

"I love you too. Be careful driving home."

With that, we say good night.

I go back into the club. I have to tell Meat and Mark about my plans. I walk over and tell the two of them I need to see them outside. They follow me out, thinking I'm sick. Hell, maybe I am sick. This hits me harder than a flu bug ever has.

"What's up, Ben?" Mark says.

"I'm going back to Olive Grove tonight."

"Is something the matter with Donna?"

"No, nothing's the matter. I've just decided I need to go back and marry her. I should have done it long before now. We're going to do it Sunday in a private ceremony. We'll do it again after the baby is born. The two of you will have to run the team. And, Meat, you'll have to catch a ride back maybe with Coy."

I can tell they have just been floored. After a pause, Meat says, "Sure, will do it, I guess..."

"Thanks. I'll give you a shout Monday. Good luck this weekend."

"Be careful, Ben!" comes from Mark.

Meat looks over to Mark and says, "He's lost his fucking mind."

"Yep."

I am in no great rush to get back. After all, I have plenty of time, and I want to get back in one piece. So I start my long drive home. I turn my new satellite radio on and find the Heart Channel 23. Yes, it's love songs. I know the guys reading this must be shocked too. Sorry, guys, I didn't intend for this to happen. Love just—wait... Hold it right there. I can't write that in this book. I won't. I refuse to write a sappy love story. I know, I know; this was supposed to be a guy book filled with drinking, sex, and other assorted lies. And boom, you find you're in a Harlequin romance novel. Strange how a story can turn.

About that time, old Seals and Crofts song starts playing. Ahh. "Darling, if you want me to be closer to you, get closer to me. Darling, if you want me to love, love only you, then love only me." I'm glad you can't hear me singing. I make William Hung from *American Idol* sound like Tony Bennett. Driving all alone, I have time to reflect. They say that before you die, your life flashes before your eyes. I don't know if that's true or not. I just know that in the next four hours, I will think about where I've been, what I've done, and who I want to be. I just have to watch out for the deer and dodge the drunks on the road.

I think back to my childhood. I think our childhood plays a major role in our development. I've said this before, but it needs to be stressed. The thing I remember most about my parents' relationship were the arguments. I know they had sex; after all, they had five children. I just want Junior to know that his parents love him and love each other. That doesn't mean that I want him to walk in during an awkward moment. The bedroom door will always be locked. But having loving parents is important. Since neither Donna nor I have a temper, at least one I have seen in her, I don't think Junior will be exposed to the fighting. At least I hope not. Donna and I communicate well with each other. And that will be important in raising our son. No visible arguments.

Damn, this sounds like a how-to-raise-a-kid guide. Sorry. When I'm working on this book, I just let it go in whichever direction it wants to go. And sometimes I need to talk to you, the readers. Since I can't see you, you're like the imaginary friends I talked to growing up. Hey, I never said I am a great author. I just write this shit down as it floats up.

But whenever I think about my childhood, I remember falling out of the tree house. I'm sure my father never thought about me getting hurt from it. Heck, it was only about ten feet up in the air. And had I not been stupid, I wouldn't have gotten hurt. Grabbing a rotten rope that I had tied to a tree limb is not the thing you win a Nobel Prize for. I was just a little hyper as a kid and did stupid thing. I'm just glad Ritalin wasn't available when I was growing up. I think far too many kids are put on drugs because parents don't want to spend the energy to raise them. Just my opinion. I often think about Jimmy's death in high school and how it has affected me. Even after my accident, I didn't think young people were supposed to die.

But no matter what I think about, I always come back to Phil. I can only imagine what I would have become had I not met him. I have no doubt I would have been fairly successful in something. But I would have never known happiness. What I learned from him was that the little things in life are what matters most. Money is great, but if you aren't truly happy, it is worthless. And to be truly happy, you have to give yourself to someone or something. I don't want you to think Phil was a saint. He wasn't. He could really be tough and, at times, a bit of a jerk. But when I think about it, so was I. He just pointed me in the right direction and kicked me in the ass to get me jump-started.

Donna is another story. When I met Donna, I thought she was, well, a prima donna. She had this aura about her that, on first meeting, was a little aloof, maybe a little cold. There was no love at first sight here but lust, of course. My god, she was beautiful. She looks a little like Ashley Judd. In fact, Ashley Judd would be great to play her in the movie—well, if they made a movie about the book. And since this will probably never get published, much less be a best seller turned into a movie, it's more of a fantasy or dream.

Back to Donna. A friend of mine named Paul had a party. Paul is a CPA. So he has a lot of people he meets through business. Donna had sold Paul and Denise (Paul's wife) a house. So that is how they became friends. Anyway, once a year, they have a large cookout on the farm they own. At that time, I was single. I had broken up with my fiancée, Sandy, a few months earlier. Sandy was a completely psycho, although she was great in bed. I could write a book just on her. But I'm sure there are books on psycho, nympho bitches already. Well, when I got to the party, Paul handed me a drink and dragged me over to meet Donna. Now I hate to be fixed up or even the appearance of being fixed up. I prefer to meet people for myself. Plus, at that time, I was going through women like Whatley goes through oysters. So I wasn't looking for a serious relationship. Paul introduced us and walked away. If you've ever gone through that, you know it can be an awkward situation.

"So you're the great Ben."

Since there was no telling what Paul had told her about me, I just played it cool. After all, she was hot.

"Great? No, not really. But better than average and like the movie I'm Gentle."

She looked me over and smiled. "I bet you are."

Now I didn't know what she meant by that crack, but it did give us an icebreaker.

I have never taken myself too seriously. In fact, I make jokes about myself often. I've found that women like guys that aren't full of themselves. In fact, if you can make a woman laugh, you'll at least get to first base on the first date. And if you're really good, you'll hit a home run. Also, guys, if you have a hard time meeting women, buy a dog. Women love dogs, especially a cute small one. It makes you look sensitive. In fact, my love for dogs and the fact I detest hunting are what Donna found adorable.

The more I talked to Donna, the more I became fascinated by her. She wasn't the typical woman I usually meet. She was different, much different. Was I excited? Does a fish swim? Hell, it was all I could do to keep the leash on Mr. Happy. Every once in a while, I could start feeling the blood flowing in. And I would start to think about one of the smelly trash cans I changed when I worked for Phil to keep from getting an erection. Trust me, a maggot-filled trash can will keep any man from getting an erection. I asked her if she would like another drink, and she said she would. I walked over to the bartender to get us another drink. Paul walked over and asked how it was going.

"What do you think, Ben? Isn't she great?"

I could tell Paul had the hots for her. But I also knew he wouldn't ever hit on her. He was a Catholic, a die-hard Catholic. Plus, he had so much money and three kids that a divorce would kill him, because CPAs love their money more than sex.

"Yeah, she's great. What's her deal?"

"Ben, she broke up with her boyfriend about a year ago. She found out he was banging a girl he worked with."

"Damn, he was a stupid fuck!"

"Yes, he was. I just thought you two would make a nice couple. But if you hurt her, I will kick your ass."

Damn! Why does everyone threaten to kick my ass? "Damn, Paul, we just met. Don't get so huffy."

With that, I walked back over to Donna.

She saw me talking to Paul and asked, "Did he fill you in on me?"

"No, not really. He just said you were a great woman and if I hurt you, he would kick my ass."

She laughed out loud.

We decided to get something to eat. One thing I always notice about women is how they eat. It they eat french fries with a fork, they're hiding something. They're trying to impress you. Eating french fries with a fork just isn't normal. I was happy to see Donna eating her fries with her fingers. That was sexy.

As the old saying goes, time flies when you're having fun. And now it was time for us to leave, and I walked with her to her car. I had to decide what to say. As we approached her Toyota, I asked, "If I asked you, would you go to dinner sometime?"

"Are you asking?"

"Would you go if I did?"

"I don't know. I haven't been asked. Think about it and call me," she said as she handed me a Post-it with her phone number on it. She even kissed me on the cheek. "Thanks for being so sweet. You're a little strange, but... you're interesting too!"

That, my friends, was the start of a wonderful relationship.

With the radio keeping me company, I continue my drive home. "The First Time Ever I Saw Your Face" begins to plays. That song is truly a classic. I can't help but think that's what will be going through my head when I see my son for the first time. Driving alone, you tend to notice a lot of things that you never pay attention to most of the time. Every mile or so, the lights reflect off a little white cross placed alongside the road. I'm know it's to mark where someone died. Some even have the names of loved ones on them. I really don't agree with that practice. Not that I don't feel for those who lost a loved one. But you just have to realize neither the body nor the spirit is there. The crosses only serve as a sad reminder of their loved one's death. Why dwell on the pain of losing someone or live in the past? The crosses may help serve to remind people to slow down and drive carefully. That would be the only benefit that I could see.

I get back to Eufaula. I'm still almost two hours away. I decide to stop and get a soda. The caffeine will help keep me awake. Not that I'm sleepy. I'm not. I have too much adrenaline flowing. I just don't want to take any chances, and there's not too many stores between Eufaula and home.

I go inside to get my Diet Pepsi and some crackers, and I walk up to the counter. The store has a bulletproof glass cage around the counters. It has a tray for you to put the money in. I have to think, *What a fucked-up world we live in*. I don't blame them for having the protective measures.

When people are killed for just a few dollars, I sure as hell wouldn't want to work in a convenience store, especially one on a back road like this. I'm sure that they had been robbed at some point to justify the cage. I clean up the beer cans that Meat had left in my truck and throw them in the trash before I pull out of the parking lot.

Back on the road again. I get a few miles up the road when I swerve to miss an armadillo crossing the road. *Damn*, I think, *I should have hit it*. As you know, I hate armadillos almost as much as snakes. Fortunately, there's not much traffic on the road. This used to be the best way to get to PC, and the traffic was heavy. But now the expressway handles most of the traffic. Now this is pretty much reduced to local traffic.

I cross over a hilltop and notice several police cars with the blue lights flashing. *Must be a license check*, I think. I'm glad I got rid of those empty beer cans now. I glance up to make sure I have my insurance card. I pull up to greet an officer, who is holding a flashlight. I roll my window down, insurance card and driver's license in hand. He motions me to go on through. I glance over, and a truck had run off the road and hit a tree. I bet he was drunk. I just hope he wasn't hurt.

I finally make it back to the Olive Grove city limit sign. It's 2:45 a.m. It's too late to go home and wake up Ford and the puppies. Plus, I don't want to set off the alarm, so I decide to get a room at the Holiday Inn. I check in and go to my room.

Since having drunk the Diet Pepsi, I'm still wired. So I turn on the television. HBO is showing *Tuesdays with Morrie*. I can't stomach to watch it. It's a great movie about a man's struggle with Alzheimer's. Since I saw it firsthand with Phil, I'll pass. I turn on Fox News. They're still talking about the London bombings. *Click*. Weather Channel has on storm stories. I watch it till I doze off.

I'm awakened by a knock at the door.

"Room service."

"Come back later." I look at the clock. It is ten fifteen. I jump up and call Donna.

"Hello."

"Donna, honey, I'm running late. I stayed at the Holiday Inn last night, and I just woke up. I'll be there as soon as I can."

"Don't rush. I'll see you when I see you."

"Thanks. See you in a few."

I check out and rush home to shower and change.

When I get home, I'm greeted by the welcoming crew. I pick Skipper up first.

"Hey, buddy, did you miss me?"

Ford says, "Why did you come back so soon?"

"To get married." I could tell he thought the same thing as Mark and Meat.

"Oh" was his only reply.

Ford, like Phil, has been great to me. He gave me the job that got me out of Georgia. And I really needed that change.

When I think about it, a lot of people have been very good to me. Maybe the Bible is right: "You reap what you sow."

I get my shower and head to Donna's. It is eleven fifteen as I pull into her drive. Damn, I hate being late. At least I did call. I'm greeted at the door. Donna is dressed in jeans and a T-shirt. I think she is getting self-conscious about showing.

"Ben, you know this is completely crazy, don't you?"

"And your point is what?"

"Nothing, really."

"Well, for your information, a lot of people think I'm crazy. Hell, maybe I am. I just realized last night that I needed you and I didn't want to wait."

With that, we get into her car. Time to go find some rings. We may have to settle for whatever they have for the time being. Donna will get her big ring later if we can't find it on the showroom floor.

As I drive away, my cell phone rings. It's Meat.

"Married yet, you bastard?"

I have to laugh at the tone in his voice. He has been a great friend.

"No, tomorrow, I think. We're on our way to find some rings."

"Well, I thought you should know we just got drilled."

I could hear laughter in the background. So I know they had won. I'll play along.

"Well, I knew you and Mark couldn't handle things. Send in boys to do a grown man's work."

"Hey, I was only joking. We won by eleven."

"I knew that."

"No, you didn't."

"Yes, I did. There's too much clowning going on in the background."

"Screw you then. Here I am, trying to keep you informed, and you bust my balls."

"No, you were trying to pull my leg, and you got caught. You're not a good liar."

"Well, good luck anyway."

"Will do! Later."

Donna looks at me and says, "Meat?"

"Who else?"

"Did they win?"

"Yes, by eleven."

"Sorry you came home now."

"Hell no. I'm going to be the biggest winner."

"You think so?"

"I know so."

There are several jewelry stores in the area, from family mom-and-pop to the big national chains. A guy is easy to buy for: a simple gold band. But I want Donna to have a nice ring, at least five karats. The only problem we face may be whether or not we can't find it today. I just hope she will settle for something in stock if we can't find what she wants. Then I can give her the nice ring at the big wedding.

Now I have to confess something. I really hate to go shopping, shopping for anything, from cars to groceries. I make it a habit to get it and go when I go somewhere. It doesn't matter if it's Wal-Mart or Winn-Dixie. The women I know and have known over the years are lookers. Maybe *browsers* is a better word. They'll pick something up and put it down, only to come back an hour later to buy it. My sister Jackie is the worst. She'll walk back and forth in a grocery store to save three cents. That drives me up the wall. "Get it and go" is my philosophy.

I've been shopping with Donna at the mall for dresses before. It lasted all of ten minutes, well, ten minutes for me. I ended up going to the music-and-movie store. Donna tried on three dresses while I was there. All three looked good on her. She really knows what her colors are and has a good sense for fashion. When she would ask how they looked, I was honest. All of them looked good on her. But she found an excuse for not buying them. Now I'm the first to admit I'm no Blackwell. Heck, I don't even know who he is, except for those best- and worst-dressed lists in the *Star* magazine.

I realized that Donna didn't need my input. She just wanted someone to say how good she looked. Well, I started to get antsy, so I decided to go to the music-and-movie store while she made up her mind.

Now had she been shopping and trying on lingerie at Victoria's Secret, I would have stayed as long as it took. God, they have some sexy stuff: crotchless panties, little red teddies. Dead armadillo, dead armadillo. Whew, I started to get excited there. You may wonder "What the hell was that about?" Well, it's hard as hell for me to write something when I have a hard-on, unless it's about having sex or jerking off.

Anyway I tell Donna where she can find me and, if I'm not there, to call me on my cell phone, hoping against hope she'll make up her mind knowing I wanted to leave. Did she? What do you think? She's a woman, isn't she? She spends hours doing her hair, putting on makeup—all the shit guys hate to wait on. She wasn't going to leave. Hell, she was in her element now. So I went to buy some movies and CDs. I still haven't bought and downloaded music yet. New technology is over my head. I bought eight movies and three CDs, to be exact. No Donna.

Since she could buzz me on my cell phone when she was ready, I went to another store: D&M video games. *I guess I could see what's new for Xbox*, I thought. Yes, I'm forty, and I still play video games. Got a problem with that? Didn't think so. Plus, *Halo* and golf games are a blast. I ended up buying a game there.

Next stop: Sporting Goods. Okay, ladies, a sporting goods store for a guy is pure heaven. I could spend some time here. I bought a new pair of cleats, a pair of tennis shoes, two pairs of batting gloves. I went over to the golf clubs. I needed a new putter. Talk about having a nice grip. It just felt good in my hands. I noticed a lady was watching me with the putter. I couldn't resist saying "Just playing playing with my putter!" I don't think she found any humor in that because she turned and walked away. Well, still no Donna. I've got to keep moving.

Next stop: JCPenney's. I walked in; they were having a sale 40 percent off in the men's department. Okay, I went crazy there: four pairs of pants, six shirts, new underwear, and even socks. Still no Donna. Damn.

Well, I was tired as hell by now. I was loaded with bags. I looked like a camel in the Sahara Desert. And this shit was starting to get heavy. I needed something to drink, so I stopped by the food court for a diet soda. All in all, I'd killed over two hours. Surely Donna was done by now. I finished the soda and went back to the ladies department, and there was Donna. Around her there must be forty dresses.

"Are you ready? I'm getting hungry."

"Yeah, let me check out."

I was wondering to myself, *Is she going to buy all these dresses?*

She reached down underneath the pile of dresses and pulled out the first one she tried on.

"Ben, will you hang up the rest of them on the rack?"

"Yes, dear," I said sarcastically.

It didn't take a rocket scientist to figure out which rack. There was only one that was completely empty.

Is there a moral to the story? You bet your sweet ass there is. Guys, let women go shopping with other women or make sure you take your blood pressure medicine, whether you need it or not.

We decide to go to the big national-chain jewelry store first. We walk in.

"My name is Jerome. How may I help you?" comes from the clerk.

"Yeah, my name is Ben, and this is my fiancée, Donna. We want to buy some wedding rings," I say.

"Follow me."

He walks around the back of the display cases to the case with the rings.

I think that he must be gay. He sort of walks that way. Before anyone gets their panties in a wad, it is just an observation. I couldn't care less about his sexual preference.

"What size ring do you wear?"

Donna gives him her ring size. He pulls out a tray.

"What about you, sir?"

"I don't know what size I wear."

He looks at me like I'm stupid because I don't know my ring size. The last ring I bought was a graduation ring, which I never wear. In fact, I really don't like wearing any jewelry at all, not even a watch.

He hands me these plastic circles to try on while he tends to Donna. I fumble around and finally find one that fits. I lay it on the counter. I decide I should fill Jerome on our plans.

"Jerome, here's the deal. We're getting married tomorrow. I know it's crazy. It was a spur-of-the-moment thing. We're also going to have a bigger ceremony after the baby is born. We need two rings. If Donna can't find the one she wants, we'll order one to use at the public ceremony."

He gives me this "what the hell was that?" look. I'm really starting to dislike this guy.

"What kind of price range are you looking at?" he says with a smirk on his face.

"Price isn't a problem."

He looks at me with a newfound respect. "Well, I do have a few rings with the stones already set." He goes to the vault and brings out a smaller box. He opens it up, and the light twinkles from the diamonds. One ring is huge. It reminds me of the one Richard Burton gave Elizabeth Taylor. It is too big, and no, we don't even ask the price. Besides, someone could hurt Donna for it.

Donna tries on all the rings. She chooses a two-karat diamond ring. I choose a simple golden band.

Jerome is about to close the box, and I say, "Wait, Jerome, I want this one too." It is a six-karat ring.

Donna looks at me and asks, "Is that for the girlfriend?"

Jerome just looks lost and bewildered.

"No, it's for you too. You wear the small one to work and this one when we're together. Plus, you have to wait till the big wedding for this one."

Donna starts to tear up. "I love you, Ben." And she kisses me on the cheek.

"Damn, Donna, not in the store. Wait till we get married."

"How will you be paying for this, sir?"

"The good ole American way, Jerome. Plastic." I throw my credit card on the counter.

He hands me the slip to sign, and we're finished.

As we start to leave, I turn to ask Jerome a question. "Got any mood rings? I'd like to have one!"

"Mood rings?"

He looks dumbfounded, so I say, "Just kidding."

How soon they forget. I remember mood rings like yesterday. I guess actually it was 1975. Jeez, I'm old.

That was easy. Thirty minutes and done.

As we walk out to the car, my cell phone rings.

"Married yet?" It is Meat.

"No, we just bought the rings."

"How many karats on Donna's?" That is none of his business, but what the hell.

"Well, I bought her two rings, total of eight carats."

I could hear the guys in the background going "What did he say?"

"Ben, that just won't work."

"What won't?"

"She has to have one ring, how many karats?"

I'm starting to get pissed at his ramblings.

"Why can't she have two rings?"

Donna looks at me strangely.

There's a pause, then Meat says, "Look, we've been killing time and drinking beer. We all picked a karat size and put up five bucks. Closest to the size wins the pot."

I have to laugh at them because I know what goes on between games; I can just picture them talking.

"Okay, I'll tell you the larger one. It is six karats."

"Fuck!" comes through the phone. "Give TJ the money, Mark. Did you tell TJ the size before you left?"

"Hell, Meat, we didn't even know till we walked in the store."

"Well, you might want to get that DNA test after all because he guessed it on the nose."

TJ gets on the line. "Thanks, Pop. I just won dinner money."

"TJ, how did you pick your number?"

"Easy. I just figured you wouldn't buy anything too big or too cheap. I also figured you had a six-inch dick, give or take."

I hear the guys laughing.

"Well, congratulations on the win. Actually, it's eight inches."

"Ben, go back to sleep."

I guess that means "in your dreams."

"Later."

Donna looks at me and says, "They must miss you."

"Yep!"

Well, that didn't take long, I think. "How 'bout some lunch, Mrs. Thompson?"

"I thought you'd never ask."

We go to get some chicken fingers and to relax a little. The restaurant isn't really busy, so we get our food quickly.

"Well, Donna, what did your parents think?"

"I haven't told them yet! I'll call tonight and tell them."

I thought that would have been the first thing she did this morning. Of course, I'm not telling my mother yet. I'll call her next week and let her know. There's no one to bring her down, and I don't have time to get her. Plus, the big wedding will be a few months after Donna gets over the birth. She probably won't agree to it till she gets her figure back anyway.

"Donna, are you sure we can get married in the chapel tomorrow?"

"Yeah, I'm pretty sure. When I get home, I'll call the minister. It's just going to be a simple service."

"Well, if not, we're going to Vegas," I say.

"But you hate to fly."

"Who said anything about flying? We'll drive."

The ride back to my house has a sense of accomplishment to it. As we walk in, Donna decides to call her parents and tell them the news. Since I don't want to hear any screaming, should there be any, I go to my office— the bathroom—to freshen up. Donna calls her parents.

"Hello."

"Hi, Mom, I just wanted to call and let you know that Ben and I bought our wedding rings today."

"Well, honey, that's great. I told Wayne you and Ben would get married eventually. Have you set a date yet?"

"Yeah, sorta."

"What does 'sorta' mean?"

"Well, we're getting married tomorrow."

There's a long pause as the handset hits the floor. "What did you just say, Donna?"

"We're getting married tomorrow."

"I thought that's what you said. How? Why tomorrow?"

"That's what we want."

I think her parents, like my mother, want the wedding before the baby is born. They had just not expressed it like my mother had.

"Okay, dear, let's think this over."

"There's nothing to think over. We only need to find somewhere to have the ceremony and someone to perform it. Ben suggested Las Vegas."

"Honey, there's no way a child of mine is getting married in Las Vegas by some Elvis impersonator. I'll call the minister and see if we can have it at the church. If not, we'll have it at our house in the backyard. You're still planning a big wedding, aren't you?"

"Yes, Mother, after the baby is born. We'll have a big hoopla wedding filled with all the ice sculptured swans and other stuff you want."

"Great. I'll call the minister and call you right back."

With that, the conversation ends. I come out of the office, wanting to know how things went. Donna is lying on the sofa with her feet up.

"Well?"

"I think it went well. Mom is going to call the minister and call me back later. She was okay with it once I told her we'd still have the big wedding later. Now all we have to do is wait for her to call back."

"What's on the agenda until then?"

"This." She reaches over and unzips my pants and begins kissing Mr. Happy.

"Ahh! You're a naughty woman, Mrs. Thomson. And that's what I love about you!"

Five minutes later, Donna's cell phone rings.

"Hi, Mom!" she says as she's wiping saliva from her mouth.

"Donna, the minister can't do the service, but Wayne's lodge brother can, and he is a justice of the peace. He'll also have the paperwork needed completed. But we can have it in the backyard in the gazebo or in the living room."

"Does the weather call for rain, Mom?"

"No, it's supposed to be sunny and warm."

"Okay, the gazebo it is."

"Donna, honey, I'll get some kind of flower arrangement from the florist, but what will you do for a dress?"

"Mom, I'll just wear one of my evening gowns."

"Do you have a white one?"

"No, Mom, but it doesn't matter, and after all, I'm pregnant. I think I have an off-white dress I can wear, if it fits!"

"Let me know if it doesn't. We can still go shopping tonight."

"Okay, Mom, I'll call you back in a little while. I have some unfinished work I need to take care of first."

"Bye, dear!"

"Bye, Mother!" Donna hangs up her phone. "Now where was I?" she says.

"Ohh! Donna, what you do to me!"

After our break is finished, Donna gets up to go through her closet. She tries on her white evening gown, but unfortunately, it wouldn't fit. I could only get the zipper about a third of the way up.

"Damn it! Now I'll have to go shopping." She picks up her cell phone and calls her mother back. "Mom, are you ready to go shopping?"

"Yes, dear, we'll be right over."

"We'll?"

"Yes, honey, your father wants to go."

"Mother, I don't want Daddy to go. But he can stay here with Ben and watch the Braves game."

"Whatever you say, hun." She hangs back up.

"Donna, I don't want to babysit your dad! Hell, he doesn't even like me."

"Well, you're stuck with him. It's time the two of you buried the hatchet anyway. Will you just do it for me?"

Since it's hard to say no to a woman who has just given you great fellatio, I cave in and agree to it. Yes, guys, I know *fellatio* sounds stupid, but she would kill me if I call it a blow job. She'll probably kill me anyway for putting it in the book. Why women hate men calling oral sex a blow job is a mystery to me. I actually think it sounds kind of erotic. *Fellatio* just sounds like a gum or venereal disease. Tell a guy you just had fellatio, and their response would be something like "Damn, did they give you a shot to clear it up, or are you still on medication?"

Okay, maybe that's an exaggeration, but it's close.

Well, Donna's parents arrive in no time flat. I already have the Braves game on when Wayne walks into the living room.

"Ben, Daddy, we'll be back later. Y'all be good."

"Yes, dear" comes out of my mouth in a slightly sarcastic manner.

"Just be careful! There are idiots on the highways now" comes from Wayne.

I could tell Donna was apprehensive about leaving the two of us alone. Well, she isn't the only one. Wayne sits down like he were waiting in line for a vasectomy. I, on the other hand, decide I should fall on the sword for Donna and try to make peace. If that doesn't work, I'd challenge him to arm wrestling.

"Wayne, I'm glad you came over. I feel like we should have had a heart-to-heart talk long ago."

"About what?"

"Well, Donna for one. Wayne, I love Donna with all my heart. And I really want to spend the rest of my life with her. I just want you to know I plan on taking great care of her, like you did in raising her. I know we probably should have gotten married right after she became pregnant. But, Wayne, I need to share the reason why I didn't ask her before now."

Wayne sits there quietly, almost in delight, as I squirm with my words.

"Wayne, my parents had a bad marriage, at least on the surface. They fought almost daily.

And to be honest, it warped me into thinking all marriages were like that. I decided I didn't want to risk that, so I always found a reason to break up with whoever I was dating at the time, regardless if it was a good or bad relationship. But with Donna, I feel completely different. I've thought about marriage even before she got pregnant, but things were perfect, and I didn't want to mess them up. And to be honest, I was afraid she'd turn me down. Now all I can think about is taking care of her and our son."

"You mean it's a boy? Clair didn't tell me that."

"Well, the last ultrasound showed what appeared to be a penis. However, the doctor said it could just be a shadow. So we don't actually know for sure."

"Well, Ben, since we're being honest, I have to tell you, I didn't want Donna to marry you. I thought you were cocky and you would do something to hurt her. You have to remember, Ben, Donna is all Clair and I have. Clair had a tough time giving birth to Donna, and afterwards the doctors said she might die if she had another child, so I had a vasectomy. So Donna will always be our baby."

"Wow! I didn't know that. Wayne, I can only promise you one thing, and that is, I will never do anything to hurt Donna. I certainly would never cheat on her. I know I must seem aloof at times, and maybe I even seem like a jackass."

He smiles at that comment.

"But I will always be there not just for her but also for our child."

"Thanks, Ben. I'm glad to hear that. I'm glad we got a chance to talk."

"Me too! Wayne, do you want some popcorn? I think Donna has some. It would go well with the game."

"Only if she has some beer to go with it."

Damn, he drinks beer. He just moved up a few more notches in my book. "Is Bud Light okay?"

"If it's cold, it's okay."

"I didn't know you drank, Wayne."

"You never asked. I don't make a habit out of it, but every once in a while, I like a cold one or two."

Well, the rest of the evening goes pretty well. The Braves go on to win 5–2.

"Wayne, you feel up to playing a trick on the girls?"

"Sure, what?"

"Well, you know they're probably worried sick that we're gonna kill each other while they're gone."

"Yeah!"

"Well, let's give them what they expect. When they pull up, let's start yelling at each other, then we'll start laughing when they try to calm us down."

"That sounds like fun. I'm in."

We sit and wait till we see the headlights pull up in the driveway.

"You ready, Wayne?"

"Fire away."

"Wayne, that's the biggest load of crap I've ever heard."

"You just don't like hearing the truth, do you, Ben?"

"Truth? You wouldn't know the truth if it hit you over the head."

The door opens, and the women rush in.

"Daddy, Ben, what in the hell is going on? I ask you to be civil, and you're ready to come to blows."

We start laughing hysterically.

"Wayne, I think we got 'em."

"Yeah, I think so."

Clair speaks up, "You guys planned this?"

"Well, yeah. We thought it would be funny. If you could have seen the looks on your faces when you walked in. Priceless!"

Clair starts to laugh. "Donna, honey, they got us. But you know what? We'll pay them back."

I could tell Donna is still a little pissed, so I say, "Donna, I really like your dad." I walk over and put my arm around Wayne. I even give him a kiss on the cheek.

"Ben, you didn't have to do that. That's pretty sick," Wayne says after he rubs his cheek. That makes Donna smile.

———

"Well, I'm glad you guys finally bonded." Donna surveys the room and notices the empty beer cans by the chairs.

"Looks like they did more than bond. They got drunk!"

I look over and say, "I resemble that remark. Well, ladies, show us what you bought. I know you're dying to."

With that, they open up the bags to show us all the new things they had bought. Donna has picked out a beautiful white dress to wear tomorrow.

"What do you think, Ben?"

"I think I wish I had bought stock in Sears—no, it's beautiful! But anything you wear, Donna, will look beautiful."

"That's so sweet, Ben" comes from Clair.

"Well, ladies, I think I'm going to leave it with you. Babysitting Wayne has worn me out, so I'm going to call it a night. I'll see all of you tomorrow at one."

Wayne shakes my hand and says, "Thanks, Ben! It was nice getting to sit down and talk man-to-man. You're welcome to join us for church tomorrow morning."

"Thanks, Wayne. I think I'll pass. My father would turn over in his grave if he knew I went to a Methodist church. He was a die-hard Baptist, you know," I say with a smile.

Wayne gives me a funny look, one of those "is he joking or what?" looks. "Well, Ben, what are you now?"

"Reformed!" I say.

"Reformed from what?"

"Pretty much everything." With that, I walk to the door.

Whew! I escaped that discussion, I think. Why is it I feel guilty for my beliefs on organized religion? I don't look down on people who go to church. So why does everyone think I'm some kind of heathen for not going? Can't I worship in my own way? I crank up the car and back out of the driveway to "Open Arms" playing on the radio. I have to smile to myself and wonder if the song by Journey is some kind of omen because tomorrow I will start on a new journey myself. While driving home, I realize that this time tomorrow, I will be a married man. Am I scared? Hell yes. I'm scared shitless. I just wish that Phil were around to talk to. While I know what he'd say, it would be nice to hear his voice. Jeez, I can't believe I just wrote that. I mean, here it is, I'm in my forties and still need someone to talk to. How pathetic is that? Of course, we all need someone to reassure us, especially when we're feeling down or up to our neck in shit. While I'm not in either, I do feel somewhat alone.

I guess no matter what our age, we'll always need our friends in special times. How would my conversation with Phil go? Something like this:

"Benny, you're doing the right thing. I know you're scared as hell. I was too! We all are. But you have seen the failures of your parents, you have seen my failures with my children. You can learn from those. You will be a good father."

"Phil, the father part I'll be fine with. It's the husband part that scares me."

"What do you mean by that?"

"Well, Donna, thinks I'm a perfect man. The truth is, I'm not! And I'm—"

"Wait a minute, fuzz nuts. If you believe that, then you really are full of shit."

"Believe what?"

"Benny, Donna knows you're not perfect! Jeez, Benny, are you still so full of yourself that you believe you're some kind of superhero? You're forty now, so it's time for you to grow the fuck up."

"Isn't that a little harsh? I mean, hell, I've been both good to and for Donna. I've never lost my temper with her. And to be honest, I am great in bed."

"You stupid, stupid, stupid sack of shit! Do you actually think giving your wife an orgasm and being nice is all there is to a marriage?"

"Phil, give me just a little credit. I'm not a complete dumbass."

"Sometimes you act like one, though."

"Oh, I forgot that you were the perfect fucking husband."

"I never said I was perfect, and the truth is, Louise knew I wasn't. We knew going into our marriage, there would be some problems. Hell, everyone has them! How many fingers am I holding up?"

"Very funny, Phil."

"How many?"

"Are you serious?"

"How many fucking fingers am I holding up?"

"Two."

"Well, if you can see them, then maybe you'll see that's there's more to marriage than great sex and being nice."

"Okay, O great one, tell me what I need to know about marriage."

"Well, Benny, since you claim to have the sex part down, here's the one thing you need to know."

"I'm waiting."

"Never hit below the belt."

"What the... What the fuck is that? I'd never hit Donna."

"I'm not talking about hitting her. At some point in your marriage, you'll have an argument. And when you do, never say anything that is hurtful or, as I like to call it, hit below the belt. You can apologize all you want, and she may forgive you. But she'll never forget what you've said, and that scar will always be there, because you can never take back something once you say it. Then after a while, when the scars get to be too much, either she'll leave you or she'll stop loving you. Benny, remember, women are more sensitive than men. If you treat her with respect and love her with every fiber of your being, you'll have a wonderful marriage. It won't be perfect, but it'll be great."

Well, that would be how one of our typical conversations would go.

As I'm pulling into my carport, I decide to call the guys in Panama City to check in on them. I call Meat's cell.

"Coach Ben!"

I am startled to hear TJ answer the phone. *Meat has to be either taking a shit or passed out drunk*, I think. "T-Jizzle, where's the Meatster?"

"Ben, he's fucking this hot-piece-of-ass waitress he picked up at the strip club."

"You're kidding me, right?"

"No, he's fucking her to death."

That son of a bitch, I think. *How could he do that to Julie?*

"Who's on the phone?"

I could tell it was Whatley's voice.

"Coach Ben," says TJ.

"Let me have the phone. Ben, how's it going?"

"Not as good as you guys, from the sound of things. Is Meat really fucking a waitress?"

"Is that what TJ told you?"

"Yeah."

"Ben, Meat passed out cold on the sofa. He has a boner that won't quit, and we're fucking with him."

Afraid to know the details but curious as hell, I couldn't help but ask what they are doing to him.

"What the hell are you guys doing to him?"

"Well, let's see, we've dripped a packet of mayonnaise on his shirt, and now we're teasing him with a feather around his ear."

"That's just wrong, Whatley."

"Well, we plan on telling him he sucked off the bouncer in the morning when he gets up. Got any better ideas, Ben?"

"Well, if you want to really fuck with him, try the old hand-in-the-water routine, and maybe he'll piss his pants."

"Damn, that's a great idea. TJ, go get some warm water."

I hear TJ come back into the room.

"Hold on, Ben, we'll tell you if he pisses himself."

I wait a few minutes and hear everyone laughing.

"Ben, that shit was on time."

I could tell it was TJ.

"His gray sweatpants turned black with piss."

"Give me the phone, you pissant. Ben, that was funny as hell. He pissed all over himself and never woke up."

"Well, I'm glad to be of service. How are y'all doing in the tournament?"

"We're three and zero. We play again at five a.m."

"Shouldn't you be trying to get some sleep?"

"Fuck sleep, we're having fun."

"All right, have fun. Just don't piss off Meat too much." I have to laugh knowing Meat will be pissed when he wakes up in the morning, in more ways than one.

"Good luck tomorrow, Ben."

"You to, What." With that, I hang up.

I walk inside to the usual pitter-patter of puppy dog feet. I realize that their lives would be changing too. Donna, the baby, and Scruffy will be moving in soon.

I'm sure the dogs will get along fine since Scruffy has spent one night here already. I just hope Scruffy doesn't eat shit. One shit eater in the family is enough.

I sit down on the sofa and turn on Fox News. The big topic is marriage, specifically gay marriage. While I'm a Republican, I couldn't care less whether two men or two women, for that matter, decide to marry each other. If you love someone and want to spend the rest of your life together, then you should be allowed to get married and enjoy the benefits of marriage. I don't think Donna and I will suffer if Tom and Gary get married too. It's much ado about nothing. Of course, it's all about sucking up to the far right in the party. The ones pushing for gay marriage are the lawyers, specifically divorce lawyers. Just think about it; their business would double if homosexuals are allowed to marry.

The only apprehensions I have would be for the children of gay couples—not because they would be mistreated in the family, but because society would look down on the kids. And of course, other kids would be cruel if they knew your parents were gay. When I was growing up, kids who were different were called names. If a boy was effeminate, he was called a faggot or queer. I don't think kids knew what they were saying or even what it meant. They were just using language they heard their parents use. I never called another kid names. I knew how it hurt me when I was picked on. I fought back, but a lot of kids can't fight back. Today when I hear of a school shooting, I always suspect that it was a kid who couldn't take the shit anymore. It really is sad. Hopefully, someday we will all learn to live together in peace and harmony. But unfortunately, I don't think it'll be in my lifetime.

Well, I guess it's time for me to turn in. I've got a big day tomorrow.

Dreams are a funny thing. That night, my imagination is working overtime. In one dream, I was at the base of a large dam when it burst. I was swept away downstream, trying to keep my head above the rushing water. If I analyze it, I could say it may have something to do with the wedding, how I'm afraid I may be getting in over my head. Of course, it could also be a memory of fishing below Buford Dam when I lived in Georgia. I often wondered what would happen if the dam ever burst. It may even be a combination of both.

In the other dream, I'm standing before a large crowd, talking from a podium. I can't see the faces, but I know I'm talking about myself. I can tell you that is something I hate to do. When I told Donna I'd hate to be interviewed by Bill O'Reilly, I wasn't joking. But it's not only him; I'd hate to be interviewed by anyone. I can't imagine the pressure I'd feel knowing millions of people were watching me. I don't know how they do it. That's another reason this book may never be submitted. I don't think I'd want to have to go on a show and talk about it. I know I'd have to defend some of my views. I'm sure some folks might take exception to the profanity in the book or maybe my views on religion. Finishing it is one thing. Talking about it is another. Sure, I may be a tough-talking son of a bitch. But I can also be a scared, shitless little boy too. I guess before I worry about the second, I should worry about finishing it first.

I awake remarkably fresh, which is a strange thing for me. I'm usually sluggish as hell and not fully awake till I have my Diet Pepsi.

I let the mongrels out to do their thing and turn on the computer. I go back to the front door to let the dogs back in. Sparky has a piece of shit in his mouth.

"Sparky, spit the poody out, you dumb little bastard."

He gives me a "fuck you" look but obeys. I get the pooper-scooper and shovels his present off the porch. *Some things truly never change*, I thought.

After feeding the dogs, I go sit down at the computer and go online. My first stop is always the Drudge Report. The headlines are about Russia and their connections to political figures here in the States. It seems like many here are hoping for a war with Russia. That is a scary thought.

Well, it's time to get started. This is the big day. I finish my Diet Pepsi and go take my morning shit, followed by shaving then showering. Now it's time for breakfast. I could have some cereal and stay on my diet, or I could drive to McDonald's and have an Egg McMuffin. Of course I choose the egg McMuffin. Hell, I plan on burning up those calories tonight anyway.

After finishing up breakfast, I still have over three hours to fill. I have to be at the house of Donna's parents. Since the dogs are sleeping, I decide to have a little quiet time for myself. I sit in the recliner and go over my life story. I know you're thinking, *This son of a bitch spends every fucking waking moment reflecting on his fucking life*. Would you wake up and smell the coffee and get a life? At least that's what I think you're thinking.

But considering I'm only in my forties, I've seen a lot of history being made, from walking on the moon to the Berlin wall coming down. Segregated schools are also a thing of the past. I remember in 1968 when I started the first grade was the first time I had ever talked to a black kid. I'm so grateful for that. I realized then that we're all the same on the inside. The only thing that separates us is the color pigment of our skin.

So many things go into making us who we are. I start to remember mine: friends, my teachers. In fact, my creative writing teacher in high school played a part in me writing this book. I wrote some short stories and some poems that she thought were good. I only did them because they were required. But I did enjoy doing them. Writing gave me a chance to let out some of the things that I kept to myself. Maybe that's why this book may never be submitted for publication. Am I a writer? No, probably not, at least in the traditional sense.

The words don't always come out the way I'd like them to. I also realize this book jumps all over the place. But in reality, that's how my life has been. I've never had an outline for my life, so why would I have one for the book? Life is about changes on the fly. And so is this book. Sorry about that, but you should know me well enough by now to understand it.

Now it's time to get dressed. I manage to get dressed in record time. I still have a little trouble from time to time with the tie. Tying a tie can be such a pain in the ass, at least with me. And if I don't get it done on the first try or two, I get frustrated and pissed off. Luckily, I get it on the first try. I'm dressed and still have time to kill, so I decide to call the boys. I dial Meat's cell.

"Hello." Damn, Meat sounds hungover bigger than hell.

"You big bastard, you sound like shit."

"Don't talk so loud."

"I'm not. What time do you guys play?"

"The game time is one."

"Shouldn't you be getting your ass out of bed then? It's getting close to one."

"Easy! Hell, we're right here at the fields. I'm getting up now, okay?"

"Good. I need someone I trust keeping the guys out of trouble."

"How are you doing, Ben? You sound tighter than a banjo string!"

Well, since I don't know how tight a banjo string is or really care, I say, "No, not really."

"You mean you're not scared to fucking death?"

I could tell Meat is coming back to life. "No! I'm at ease with things now."

"Goddamn, you sound like a man who has just been told he has a terminal disease."

"Well, excuse me, dickhead. At least I didn't piss on myself last night."

"Who told you about that?"

"Whatley and TJ."

"Those motherfuckers. I bet they poured piss on me while I was sleeping."

"No, it was your own piss. They put your hand in water while you passed out."

"Fuck!"

"Sorry, you shouldn't have passed out first."

"You probably put them up to it, didn't you?"

"Well, you did start all the shit with the 'Ben's Candid a Camera' bullshit."

"That's just wrong. Paybacks are hell, big boy!"

"No, Meat, we're fucking even now. Truce?"

"Truce!"

"I'll give you a call later after the wedding."

"Good luck! You'll need it."

With that, I hang up.

The Davis house is a typical ranch that makes up the subdivision. Sort of reminds me of the *Brady Bunch* house. Typical seventies model.

As I step out of the truck, I'm greeted by Wayne.

"Ready, big fella?"

"Of course! But the big question is, are you ready?"

"For what?"

"Ready to have a Republican for a son-in-law."

"Well, I had hoped Donna would marry one of the Kennedys. But then I'd have to deal with a Yankee son-in-law. So yeah, I can live with it. It just means I expect an expensive Christmas present now since you Republicans have all the money."

"Well, Wayne, I'll buy you the most expensive fruitcake made."

He smiles at me and says, "I actually like fruitcake."

"So do I! Especially if it's soaked in rum."

"Exactly! Ben, I have orders to take you downstairs so you can't see Donna. You know how superstitious women are."

"I was wondering about that. That is fine with me."

With that, we walk around the backyard to the outside entrance. I glance over to the gazebo to see it is decorated with flowers. It is beautiful. Once inside, my eyes begin to survey the room. Donna is right; Wayne has sports memorabilia all around: autographed jerseys, balls, and photos. I have to admit, I am impressed, and I am not impressed easily.

Wayne sees me looking around and says, "Ben, this is my room. This is the only room Clair lets me do what I want to. The rest of the house is filled with all her froufrou stuff."

Having never been inside their house, I find it quite interesting. It reminds me so much of my basement, except he doesn't have an inflatable doll in the corner.

My basement has a bar, a pool table, a big-screen television—a typical man cave. I am quite taken by the fact he has a model train set as well as an old slot car track. I had both growing up and used to love racing with my friends.

"Does this still work?" I ask, pointing to the car track.

"Sure. Do you want to race?"

"Sure. But I have to warn you, I was the champion of Pinecrest Drive."

"Good, then I won't have to hold back." Wayne turns the power on, and we start our race.

"Ten laps! Ready, set, go!" comes from his lips.

I'm not sure how many races we ran, but I know I lost the first three. Actually, I lost them badly. I won the fourth, but I suspect he threw the race.

Suddenly, I hear someone say "What's up, bastard?"

I look up, and it's Meat and the softball team. "What the? What the hell are you doing here?"

Meat looks at me and says, "Well, I awoke this morning at five a.m. to use the bathroom. I realize I had wet myself, so I took a shower. I was wide awake after that, and I started thinking about you and Donna. I didn't want to miss the wedding, so I decided to wake Whatley and tell him I was leaving. He also decided that the wedding was more important than a softball tournament, as did the rest of the team. So we told the complex director we were going to forfeit the tournament. And here we are."

I was speechless. It's something that rarely happens to me. The guys all introduce themselves to Wayne.

When they have finished, Wayne looks at me and says, "That's some motley crew you've got, Ben."

About that time I heard "I'm Whatley, Tom Whatley! You mean to tell me you couldn't do better than this guy for your daughter? Some father you are." Whatley smiles.

I look over at Wayne.

Wayne says, "At least Donna didn't marry a lesbian!"

I have to laugh out loud because I've always considered myself a lesbian. Why? Kind of obvious, I hope.

"The hell she isn't" comes from Whatley.

To try to change the topic of conversation, I ask about the wives and girlfriends. "Where are the ladies?"

"Upstairs with Donna" comes from Mark.

About that time, I hear the doorbell. I look down at my watch, and it is four o'clock. It must be the justice of the peace.

Clair opens the door and says, "The justice of the peace is here. Time to get started."

With that, the guys go outside, and Wayne walks up the stairs to be with Donna.

Meat looks at me and says, "Give me the ring. I'm going to be the best man."

So I hand him the ring.

The justice of the peace walks down to meet me. We go over all the details in record fashion. He is a nice guy. His name is Bill Frazier. He is probably in his midfifties, with snow-white hair, looks a little like Cary Grant.

We leave to go to the backyard. Jeez, it's hotter than hell outside. Being in this suit doesn't help matters either. Since we have no music for the bride's entrance, we turn to the sliding glass door at the sound of it being opened.

There she is, in all her splendor, the woman I want to spend the rest of my life and all of eternity with. Donna and Wayne slowly make their way to the gazebo.

Donna has never looked more beautiful in her life. As they arrive at the gazebo, Wayne kisses Donna on the cheek and gives Donna's hand to me. There's a tear that slowly rolls down his cheek as he makes his way over to stand next to Clair. Donna and I turn to face the justice.

"Dearly beloved, we are gathered here" comes from his mouth. He turns to Donna and has her repeat after him.

To be honest, I don't hear much of what he says. I'm mesmerized by her beauty. Finally, I hear her say "I do."

He then turns to me and says, "Ben, do you take this woman to be your lawfully wedded wife from this day forward to love, honor, and cherish, for better or worse, in sickness and in health and forsaking all others?"

I look at Donna and wink then look back up at him and say, "I do... and then some."

"Well, I now pronounce you man and wife. You may kiss the bride."

I give Donna a soft little kiss out of respect for everyone there but mostly her parents. I've been to a wedding where the guy practically gives his future wife a tonsillectomy. I've always thought it is tasteless to slobber all over each other in front of friends and family and, more importantly, God.

Since the wedding is on the spur of the moment and we don't have a reception set up, we all go inside. Clair has managed to get a wedding cake on the spur of the moment. It is not one of the fancy three- or four-tiered cakes like you always see, but it does have two tiers. Donna and I cut the cake. We also have some finger sandwiches and punch that Donna's friends from work had made. So we all just sit around and swap stories. Most, of course, are about weddings, some of the funnier things we've seen over the years.

My sister got married in one of the most severe storms I've ever seen. They also got married in my parents' house. My mother, who is terrified of storms and who would always make us go to the basement if a storm got bad, was scared to death. During the service, we had a silver maple tree blow over in the front yard. I was just sure my mother was going to make them finish the service in the basement. But they got through it okay. It was, however, a bit of an omen. They did have a stormy marriage for a while, but now they are pretty happy together.

We also didn't have time to plan a honeymoon either. Hell, we're not even positive which house we'll keep. I'm sure it'll be mine since I have twenty acres with my house and Donna lives in a cramped subdivision. Mine would also be better to raise a family in, and of course, it is better for the dogs. But not a lot of women like log homes. But fortunately, Donna does. At least she says so. And I'll even let her decorate the upstairs however she wants to. But the basement is mine!

After a little while, people start to leave. And it's time for us to leave too. We say goodbye to everyone. Wayne and Clair hug and kiss Donna.

Clair hugs me and says, "Promise me you'll take care of my baby!"

"Clair, I'll not only love her, but I promise I'll honor my vows. So yes, I will always take care of her."

With that, we walk out to the car.

"Whew!"

"What was that for, Ben?"

"I thought the guys may have trashed the car."

"No, Momma warned them when they showed up not to decorate it."

"Your mother is a saint!"

"Yeah, she's okay. She really does love you too."

"Are you ready to go home, Mrs. Thompson?"

"Which one?"

"Ours! My old house?"

"You know, Ben, we'll have to do some remodeling if we live in it."

"Whatever you want, dear."

"There you go, already placating me," she says with a smile.

"Hey, I'm officially pussy whipped now. I don't have a choice."

"Yes, you are! Ben, tell me the truth. Did we do the right thing?"

I look at her and have to hold back the tears that are filling my eyes. "Yes, we did. I just wish I'd realized earlier how much I needed you so we could have had that big, beautiful wedding you've always wanted because, Donna, I've always known that I loved you. I'm just sorry that today wasn't perfect, but I promise I'll make it up to you."

"Who said it wasn't perfect? It was to me."

"Well, Mrs. Thompson, you're not hard to please then, are you?"

"I settled for you, didn't I?"

"Settled? You got the cream of the crop, lady."

"Whatever you say, sweetheart!"

"Now who's placating who?"

"Exactly!"

Before we can go home, we have to go by Donna's for Scruffy, some of her clothes, and god forbid, I forget, her makeup. We pull into her drive and exit the car.

"Well, are you going to miss it?"

"What?"

"The house."

"No, I think it will be an easy sell. What do you think about holding on to it and renting it out?"

"Donna, I'd hate to be a landlord. People break things and call at all times during the night. Plus, you may get tenants who don't pay the rent. Then you get stuck dealing with lawyers. It's just not worth it."

Donna starts laughing.

"What's that about?"

"We sound like an old married couple."

"Yeah, we do!"

Donna opens up the door. Scruffy starts barking and jumping up and down.

"Ben, do you realize we're going to have four indoor dogs?"

"Yeah! But it could be worse."

"How's that?"

"We could have five."

"You're so smart. I knew there was some reason I married you."

"I thought you married me for the great sex."

"That too!"

If you hadn't guessed by now, I have an erection that won't quit. In fact, I've been fighting one since she and her father walked toward the gazebo at the wedding.

"Mrs. Thompson, I'm a little nervous to ask, but I'd want to make love to you. But I have to let you know, I've never been with a married woman before."

"Honey, it's just like riding a bicycle. You never forget how."

"Is that so?"

"Oh yes."

I start to kiss her neck from behind as my hand cups her breasts.

"Will you ride me then?"

"I thought you'd never ask. But you do need to take Scruffy for a walk first."

"Damn! Okay."

"I'll be here waiting on you when you get back."

I put the leash on Scruffy, and we walk around the front yard as he marks each bush and tree.

"Scruffy old boy, your life is about to change, and you don't know it."

Scruffy looks up at me when he hears his name. He gives me one of those dog "what the fuck are you talking about?" looks. He finishes doing number one and starts walking in circles. I know from experience that means he has to do number two as well. After he finishes, he turns to inspect his poop. He sniffs it then hikes his leg one final time.

"Good boy, Scruff!"

I'm glad he's not a shit eater. I don't think our household could deal with two of them. Once inside, I remove the leash. I look up to see Donna with a towel wrapped around her.

"Want to grab a quick shower, big boy, then let Mrs. T take you all the way?"

"Is that a proposition, Mrs. Thompson? Or are you just teasing a very horny young man?" Donna's reply is in her Greta Garbo voice. "Darlink, I aim to please, not tease. Now let me inspect your tool." She unzips my zipper to show a bulge in my underwear.

"Is that good enough to get the job done, ma'am?"

"Yez, it tiz." She drops the towel wrapped around her to the floor. Her breasts are simply beautiful now.

I can tell they are starting to get larger for the baby. But since Junior isn't here yet, I get the pleasure. Her nipples are hard, hard from pure excitement. She throws her arms around me and gives me a soft, gentle kiss.

"I love you, Mr. Thompson."

"I love you too, Mrs. Thompson."

I look down and see Scruffy wagging his tail, looking up at us.

"I love you too, Scruffy."

We kiss gently and stroke each other's sensitive areas. Then my hand slides down her body till it finds her most sensitive spot, what I like to call my glorious heaven. I take my finger and slide it between the lips that guard her door to find it delightfully wet already.

"Hmm, someone is a wee bit excited, aren't they?"

"Well, I was thinking about Tom Cruise in *Top Gun*."

"Whatever gets you off, baby."

"Let me see if I can get you off."

With that, we go to bed.

Making love to a woman that you're in love with may be the closest thing to heaven on earth. I say that because I do have quite a bit of experience in the sexual realm. However, I'm nowhere near the Wilt Chamberlain numbers. I can only estimate that I've made love to about a hundred women, give or take a few. I think Wilt claimed to have bedded twenty thousand. I didn't read his book, so that figure could be wrong. Most of mine were in the late seventies to early eighties. When I was in my late teens to early twenties and before AIDS became a household word, at that point in my life, it was purely for sexual fulfillment. Love was never an issue.

A lot of the girls were from my high school days; others, I met at bars. And let me tell you this. Any parent who thinks their children aren't having sex should have their head examined. This is only an estimate on my part. But I'd say 70 percent of the girls who were juniors and seniors were having sex, at least in my school. And I graduated high school in 1980. A lot of the freshmen and sophomores would lose their virginity to the guys who were juniors and seniors, thinking it would get them noticed and accepted by the in crowd. The guys would have sex a few times with them and move on to the next girl, just like playing musical chairs. At that age, guys are driven purely by their testosterone. I'm sure it broke a lot of the young girls' hearts.

I usually dated the same girl for quite a while. I guess I've always wanted monogamy. The problem I always had was with girls falling in love with me. Love scared the shit out of me then. I wanted to make love, not be loved. And when a girl would say she loved me and wanted to spend the rest of her life with me, well, it was time for me to move on. I knew at an early age that teenagers didn't know what love was, at least not the guys. It is true—at least I believe it's true—that girls mature much earlier than guys. Hell, I'm in my forties, and I can still be immature. I'm not making excuses because I like being a bit childish from time to time. But girls are more grounded at an earlier age.

After high school came several years of going to the bars. The bars were like being locked into a toy store for a night. So much to choose from and oh so much to play with, because everyone was there for sex. Sure, some of the women would only have a drink with you. But if you really wanted to, you could pick up a woman rather easily. I think the kids today call it hooking up.

Sex truly is and will always be the human condition. After all, we all are animals. And sex is the driving force in the animal kingdom.

But at some point, when I was about twenty-two or so, my desire for just sex started to wane. I would come up with excuses to tell my buddies so I could skip out on the bar nights. On Friday and Saturday night, if I didn't have a date, I'd drive up to Lake Lanier and park my car and stare out across the lake at the water. The lights from the boats were my sole companion. The moon was my lover. (Yeah, I know it does sounds like a Little River Band song.) I don't know if I was depressed or merely searching for something, possibly the meaning of life. You see, I was at a crossroads in my life, and I had to decide who and what I wanted out of life. The moon shining on the water had such a peace about it, a sweet serenity that swept me away for hours. I guess I had hoped God would come down and tell me all the answers that I sought, like in the story of Moses in the Bible, but it didn't happen. What did eventually happen was,

I found this inner peace in myself. I learned to accept that I was different, that I didn't need anyone else's approval. Nor would I ever try to impress anyone with lies. I would always be myself. Like it or not, this is who I am. This is what I believe.

While I wasn't suicidal at that time, I do understand now why so many teenagers commit suicide in their teens. They're lost, searching for their own meaning of life. The responsibility of being an adult is sometimes a tough step for a young man or woman to make. Who are they? What do they want to do for the rest of their lives? Who do they want to spend the rest of their lives with? These are all tough enough decisions to make, especially when alone.

I came to realize that I wouldn't find love in a bar. Nor would I find it in a bottle of booze. Hell, I might never find it at all. But I knew that if I ever did, I would not let her go. That was many, many years before Donna came into my life. My favorite line in a movie was spoken by, yes, Tom Cruise. The line was "You complete me." I think it was in *Jerry Maguire*. Well, that is what Donna has done. She has not only completed me; she has showed me what unconditional love truly is. I glance over at her now as she lies sleeping, with Scruffy sleeping at her feet. What a beautiful sight it is to see. Only her head and left shoulder are visible to the eyes. But her love still fills the room. I bend over to kiss her naked shoulder, and then I too drift off to sleep.

Monday morning comes too early. Donna wakes me as she's stirring to get up. I can hear the shower running. She is going to work because she'll take time off for maternity leave soon enough. So I'll have to make many of the decisions about the houses. The next few weeks, we'll be moving and selling furniture we can't use. I'm lying in bed with this massive pee hard-on trying to psyche myself up to at least get up to go empty my bladder. Donna walks into the room.

"Ben, how did you sleep?" She notices my erection.

"Wow! I thought we emptied that last night?"

"We did! That's just a pee hard."

"Pee hard?"

"Yeah, sometimes men wake up needing to pee real bad and they have an erection like this. Once you take a leak, it goes down." I get up out of bed and make my way to the toilet.

Donna follows me into the bathroom to put on her lipstick. "Mind if I watch?"

"Watch what?"

"You peeing! I've never seen a man pee before."

"Suit yourself! Hell, you can hold it if you want to."

"What do I do?"

"Well, you aim it towards the water like a water hose. That's good! Now you have to say this: 'Magic penis so full of pee, come on out and release from thee.'"

"You don't say that, do you?"

"Yes, I do. Some guys have to talk to it to get it started, some have to even run water to get it started."

"I'm not going to say that. It's totally stupid, and you're just screwing with me."

"My god, do you think Scruffy is going to tell the neighborhood dogs his masters say a chant before pissing and they'll, in turn, tell their masters? I don't think so. Besides, it's cute. Come on, Donna honey, do it for me."

"You won't tell anyone, will you?"

"Of course not."

"Okay! Magic penis so full of pee, come on out and release from thee."

With that, the urine begins to flow. It scares Donna, and she releases her grip, and piss goes all over the toilet before I could grab it and get it in control.

"What the hell was that, Donna?"

"It startled me."

"It didn't startle you. You got scared like it was a snake that was about to bite you."

"Well, I told you I just wanted to watch. I didn't expect to feel it move like that. You men have some kind of weird plumbing."

"I guess you expect me to clean it up too?"

"Well, it is your pee."

I just look at her and say, "Women!" I brush my teeth and give her a kiss goodbye and grab the mop bucket and the Mr. Clean.

With Donna off to work, I plan my day. I have to make arrangements for movers. And I also have to clear out a closet or three for Donna's clothes. I decide to take Scruffy with me. *The little bastard might as well get used to his new home*, I think.

On the way home, I pick the other dogs up as well. Ford has kept them. So I open the back seat and put Skipper and Dusty in. They're getting old and can no longer jump that high. Sparky, on the other hand, can jump like Michael Jordan. Off to the house. Sparky jumps to the middle console that's between the front seat and sees Scruffy. Of course, they do what all dogs do: they sniff each other's nose then each other's ass. I wonder if dogs notice the size of other dogs' dicks. Hey, that's an honest thought. Do dogs have penis envy? Maybe the dog psychics should ask that to a dog on their television show. Like I said, this book is filled with a lot of useless shit that fascinates me.

I get home and let the dogs out. Skipper and Dusty hike their legs and head for the front door. Scruffy runs down to the pond then back up to me. Sparky gives him an "Are you fucking crazy? It's hot as hell out here, and you're making us all look bad" look. Once Scruffy settles down, I open the door, and all the dogs head for the water bowl. Scruffy walks around in awe, sort of like I do when I go to a new porn shop. The dogs settle in their beds, and I retrieve an old bed out of the shed for Scruffy.

Finally, I can get started. I go to my desk and start looking up movers. To be honest, I hate moving. Not that I've done a lot of it myself. I've helped friends move over the years, but my only move was from Linwood to Olive Grove. And I only brought a TV and clothes with me, so it wasn't a big deal. I will admit to you I've quit helping people move. I've had enough sore backs that I've finally said "No more." I'd rather pay someone than do it myself, and so can they. Lazy? You bet your sweet ass I am. But I no longer have a sore back. I finally settle on a mover after a number of calls.

Now I only have to set the date up, and until Donna decides what she wants to keep, I can't do that, so I decide to have some breakfast. Since I've started my diet, I've lost only ten pounds. Of course, I've cheated, but ten pounds is still ten pounds. I haven't had breakfast yet, so I'll have a little cereal and catch up on the news. The news is about polygamy, mainly polygamy cults. This one is in Texas. Is it just me, or does Texas seem to have more insane, whacked-out cult leaders living there or what? Remember David Koresh. One look at him should have set the alarm bells off for any would-be follower. But of course, they were as crazy as he was. I am just sorry so many innocent children died in the fire.

First off, any man who has more than one wife is a fucking idiot. Sex with three women is one thing, but married to three? No fucking way, Jose. First, there's the jealousy issue. Having three wives living that close together would be like locking Ann Coulter, Hillary Clinton, and Nancy Pelosi in a room. It would be one big catfight. However, I think Ann would win that fight easily. She is one tough woman. But having three wives, you also have to deal with three times the PMS. That alone would scare any rational man away. Dealing with Satan once a month is bad enough, but three times a month? No fucking way! Then you have all the children to deal with. Can you imagine little Tommy asking his mother, wife number 1, "Where's Daddy?"

"He's fucking wife number 3 today."

How could you possibly give enough time to your children? Of course, some Mormons still believe in polygamy and practice it today. I will have to say in defense of the Mormons that most have condemned the practice of polygamy. But I also have to be honest with all of you. One woman is enough for this man. I couldn't handle three women at the same time. I'm not ashamed to admit it either, because Pfizer doesn't make enough Viagra to keep me up for the challenge. My balls hurt now just thinking about trying to satisfy three women. I mean, a man only has so much semen to go around. Okay, enough about my balls and semen. Back to the work.

Okay, I admit I'm a bit like my father. He was a pack rat, and so am I. I have more clothes than I could possibly wear. Of course, in my defense, some are my fat, semifat, and thin clothes. Since it will be a while before I can wear any of my thin pants, I'll store them in a trunk in the shed. Hopefully, I'll be in them sometime this year. Yeah, right! When you're cleaning up, you'll find more shit that you've thought you've lost in the strangest fucking places. I've found several socks without its mate in the corner of the closet. Of course, I'd already thrown away the matching sock because I thought I had lost this one, so now these can be thrown away too. I'm sure Sparky was the one who hid them there since I found his chew toys along with some milk bones beside them.

I've also found some back issues of *Playboy* and *Penthouse* in the closet. I can't throw them away because they'll be collector's items one day, so I'll take them to the shed with the pants. One day, Junior will probably find them like I found my father's hidden in the toolshed. But that's okay. If he is anything like me, he'll be asking for the keys to the shed so he can work on his bike. At least that was my excuse. I'd go down to the shed to work on my bike and beat off like a monkey in the zoo. Made you wince, didn't I? At least I carried some paper towels with me. I found out the hard way my father's grease rags were full of black grease. And trust me, trying to wash black grease off your dick with Dial soap ain't going to happen. You almost have to use industrial cleaner to get that shit off. I know; I have firsthand experience. Damn, that made me laugh. I hope you got it.

The phone rings. It's my mother. *Oh shit*, I think. I could feel my asshole puckering up. Well, she'll be hurt and pissed when I tell her about the wedding, but I guess I'd better get it over with. I'll just tell her we got the justice of the peace to do it on the spur of the moment so the baby wouldn't be a bastard. That'll make her Baptist side happy. Besides, my mother and father were married by a justice of the peace. Like father, like son. Besides, I'll let her know we're going to have a big wedding later on.

I pick up the phone.

"Hi, Mother."

"Benny, I just called to let you know David Jones passed away."

I have no clue who she is talking about.

"He used to sit beside your father at church with the other deacons."

"Oh! Well, I'm sorry to hear that. But I'm glad you called because I was about to call you. There's something I need to tell you."

"What's that?"

"Well, Donna and I got married by the justice of the peace this past weekend. It was a spur-of-the-moment thing."

After a long pause, she says, "Well, I'm glad to hear that. I've been praying you'd settle down. I just hope Donna doesn't turn out to be like the sluts you used to date."

"No, Mother, she is a sweet, loving woman."

"Well, I still want to meet her soon."

"Well, I'll get her to give you a call sometime this week."

"Well, Benny, I'll talk to you later. I have other calls to make. Love you!"

"I love you too, Mother."

Whew! That went better than I had thought it would. I guess Donna will have to call her now. I know it may sound like I don't love my mother, but I do. The problem is, she and I are completely different. I'm laid-back, whereas my mother is hyper as hell. Part of her problem can be attributed to a thyroid problem—actually, thyroid cancer. She had her thyroid removed years ago, and she has to take medication for it as well as for lupus and congestive heart failure. So her health is always an issue.

In fact, that's the main reason I own a cell phone now. Since I shared the first poem I ever wrote, the one about abortion, which probably will be edited out (I'm still debating about that), I might as well share the second, which I wrote for my mother on Mother's Day 1979. It's titled—what else?—"Mother's Day Poem":

Mother's Day Poem
Sometimes for me it's hard to say
How much I love someone
Or just a simple thank-you
For something they may have done.
Mother, the job of raising us
May have started with our birth.
And I know I can never repay
What that job was really worth.
Although at times, I may get mad
And think you worry way too much,
I thank God every chance I get
For you and your loving touch.
Mother, there's just one thing more
That I need to say:
Thank you, and I love you.
Have a happy Mother's Day.

So there you have it, ladies. I'm really not the evil son some of you thought I was, am I? I'm also not much of a poet either. But if you bought this book, you already know that. But I do know a lot of words that rhyme with *truck*.

Since I've started writing this book, I discovered something about myself and about other writers. One is, writing a book is hard as hell, much harder than I thought it would be. So I'm winging it! I know some authors can turn out several novels every year. I can't, nor will I try because it's hard for me to stay focused, and it's impossible for me to force myself to write. I really do have to be in the mood. Maybe if I knew what the fuck I was doing, it might be a little easier. But since I don't and since I have no outline, it's been a struggle.

But writing this book (and for me, it's hard to call it a book, much less a novel), I've learned I do have a resolve and patience, more than I thought anyway. I will face a dilemma at some point, and that is, do I want to risk getting turned down by a publishing company by submitting it for publication? If you haven't noticed, I have an ego the size of the Grand Canyon, and I don't want any blows to it primarily because I don't handle rejection very well. In fact, I can't remember being rejected ever.

And to be honest, I know this isn't like any book I've ever read. Granted, I only read a few books a year, usually something paranormal or maybe a mystery novel. I know that most mystery novels are similar in nature. It may be because fiction writers know how to write with an outline. Well, I might be able to do that if I tried, but I don't want to because I know that I can only write one way: from within. While there is some fiction in this book, most of the crazy, unbelievable things are true.

But if I'm being completely honest with myself and if I were a publishing company, I wouldn't publish this book. Why? Well, first, I'm an unknown author. And second, the story has very little rhyme or reason. And third, what idiot author talks to the readers while writing (well, besides me)? And finally, I would have to go out and defend it. I know that if published groups would come out of the woodwork to crucify it because of the profanity and subject matter without trying to understand it, no matter what I would say in its defense, it wouldn't change their minds. And while I wouldn't mind a good fight, I have to ask myself, is it worth it? While I don't find the word *fuck* offensive, some people do. I certainly never say it in public or around children, just around my friends, which, if you're reading this, I hope you are. My friends know me and accept the fact I'm a little nuts. But hell, most of them are too. I'm sorry to bore you with this shit again, but it was on my mind and I needed a break.

I haul the last load to the storage. Now I need to feed the dogs. I get the dogs fed and throw a Healthy Choice dinner in the microwave when the phone rings. It's Donna.

"Hello, darling," I say in my best Conway Twitty voice.

"Hi, Ben. I'm calling to see if you can meet me at my house so I can bring over my clothes this afternoon."

"Sure, just give me a call when you leave work."

"Can you go over and take Scruffy out?"

"I won't have to. He is here with me now. In fact, he just finished eating."

"Great! How is he getting along with your dogs?"

"Just fine. He and Sparky are best friends now."

"Okay, well, let me run. I need to find some boxes for packing."

"Love you!"

"Love you too!"

The timer goes off, and I go remove my lunch from the oven. The dogs come over to the table to inspect the situation. Skipper sits up and begs.

"No, Skipper, you've eaten already. This is my lunch. Okay, damn it, I'll save all of you a little taste."

The phone rings again.

"Fuck! Will you people let me eat in peace?"

It's Meat.

"Hello!"

"You sound pissed off. What flew up your ass?"

"Nothing. I'm trying to eat. That's all."

"Well, excuse me. It's not like you'll starve to fucking death missing a meal."

"You're a fine one to talk with your watermelon head. There's enough water in that head that you could survive being lost in the desert like a camel and never get dehydrated."

"Oh, always bringing up my big head. That's not all that's big, you know."

"Fuck you, Meat! What do you want?"

"Well, I was calling to see if you need help loading Donna's stuff up later. We have late games tonight, so I could help till about a quarter till eight. Donna told Julie you were going over, and Julie insisted I call to offer my help."

"Thanks, but I don't know what time we're doing it yet."

"Well, I'm not offering now anyway. Not until you apologize for calling me a watermelon head."

"Jeez, you big fucking baby, I'm sorry."

"Okay, I'll help, but you're buying the beer."

"Okay then. I'll buy the beer."

"Give me a shout when you're on your way."

"Will do!"

I leave the phone off the hook in hopes that I can eat in peace.

I sit down at the table and cut four pieces of chicken off and set it aside along with four green beans for the you-know-whos. After eating, I have very little left to do till I meet Donna this evening. So I decide I'll try to find some boxes myself. I go to all the manufacturing companies that I know in town and manage to find a truckload of boxes in the Dumpsters.

I will go ahead and take them to Donna's. On the way, I stop and buy a case of beer for Meat. Okay, I may drink one or two of them. But that's it. My final stop is the diet center to get a B$_{12}$ shot. God, I hate those damn needles. I have the option of getting the shots in the arm or hip. I always try to get them in the hip. That way, I can't see the needle go in. And it's because I have more fat there than in my arm. But damn, do they ever hurt. I then take my sore ass back home and wait for Donna to call. It's hard to believe so much has happened the last four days. It's also hard to believe what the next few weeks have in store. Donna and I have to make some decisions on what furniture stays and what goes. But for now, I'm going to relax, which is what I do best anyway. It's four o'clock, and the phone rings. It's Donna.

"Hello, baby cakes."

"Hi, Ben, just wanted you to know I'm leaving work now. I'm on my way."

"Okay, I'll see you there."

I call Meat and get his voice mail and leave him a message. Before I leave, I decide to let the dogs out to do their business one more time.

"Who needs to winky dink?"

Don't ask; I have no idea what that means. I just try to teach the dogs a new word every once in a while. I also know it's not a real word, but they don't know that. At least I don't think they do. The dogs think it means to piss. But everything I say to them, they think it means to piss. I let the dogs back inside and lock the door.

Donna is just getting out of her car as I pull up. She unlocks the door and walks inside. There she sees the boxes.

"Ben, that's so thoughtful. I could only find a few boxes. Most of the places had thrown them in the Dumpster already. And I wasn't about to use a box that had been in a Dumpster. Where did you find them?"

Realizing that these were perfectly good boxes but that she had a problem using boxes that had been in a Dumpster, I do what any smart man would do: I lied. But only a little white lie, mind you.

"Well, dear, you do know I have connections with a lot of local manufacturing companies, and I got them to save them for me."

Now, ladies, don't get pissy on a technicality. I made sure none of the boxes had any shit on them before I loaded them up. They were clean enough to eat off—well, almost! We walk into the bedroom, and she starts pulling clothes off the rod, hanger and all.

179

"Donna, do you have an old quilt or blanket that I can lay in the back of my truck?"

"Yeah, in the linen closet. What do you need it for?"

"Well, we can lay all of your dresses flat and cover them up. And if we need to, we'll weigh them down with a box. That way, nothing will get wrinkled and we can just hang them back up when we get there."

"Aren't you so smart?"

I smile, knowing she is trying to use her female psychology. I know the game, so I play right along.

"Well, just a little."

The truck is loaded, so I make the first of many trips. Donna stays and packs up her personal shit as I pull out the drive. Since the closets are clear, it is easy just to hang up her clothing. I will let her straighten things out later, since I know she has a particular order for everything.

When I arrive back at Donna's, I see that Julie's car is in the driveway. Meat must be with her. I walk in and see Julie.

"Where's Meat?"

"In the bathroom. He's been in there since we got here."

Oh shit, I know the big bastard is probably dropping a bomb in there because he's too old to be spanking the monkey. I hear a flush and a reflush and a final flush. Then I hear the sound of an aerosol can being sprayed, followed by the sound of running water. He then walks out of the bathroom.

Before I can say anything, he says, "Fucking low-flow toilets aren't worth a shit."

I laugh because it was funny as hell but also true. Whoever came up with the low-flow toilets and passed the laws making them be used in new dwellings should be shot. I could see them being used in urinals because piss is just a one flusher. So all you need is a little water. But if someone like Meat takes one of his mother of all shits, one flush simply won't do. Hell, I'm surprised it only took him three. If the government does a survey on water usage on low flows, my guess would be that people use more water on a low-flow toilet, having to flush it more than the older toilets, which I have. Since most of the government is full of shit, they should know it takes a lot of water to flush it down. I guarantee you, the low-flow law came from a democratic environmentalist like a Al Gore. It's my opinion that low-flow toilets and global warming are two of the greatest hoaxes ever perpetrated on America.

"What the hell are you smiling about?" Meat says.

"Nothing, dude."

Meat and I make several more trips over to the house with the clothing. Finally, we finish up at six.

"How about some dinner, folks?"

Since the softball games are still a couple of hours away, we all agree to go out to eat. We choose a Thai restaurant. I have to admit I love Thai food.

Meat and I sit quietly, stuffing our faces with food, while the ladies talk about maternity clothes, baby clothes, and other things that don't interest us. Every once in a while, Julie would ask Meat a question, and he would answer it with his mouth full. If it isn't full, he'd take a bite. His response is either "unhoe" or "uh-huh," which I think is "I don't know" and "yes." I realize Meat did that because he wasn't paying attention to their conversation either. He only responded when he heard his name mentioned, sort of like Pavlov's dog and the bell. I have to give the big guy credit; that was brilliant. I'll definitely have to remember it.

We finish up our meal and head back to the house, where Julie will stay with Donna, while I go to the ball game with Meat tonight. Meat throws his gear in the truck, and we make our way to the ballpark.

"Meat, that was fucking brilliant!" I realize I am paying him a compliment but not knowing what the hell for.

He replies, "Yes, it was. But I'm not sure what you're referring to."

"The way you always mumbled with food in your mouth when Julie asked you a question. I knew you had no idea what she asked."

"Well, you need to learn these things. It took me years to develop and master that technique. Carla used to get pissed if I didn't listen to her when she asked a question. Usually, it was during a football game. She would walk in and ask some dumb question, and I'd say 'Yes, dear,' thinking it would pacify her and get her off my back. You know I don't want to be disturbed during a football game."

"That is true."

"Well, finally, she caught on to what I was doing. One Saturday during a football game, she asked if I'd ever fucked a goat. I said my typical 'Yes, dear,' and she threw the remote and hit me in the head. After that, we didn't have sex for a week."

"Damn, that's tough."

"Well, not really. I just realized I had to change my strategy often."

"That's true! You throw a batter nothing but fastballs, eventually he'll hit a home run or, in your case, hit you in the head. You have to throw the curve or a changeup every once in a while to mix things up."

"Exactly my point, and since my divorce with Carla, I use the strategy on Julie. And it's worked every time—so far!"

I make a fist and reach across the seat to meet his fist. It's sort of an adult male high five.

We pull into the complex parking lot. Some of the guys are already there drinking beer. As we get out of the truck, we hear "What's up, you pussy-whipped, married motherfucker?" It is coming from TJ.

"Not much, you hand-whipped, no-hitting, big-nosed bastard."

"That's funny! Hey, Ben, got milk?" I look over at TJ, realizing he was referring to Donna's breasts. "No, but I have the Oreos waiting!"

The guys get a chuckle out of that. Of course, I do too.

With the wedding and pregnancy and everything else going on, I have turned the coaching duties over to Mark and Meat. I know my plate is too full to coach full-time. Maybe I should have realized that earlier, but hey, I'm a dumb sack of poop. Just ask Wayne. I will coach and help out when I can because I know I will need a diversion from the real world.

Well, game time is near, and we walk down toward the field. The guys are all joking around. Mark makes the lineup out, and I take it upstairs for the scorekeeper.

Softball is like church in one way. You get to see and talk to friends once a week. But unlike church, there's no pressure to conform. Everyone is accepted as they are at the ballpark. What they do in their personal life is their business, unlike at church, where everyone knows your business.

The guys put up eight runs in the first. The team is clearly the best team in the league. I used to feel sorry for the opponents we play, especially the ones we beat so badly. But I remember being on teams that got beaten like that too. Only one team can be the best. If you're not it, then it gives you something to shoot for. Same thing happens in everyday life. It's like the old military slogan: "Be all you can be!" The guys go on to run rule both teams; the first game they won 24–5 in four innings. The second they won 26–2 in three innings.

Afterward, we sit around and drink a beer and talk. Honestly, this is the most important time for us. It's therapeutic for us to discuss what's going on in our day-to-day lives. We ask for and give each other advice. There again is the similarity to a church, except we all take on the role of the minister—me, probably more so than others simply because I'm older—or an elder in the church of softball.

One thing we are not is judgmental. I'm certainly not. I know the guys have to live their own lives and learn from their own mistakes. And some are making huge ones. A couple of the guys are having affairs with other women. In one case, his wife found out about it. Needless to say, he is going through hell. He has to decide to stay and go to marriage counseling or get a divorce. I know I can't tell him what to do. My thoughts are it's probably too late to save the marriage. Even if they stick together, there'll always be that cloud hanging over their heads. I've always said it's easy to forgive but impossible to forget, especially for women. When you betray someone you love, some—if not all—of that love is lost. And all the respect and trust are gone. And no matter how hard you try, you'll never find or rekindle it.

I can somewhat understand why some men cheat. They're missing the passion they once had with their wives. At least that's what most say. Maybe they're not getting enough or any sex anymore, because it does take two to tango. But mostly I think guys just need to be wanted. That said, however, I can't put the blame on all wives. Some men are just jerks and only care about getting their dicks wet. Those are the guys who get what they deserve.

We pack up and head toward home. We get back to my house and go inside. Donna and Julie are sitting on the sofa with dogs on each side.

My first thought is *This should be a Norman Rockwell painting.*

Donna looks up and says, "How'd it go?"

"We won both games."

"Did you girls solve the world's problem?"

"No, just what we want to do to the house," Donna says.

I'm thinking, *Oh shit, here we go.*

About that time, Meat speaks up, "Do whatever you want to upstairs, but the basement stays as it is. Hell, the state should place a historical marker on the basement door."

"Don't worry, you boys can keep your playhouse."

Whew! That was a relief.

Looking at Donna, I ask, "What did you decide?"

"Just on what new floor covering, paint, drapes, and furniture are needed to spruce this place up."

"What furniture?"

"Mine! Except we'll keep one of your bedroom suites."

"Okay, I can live with that," I say, even though her furniture is a bit frilly.

Meat senses that this would be a good time for them to leave.

"Julie, we need to go."

With that, they get up to leave.

As they drive off, Donna looks at me and says, "Are you okay with the changes? I mean, this is your house."

"No, Donna, this is our house. You leave the basement alone, and you can do anything you want except paint anything pink. "However, I'd prefer us to buy new living room furniture. I'm not fond of sitting on a floral-print sofa."

"Deal! We can have a big yard sell and get rid of some things from both houses."

"Well, if you want a yard sell, Donna, you'll have to deal with it. I hate yard sells because only cheap people looking for a deal go to them. But if you want to deal with them, you can keep all the money out of it. The other thing is, I'm not moving furniture. We'll hire movers first."

"Damn, Ben, you're so easy to deal with."

"It's because I'm pussy whipped."

"Yes, you are! You want to play with it? You know it has your name on it!"

"I want to do more than just play with it, Mrs. Thompson."

After making love, Donna lies in my arms, and we begin to talk. Of course, we have four dogs who have joined us. Good thing I have a king-size bed.

"Donna, I talked to my mother today. I told her we got married."

"How did she take it? I mean, not being at the service."

"Well, I told her we planned to have a large wedding later."

"What did she say?"

"She was surprisingly okay with it. I did tell her you'd call her and talk."

"That's no problem. I'll call her this week. Maybe you can drive up and bring her back for the yard sale."

"I'd rather not!"

"Don't be such a wus."

"I'm not a wus! I just like being the equator."

"What does that mean?"

"Well, you're the north pole, she's the south pole. I'm in the middle, where it's safe. If the poles shift from position or they ever meet, then all hell breaks loose on earth. You know, earthquakes, tidal waves, your basic mass-destruction shit."

"Ben, you watch too much Discovery Channel!"

"Maybe, but I like having the two of you at separate ends of my world. Besides, my mother really is like the television character Maude on steroids."

"Well, I'll call her and talk to her."

"Thanks!" I reach over to turn off the light.

"Good night, John Boy. Good night, Skipper. Good night, Dusty. Good night, Sparky. Good night, Scruffy. Good night, Junior, and good night, my sweet darling." Whew!

"What was that about?"

"Hey, it worked on the Waltons."

"Ben, you're too much! Now go to sleep."

"Good night, my sweet little pussy!"

"Ben!"

"Sorry, dear! I didn't want it to feel left out." I end by whispering "Good night, Mr. Happy. You did a great job tonight." I look under the cover, and he gives me a thumbs-up and a wink. Okay, so I made that up. Jeez!

Donna manages to go to sleep before I do. My mind begins racing around like it always does. My body can be dead tired, but my brain stays in overdrive. It really is hard for me to go to sleep most nights. Usually I'd lie in bed and watch TV till I fell asleep. But now with Donna, I don't think that would work too well. So I lie in bed and start solving the world's problems yet again. I'm almost asleep when I hear this startling sound: snoring. Donna is snoring—not just any kind of snoring, but snoring like a fleet of sailors after pulling a weekend drunk. It scares Dusty and Sparky so bad they crawl up next to me like they do in a thunderstorm. Damn! I just lie there watching the numbers on the clock change. Somewhere between three o'clock and three thirty, my body just says "fuck it," and off I go to sleep.

The dogs wake me up about seven thirty to go out and do their business. Donna is already up, getting ready for work.

"How did you sleep, darling?"

"I slept fine till you woke me up snoring about 4:00 a.m."

"I woke you up snoring?"

"Yes, you did. You snore like a freight train! Damn, Donna, you kept me up snoring. I didn't go to sleep till after three."

"Ben, I don't snore. You're just saying that because I said you snore."

"Yes, you do. You snore like a seventy-year-old hobo with emphysema."

"I do not."

"Yes, you do. You just don't hear yourself. I bet at Georgia Tech, their Richter scale went off. They probably thought there was an earthquake centered in central Alabama."

"Then how come you didn't wake me last night in my old house? I had to be snoring then too."

"Maybe your bed is snore-proof."

"That's just crazy. But if it's any consolation, I couldn't go back to sleep after you woke me."

"Donna, I have a suggestion to make."

"What's that?"

"Separate bedrooms."

"Ben, we're married. Married couples are supposed to sleep in the same bed."

"Not necessarily. A lot of couples sleep in separate bedrooms for this very reason. It doesn't mean you can't come in and get in bed with me in the mornings for a little snuggle time or to make love. The same thing for me coming and getting into your bed. We don't have to lock the doors. But we would sleep better."

"But we were planning to turn the other room into a nursery for the baby."

"Not anymore, we're not. I'll get a contractor started on adding another room for Junior."

"Well, that actually makes sense. But I want my own bedroom suite in there."

"Consider it done. I'll pay the movers whatever it takes to get it done today. They can leave that old suite in your garage to be sold at the yard sell."

"Okay, well, I'm off to work. See you tonight."

I let the dogs back in and watch her drive off.

"Okay, boys, I'm going back to bed to get some more sleep. Who wants to join me?"

I get back up at ten thirty, feed the dogs, and start making calls to movers. Whatever it takes, I'm determined to pay to get the furniture moved today. Some of you may think this is crazy, that we'd get used to each other snoring. Bullshit! I'm sorry I don't share your sentiment at all. I've slept alone over forty years, and I'm pretty well-set in my ways. My routine has been the same for all those years. Sure, I've shared my bed a few nights with women and with Donna on several occasions. But that was for only one night at a time and not a lifetime. I truly love Donna, but now we've both decided we can't stand to sleep with each other, which I think is a good thing. At least we were honest and both agreed on it. We can always make love before we turn in or early in the morning. Either way, we'll have more energy, and we'll both have a good night's sleep either before or after making love. Besides, who can fuck and sleep at the same time? I've never heard of it. I've heard of people sleepwalking but never of a man inserting his penis in his lover while he was asleep. I've had some women who fucked like they were asleep or dead, on more than one occasion, actually. Hell, I may have even put some women to sleep while making love to them when I was younger. I even awoke once with a pee hard while I snuggled up to Donna from behind. Mr. Happy was snuggled between the cheeks of her ass.

Damn, that's an erotic thought. Grandma naked, Grandma naked! Whew! That was a close call. Mr. Happy almost sprang into action.

Speaking of action, that's who I got to move the furniture: Action Movers. They'll be here at three o'clock. I have some time to kill before the movers get here, so I'll work on this book. My other project has hit a snag, and to be honest, I don't want to work in a hot barn. The temperature here in central Alabama is getting hot, in the nineties every day. Plus, I'd have to deal with the mosquitoes in the barn too. I know you think I'm a wus. You know what? I don't care. Besides, I need to finish the book.

You folks may wonder when I do actually have time to work on the book, which is what I always wonder about when I read a book. What time of day do authors write? Since authors only write a story, you don't know what they're going through in their day-to-day process. Do they get writer's block? Have they just fucked someone on their desk and spilled their coffee? Okay, maybe only I think about that one. It is a nice fantasy to think about. I mean, I'd love to have Donna walk in buck naked with a can of whipped cream while I'm working on this. It would be a nice diversion. But unfortunately, it hasn't happened—yet! But when it comes to writing, I have to write when the mood hits me. Some writers can start at 9:00 a.m. and quit at five o'clock. If I try that, I'd end up playing *Spider Solitaire* most of the time.

It really is a shame they don't make Cialis for the brain to get you up and started. If they did, I'd be a junkie. I love the ad: "When the time is right, you'll be ready." Imagine popping a pill and writing five pages before lunch. How cool would that be? Unfortunately, it doesn't work that way. So what I do is, when I get tired of surfing the web, I click on the book and read whatever I wrote last, usually the last five or six pages. Sometimes I'm shocked by what I wrote, other times, amused. I usually end up making a few changes, then after that, I pick up where I left off, unless I decide to completely go in another direction, which is what I'm doing now. But like I've said, I go whatever direction the book takes me.

The truth is, if writers had to pass a test to write the way you have to in order to get a driver's license, I'd be stuck riding on public transportation. I think what I like about the way I'm writing this is that you're going along for the ride with me. Most writers want to drive you and throw twists and turns in just to keep you guessing, maybe even an occasional roadblock. At least here you're a copilot riding with me down the road in this fog I'm in. And trust me, the fog is pretty thick. At least I do have my lights on. My only fear is, at some point, I may run out of gas or maybe even break down. I'm sure you're probably asking the same question right now that I am: Why in the hell did he just write that shit? Your guess is as good as mine.

Well, it's almost time for the movers. I'd better get ready. The movers show up on time, which may be a first. There are three of them: one white guy and two Latinos. I only notice because the white guy speaks to them in Spanish. I know that only because I took Spanish for a year in high school. In fact, I was a straight A student, which means I didn't understand a damn thing they said. It's true when they say "use it or lose it." And to be honest, I can recall very little of what I learned from Mrs. O'Neal's Spanish class. So yes, it's lost. They start moving out the furniture from what used to be the guest bedroom. That will become Donna's bedroom for now. They safely load everything on the truck. Then they follow me over to Donna's house to unload it in the garage.

I have to admit the Latino guys are working their asses off. But I do have to be honest about something. With all the illegal-alien controversy on the news, I have to wonder to myself if they're here legally or not. The white guy must be the foreman because he isn't doing anything but giving directions. Now honestly, I have no problem with foreign workers. I'm actually glad they are people who want to work. But I do understand the fear so many people have about people coming into this country illegally. We do need to know who is coming in and if they have any criminal records or if they're possibly linked to terrorist groups.

That said, I can also understand the men needing to support their families in Mexico. Here's what I don't understand: Why can't the government make it easier for would-be honest workers to enter the country legally? Why is there so much goddamn red tape? There has to be a faster way to have background checks. If we worked with the Mexican government better, you would think it would be easier to get approval. We really do need the workers. Hell, few people will take jobs that pay minimum wage. And I would be willing to bet these guys aren't close to making that. In one sense, it's slave labor. It's not much different from the young children and women forced to work in overseas sweat shop. But you don't hear many Americans bitching about that here with the illegal aliens. They merely bitch about their legal status. The companies that hire them probably don't pay payroll tax. The workers also have no insurance. It would benefit everyone if they come here legally. I understand that the cost of goods may go up some. Things like produce and even lawn service would increase, but it would make our country much safer. Isn't that what we all want anyway?

Jeez, I just realized I sound like a Democrat. That's a scary thought.

We get back to the house and unload Donna's bedroom suite. Not a single scratch. I write a check to the moving company and tip both the Latino guys for their service. I go ahead and make up her bed. I also go and cut a single red rose from a bush in the yard. I lay it in front of the throw pillows in hope for an invitation there later.

I also start dinner. I want us to have a meal in our home together. To be honest, I'm tired of eating out so much. It'll be a simple meal: pork chops, some seasoned rice, and a salad. Hell, I may light a candle for good measure because I have a strategic plan. After dinner just after dark, I'm going to try to talk Donna into going skinny-dipping. We've never done that together. Yeah, we've taken plenty of showers together but never a swim—naked! How erotic is that?

Maggots... maggots in a dead possum. Sorry, Mr. Happy started to move, and I can't cook with an erection. I'd be banging Mr. Happy's head into the stove while I'm trying to cook, and that might piss him off enough to go AWOL later. And you can't play navy SEAL with an AWOL pecker. So for now, it's down periscope—damn the torpedoes—and full speed ahead. God, I love navy jargon. Thanks, Captain Mealy.

Donna arrives home a little after five o'clock. She looks exhausted.

I greet her with a kiss. "How was your day?"

"Tiresome. I showed one couple six different houses. In each one, the husband found something wrong."

"That jerk! Just like a man, can't make up his mind."

Donna looks at me and smiles. "Something smells good."

"Well, I'm making dinner for my love."

"Okay, mister, what's up your sleeve?"

"Why do you always think I have some sort of agenda?"

"Maybe because you always do."

"No, I just wanted us to have our first dinner at home together. Plus, I want you to see something." With that, I take her by her hand and walk her to the bedroom.

"Wow! You got it moved."

"Of course, I did. You didn't think I'd lie around all day and watch soap operas, did you?"

"I'm so impressed—and oh, how sweet. A rose. For me?"

"Actually, I cut that for the woman I had in here at lunch—of course, it's for you."

"Ben, you're so adorable."

"Donna, 'adorable' is for puppies. How about 'the sexiest man alive'?"

"Whatever floats your boat, Ben."

"Speaking of boats, what do you know about navy SEALs?"

"Not much really."

I smile, knowing what lies ahead.

"Well, you come and stretch out while I set the table."

Donna sits down to be greeted by four excited dogs.

"Are you ready to eat, my lady?"

"Yes, let me wash puppy dog off my hands first."

She walks back out of the bathroom just as I'm blowing out the match that I had used to light the candle.

"How romantic, Ben."

"Nothing but the best for you, my dear."

"I could get used to this."

"Well, don't! I can't do this chef shit every day."

"But you have such a nice big spatula, Ben."

"If you think flattery will get you somewhere, you're absolutely correct. Plus, you do have such a wonderful mixing bowl that my big spatula just loves."

"Oh, my little doughboy. Just don't say I have one in the oven."

"One what?"

She laughs as we finish up dinner.

"Well, Chef Thompson, what's for dessert?"

"You mean now or later?"

"Ben, I'm talking about something to eat!"

"So am I!"

"Ben, I mean, like, food."

"Oh! I think there's some ice cream in the freezer."

I go into the kitchen and fill a cup up with ice cream. I walk back into the living room and hand her the cup.

"You're not having any?"

"No, I'm pretty full."

"Mmm! It's good. Sure you don't want a taste?"

I walk over to her. She has a spoonful of butter pecan ice cream on the spoon waiting for me.

"I don't need that." I place the spoon back into the cup. I bend over to kiss her lips. "Mmm, that is good!"

I could still taste the ice cream that was on her sticky lips.

"What are you doing, mister?"

"Just sampling one of the many Baskin-Robbins thirty-one flavors."

"What is your favorite?"

"It's a new flavor called pussy fruit passion."

"Would I like it?"

"No, most women don't like it unless they have a wallet with a chain in their pocket."

"I don't know. I like the way I taste."

"Well, that makes two of us. Donna, how would you like a dip in the pool?"

"My bathing suits are still packed up."

"You do not need a bathing suit. You live in the country now. It's dark, and the water is perfect. What do you say?"

"What if someone drives up?"

"Fuck 'em! All my friends know to call before they come over because of the dogs. So if anyone drives up unannounced, it would have to be Jehovah's Witnesses or someone lost."

"No one would see us?"

"No! Except maybe an owl or deer."

"Okay, let me undress and get some towels."

We get undressed and wrap a towel around us and head for the pool.

If you didn't already know, I'm fighting off an erection. I mean, I don't want it to seem too obvious. I guess I could hang a towel on it and get a laugh. But then the game plan would be changed. Besides, this is, hopefully, only foreplay. I walk in first step-by-step. The water is a little cool but not bad. I reach my hand up to help her down the steps.

"Burrr! This is cold!"

"Oh, Donna, it's eighty-two degrees. You'll get used to it. Here, let me warm you up." With that, I put my arms around her and give her a soft kiss. "How's that?"

"Not bad, actually."

"See, I—"

"Don't say 'I told you so.'"

"I wasn't going to say that!"

"Yes, you were."

"No, I was going to say 'See, I... think the water temperature is fine.'"

"You paused after saying 'See, I.' And besides, that statement makes no sense."

"It didn't, did it?"

"No, it didn't."

"Well, dear, you missed your calling. You should have been a teacher."

"Why a teacher?"

"Well, you like correcting things and you're hot. So the male students would love taking your class."

"And what would I teach?"

"What else? Sex education. I'm sure, after class, all the young boys would rush to the bathroom between periods to whack off. You do have that effect on men, you know."

"Did you ever whack off at school?"

"Hell yeah, sometimes two or three times a day. I even had a wet dream in study hall once."

"You didn't!"

"Of course, I did. Hell, in study hall, you could study or sleep. One day, I took a nap and woke up with Mr. Happy glued to my shorts."

"What did you do?"

"I never took another nap in class."

"I mean about the semen in your shorts?"

"After class, I went to the bathroom and took them off and washed up. Then I took the semen-filled underwear and put them in Ms. Blakely's bottom drawer as a gift."

"Why her?"

"Well, that's who I was fucking in my dream."

"That made a lot of sense!"

"Well, it did at that time. I'm just glad they didn't have DNA testing then. She wasn't amused, and the principal investigated to try to find out who did it. He was pissed!"

"Could you blame him?"

"No, but I'm sure it was out of jealousy because he was banging her at that time."

"Well, I'm glad to see you have grown up a lot since then."

"Yeah, I have. You want to play navy SEAL now?"

"What's that?"

"This." I sit Donna on the second step and take a deep breath. I go underwater and spread her legs and start blowing bubbles from underneath the water that passed across her clitoris. I came up for air.

"How was that?"

"I think you failed your mission."

"Damn! And I thought it was a great idea too. I guess I'm your prisoner now. You want to tie me up and interrogate me now?"

"You still have some of that semen-under-shorted little boy in you."

"Well, I do still have a lot of semen."

"Let's go inside, and you can show me, big boy."

We wrap ourselves up with the towels and walk inside, hand in hand. Once inside, we head for the shower to wash the chlorine off. After the shower, we put on robes and snuggle up on the sofa together.

It's too early for bed, and to be honest, the water had a calming effect on Mr. Happy. I guess you could say it was a tranquil moment. We couldn't find anything we cared to watch on the television, so we talk. Donna brings up the book.

"How's the book coming along?"

"Okay, I guess. I putz with it every now and then."

"Can I read it?"

I think, *Should I let her read it or not? If I don't, she'll get pissed. If I do, she may find fault with it. I guess I do need someone to read it and let me know what they think.* "Donna, if you want to, you can, but I have to warn you, it is graphic."

"I can handle it. Besides, I'm it. You told me that."

"Well, if you want to read it, it's on the computer in a file. Just don't go and rewrite it."

"I won't! I promise."

With that, we walk to the office, and I load up the file.

"There, but don't say I didn't warn you, and don't go out tomorrow looking for a divorce lawyer. I'm not even sure if I want it published."

She starts reading, and I leave the room. I can't bear watching her read it. I'll go watch the Weather Channel and maybe play solitaire on the computer. I admit I'm nervous as hell, wondering what she'll think, what she'll say. I try to keep my mind off the subject.

After about two hours, I have to check on her. I am filled with a nervous curiosity. After all, she could have had a heart attack when she read about the exploding ass. Oh, wait, I took that out. Whew!

I walk into the office. She is still reading and doesn't hear me.

"Well?"

"It's definitely you. Rude, crude, and nude. But it's actually better than I thought."

"Is that a compliment or criticism?"

"A compliment, I guess."

"What's wrong with it?"

"Well, you don't write an intimate love scene very well."

"Well, I didn't want to go into detail about our love life. Some things are sacred."

"Well, the love scenes are sort of bland and short."

"Well, excuse me for not reading Harlequin romances when I was growing up. I tried to leave something for the reader's imagination."

"Well, you did."

I could tell she was teasing me, so I offer her a challenge.

"Well, Ms. Know-It-All, you write a love scene, and I'll put it into the book just as you write it."

"Okay, you're on, Ben"

"Fine! Now can we go to bed? It's after eleven."

"Go ahead. I've got work to do."

"You're going to write it now?"

"Yes, I'll turn in, in a little while."

"Don't you need some inspiration for your love scene?"

"No. I watched *Top Gun* last week."

"Oh, that one hurt."

"I thought it might," she says with a grin.

I give her a kiss good night. "Love you!"

"Love you too!"

"Donna, be kind to me in your scene."

"Darling, I'll make the readers think you're a sex god."

"Sex god may be too much. Just be honest, and if that doesn't work, embellish me as much as possible."

"You mean lie?"

"Hey, it's fiction. At least that's my story, and I'm sticking to it."

With that, I turn in. I lie awake in bed, wondering what she is writing. My mind is full of possibilities. I lie there, waiting to hear her footsteps walk across the floor. My brain tells me to pretend I'm asleep when I do hear her, just in case she looks in, so she doesn't know I'm giving her writing too much thought. I try to think about the softball team, about the upcoming tournaments. I force myself to think about the new construction for Junior's room. Hell, I try to settle on a name for the poor kid. Junior is hardly a name for him. But my mind stays on her words.

Being a man, well, being me, I always wonder about women. I've heard of a woman faking orgasm before, like in the *Seinfeld* episode. I wonder if Donna has ever faked one. Honestly, how do we know? A man ejaculates when he reaches orgasm, so there's no faking that. But women are different. I can feel Donna's orgasms, so I'm pretty sure she isn't faking it. But now I can't be sure. I will admit it's hard to write about sex, especially when it's someone you care about and all you want to do is protect them.

But I told Donna to do her thing, so whatever comes. Sorry, bad choice of words. Whatever she writes will go in the book without editing. Hell, I've spilled my own guts, so you pretty much know who I am, at least in a fictional sense. I guess we'll have to wait for morning to find out about Donna.

Morning has broken, to quote a Cat Stevens song, and the dogs are ready for their morning business. I get up to fix their breakfast and wake Donna for work.

I walk into her room. Her bed is made. I walk into the office, and I see her asleep on the sofa. I walk over and kiss her on the cheek.

"Good morning, Laura Loving."

"Good morning! Who's Laura Loving?"

"That's just a name of a fictional romance writer that popped in my head. It's seven thirty, time for Sleeping Beauty to wake up and get ready for work."

"I'm not going in today. I stayed up just about all night writing like an idiot."

"Damn, that must be some love scene."

"You can read it later. Right now I'd love for you to take me to breakfast."

"Where do you want to go?"

"Waffle House."

Donna changes her clothes, and we're off to the Waffle House. All through breakfast, my thoughts are on what she has written. But I've decided not to bring the subject up. I don't want her to know I'm scared shitless about what she has written. So our breakfast is spent reading the paper and stuffing our faces with ham-and-cheese omelets and hash browns.

After breakfast, we go back home, and Donna calls in to work. Then she decides to go to bed to catch up on her sleep.

"Ben, if you want to read what I've written, it's in a separate file titled 'LS.'"

"I take it that stands for 'love scene.'"

"You got it, Einstein."

With that, I make my way to the office with the anticipation of a seven-year-old on Christmas morning.

Did Santa think I was naughty or nice? Hopefully, a little of both. I turn on the computer and click on the file. To say I am shocked is an understatement. This demure petite, little woman I love wrote a scene that would be better served in the *Penthouse* forum or in an article of *Cosmopolitan*. I never knew she could express herself in that way. To be honest, when I read it, my dick got harder than it ever has, which is scary, considering it's usually like a rock. Maybe it is the fact that I know this is true, that we did all the things she wrote about. While I am concerned about our privacy and want to protect her from scorn from her family and friends, she threw all caution to the wind.

After reading it, I walk into her bedroom to ask her if she is sure she wants me to put it in the book. She assures me she does. In fact, she asks me to join her in bed. Maybe it is the bulge in my pants she saw. Maybe it is simply the need to work off the sexual frustration she felt while writing her love scene. Either way, it is for my benefit. And who am I to argue? Since I can't describe lovemaking as well as she can, I will just say that this is her description that we replayed that morning. This is what Donna wrote without my editing:

When you come into the room, I get aroused just by how you call my name with that question mark drawl "Donna?" It's a carnal warning, I think. "Danger!" My brain tells it's a wicked, predaceous, heat-seeking alien approaching.

Phallic name: Mr. Happy—loaded, armed, and ready. On the face of it, our welcome, like our first kiss, is tender and gentle, polite in nature. But loving you has always been a wonderful challenge.

I'm so expectant, excited, tortured, and needy, while you are always a picture of self-assurance. My favorite fantasy comes true when it's my turn and you lie on your back vulnerable. You're stretched out for my pleasure.

On all fours, I crawl up between your hairy legs. My palms cover your nipples, and a smile spreads across your face in a lustful wait. I feel like a trained animal, a courtesan gone wild, a tigress in heat primed to seduce you, to get you ready to spill your seed inside me. My nerves are raw, my swollen tissue burning for what I want. I brush my lips across your face, your eyelids. I lick across your slightly parted mouth and draw your lower lip into my mouth. I'd love to bite. Instead I suck on your lip and spar with your tongue. I try to let you know how badly I want you to fuck me. My pussy feels painlessly empty. My breath comes in gasps. I whisper my longing in your ear. My wet tongue rims around its outer edge then pointedly thrusts into your ear to mimic what I want you to do to my pussy.

You respond with a slight spasm and a gasp. When you pull me close, I feel wet, wild, and wonderful. Now I do bite, ever so carefully, your earlobes, sucking and licking along the way down your neck. Then you guide my head back to your eagerly awaiting lips. We kiss for what seems like an hour till I finally push backward and continue my descent down your body, settling on your chest.

My mouth moves back and forth from one nipple to the other, sucking hard, biting firmly, but careful not to bite too hard. Slowly, surely, I inch my way down your stomach, noting your reaction to every move I make. When my hands reach lower and your erection reaches higher, I give it a playful squeeze, and you raise your hips in invitation. I squeeze a little harder, and I hear "Jesus, Donna, I'm dying here!"

I release my grip and stroke the captive Mr. Happy with my fingers. I think, *Oh no, my darling, you are dying only caught in my web of lust.* I inch lower to cup your balls and lift their weighty sac. I'm as feverish as you to move. I want to crawl inside you. I want to kiss you everywhere, taste you everywhere.

I lift my head and look at your beautiful erection. I kiss its velvet head. A salty liquid droplet of love awaits my tongue. I take the head into my mouth, running my tongue around its rim. I am lost in my need as my mouth plays up and down in juicy, lusty joy, as my brain turns to Jell-O. My tongue dances to its own rhythm. Sensations from your swollen cock short-circuit through my brain, down to my burning, aching interior as I sip from the holy grail of your erection. This is heaven and all mine. I don't know how long I followed my heart and my mouth, but when my need and your need become one and the same, I rise from your saliva-coated erection.

You lick your fingertips and guide yourself to me and the gates of paradise that are opened to receive. "Is this what you want?" you say.

"Yes, please," I say as inch by blessed inch fills me to the hilt, the sensitive tissue giving way to your glorious cock. I cannot move. It is too charged, too perfect. But ever so slowly, I begin the dance of mating, as old as mankind, undulating against your lower body. I feel strong and happy, and I take all that is yours to give.

I'm a woman on top, moving at my own speed in concert with my soul. I give to you as you give to me, and I move as long as it takes when the now explodes. A megawatt jolt shoots outward to the stars, and I fly apart into a million shards of crystal stardust.

Minutes seem like an eternity. Then ever so slowly, like a silver cloud of joy and satiation, I drift earthward. The treasured sensations begin to fade away. I am exhausted, slumped over your warm body. Then I'm aware we are still joined, and I'm tingly and filled with little aftershocks. You, my darling, are making magic: half thrusts in rapid succession, quick small movements to awake my dying orgasm. It is beautiful and lyrical, and I love it. "More," I whisper.

"Thank you!" I say. You keep a perfect tempo till the perfect time when one long thrust seats you fast against my cervix, your hard cock pressed deep inside of me. It is too much, too good. The tears welling up behind my eyelids spill over. I know I am crying. I cannot hold back my emotional collapse. I struggle to get my breath. It's not original or inspired, but I just roll off you into your awaiting arms. I am spent and immoveable. With a very warm mouth against my ear, I hear tender, whispered words: "How about a little time-out?" There is a masculine strength and endurance behind your silent smile. My god, I think this man is not finished. This man is alert. He has just begun to play. As I regain mental clarity, I realize I'm the luckiest woman in the universe.

Okay! Is that not some hot shit? I bet you guys got a boner, didn't you? Hell, I did. And the ladies probably got wet too.

And to think I was worried what she was going to write. I knew I was a pretty good lover, but my word, I didn't know I was a freaking sex god.

Maybe I should scrap the book and host my own sex talk show (*Talk Sex with Ben*) or maybe make my own instruction videos (*Ben There Done That*). Some of you may think I wrote that, but I promise you I didn't. Honest!

I wish I could take credit, but that's way over my literary head. That "shards of stardust" line—no way I could make that shit up. Donna, you are an incredible inspiration. And I love you. That's the last I'll talk about our sex life in the book—well, at least for a while.

Time to get to work. As Donna lies near comatose in sleep, I decide I need to get some yard work done. I've gotten behind on my spraying. I hate weeds, and they are starting to take over my flower beds. I'm too lazy to pull them, so I spray a lot of Roundup. With all the softball and wedding stuff behind me for now, I can work on getting my yard cleaned up.

Plus, I have to get a contractor started on the addition to the house, Junior's room. I realize there's no way to complete it before he comes into the world, so his crib will be in Donna's bedroom for a while. The problem with the addition is that it will have to be done to match the house, which is a log home. The builder who built my house is no longer in business, so I have a call into Jim Barna log homes. The logs for my home came from them in a kit form. I just need to find out who has the franchise locally so I can get them started on the room. I have my cell phone with me in case they call.

While I'm out spraying a bed near the pond, I almost step on a rather large snake. It scared the shit out of me. One moment, I'm looking for weeds; the next, I'm jumping out of the way of a fricking anaconda. Okay, it may not have been quite that big, but it is huge, considering I have forty pounds of spraying gear on. I damn near broke my neck getting away from it. I have to admit that for an out-of-shape forty-year-old, I'm still light on my feet. Once I am at a safe distance, which, for me, means back on the porch, I notice a meter reader pulling in. Since I have two meters (one on the house, the other at the barn), I warn him about the snake. He would be walking close to the bed on the way toward the barn. I watch him check the house meter first. Then he makes his way toward the barn. When he gets to the flower bed, I watch in amazement as he reaches down to pick up the snake. He starts walking back up the hill toward me.

"It's just a rat snake. It's harmless."

I have admitted I hate snakes. There is no good snake. Actually, there is: a dead one. I finally yell at him not to bring that snake up near me.

He looks befuddled. "It's a good snake. It eats mice."

"I don't care what it eats. It's about to die. Besides, I have cats that eat mice. I don't need no snake helping them."

"Don't kill it. I'll take it with me."

"Okay! If you want to play crocodile hunter, go right ahead. But if you put him down, I'm going to get my shotgun and blow him to bits."

I watch as he takes the snake and puts him in a box in the cab of his truck. My first thought is, *What an idiot*. Actually, that is my only thought.

Since my near-death experience, I suddenly have the urge to take a leak. I'm just happy I didn't piss my pants. I go into the basement to relieve myself.

Just as I am finishing up, the phone rings. It's Whatley.

"What's up, Monster?" That's his pet name for his penis.

I know, I know; you should never call another man by his penis nickname, but he also uses it to describe his hitting ability, so I'm covered there.

"Ben, Denise and I have decided to have the guys from the team over for a cookout Friday night. I'd like it if you and Donna can come. Can you make it?"

"I think so, but I'll have to run it by her first."

"All right, let me know if you can't make it."

"Will do."

With that, we hang up. After hanging up, I realize something I hadn't thought of before: guys have short conversations on the telephone. Think about it. We call, we get down to business, then we hang up. Short and sweet. No BS. Women, on the other hand, can talk for hours with each other. I once heard Donna and one of her friends talk for over an hour about makeup. I know most guys don't wear makeup. Yes, I realize maybe a few do. But what could you possible talk about for an hour? Eyeshadow, lipstick, that war paint stuff they smear on their cheeks. Sorry I can't remember what that stuff is called. Seriously, that amazes me. My mother may be the worst. I swear, she is on the phone her every waking moment.

The phone rings again. The number is from out of state.

I answer, "Hello."

"Mr. Thompson, this is Davis Jasper returning your call about log homes."

"Yes, sir. I need to add a room to my house and need to find out who has the franchise for this area so I can give him a call."

"You're in Alabama?"

"Yes, sir."

"Then Homer Wilkinson is who you need to call."

He gives me his number, and we hang up. There you go, short and sweet.

I give Mr. Wilkinson a call. He is building a log home near Lake Martin, which is only about forty-five minutes from here, so he agrees to stop by after five today.

I get back on my spraying, hoping to finish up before it gets too hot. While the backpack sprayer beats the hell out of the old three-gallon handheld sprayers, they do wear you down. My backpack sprayer, when full, weighs over forty pounds, which is thirty-five pounds too much for me.

I finish up and go into the house to take a shower. Sleeping Beauty is awake from her nap.

"Hi, baby, did you sleep okay?"

She yawns and stretches. "Yeah, I did. I didn't know writing was so tiresome."

"Well, I put what you wrote in the book exactly as you wrote it. Are you really sure you want the intimate stuff in? I mean, it was from your point of view, and your friends may read it."

"Ben, you've poured your soul on the line in the book. Why shouldn't I? We're married, and even if we weren't, people make love all the time. Besides, you are a great lover, and I don't care if the world knows that. Just make sure I'm the only one who gets to find out."

I think back to a shirt my brother used to have. It had a picture of a basset hound on it with the saying "I may not be rich, tough, or beautiful. But I'm faithful."

"Donna, Mr. Happy knows he only has one playground he's allowed to play on."

"Well, just make sure he doesn't fall off the slide. And if he ever decides to swing on another playground, I'll whack him with the monkey bars."

I thought it was funny she used all the playground analogies. I also realize she may be a little jealous. "Are you jealous?"

"Of course not."

"Well, you sound a little jealous."

"Well, it's just you make the Donna in the book so perfect. I'm not that way."

"You are to me. Granted, you turn into the exorcist sometimes with PMS. But hell, most women do that."

"You never say anything to me when I have PMS."

"Donna, I'm not stupid. I know that would only piss you off even more. Besides, I just don't pay it any attention."

"You don't?"

"No, I realize it's the hormones going apeshit in your body. Besides, I sort of like both the Dr. Jekyll and Mrs. Hyde of your personality, especially that great-lookin' ass Mrs. Hyde has."

"Doesn't Dr. Jekyll have a great ass too?"

"Of course, but Mrs. Hyde has this 'I'm going to fuck you to death' attitude, whereas Dr. Jekyll is more laid-back."

"Do all men think about sex as much as you do, Ben?"

"Probably. But we also think about sports too."

"Well, I'm just glad I'm a woman."

"I am too. I mean, I'm glad you're a woman."

"Thanks, Ben. I think I may go into work for a few hours now that I've gotten some rest."

"Go ahead. I have a contractor coming in to talk about the addition to the house."

Donna gets dressed and leaves for work.

I go into the house and start a rough sketch of the house addition. My thoughts are *I can enclose the carport and tie it into the house since the foundation is already there.* And building another carport or garage is no big deal. But like everything I do, I decide to add an extra bathroom and an office/library. I really do need a bigger office. Not that I do much in it other than surf the internet and work on this book. But it would be cool to have nonetheless. Donna and I have decided that the addition will be my project and the house redecoration will be her project. That way, we don't step on each other's toes. The way I look at it is, she can't make a log home look too frilly. Plus, she does have pretty good taste. I mean, she found me, didn't she? Don't answer that.

The phone rings; it's Meat.

"What's up you, bastard?"

"Not a damn thing. I don't have a case to do for several hours, so I thought I'd come over and hang out just to kill some time. Got any new movies?"

"Yeah, I picked up *16 Blocks*, the Bruce Willis movie, and *Kiss Kiss Bang Bang*. Both are action movies."

"Cool. I'll be right over."

For the past couple of years, Meat has been working as a pacemaker rep or a heart technician. I'm not sure exactly what his title is. I just know he sells pacemakers and defibrillators and assists the doctors when they put them in or, as he calls them, do a case. He's good at what he does and makes good money doing it. I couldn't do it simply because people die sometimes. I couldn't handle that part. But he does well with it and enjoys it.

I hear the basement door open. "Is that you, Meat?"

"Who else would it be?"

"Halle Berry or maybe Ashley Judd?"

"Yeah right! What have you been smoking?"

"Fuck you!"

"Yeah, you'd like to." I catch a whiff of fried chicken. "What's that smell?"

"Just a little KFC. I thought we'd need a snack watching television."

"That's what I like about you. You're always thinking."

"That's what I get paid to do! Whatcha doing? Working on the book?"

"Yeah. Hey, come here. I want you to read something that Donna wrote."

"What is it?"

"I let her read the book, and she said it was good but that I didn't know how to write a love scene."

"What did she write that was too short? Like it probably is."

"Kiss my ass, Jethro. You can't read it now."

"I don't want to read it anyway."

"Yes, you do."

"Okay, maybe I do. Move over."

Guys really are interested in sex. I know he would be anyway. As he starts reading, I could tell he is impressed.

"Donna really wrote that, didn't she?"

"Yeah, she did."

"Well, I could tell she wrote it because you would never have come up with that 'shards of crystal stardust' line. Plus, it's fucking good."

"And mine isn't?"

"I'm just saying hers is fucking hot. I didn't think you had that kind of ability in bed. I'm impressed." He reaches over, and we bang fists together. "Hell, that even got Mr. Ed stirring."

Yep, you got it. That's his pet name for his pecker.

"Well, I'm going over to the television. Adjust yourself and don't stick your hand in the bucket of chicken till I get mine out first." I go and load up the movie.

While I love watching movies on DVD, I hate all the coming attraction previews, and I also hate all that copyright-protection bullshit that they have before the movie comes on. Hell, everyone knows copying a movie is stealing. And you shouldn't buy or sell pirated movies. Enough already. Does Hollywood think their little scene before a movie starts is going to deter a criminal? I'm sure the criminals think it's funny. If you want to do something, throw their asses in prison and throw away the key. Just don't take fifteen minutes of my time with all your bullshit. I buy a movie to watch it, not watch previews or get a lesson in law. Do I believe the motion picture industry will take my advice? Hell no, but it feels good getting it off my chest.

"Meat, the movie is about to start."

Meat walks in and gets into his chair and grabs the bucket of KFC. "Hit it."

I have to admit Bruce Willis is one of my favorite actors. He may not be a great actor in a Shakespearean sense. And I think he would admit that he's no Laurence Olivier. But he knows what he does best, and that's action movies and thrillers. I can't ever remember being disappointed in one of his movies. And I've been a fan since *Moonlighting* came on television. My favorite episode was "Atomic Shakespeare," or their version of *Taming of the Shrew*. While the movie *16 Blocks* isn't as good as, say, the *Die Hard* movies, it's still pretty good. Of course, like most movies, they're predictable. But if you blow up enough automobiles and kill enough bad guys, that's okay.

After the movie ends, Meat gets up to leave. I have to get ready for Mr. Wilkinson too.

"Later, you lucky bastard."

I could tell Meat is still thinking about the sex scene. And maybe he is just a little envious too. I go outside to empty the skimmer in the pool and also to make sure no snakes are in it. Damn, I wish I hadn't seen that snake. I'll probably dream about it tonight.

And if you think I'm bad, let me tell you, Meat is ten times worse. Meat, another friend named Teddy, and I were fishing on Lake Harding one summer afternoon when a water moccasin swam right toward the boat. Teddy decided he'd pick it up. Why? Well, Teddy is crazy. And he was probably going to show off since he knew both Meat and I hated snakes. Meat warned him not to do so, but Teddy bent down to pick the snake up. Meat grabbed the boat oar and threatened to knock Teddy overboard if he brought that snake in the boat. What happened? I said Teddy was crazy, not stupid. He left the snake alone and handed us both a beer for upsetting us.

While I'm on the subject of snakes, I have to tell you a story about the pet blue jay I used to have. His name was Phil. Yeah, I named him after my boss because he was always around watching what I was doing when I'd be working outside. Phil made himself a pet. One day while I was out walking with the dogs, he flew down on the ground at my feet. I could tell he was a young male, less than a year old. And the dogs didn't seem to be scared of him at all. At that time, I had a bag of peanuts in my pocket that I was eating, so I tossed one in his direction. He hopped up to it and ate it. I started back to the house, and he followed. At that time, I didn't have the two outdoor cats that I have now. Anyway he flew down to the railing on my porch and sat there. He watched my every move as I watched him in total amazement. I realize this is supposed to be about snakes, and it will be, so bear with me. Realizing that blue jays are pretty mean birds, I was fascinated how tame he was. So I went in the house and got some raw peanuts, crackers, and bread and put them out for him, along with a bowl of water.

Well, after that, Phil started to hang around. He would fly down and land on my shoulder if I was working in the yard or fishing. If I was on the riding mower, he would perch on the steering wheel. In fact, whenever someone would pull up to the house, if the car window was open, he'd fly in and perch on the steering wheel. If the window was up, he'd perch on the side mirror. He even got so he would land on the door knocker and peck on the window when he wanted in the house. My friends were amazed. And to be honest, so was I.

One morning, when I let the dogs out to do their business, Sparky decided to take a milk bone treat outside with him. Phil flew down and snatched it from his mouth. He scared Sparky so bad that his head would pivot back and forth in a nervous panic whenever he had to go outside.

Well, one summer day, I heard Phil going crazy outside on the railing. I opened the door to see a large snake curled around the top of one of the rockers on the porch. I knew he wanted Phil for lunch. And Phil knew the snake wanted him for lunch, and he was going ballistic, jumping up and down, squawking like hell. So I walked out to the barn to get a brush ax. Phil followed. As I was walking back, I noticed Phil perched on the handle of the ax that I had over my shoulder. When I got back to the porch, Phil hopped back onto the railing far away from the snake. I took the ax and chopped the head off the snake. When Phil saw the head hit the porch, he flew down at the snake's head and started squawking at it, like he was telling the snake to take that shit. My ESP read his bird brain, and I swear he said "You done fucked with the wrong bird today, asshole." I swear I could read his mind and that's what he was saying.

Anyway it happened one more time that summer. Phil was squawking on the porch in a panic. I opened the door just in time to see a snake going into a box I keep on the porch that contains old work shoes. I gave him the ole thumbs-up, and we again gave the snake the guillotine treatment. I started to wonder if Phil would squawk because he was frightened or if he was warning me. I really think he was warning me.

Well, Phil hung around almost three years. I noticed he started coming less and less. When he did, he had a female with him. He'd take food from my hand and fly up to give it to her. She would then fly away. After a while, he stopped coming at all. I guess his mate gave him too much hell about being away from the nest all the time and about being out with his buddies instead of out working and putting food on the table. But now every time I see a male blue jay on the property, I like to think it's Phil. And who knows? It may just be.

I see a truck coming down the drive. I look at the time on my cell phone, and it's a little after five. It must be Mr. Wilkinson. A man in blue jean coveralls gets out.

Well, he looks like a Homer, I thought.

"Are you, Mr. Thompson?"

"Yes, I am. You must be Mr. Wilkinson."

"Yes, but everyone calls me Homer."

"Well then, you can call me Ben, Homer. Here's what I have in mind."

We walk over toward the carport. I tell him my plan for converting the carport into a room for Junior and how we can tie it into the house through the bathroom and use the additional space in between for my office.

He sees no problem with it and then suggests an architect who can draw up the plans. They need the plans to get the kit of logs ready. He also tells me they would have the logs up and the roof dried in, in less than two weeks after they start. I remember it only took a few weeks for the logs to be stacked on this house. The logs came in a flatbed tractor trailer.

What takes so long on a log home is the electrical and plumbing. So I agree to call the architect and get the ball rolling. About that time, Donna drives up.

"Homer, this is my wife, Donna. Donna, this is Homer, our contractor."

"Nice to meet you, Homer."

"Nice to meet you too, Mrs. Thompson."

With that, Donna walks into the house.

"You did purty good there, Ben."

Smiling, I say, "Yeah, I did."

Homer leaves, and I walk inside.

"What did he say, Ben?"

"He said I did purty good."

"What did he say about the addition?"

"I have to get an architect to draw up the plans then send them to the manufacturer to get the kit put together. He also said that it would take them a couple of weeks to put everything together."

"What kind of time frame are we looking at?"

"Probably about two to three months to completion. We'll have to make do till then. There'll also be a mess around here for a while once they start."

"That's not bad at all then."

"No, it isn't. How's it going with the painters and floor contractors?"

"I haven't really started looking for contractors, but I have made choices on colors and style of flooring."

"Great. Just make sure you get what you want. I don't want to redo it in a year or two."

"Aye, aye, Captain."

"Donna, I'm serious. I hate the smell of new paint. And the only reason I bring it up is, a friend of mine has a wife that paints everything once, if not twice, a year."

"Ben, I hate the smell of paint too, so don't worry. Did he really say you did purty good?"

"That was his exact words. What else would someone named Homer from the South say?"

"Well, that sweet man."

"Hey, what about me? I've worked myself to a frazzle today."

"Frazzle?"

"Hey, I'm from the South too. I mean, I just didn't fall off the turnip truck today, dear."

"Now you're just mocking the South."

"No, I'm not. I was hoping to hear I'm a sweet man too."

"Ben, you're better than sweet, you're delicious." She puts her arms around me. "That's what I'm talking about, Donna."

She whispers into my ear, "What's for dinner?"

"Whatever you want as long as we go out. I'm plumb tuckered out and don't feel like cooking."

"Well, my little hillbilly, we'll go out. Just let me change first."

I feed the dogs and sit and wait for Donna. Some of you Southerners may be mad I made fun of some of the Southern expressions. I didn't. I'm proud to be a Southern boy. I just used the expressions my grandmother used the most, the ones that used to make me smile. And just so you know, I grew up on turnip greens and black-eyed peas, country ham, and white gravy. Not only that, my father owned every Merle Haggard and George Jones 8-track tape available, while my mother listened to Conway Twitty and Loretta Lynn records. When I would go to the family cabin in the North Georgia Mountains as a boy with my parents, they would invite the local people over for a cookout. And after eating, they'd make music and drink moonshine. And some of those countryfolks made the Darling family on *The Andy Griffith Show* look like Rhodes scholars.

When I look back on those experiences though, I realize those were some of the best times I've ever had. I also realize it's not where you came from; it's where you go in life that's important. But it's also important you never forget where you came from. And I never will. While the South still gets looked down upon from the media, it's a great place to live and raise a family. While we can't take back some of its history, the intolerance toward our brothers and sisters of color or slavery, we can learn from it. Out of the intolerance came leaders like Martin Luther King and Rosa Parks, who opened not only our eyes here in the United States but also the world's that all men and women are truly created equal.

"Ben, I'm ready."

"Coming, dear!"

Speaking of country food, we decide to eat at the Cracker Barrel. I order fried steak that is smothered in white gravy. Donna orders the fried catfish fillets. I have to admit I don't eat much fish, seafood absolutely. Crab, shrimp, lobster—love it all. But most fish is, well, rather tasteless. And knowing a catfish will eat any dead, rotting shit doesn't help matters none. Having caught them and seeing what they look like, I'd almost as soon eat an armadillo—I said *almost*!

At dinner, the topic of conversation is the book. Why? I don't know. I sort of wish I hadn't let Donna read it so soon. When we get into the car to leave, we get into a discussion about my language.

"Ben, why do say *fuck* so much? You say it in the book, and you even say it around your friends. Don't you know some people find it offensive?"

"Donna, first off, I'd like to meet the first person who deemed the word *fuck* offensive. He was probably some pedophile priest or some other religious nutjob. Nowhere in the Bible does it say *fuck* is a naughty word. And to be honest, I don't find it offensive. I don't say it around people I don't know for the reason you mentioned, and I certainly don't say it around children. But I do think it's a great adjective. I mean, which makes the point better: 'He's an idiot' or 'He's a fucking idiot'? I rest my case."

"Well, would you say it around our son? And what would you do if you heard him say it?"

"Donna, those are hypothetical questions, but I'll answer them. First, no, I won't say it around him. But he's going to hear it, probably before he starts school. Second, if he says it, I'll sit his ass down and tell him that's a grown-up word and if he uses it again, I'll make him plow the back forty."

"Go ahead and make jokes about it."

"Donna, there are certain bridges we'll cross if and when we get there. We can't plan for everything. I know you want to, but we just can't."

She gives me a "you're not getting any tonight look" and sits back in her seat.

When we get back to the house, Donna walks outside with the dogs to watch them while they do their business. Since there are coyotes in the area, we always go out at night with the dogs. Donna is standing on the porch with her arms crossed, but I feel she's in another place. She has something on her mind that's bothering her. And it's my job to find out what it is. I walk outside and put my arms around her.

"Donna, what's really the matter? I know something is bothering you."

"Ben, I'm sorry about tonight. I guess I'm just afraid."

"Donna, you have nothing to be sorry for, nor do you have anything to fear."

"I'm just worried I won't be a good mother. I know you'll be a great father because you're such a down-to-earth person, but maybe in some way, I wish I hadn't gotten pregnant. It has turned our world upside down. I feel like I trapped you, and I can't let go of this guilt I have."

I turn Donna around to face me. I try to think of what to say to ease her mind. "That's bullshit, Donna, and you should know it. Yes, you trapped me that first day we met—not because you were pregnant then, but because I saw in you the perfect woman for me. I don't know what else I can say to erase whatever guilt you feel. But I will tell you right now that I feel like I've won the lottery. I am the luckiest man in the world. And that bullshit about not being a good mother is—excuse my language—fucking ridiculous. Yes, our world has changed forever, but it is for the best. And the sooner you realize that, the better you'll feel. And since you are carrying our child and he can feel your emotions, I suggest you get your shit together, if not for yourself, then for him."

"I love you, Ben."

"You better because you're fucking stuck with me, at least in this lifetime."

"I even like hearing you say *fucking*."

"I told you that it's a great adjective, didn't I? It's also erotic, isn't it? All right, you little bastards, hurry up. The mosquitoes are biting my ass."

The dogs all trot toward the porch.

"Damn, I hope Junior minds that well, Donna."

"He won't! He'll be stubborn just like his daddy."

"Well, he'll get taken to the woodshed then."

"No, he won't. You know you'll never spank him."

"But I will take his Xbox away."

About that time, he kicked.

"Ben, I think Junior is tired of us talking about him and wants us to stop."

I put my arm around Donna, and we walk back inside. I smile, thinking that the kid will probably be a chip off the old block. I just hope he doesn't get sent to the principal's office his first day of school like I did. I guess I'd better plan for the worst. We get back inside and stretch out with our fur family.

"Ben, do you think the dogs will accept Junior?"

"If they don't, we'll have to put Junior up for adoption."

"Ben!"

"Just kidding, dear. I'm sure everything will work out fine."

The phone rings.

"Hello, Coach Ben." It is the voice of Bryan.

"Hello, Bryan. How are you doing?"

"Okay, I guess."

After a long pause, I realize something is on his mind. "What can I do for you, Bryan?"

"Coach Ben, I was... I was wondering if I could come back on the team. I know you filled my spot already, but I just want to be back on the team. If I don't get to play, that's okay, I understand, because I was the knucklehead who made the decision to leave."

I could tell he is choked up. And it is probably all he could do to call.

"Bryan, if you come back, the guys may give you a hard time, at least for a while. And you're right. You won't get as much playing time as before. But yes, you can come back."

"Thanks, Coach Ben. I won't let you down again. I promise."

"I know, Bryan, I know."

With that, we hang up.

I go back and sit down beside Donna.

"Who was that?"

"Bryan."

"Isn't he the guy who quit to go play with another team? And you let him back on the team without talking to the guys first?"

"Yep!"

"Are you crazy?"

"Yep!"

"Would you stop saying yep and tell me what you think? Won't the guys resent him?"

"Donna, the softball team isn't a democracy. I am—well, was—the coach, and I am still the sponsor and the leader. It's my decision and mine alone. I will tell the guys if they have a problem with it, they can leave."

"I just think you're asking for unnecessary trouble."

"Donna, I always knew Bryan would come back. I never even took him off the roster."

"How did you know?"

"Just a gut feeling. I was that young once. And I made some dumb decisions. Bryan just got caught up in that old 'grass is greener on the other side' shit. He knows now it isn't. The guys will eventually understand."

"Well, if you think so."

"I know so!"

I decide to call the guys tonight so they can hear it from my mouth. I call Mark first. "Hello."

"Mark, this is Ben. I just wanted you to know I let Bryan back on the team."

"What the hell for? He left us to go play for Roscoe's, and we've already replaced him."

"Mark, Bryan is young and foolish."

"And your point is?"

"Well, that he got caught up in something he wasn't ready for. I think we can ease him back into some playing time. We just won't let him start right away. It will give us a bench so we can rest some guys. It's hard to play three or four games in a row in this heat without rest anyway."

"Ben, I can live with it, but I don't like it. And Meat will go through the roof when you tell him."

"I can handle Meat."

"Well, good luck. You're gonna need it."

"Thanks, Mark. Talk to you later."

With that, we hang up. One down and a team to go.

I'd better call Meat. Mark is right; he may be a tough sell. I dial his number.

"What the hell were you thinking about?"

"Hello to you too."

"You're a dumb bastard for letting Bryan back on the team."

"How the hell did you find out so soon?"

"Kroy called me. And he's as pissed as I am."

Bryan must have called Kroy since they're brothers, I thought. "Will you calm down?"

"No! Not until you can give me a reason for letting that turncoat back on the team. That's just fucking bullshit."

"Are you finished yet?"

"No, I'm not."

"Well, when you finish, I'll tell you why."

"You can't possibly have a good answer unless you claim temporary insanity. Did you get hit on the head by something falling from the sky? You know this is going to fuck up the team chemistry. You're going to have guys talking about it with one another. Guys will be choosing sides. It's going to be hell."

"Meat, would you just listen to yourself? You are acting like you're seven years old. How fucking old are you?"

"You know how old I am. I'm thirty-six."

"How old is Bryan?"

"I think he's about twenty-one. Why?"

"Did you not ever do anything stupid when you were twenty-one?"

"That's beside the point."

"No, dipshit, that's exactly the point. Bryan made a mistake. He realized the mistake and apologized for it. You're acting like he gave up government secrets or something. This isn't real life. It's men's slow-pitch softball. It's a fucking game that allows grown men to act like boys and have fun. But it's time for you and everyone else to realize I make the decisions who's on the team. And Bryan is back on the team. I don't want to hear anything else about it. You're my best friend and should give me the benefit of the doubt."

"Sorry! You're right. I'll live with it."

"Thanks then. Just stand by my decision and stand with me on it."

"All right, bro."

"I'll make some calls too."

"Thanks!"

With that, I hang up the phone. *That went well*, I think.

"I take it Bill wasn't happy with your decision?"

"No, he wasn't. But, Donna, you can't let the inmates run the asylum. I'm sure they'll talk behind my back till they get over it."

"Ben, you barely know Bryan. Why stick out your neck with the team for him? Are you trying to prove a point?"

"Maybe, maybe not. I did stupid things when I was at his age. I had someone to kick me in the ass but who also stuck by me. So I feel the need to return the favor."

"You're talking about Phil?"

"Yeah, him and my father too. I didn't realize till after my father died everything he had to deal with. Alcohol was his means to escape. We had some great talks at the cabin after I had grown up. I mean, the man raised a boatload of kids. And my parents didn't have a lot of money, so it was tough on him, I'm sure. He was harsh at times, but in his way, he loved us very much. Phil had an edge too. But once you got to know him, he was a kind and gentle man. He taught me a lot. He saw something in me that I didn't know existed. But more importantly, he made me see it. He also gave me several chances when I'd fuck up. That's why it's important for me to give Bryan a second chance."

"Well, darling, that's why I love you."

"You mean, it's not because of my sexual prowess?"

"Darling, I wrote the scene in your book, didn't I? That was true. But I love you not for your ability to give me orgasms but because underneath all that external macho crap lies a sweet, loving man."

"Don't ever say that shit in public, Donna. It'll ruin my image. I like being known as a jerk."

"Ben, no one thinks you're a jerk."

"Sure, they do. How about the Jehovah's Witnesses who saw me naked that day?"

"Well, they may, but they probably just think you were upset at having a small pecker."

"Hey, that's below the belt." I stand up and drop my pants. "That's not small. And it's not even hard."

"No, that's actually impressive, but the cold water made it shrink. I saw it after our swim, and it looked a wee bit small."

"That does it. I'm getting a heating system for the pool."

"Darling, I'm kidding. You know I can't take all of it now."

"Don't placate me."

"I'm not, darling. Jeez, what is it about guys and their penis sizes?"

"Yeah, well, it's the same with women and breast size."

"What about breast size? You don't like mine?"

"I love yours. I'd probably divorce you if you wanted implants."

"So what's the point?"

"Look at how many women get them that don't need them, how many millions, if not billions, are spent for bigger tits. A guy simply can't get a balloon filled with water shoved inside his dick to make it bigger and longer. We're stuck with whatever God gives us."

"That's not true. I read there's a surgery to make the penis longer."

"Donna, no man in his right mind would let someone cut on his dick. The few who do probably really do need it."

"So you're saying both men and women have insecurities?"

"That's exactly what I'm saying!"

"You could have just said that and not gone on a tangent about tits and peckers."

"Say that again?"

"Say what, Ben?"

"Tits and peckers! It just sounds sexy the way you say it."

"Mister, you have a one-track mind."

"Donna, we should still be in the honeymoon phase of our relationship. I mean, we could be on a cruise right now rocking the boat. But we're just two old farts sitting around, talking about the good old days."

"The good old days was this morning. And I'm still sensitive down there."

"Down where?"

"Down there."

"You have to say the word."

"My vagina is still sensitive."

"That's not the word I'm looking for. Cover your ears, Junior. Mama's gonna say a naughty word."

"Ben, I'm not going to say it."

"You say it, or I'm going to tickle your feet till you do."

"You wouldn't!"

"Oh, wouldn't I?"

"You tickle my feet, I'll probably piss my pants."

"That's even better." I take off her shoe.

"I'm going to start tickling on the count of three. One... Two..."

"Okay, my pussy is still sensitive. It still tingles from making love this morning."

"Bingo! We have a winner. See? That didn't hurt a bit."

"You guys and your profanity."

"*Pussy* is an erotic word and not profanity."

"I guess you think *twat* and *cunt* are also cute little words."

"Yeah, I do. I think "hot little twat" and "cute little cunt" are both great words used correctly. *Vagina*, on the other hand, sounds ugly. I could never tell you I wanted to eat your vagina. That sounds like an organ, sort of like a pancreas. But I could tell you I want to kiss your cute little cunt or lick your hot twat without a problem."

"And *pussy*?"

"That's the crème de la crème. That's like a dessert. I could definitely eat your pussy."

"The way you say it almost makes sense."

"Thanks! I think... Let's turn in."

"Do I hear a kitty purring?"

"No, that's your country fried steak talking."

Morning arrives. I awake to the sound of rain on the metal roof. The sound of rain is so soothing. But this rain may just turn out to be a hindrance for me today because I need to meet with the architect and get him started. Luckily, I've kept the old blueprints of the house, so that should give him a head start. I'll also take some pictures of the carport at all the different angles if it stops raining.

I hear the blow-dryer going in the bathroom. Damn, Donna does mornings better than I do. I get up and stretch.

"Okay, boys, go pee on the car tires."

My dogs hate rain. When it's raining and they need to do their business, they go outside and piss or shit on the carport, which is okay with me. I keep a small shovel on the carport just for that reason, because nothing smells as bad as a wet dog—well, except maybe a yeast infection. But that's a whole different ball game.

I go in the bathroom and brush my teeth. I don't think I have mentioned this before in the book, and I'm sure some of you ladies are dying to know about this, so I'll tell you. I sleep in the nude. I can't stand anything between me and the sheets. Donna, on the other hand, sleeps in a nightgown. I just can't stand the thought of my underwear getting in the crack of my ass. The fact is, I have been sleeping nude ever since my brother got married and left home. It just made masturbating and scratching my balls easier. I think I still shock Donna sometimes when I get up naked in the mornings. Of course, once Junior arrives, I'll have to be more careful about my nudity. I'd hate to warp his psyche. I finish brushing my teeth and turn the shower on.

"Donna, will you let the dogs back in, please?"

"Yeah, I'll do it now."

I take my morning wake-up shower, which usually lasts fifteen minutes or until the hot water runs out. I step out to dry off as Donna is putting the finishing touches of her makeup on.

"Damn," I say.

"What's the matter, Ben?"

"I'm getting old, that's what's the matter."

"Why do you say that?"

"I'm getting gray pubic hair. I wonder if they make Just for Men for the privates like they do for mustaches and beards."

"Ben, don't ever say anything about me being vain again."

"Well, just look at all the white hair down there. My dick almost looks like Santa's beard."

"What do you want me to do about it?"

"Well, you could start by looking."

"Jeez! Yes, you're getting gray pubic hair—big deal. You know the hair on your head has a lot of gray in it too."

"Yeah, but that makes me look distinguished. Gray pubic hair makes me look old."

"Well then, just shave it all off like I do. No one will know you have a bald Happy Herman. You don't go to a gym where other guys see your penis."

"True, but then it would look like a bald-headed rat when it's limp. Plus, who knows? I might be in an accident where the paramedics might have to take off my pants and underwear to stop bleeding or something. They might think I'm a weirdo or something if there's no pubic hair."

"Suit yourself, but if you asked me, it would make it look bigger. Plus, you already shave your testicles."

"You really think so?"

"Do whatever makes you feel good, sweetie. I've got to run or I'll be late for work."

"Donna, remember, tonight we're going over to the Whatleys for a cookout. And be careful driving. It's pouring outside."

To be honest, when it rains and I have to drive in it, I always remember that that's how Jimmy died. I don't dwell on his death; I certainly hope not at least. But by remembering it, I think I'm reminded to drive a little more safely.

The rain lets up, and I take a few photos that I download and print off on the computer. I also take some photos of the house that I had taken last spring so he could get an idea of the layout.

I feed the dogs, and I'm off to the architect's office. The architect is named Leonard Chapman. I arrive, and he takes me back into his office. He has little model buildings scattered around his office. I realize they're not toys but scale model of houses and office buildings he's designed. Some are actually quite interesting. We spread out the blueprints and go over all the details. He sees no problem with the addition. Actually, I think he is disappointed how easy it is going to be. He tells me he would have something for me to look at by the end of next week, which pleases me.

I leave and go back home, stopping off only to buy beer for Whatley's party. I get back home with nothing to do, so I put with the book and surf the internet.

Donna calls around noon and informs me she called my mother and found her perfectly charming. I guess my mother didn't call her a slut then.

My first thought is *Yeah, charming like a cobra.*

But my mother has agreed to help her with the yard sell and is eager to meet her. The thought of the two of them together scares the living shit out of me. I had written "the living crap out of me" first since Donna thinks I use too much profanity. But that sounded stupid, so I changed it to "living shit." I think you'll agree that sounds better. So much for trying not to be vulgar.

I'm sure my mother will tell Donna all the "when Benny was a little boy" stories. And I'm sure she'll tell her about all my ex-girlfriends, all of whom she hated. They really weren't sluts. They just liked sex—a lot! This moved them to the front of my class when it came to dating. I'm not ashamed to say that my dick dictated whom I went out with when I was in high school. And even the Bible says it's better to cast your seed in the belly of a whore than on the ground or something to that effect. So I tried to follow that directive. Of course, I always used a condom. So I actually never planted the seed, but boy, did I cast out a lot. Okay, enough on that. Time to get the beer iced down for tonight's party.

Donna arrives home promptly at five. She then begins her makeover process, which starts with a shower then the whole hair-and-makeup routine. I'm all ready to go, so I know I'll be in for a wait. I guess that after a while, guys just learn to be patient waiting on women. I am still finding that out.

I'm just thankful I have video games. Even in my forties, a lot of my friends and I play games on the Xbox. In fact, I still play on a 360 system. When we have a group of guys, we play *Halo*. When I'm by myself, I always play one of the war games, of which there are many. I can fly a bomber on one game or I can be a navy SEAL. It's not much different from when I was a kid playing army with my plastic soldiers by the creek.

After high school, I thought about joining the navy or air force. I scored well on the military test, and I was recruited by all four branches of the armed services. I chose to go to college, which, for me, was the right thing to do. If you haven't guessed yet, I don't take orders well. I was pretty sure I would probably get in trouble by punching some sergeant in the mouth. Watching *An Officer and a Gentleman* and *Stripes* actually persuaded me against joining. Sergeant Hulka in *Stripes* was such a jerk, and even though it was a comedy, I could still imagine that was what most sergeants were like.

But men and women who do serve in the armed forces deserve our greatest respect. It takes someone special to put their lives in danger just so we can maintain our freedom. The soldiers, along with police officers and firemen, don't get enough credit for what they do. You only hear about them when a tragedy strikes, like 9/11, or when they do something wrong like the Rodney King beating. But most are loyal, law-abiding servants to our country. And if you ever see one on the street or in the grocery store, you should thank them for their work and dedication. I'm sure they'd love to hear that. I try to always make it a point to say thanks.

After an hour and a half, Donna is ready. We get to the Whatleys about a quarter till seven. Todd and Holly are already there, as are Rusti and Mark. The Monster already has the grill fired up out back. I go outside where the guys are watching Whatley cook and drinking beer. Of course, I have my own cooler in hand. I can actually drink all I want tonight since I have a designated driver in Donna. That's one good thing about a pregnant wife. She can't have alcohol. Whatley and Todd both question why I let Bryan back on the team. They accept the fact it was my decision. However, I don't think they were necessarily thrilled with it though.

Since Whatley joined the team late, I don't think he really cared one way or the other. But he picks on me about it. One by one, the other guys show. Some, with their wives; others, with their girlfriends. Whatley has three dogs that stay in the house. But since there will be a lot of visitors, they put them outside in a fenced-in kennel area of the yard. Their backyard is also fenced. One is a golden retriever puppy, and the other two are Brittanys. They start to raise hell, so Todd asks if he can let them out to run around in the yard. Whatley agrees to it. He is hesitant to because after the rain, he doesn't want them to track mud or dirt in the house. So we have to watch the door in case someone comes out so the dogs wouldn't run inside tracking dirt. The dogs stay with us on the patio and even start retrieving an old tennis ball we throw.

Well, the beer starts taking its toll on my kidneys, and I need to take a leak.

"Whatley, where's your bathroom? I need to take a leak."

"Just go around the side of the house. There's a rock garden with nothing planted in it. I piss there all the time. If you go inside, the dogs may slip in."

Well, that actually makes sense. God knows I don't want Denise pissed at me for letting the dogs inside, so I go around the side of the house and turn Mr. Happy loose. Just as I get well into my pissing mode, the golden retriever puppy runs between my legs and gets a stream of piss on its head and back before I can pinch the flow off. It doesn't seem to bother him too much. Well, I walk around and tell Whatley his dog ran between my legs and got a little piss on his back. Whatley hands me the water hose, and I spray him off. Well then, Holly walks out a few minutes later, and of course, the dog wants some attention. She bends down to pet him and notices the dog is wet.

"Did it rain again?"

Todd says, "No, Ben, pissed on the dog."

"Ben, that's sick, and it's on my hands."

Well before we could explain, we hosed the dog off, and Denise comes out.

Holly says, "Ben pissed on your dog."

"You pissed on my dog?"

"It was an accident! Tom told me to piss around the corner of the house because he was afraid the dog might slip in and track dirt in. Then the dog ran between my legs from behind before I could stop the piss."

"Tom Whatley, you stupid idiot. Don't you know that's what bathrooms are for?"

"Hey, he pissed on the dog, not me."

Then Holly tells Todd, "Why didn't you tell me before I petted the dog?"

Of course, Donna walks out to see what all the commotion is about.

"Ben, how could you piss on her dog?"

"It was an accident."

Finally, Mark whistles and says, "We washed the dog off before Holly petted it. She only got water on her hands."

About that time, Meat and Julie show up. "What did we miss?"

"Bad question, bro."

"Ben pissed on my dog."

Meat gives me a "what the fuck" look.

And I shrug my shoulders.

"Did the dog consent to the golden shower? That must be some freaky dog you have, Denise."

Denise punches Meat in the arm.

"What was that for? I wasn't the one who pissed on your dog, he did." He points at me. "That's for being an insensitive jerk."

The ladies storm off inside.

Whatley looks around and says, "Well, that went well, don't you think? Looks like none of us will be getting any anytime soon."

"True."

What happened after that? Well, we did what most red-blooded males would do: we drank ourselves into a stupor. Hell, if the wives were pissed anyway, we might as well take advantage of it. I mean, how much more can they get pissed than they already are? Honestly, after a while, the wives settled down. After all, we had all the food outside with us. So if there's a moral to this story, this is it: it's better to be pissed off than pissed on, because if you get pissed on, the shit will really hit the fan.

In the car on the drive home, Donna questions me on the incident.

"Ben, what happened back there?"

"Donna, it was just as I said. I asked Whatley where the bathroom was, and he told me to go around the corner. I never saw the dog till he got pissed on."

"What is it with men and peeing outside?"

"It's actually no big deal, really. At least we're housebroken. Besides, we can pee standing up, and we don't even have to hike our legs."

"Well, Denise was pissed." She laughs when she saw the irony in her statement.

"Well, I'm sorry sometimes shit happens."

"Well, I'm sure Tom will catch hell tonight."

"I'm sure he will. But that's the trade-off when you marry a beautiful woman."

"What's the trade-off?"

"Most women have a built-in bitch factor. Beautiful women have more of it than an ugly woman."

"Do I have it, Ben?"

"I said most women, not you. You're just a little weird."

"Weird in what way?"

"Darling, I love you, but don't you think the fact you peel grapes makes you just a little weird?"

"No! The skin upsets my stomach. Besides, you're the one who's really weird."

"I never said I wasn't."

"Oh, so you mean you don't mind being called weird?"

"No, I'd prefer the word *different*. But you can call me anything you want to."

"Why?"

"Because I love you. And I admit I'm a little out there."

"I guess I love you too, even if you have a dog that eats poop and you like to piss on dogs."

"Thanks, dear. That's the nicest thing you've ever said to me."

"You're welcome!"

We get home and turn in for the evening. Just another boring day in my life, and I wouldn't trade it for anything. Well, I guess you've noticed by now that I live a less-than-perfect life. And by no means is our life ordinary.

Next weekend, we have a tournament in Ashton, and my mother is coming to visit to help with the yard sell. The sad thing about it is, I'm more concerned about the yard sell. I will go to the tournament just to monitor how the team accepts Bryan back. At least that will be my excuse to Donna. I really don't want to be a referee at the yard sell. I would just as soon give the junk to Goodwill than to try to make a few hundred dollars.

Before you flea-market, yard-sale junkies get your panties au gratin, let me explain. Yes, you may find a bargain or two from time to time. Hell, back in the seventies, I hit the mother lode of baseball cards at a yard sell my mother dragged me to. But for the most part, they had nothing but junk: old clothes, junky furniture. And in the last flea market I went to, a guy had an old 8-track tape player and a boxful of 8-track tapes. Nothing but pure junk! So okay, yeah, I bought the Styx's *Pieces of Eight* and the

Foghat's *Fool for the City* tape for a dollar apiece. But that was for nostalgia's sake. And I even found a second-year *GI Joe*, but hell, I collected those.

The six-pack of Billy Beer I bought would be an interesting item for the bar in the basement, because I really liked Billy Carter. He was a true man's man. In fact, he should have been elected president instead of Jimmy. Jimmy was an idiot—still is, in fact. The point I'm trying to make is, I almost got sucked into buying a bunch of junk I didn't need.

One rather large woman almost talked me into buying a lava light. Yes, I already had one and didn't need another, even though it was only three dollars and a great deal. I had the balls to say no even though it might have looked good in Junior's room when it's finished.

However, some people get roped in buying stuff they don't need. They fall prey to a half-assed sales pitch from someone named Clyde. Then what happens? They have a yard sell to get rid of it. It's a never-ending circle of sheer stupidity, and I refuse to take part. I hope this lesson will give you all the strength to just say no.

Saturday morning, and I have nothing to do except watch baseball with the Meatster. Donna is getting ready to go furniture shopping with Julie. I go downstairs with the munchies for the day. I decide to call Whatley and make sure Denise doesn't give him the Lorena Bobbitt treatment. I don't dare call him at home because, honestly, I am afraid to talk to Denise, so I call his cell instead. Yes, I'm scared of her.

He answers.

"What's up, Whatley?"

"Not my dick, that's for damn sure. I think Denise put a No Trespassing sign on her poo nanny."

"Ouch! Sorry, dude. Anything I can do?"

"I think you did enough." Then he starts laughing.

"I've pissed on that dumb little bastard before, so don't worry about it. Denise took them all to be bathed."

"Well, I don't mind paying for it."

"Fuck it! What have you got going on, Ben?"

"Meat is coming over to watch a ball game while Julie and Donna go furniture shopping."

"Damn, that sounds like a blast."

"Well, you're welcome to join us. Hell, Denise may want to go furniture shopping with the girls."

"I'll ask her when she gets back."

"No way. You ask her, she won't do it. I'll get Donna to invite her. She may go for that."

"Damn, Ben, you're brilliant."

"That's what I get paid for. Give me a shout back after Denise hears from Donna."

"Will do!"

I go upstairs and ask Donna if she minds calling Denise to see if she'll go with her. I tell her she may be able to smooth things out for me. She happily agrees and calls Joann's cell. They talk for a few minutes, and Donna gives me the thumbs-up. Now I only have to wait for Whatley's call. I go back downstairs. After getting dressed, Donna comes downstairs. It's really the first time she's ever seen what we guys like to call paradise. I think she may have seen it before, but this is her first as my wife.

"So this is the He-Man Woman-Haters Clubhouse?"

"More or less, except we do love us some women."

"Yeah, I can tell with the *Playboys* and *Penthouses* all over the floor."

"Tom and Denise are on their way over."

"Ben, are you sure you want me to buy new furniture?"

"Sure. Your stuff is too frilly for a log home, and mine has twelve years of puppy dog abuse."

"And you trust me to pick it out?"

"Absolutely! But just remember, we have dogs and a newborn on the way, so it should be easy to clean."

Donna surveys the room. "Did you know you have two autographed books by Anne Rice?"

"Yes."

"They're the same book?"

"I know. She was in Atlanta, and she doesn't travel there often, so I bought two."

"What the heck for?"

"I might trade one for something or maybe give one as a gift."

"You want to donate one for the yard sell?"

"Donna, everything down here is here for a reason. Some things are collectibles and may appear to be junk. Others are just junk that I collect."

"Like that?" She points to an inflatable love doll that had gone flat. It had a hole in it when we opened it.

"That was a gift from the softball team. It's just for amusement. You want it for your yard sell?"

"Are you kidding me? I can just imagine your mother selling it to some hobo-looking man."

"Hey, hobos need lovin' too! But that would be too funny."

"What about all those CDs and DVDs?"

"Sorry, dear, I'm keeping them."

"There must be over a thousand of each."

"Actually, a little over eighteen hundred DVDs and twelve hundred CDs. Donna, you have to remember, this is a sacred place for me."

"I know, I know. Actually, it is kind of cute and cozy."

"See? You're starting to feel its magic."

"No, it's the stale air down here. You know you could use some air freshener."

"We have some Lysol in the bathroom we spray when someone drops a bomb."

About that time, Meat walks in. He sees Donna. He starts making all these jesters like a third-base coach, pulling on his ear, patting himself on the chest, and ends up grabbing his ball.

Donna seems amused and asks, "What the hell was all that about?"

"To ward off evil spirits. Wives aren't allowed in the temple. Girlfriends are okay, but not wives. It'll curse the chi in here."

"Dave, you make about as much sense as Ben does."

We reach over and bang knuckles.

"Dave, is Julie here?"

"Yeah, she is upstairs."

"Well, I'll go up there and wait for Denise with her. God, I hope Lacy doesn't grow up to be like you because you guys are so childish."

With that, she walks up the stairs.

"Women!"

"Yep!"

After a few minutes, Whatley comes strolling in.

"What's up, Ben and Meat, you big dumb bastard?"

"You keep talking to me like that, and I'll cut off whatever balls Denise left."

"What are you talking about, Meat? We had sex this morning."

"Yeah, you and your right hand."

"No, I used my left. It was like getting some strange."

226

We all laugh, knowing he is probably serious.

"Well, Ben, how does it feel to be married?"

"The same way it felt being single. I mean, hell, I haven't changed any."

Whatley looks at Meat and says, "He just doesn't know, does he?"

Meat shakes his head.

"Doesn't know what?"

"How once you're married, the wife slowly tightens the collar around your neck. The next thing you know, you're on a choke leash, and you have her name branded on your ass, at least until you're divorced."

"That's bullshit!"

"All right. Just remember, the Monster warned you."

Meat looks at me and says, "He's right, Ben."

"I know I'm right. Ben will just have to find out the hard way. It'll start out on a Saturday when you have plans fishing, playing softball, something you enjoy. Then the old lady will say 'I need you to stay home and fix the irrigation' or some other bullshit problem. Next thing you know, your balls are in a jar in the nightstand right beside her dildo. It'll be such a slow progression you won't notice it till *boom!* You wake up and you don't know yourself anymore. You'll be a shell of your former self."

Meat nods.

"He's right, Ben!"

"Will you stop agreeing with every fucking thing he says? First, Donna isn't like that."

"I've heard that shit before, Ben. All newly married men say that when they first get married."

"Well, she isn't like that. First, she loves sex, and second, she respects me."

Meat looks over at Whatley and says, "She does love sex."

"How the fuck do you know?"

"Let him read it, Ben"

I take Whatley over to the computer and let him read Donna's sex scene. Whatley starts to read it. Every once in a while, he looks over at me.

When he finishes, he turns and says, "Ben, that's some hot shit. I would have never guessed that Donna was a freak. I'm fucking impressed! And I don't get impressed often. If I were you, I'd just gift wrap my balls and say 'Here. Take them! They're yours.' Did she really write that?"

"Yep."

"You're the fucking man."

"Yes, I am."

We go sit down and watch the game of the week, the Yankees versus the Red Sox, and proceed to drink masses amounts of beer.

After about three hours, the phone rings; it's Donna.

"Ben, are you guys hungry?"

"As a matter of fact, we are getting hungry."

"Well, we'll pick up some pizzas and bring them home. Need anything else?"

"Yeah, I think we need some more beer, if you don't mind."

"No problem. We'll be there shortly. Love you, Ben."

"I love you too."

The guys have overheard the conversation.

Meat looks at me at says, "Where do I sign up?"

"For what?"

"The course on wife-obedience training. I need to learn how to train women like that."

"No training is required. You just have to know how to treat them."

"How's that?"

"With respect."

"Then you're pussy whipped!"

"Yeah, maybe, but the pussy is good, and she brings beer."

"Bastard!"

We hear the dogs barking and look out the window to see the girls getting out of the car.

"Here's how you do it." I walk outside and go to meet the girls.

"Need any help, ladies?"

"Thank you! That's so sweet, Ben! The beer is in the trunk" comes from Donna.

I open the trunk and start helping unload. I glance over to Meat and Whatley and yell, "Don't just fucking stand there! Give the girls a hand!"

Meat gives me his famous "I hate you, you bastard" look.

We all go inside and start eating the pizzas.

I start out the conversation with "Donna, did you find any furniture you liked?"

"I found a living room suite I really liked, but it was a bit pricey, so I didn't buy it."

"If you liked it, you should have bought it."

"Well, I wanted you to see it first."

I look at Meat and Whatley, and they're shaking their heads. I can only imagine it was from hearing Donna being so considerate and waiting for me to be with her to buy it.

"Honey, after we eat, call and tell them you want it. Consider it one of our wedding presents to each other."

"Are you sure?"

"Yes, I'm sure."

Denise looks over at me. She hasn't spoken to me since she bitched me out for pissing on her dog. "Ben, even though you used my dog for a urinal, you're all right."

"Whew!"

We finish up eating the pizza, and the girls decide to go back and buy the furniture instead of just calling them and giving a credit card number over the phone like I would have. But that is okay with us. It just means more time for us to drink beer.

Whatley, Meat, and I go back downstairs.

"I hate you, Ben. I mean, I really fucking hate you."

"Why? Whatley."

"You have raised the fucking bar so high that we'll never meet expectations now."

"Well, it's not like you were meeting them before."

"Yeah, but the women didn't know Mr. Perfect existed. Jeez, you're such a kiss ass."

"Like I told you, bastards, I let Donna do her thing, and she lets me do mine. That's why my balls will never be in her nightstand drawer beside her dildos. In fact, she'll never need a dildo either. Besides, look at it this way. It doesn't matter if you're married or single. You're always going to be spending money on a woman. And if you're single, you're going to spend money on either your date or a hooker. That can be dangerous. I figure I have the best of both worlds. Donna is loving and considerate, and she almost fucks me to death. What more is there to be found in a woman?"

"What you're saying is, we're going to pay for it one way or the other, so we might as well let them have all the money and they'll give us more pussy?"-

"Well, within reason. I know Donna is conservative with money. Plus, I trust her. Call Denise and tell her to see if there is anything she wants at the furniture store. I guarantee you'll get some poo nanny tonight regardless of whether she buys anything or not."

"What if she buys out the store?"

"Then that's your fault, not mine. I'm just saying women want to be trusted."

Whatley pulls out his cell phone and calls Denise.

"Hello."

"Denise, while you're out shopping, see if there's anything we need for the house."

"Really?"

Whatley looks at me. "Yeah, really." He hangs up the phone.

"This shit better work."

Meat has been too damn quiet. I know he has something to say. He finally speaks up.

"You guys disgust me. I'm glad I'm divorced now."

"Both of you are so fucking whipped it ain't funny."

"How's that Jiffy Lube?"

"Jiffy Lube? What's up with that?"

"Hell, you have so much grease on your hands all the time you might as well work at a Jiffy Lube."

"Funny, Ben."

"I'm serious, Meat. If you were smart, you'd do whatever you needed to, to hang on to Julie before she dumps you for someone better."

"Dumps me for someone better? You've got to be kidding. She knows I'm the real deal."

"Look at yourself, Meat. You're no George Clooney."

"Fuck you. I've been divorced less than a year, and I'm going to savor all I can before I get married again. And that's if I do."

"I'm not saying to get married, at least right away. But let her know you care."

"Why is it all you married guys want their single friends to get married? Is it so they'll have someone to be miserable with?"

Whatley chimes in with a yep.

"I'm just saying, do something special for her, like buy her earrings or take her on a long weekend trip, just you and her."

Whatley chimes in, "Ben, you sound like Dr. Phil. Do us both a favor and hand us a beer and shut the hell up."

The two of them bang fists together, and I shut the hell up. Calling me Dr. Phil was a low blow. We turn on ESPN and kick back till the girls come home.

———

When the girls get back, Donna is excited to show me the living room suite and kitchen table she bought. She has taken a picture with her cell phone. I'm still amazed at what all you can do with a cell phone. It probably won't be long before they'll come equipped with a dildo or pocket pussy.

Denise informs What that she bought two new lamps for their bedroom nightstands. She even gives him a hug and kiss. As the Whatleys leave, he gives me a thumbs-up. I guess he may even get to sleep back in his bed tonight. Julie and Meat leave as well.

"Drive carefully, Julie! Take care of Jiffy Lube."

She looks over at Meat, and he replies, "Don't ask."

Donna and I walk back inside.

"Well, dear, do you feel better?"

"Yeah, the girls were a lot of fun. How did it go with the guys?"

"Pretty much the same ole shit."

"Ben, they are supposed to deliver the furniture Monday. Is that okay?"

"Yeah, I'll try to make a deal with them when they come out with the new furniture and see if they'll drop the old suit off in your old garage for the yard sell.

"When will you be driving up to pick up your mother?"

"I'll probably leave Friday morning around ten. That way, I can miss the rush hour traffic both ways."

"That's a good idea, Ben."

"That's all I know, dear."

"Ben, if I didn't know you better, I'd say you were a narcissist."

"Well, Donna, we should love ourselves. And I do. But I would never sit around and look at myself in a pool of water."

"Why not?"

"Because a mirror gives you a much-clearer image."

"What do you see when you look in a mirror?"

"One lucky son of a bitch."

"Really! Tell me why?"

"Well, I'm healthy, wealthy, and wise. What else is there?"

"Anything else, O great one?"

"Well, of course, I also have you, Junior, and the dogs who love me."

"Well, you know, Ben, I just happened to settle for you. It's not like I couldn't have done better."

"Is that a fact?"

"Yeah, who knows, Tom Cruise may be available in a couple of years."

"Well, Donna, after the book is published, I'm sure I'll have all the actresses in Hollywood beating down my door. Who knows, Halle Berry may want my special attention."

"Attention! That's all you would get—if that."

"Maybe, maybe not. I have a particular sex scene that you wrote that I can use as a sexual recommendation."

"Ben, you're the one who told me the book was fiction, so that's what I wrote."

"Fiction? Is this fiction?" I pull her close and kiss her neck. And then I flick my tongue across her ear.

She pushes me back. "Stop that! You know it drives me crazy."

Our eyes meet as I smile. "I rest my case."

I guess you can say I finally beat her at her own game. Let's go in.

The thought of my mother coming down to visit is scary. I know Donna can handle her, but I don't know if I can. For a mother and son, we are completely different. Hell, she's even a Democrat. I used to think that there had to be some mix-up at the hospital. But I was the only child born that day in that hospital, so that takes away that excuse. I'm conservative with money, where she is not. I can keep my emotions in check; she doesn't. Don't get me wrong, I love her, and she is a good mother. But she tries to be controlling. And I won't let her. In so many ways, I'm like my father.

My parents' marriage made me want to study relationships and sexual behavior, just to see if they were normal or not. I became fascinated, almost obsessed, in reading and learning all I could. There have been many books written on the subjects, and honestly, I've read my share. Whether it's husbands and wives, parents and children, or just books on friendships, my conclusions are pretty simple: a lot of people are fucked up. Whenever I hear about an abusive spouse who either beats or kills their partner or a parent who kills a child, I'm shocked yet amazed. How can this happen in America? Don't other people see the warning signs? We turn a blind eye to a problem if it involves someone we know, thinking they will resolve their own problems instead of getting involved. We use excuses like "It's none of my business." But if someone is in danger, especially a child, it is our business. A wife has the ability to leave and seek help. A child doesn't.

It's my belief that if a child is hurt or killed by one of their parents, then the other parent is almost as guilty. If you live with someone, you get to know them, to understand them. If you haven't, then you're an idiot. And don't tell me there aren't warning signs of mental illness or depression.

There is! I truly believe anyone who harms a child should be executed the day they're found guilty.

That includes sexual offenders. I still can't believe we release sexual offenders back into society. How many repeat offenders do it again once they're out of prison? I'd love to know. Too many sick fuckers are let out of prison daily. These pieces of shit prey on innocent women and children. And if the excuse for letting them out of the jails is overcrowding, then execute them! You cannot rehabilitate a piece of shit. Shit will always be shit no matter what you do to it or how you try to cover it up. I hate it when some defense lawyer tries to use the old "Well, he was abused as a child" defense or "He is mentally incompetent." That is total bullshit. If a man or woman was abused as a child, then they know how it feels. Basically, they're saying, "I suffered, so I had to make that child suffer."

Here's what I believe. It's my belief that we all know right from wrong. Even at an early age, we begin to understand it. Even most mentally unstable people know that murder is wrong. Harming a child is wrong. Maybe the Bible is right. I do believe in "An eye for an eye." While I can't kill an innocent animal, I sure as hell could throw a switch to execute a piece of shit in a heartbeat. If someone harmed my child or wife, I would see to it they died. If it meant hiring someone to do it in prison or even if I had to hunt them down and do it myself, I would not rest till I had closure. If I went to jail for it, so be it.

And if I were ever on a jury and a man had hunted down and killed someone who harmed his wife or child, my vote would be "not guilty" regardless of evidence of premeditation. Our judicial system is flawed when a judge will give a pedophile a six-month sentence. I say castrate the fucker and throw him in the general population in prison. I guarantee you, the inmates will do the dirty work and enjoy doing it. In fact, that's what should happen. They took care of Jeffrey Dahmer, didn't they? Whew! Sorry about that. But by now you know I get on my soapbox from time to time.

Back to my mother, I realize I'll have to talk to her. With Donna pregnant, she doesn't need any potential problems, because my mother, no matter how well intended, can be overbearing at times. It's not that she means to be. She just comes across that way sometimes. A mother's job starts before birth. But at some point, they have to realize that their child is grown and needs to fend for themselves. As I was growing up, my mother did a lot for me. She was even the den mother for my Cub Scout group that got booted out of the Scouts. I feel sorry for that because I know it embarrassed her, but we were only a group for a short period of time before we got the axe.

What happened? I'll start at the beginning. My mother had me (the angel) and about seven future inmates and one special-needs kid, so she had the bottom of the barrel of kids that the other mother refused to take. That's what happens when you don't show up for the first meeting. And she didn't. We were more like a gang than Cub Scouts den now that I think about it. We were, for lack of a better word, little hellions. Anyway our first project was to make something out of popsicle sticks. Each den had to submit one. Well, Steve from our group is the only one of us who actually did one, so his got submitted from our den. I think our den number was something like 666, which should have been an omen for my mother, the Baptist.

Anyway the Saturday before the next meeting, we had a group meeting at our house, which, by the way, was only a block from the Scout hut where all the projects were. You can probably see where this is going, can't you? Well, my mother left to go somewhere. Seems like it was an Amway meeting or something. Well, when she left us alone, which wasn't a smart thing to do, all the guys decided to go to the Scout hut and go through the window and destroy all the other projects except for Steve's. That way, we would be assured of winning the competition. Hey, at that age, it seemed pretty smart. We were only seven or eight years old at that time. Well, the group talked me and Ray (the special-needs kid) into serving as lookouts. So we actually never broke into the Scout hut. I guess we were accessories to the crime. The guys broke all the projects except for Steve's.

Well, that Tuesday night at the meeting, we were called into a separate room, where we were questioned at length. I really should say *interrogated*. Finally, this kid named Johnny cracked under the pressure and ratted us out. The thing that still pisses me off the most is that it was his idea. Our whole den was booted out except for Ray. He got transferred to another den. His parents must have hired a lawyer to say he didn't understand what the hell he was doing.

Well, Ray eventually made Eagle Scout, and the last I heard, he was in Congress. The sad thing about that is, he probably has the highest IQ there. So maybe being slow or claiming temporary insanity does work. Maybe it was affirmative action that helped Ray make it to the top. The other guys? Well, they either are dead, are in jail, or have served time—one for manslaughter, a couple of the others for drugs, one for armed robbery, and the rest for trivial dumb shit. As you can see, I turned out the best of the group.

Of course, it didn't stop my father from taking me to the woodshed. And trust me, it wasn't to chop wood. It was a couple of days before I could sit down without pain. It was the first of only two paddlings he ever gave me. Of course, the Georgia public school system made up for him. My best guess is, I got paddled about sixty times in twelve years. And of course, I never did anything to deserve any of them. Well, maybe I did, but it wasn't my fault!

As you can see, I was a little hyper as a kid. Had it not been for getting involved in sports, I'd have probably done a lot worse. Sports, particularly baseball and football, let me spend most of my energy. Unlike kids today with their video games that stay inside playing games and eating leftover pizza, I was outside riding my bike, swimming, and shooting basketball when I wasn't playing in a recreational league. Of course, I was skinny as hell. I could not even put on weight in high school. The most I weighed in high school was 160 pounds. And that was because I started lifting weights.

It's funny when I think back to the high school football team. We only had few guys who played that weighed over two hundred pounds. Today the football players are huge. Of course, back when I was in school, kids weren't doing steroids. And of course, growth hormones weren't being injected either, not in humans or into livestock.

Since steroids and human growth hormones have been in the news lately, I guess I should comment on them. Athletes have been using them for decades. My guess is, it started in the seventies for some professional athletes, maybe even the sixties for professional bodybuilding. If you look at photos of professional bodybuilders in the fifties, then jump to the late sixties; you'll see a huge difference in size. In the late sixties, guys looked inflated, like someone stuck a needle in them and filled them with air. Of course, they did stick a needle in them. It was just steroids instead of air. Professional football players were probably next. In the seventies, they started getting huge.

I also believe it was in the seventies that some major-league baseball players started using them. I say this because in the early eighties, some of my friends started using them as well. In just a few months, they put on a lot of muscle. One old teammate even became a professional bodybuilder.

He won several regional titles. Of course, by 1991, he needed a liver transplant, and he died from heart-related problems in 2001. When my friends started doing them, I have to admit I was envious of their muscle development. But I just couldn't do them. No, it's not because I was morally superior. It was because I couldn't afford to buy them. If I had the money at that time, I probably would have used them too. Now I'm glad I was struggling to make ends meet.

But with all the steroid news about major-league baseball, no one is talking about young high school athletes who are using them. I've seen a few stories on the subject but not nearly enough. Why? These kids aren't famous. It doesn't have the same headline, rating, grabbing attention the professional baseball story does. I can easily spot a kid or even an adult who uses them.

And I can also tell you a lot of softball players use them too. I see that at tournaments. Some guys I've known over the years will use them during the winter, and when I see them again in the spring, I don't recognize them. It's pretty easy to know what they're doing. I've even had guys on my team who used them. When I asked them, they denied it. But I knew they did.

It's my guess, and it's purely a guess that 15–20 percent of guys who play tournament ball use steroids. And honestly, that could be low. One year, I had four guys whom I was sure were on them at some point in the season. Four out of twelve is 33 percent. However, I don't think that is the norm. I knew they were doing them because of their mood swings, and their muscles would balloon up and then would shrink back down. I could tell when they cycled both on and off. It's not a tough thing to notice. I tried talking to them, but they refused to listen, so there was little that I can do as a friend or a coach except hope they quit before they did major damage to their bodies. I think parents need to keep an eye out on their children. If Dave and Kathy are getting rapid muscle development, don't be afraid to find out what they are doing, even if it means testing them, because it's better to test them now than burying them in twenty years. Sometimes love can be tough.

Of course, steroids are just one of the many drugs that are out there just waiting for some insecure young man or woman to try and then get addicted to. Crack, meth, acid, GHB, heroin are not only addictive but deadly. It seems like meth is the most popular drug of choice lately. Honestly, I don't know anyone who uses those drugs. I certainly haven't tried, nor will I ever try them because I've always hated the feeling of being high. And I certainly don't need to go on any trip. Marijuana is a different topic. I tried it several times, but I didn't like the feeling it gave me. Instead of feeling high, I felt tired and stupid. Plus, it made me hungry as hell. And I can tell you as a fat, stupid, lazy guy, I don't need any help in those departments.

That's not to say it doesn't have any benefits medically. If I had cancer and was undergoing chemo, I'd smoke it in a heartbeat. I know someone who went through chemo and swears that pot kept her alive. And no, she doesn't smoke it now. She was so sick from nausea that was caused by the chemo that she considered suicide. Yes, I know there's some drug made from marijuana that they give cancer patients that is supposed to work as well. But for her, it didn't.

Now this may sound hypocritical, but I think marijuana should be legalized. Why? Pot is almost as easy to buy as a diet soda. And the people who want it will get it somehow. Now you're probably thinking *Yeah, but you could say that about all drugs.* True! But the effects from pot are no worse than those from drinking alcohol. And alcohol is legal. The other drugs are deadly. The revenue raised in the form of a tax could even be earmarked for drug abuse counseling and even in the treatment of those addicted who need help. Yes, that's fucking hypocritical. But right now, the government is just sitting around, twiddling its thumbs. Just Say No! doesn't cut it anymore. I thought it was stupid when I first heard it, and I loved the Reagans.

With Junior on the way, I realize someday I may have to deal with all this shit. I survived growing up. But I'm not going to sit around and act like drug use doesn't go on, because it does. Junior will be faced with decisions, from drug use to sex. So I'm going to be informed on the issues, and so will he, because I know from experience it's hard to say no if your friends do it. And I'm not going to hide under a rock while he makes dangerous mistakes.

Sex is another issue. I didn't have to deal with AIDS in the seventies. It might have been around, but it wasn't national news. So Junior will know that if he wants to have sex, he'd better use a condom, even if I have to buy them for him. And trust me, if I have a good reason to think he is doing any drugs or drinking, I will force him to take a test. And if he fails it, I'll lock him away in a drug treatment program. Too harsh? Maybe, but as a parent, we can't always be best friends with our children. We have to look out for them even if it means pissing them off. I think the key to raising a good child is to start talking to them at an early age. Just like in a marriage, communication is the key.

I think Junior will be well-adjusted, and hopefully, he won't fall into the pitfalls of drugs. I think if you reward a child and tell them you love them and you're there for them, they tend to turn out okay. Will he fuck up? I'm sure he will. I did!

Tuesday morning, I wake up actually feeling good, at least for a change. Donna is almost ready for work, so I guess sex is out of the question. I step on the scales. Damn! My diet is going slowly. Maybe if I could fight the temptation to eat something that tastes good, I could lose weight faster. Having a pregnant wife eating in front of me doesn't help either. But I've decided I have to push myself. I have to. Donna is thirty-six, and she was in great shape before the pregnancy. I'm forty-four, and just like an old car, I could stand a tune-up and some bodywork. Donna says the age difference doesn't matter. But I know it does, at least to me.

I know women usually outlive men, and the fact I'm eight years older means I will be gone long before she does. That doesn't bother me. What does is having diabetes or heart problems that drag out for years. I want to be able to play toss with Junior and do things with him. And the fear of health problems keeping me from doing those things really does scare me. I also don't want Donna to have to care for me like my mother did for my father. I want to be healthy enough to make love to her till we're in the old folks' home together. But the thought of my father lying in bed for four years and my mother and sisters caring for him often plays in my mind. I would never let Donna do that. I have a living will, so if I ever get in that shape, someone will pull the plug. My father didn't have one. My mother had his power of attorney, but she couldn't bring herself to have his feeding tube removed and starve him to death. I have to admit that would be tough to do to someone you love.

His last stroke had left him unable to talk or feed himself. He also had to wear adult diapers and be changed like a baby. I watched a strong, virile man waste away to nothing. The biggest problem was knowing he never wanted to be in that position.

I don't blame my mother. She loved him, and she cared for him like he was a baby. But several times in past years, he told me he never wanted to live like that. His sister, my aunt, had died that way in a diabetic coma.

The problem was, he didn't fill out all the necessary paperwork. I have! So Donna will never have to make that decision. While I'm not preoccupied with death, I'm not afraid of it either. My only fear is having a slow, painful death that wears on my family. That's why getting healthy is important.

I want to enjoy life, to live it to its fullest. Then when I can no longer enjoy it, I want to die. Of course, I don't get to make those decisions. But I can decide to push myself more to lose this weight. When Donna and I renew our vows after Junior is born, I want to look good in the wedding photos. I guess I'll use that for my motivation. Hell, if this book gets published, they may want a photo for it. I don't want to be fat.

Okay, people, I'm sorry for that depressing shit I just wrote. I just reread it. Like I've said, I write shit down as it floats up. And that includes depressing shit from time to time. Maybe the editor will remove it. If not, maybe you're starting to see the many facets of my personality. This side usually stays buried inside, locked away in a secret vault inside my brain. I'm sure even you, the readers, have your down moments. We all do. So please excuse me when I express mine. I know while reading this book, you have to ask yourself, Where the fuck did that shit come from? Hell, I say it all the time as I'm writing it down. Trust me, I don't have a clue where it comes from. Every day when I work on this book, I'm amazed at the shit I write down. I just scratch my head. Okay, sometimes I scratch my nuts and then start back to writing. I can only imagine what the reviews of the book will be. I would imagine that they would go something like this:

> *A Season in My Life* is the nearest nothing that's ever been published. After reading it, you'll scratch your head and say "What the fuck was that all about?" Mr. Thompson is in dire need of professional help. He's fucking nuts! However, the book is a must read because it's so bad it's good. My god, it's rubbed off on me; I'm starting to sound like him.

At least that would be my perfect review. Damn, I'm starting to get back to my old self now. I'm getting my mojo back. It could just be that I'm horny since I didn't get any lovin' this morning.

Do you think masturbating is cheating? I didn't think so either. I'll be back in a little while.

Whew! I feel better now. Since I'm on the subject of masturbation and my mother is coming to visit, I should tell you she caught me jerking off once. My father caught me once after I had used the VapoRub, but I had finished by the time he walked in. God, I can't believe I'm about to write this down. My mother caught me jerking off using a piece of bologna. Stop laughing! It's true in a fictional sense. Like Ripley's, you can believe it or not. I was about twelve, and I had already found my father's stash of porn in the toolshed. Well, all the ladies shown in the magazines had pink pussies.

Anyway one summer day, before the public pool opened, I decided to work on my bike, a.k.a. looking at Pop's porn while choking the cobra. I opened the fridge to get a soda and saw this pack of bologna. It was pink like the pussies in the *Hustler* magazines. Well, at twelve, seeing the bologna gave me an erection, so I made a sandwich as my mother talked on the phone in the kitchen. There were two pieces of bread and two pieces of bologna. No mustard. I did remember the VapoRub incident. I wasn't totally stupid.

So I took my sandwich and soda to the shed. My bike stayed there. I went inside, got the magazines from their hiding place, and proceeded to open the sandwich up and remove the bologna. I laid the bologna in my hand and then wrapped it around Mr. Happy. It was cold but actually felt pretty damn good. I began jerking off. Well, the first piece started falling apart, so I switched to the second piece. I was getting close!

About that time, my mother walked in. "Danny, could I get you to..." She didn't finish her sentence, but I had just finished and didn't have time to cover up the semen-covered bologna. She turned and walked away, mumbling to herself, something about raising a son who was a pervert. Of course, she called my father and told him the news.

And yes, we had another one of those father-and-son chats. He basically told me it was natural to beat off but not to use his lunch meat to do it with. He also bought a large jar of Vaseline that he kept from then on in the shed along with some paper towels.

My mother avoided me for a week or so after that. She was really embarrassed. My father thought it was actually funny. Once after I had grown up and when we were at the cabin, he told me stories of stealing watermelons in the summer with his friends as a kid not to eat but to fuck. He said they would cut a round hole in it then fuck it. Then after they were finished, they'd throw them in a ditch in the woods. He also said it felt good. The melons were nice and hot, and of course, they were wet. We both laughed about it.

My father was pretty good at laughing at shit that upset my mother. Like the old saying goes, the fruit doesn't fall far from the tree. And in some ways, I am a chip off the old block. So, guys, don't laugh and don't knock something till you try. And if you're going to try it, let me know so I can buy stock in Oscar Mayer.

Well, it's 6:00 a.m. Thursday morning. I actually awake before Donna. I let the dogs out, and I brush my teeth and fix the dogs their breakfast. I let the dogs back in so they can eat, and I crawl in bed with Donna. She awakes as I slide between the sheets.

"What time is it, Ben?"

"Six a.m."

"What are you doing awake this early?"

"I just woke up and thought we could snuggle since we didn't get to yesterday."

"Is that all?"

"For now, yeah. I just wanted you to know that I loved you."

"This doesn't have anything to do with your mother coming down tomorrow, does it?"

"Actually, no, it doesn't. I just realized I have to get my shit together concerning my weight problem."

"Ben, we've been through this."

"Hold it right there. It's not about the weight, it's about my health. Donna, I'm forty-four. I'll be at least sixty-two when Junior graduates high school, older than most of the other fathers there."

"Ben, you can't go back in time and change your age."

"I know that. I'm just concerned about my health. I want to make sure I'm around for the both of you. I don't want Junior being ashamed of his broken-down old man for a father. Nor do I want you to have to take care of me like my mother had to care for my father."

"So it is about your mother's visit!"

"Not completely. Maybe it helped me realize that I am in piss-poor shape and that down the road, I could have major health problems."

"What can I do to help, Ben?"

"You're doing it. Just love me and give me strength. And tell me when I need a face-lift."

"A face-lift? Ben, men don't get those unless they're actors."

"Darling, just because I'm getting older doesn't mean I have to look old. I'm not ever going to look old. I mean, I don't want a face like a softball glove old. And I do need to start eating healthier and get rid of the excess body fat."

"Ben, I'll do whatever you want me to."

"Thanks. That's what I needed to hear."

I realized after we got up how much my life has changed for the better. Now if I can get through this weekend, all will be great. We have decided to eat more meals at home from now on. Donna can still eat to her heart's content, and I can eat healthier. By not going out, I won't be tempted to eat things I shouldn't. I will also stop drinking beer with the guys. And this morning, I'll go grocery shopping to get enough food to last through my mother's visit. Now just to survive the weekend.

Friday morning, and I'm off to Atlanta to pick up my mother. God, I dread the drive up. You don't realize how crazy drivers are till you drive in Atlanta. Drivers will cut across five lanes of traffic without thinking how dangerous it is. Those people don't deserve a ticket; they should be shot. Once, I got run off the road by some idiot in a Miata crossing several lanes at once. I was in my truck. I should have hit him, but I know it would have probably killed him, so I swerved to miss him and ran off the road, almost losing control myself. Was I pissed? You bet your sweet ass I was pissed. If I had caught up with him, I would have beaten his ass. So I can understand road rage. Not that it's right, but I can understand it. I make it to my mother's without any near-death experiences.

She has her bags already packed, and we leave for the drive back down. Driving Mother anywhere is nerve-racking. She is the worst backseat driver in the world. If you could create a ride at an amusement park based on driving her around town, it would be more frightening than any ride at Six Flags. She constantly tells you how to drive: "You're going too fast! You have a truck on your bumper!" She drives me up the fucking wall. So I always turn up the radio to drown her out. My mother has always been critical of men drivers. So I'm sure that's where my criticism of women drivers comes from.

My mother may have never been in an accident, but I'm sure she's caused many! She drives with two feet, using her left foot to brake! How crazy is that? She used to scare the shit out of me when I was a kid. I can't count how many times I had been riding with her when some driver would pass and give her the ole middle finger salute!

I remember once a guy in a convertible pulling up at a red light and asking her where she got her driver's license—at fucking Kmart! He was pissed because she changed lanes without checking her blind spots and almost ran him off the road. Of course, to her defense, I would say there are not enough mirrors in the home of a narcissist to help her cover her blind spots.

Since I was rear-ended by a woman putting on lipstick, I find myself scared of women drivers. Sure, men have been known to eat and drink while driving. Some men even talk on the cell phone. But men, on the whole, don't multitask while driving like women do. A woman will talk on the phone while putting on makeup and changing radio stations. A man will take a bite out of a burger then put it down to take a drink of Cola. Women think they have to do it all at once.

We finally make it to Olive Grove and in one piece, except my nerves are shot and I have a sudden urge to take a shit. A long, leisurely three-day shit. What else would I do? Even I realize I need to get my shit back together. Damn, this is going to be a long fucking weekend, which reminds me, I'd better stock up on antacid.

On arrival, we are greeted by Donna and the dogs.

"Hi, Mrs. Thompson. I'm Donna. I'm glad we get to finally meet."

I think, *She's already kissing Mother's ass.* I mean, who else would my mother think she is? My nanny?

"Well, it's nice to meet you too, dear."

I can't help but notice my mother is staring at Donna's belly.

"When are you due, Donna?"

"In about eight weeks."

"Well, you know that will make number ten and eight great-grandchildren."

"You look too young to have so many, Mrs. Thompson!"

"Call me Georgia or Mom now, Donna. After all, we're family now."

God, I think I'm going to be sick. I know I have to say something.

"Let's all go in. It's hot as shit out here."

"There you go with that trashy mouth, Benny."

"Mother, I go by Ben now."

"You'll always be Benny to me."

We walk inside, and I take Mother's bags downstairs to the guest room.

This is going to be a long fucking weekend, I think, *pornography.*

I pick up the scattered pornography off the floor and lock the inflatable doll in a trunk.

I think, *Damn, I'm still picking up my toys for Mother!*

I make my way back upstairs. Donna has already made Mother a cup of coffee, and they're making small talk. And I do mean small talk. Mother is telling Donna all the "when Benny was a little boy" stories.

"Well, you know, Georgia, we're expecting a boy."

"Well, if he's anything like Benny, he'll be a handful. Benny was into everything."

"Mother, I'm sitting right here. You don't have to be so negative. Jeez!"

"Ben, be nice to your mother. I want to hear all about your childhood."

"Well, I'm sure you will. I've got some work to do outside. I'll be at the barn if you need me."

"I'm sure you do!" comes from my mother.

With that, I leave. I'm sure Donna will have heard my life story in 4-D by the time I come back in. But it's not like I've hidden anything about myself. All of you pretty much know everything about me by now. But I do feel kind of strange, like I've lost control. I know you think I'm overreacting. Maybe I am, but if you remember in the Garden of Eden, Adam and Eve didn't have to contend with a mother or mother-in-law, although they did have the talking snake to contend with. No, I'm not making any comparison. Well, maybe a little.

I get to the barn and start working on my Weed eater. It doesn't need a lot of work, but I change the spark plug and replace the line anyway. Heck, I might as well work on my rod and reels too. It's going to be a long weekend.

After a couple of hours, I go back to the house. It's getting hot, so I might as well work on the book. At least it's cool inside. I go inside. Mother is showing Donna pictures of me growing up.

"Ben, you were so adorable as a little boy. I love the picture of you in the cowboy hat riding the bicycle with training wheels."

"I'm glad you're having fun."

"Donna, this is my favorite. Benny was pudgy then too."

Without seeing the photo, I knew it was the one of me at about eight months naked. She shows that one to everybody. I was fat and bald. Thank God I was on my belly when they took the picture. I'm glad people don't take nude pictures of their babies anymore. They really should be put in jail for that.

"Well, ladies, I'm going to go work on my book. You know where I'm at if you need me."

With that, I go to my office. Okay, I admit it. Maybe I don't understand women as much as I thought. Then again, maybe I understand them too much. I realize that Donna is just trying to make my mother feel comfortable. I appreciate that. I really do. And I'm happy my mother is being nice to Donna. I just hope there are no fireworks. So yes, I'll be on pins and needles all weekend.

I think I'll give Meat a call.

"What's up, bro?"

"Meat, I feel like crap."

"I take it your mother is there."

"How did you guess?"

"You didn't say shit."

"Damn, you're good."

"You feel like your world is upside down, don't you?"

"Yeah, I do."

"Well, that's because it is. Two women you love in the same house. That's some scary shit for any of us to take."

"Thanks, Meat, for making me feel better."

"Don't mention it. Besides, if they blow up and have a fight, you won't have to worry about it anymore."

"What if they get along and like each other?"

"Then you're pretty much fucked for the rest of your life."

When he said that, a little light bulb turned on in my head. Maybe he's right. Maybe I'm afraid they'll like each other. Damn, I hadn't thought about it that way.

"Ben, are you still there?"

"Yeah, I just lost my train of thought."

"Well, if you need a place to crash, you can stay at my place."

"And leave the two of them alone? No fucking way."

Like the old disco song, I will survive.

I decide to go upstairs and decide to stand my ground, which probably means being a verbal punching bag. I walk into the living room.

"Benny, Donna tells me you haven't decided on a name for your son yet."

"No, Mother, but we'll get around to it."

"What about naming him after your father?"

"Absolutely not! He will not grow up being compared to anyone. I think he needs his own identity, and if you name a child after a relative, then he will always be compared to them."

Donna speaks up. "I like Gabriel and calling him Gabe."

"Too biblical."

"What's wrong with a biblical name, Benny? Benjamin is a biblical name."

"Yes, it is, but you named me Benny, remember? After the family doctor."

My mother smirks.

"Mother, a child needs his own identity. Parents get too caught up naming their children. If I had to pick a name, I'd say Grant. It's not overused, and no one in the family is named that. It's also not too hip."

Donna gives me a "no way in hell" look.

"How about some lunch?" I say, trying to change the subject.

"Sounds good to me" comes from Donna.

Mother decides to go downstairs and freshen up first.

Donna grabs me by the arm. "Ben, what's wrong with you? You're being rude to your mother."

"I don't know. I just feel like I always have to defend myself and my decisions."

"Ben, she told me all about how you've helped her financially when your father was ill and how proud she was of you. And then you come in with your ass on your shoulders."

"I'm sorry."

"Don't tell me, tell her. How would you feel if something happened to her? I'll tell you how you would feel—guilty!"

"Damn, Donna, I'm trying."

"No, you're not. Something is bothering you and has been for a long time. You need to come to grips with whatever it is and deal with it. Your mother is a sweet lady who adores you. And you need to talk to her. She may not always be around."

I bend over to kiss her. "You're right."

"I know I'm right."

"I just said that."

"You did, but you didn't mean it."

"Yes, I did. I just wish you were wrong once in a while. You're too damn perfect."

"I am?"

"Yes, you are. And if my book ever gets published, people will think you're perfect. And that being said, no woman is truly perfect."

"What is that supposed to mean?"

"That we all have flaws, even you, dear."

"Is that right? What's mine?"

"You respond to what I say far too often with a question."

"Really?"

"I rest my case."

"Ben, you're a smart-ass."

"It beats being a dumbass, but I'll go talk to my mother."

With that, I walk downstairs. Walking down the stairs, I try to gather my thoughts together. While Donna is right, that something is bothering me, I'm not sure what it is. I walk into the basement.

"Mother?"

"Yes, Benny, I'll be ready in a minute." She walks into the den area.

"Are we ready?"

"In a minute. Donna is freshening up. Mother, I need to talk to you."

"Is everything all right?"

"Yes and no."

"What does that mean, honey?"

"I don't know. I'm sorry if I was rude to you upstairs. I didn't mean to be."

"Well, you're just nervous about being a daddy."

"Yeah, that's true but..."

"But what?"

"Well, to be honest, I'm afraid of the whole marriage thing. To be honest, I don't want to have a marriage like yours and Dad's. I don't want my son growing up to see his parents fighting and saying nasty things to each other."

"Yes, we had our share of arguments, but we also had our good moments too."

"Well, I don't ever remember seeing them—well, not until Dad had his last stroke."

"Benny, your father was complex, much in the same way you are. He didn't show his emotion unless he was mad. Then he would explode."

"That's what I'm talking about. You don't know the impact seeing the two of you fighting had on me. In a way, it caused me to fear relationships."

"Benny, all married couples fight."

"That's not true, at least not to the degree that your arguments went to."

"Well, you turned out all right. And look at how many different girls you dated."

"The key word there is *dated*. I never allowed any of the women into my heart out of the fear it would turn into a terrible relationship like you and Pop had. It took me years to realize that not all relationships were like that."

"You keep saying we had a bad relationship."

"You did! You may not realize it now. But remember, you filed for two divorces. Parents shouldn't fight in front of their kids. And somehow I always felt like it was my fault. I used to wish I had never been born."

"Benny, if you want me to say we made mistakes, I will, because we did. But we did love each other very much. After all, we had five children."

"Mother, having children doesn't mean you love someone. It just means you didn't use birth control and you both were horny."

"What is it you want me to say then?"

"Nothing! I just wanted you to know what growing up in hell was like. I used to wish I had different parents. I would daydream about having parents like I would see on television, parents who loved each other and knew how to show love to each other and their children."

"We loved all our children."

"Yes, you did, but you never displayed love toward each other till Dad had his last stroke."

"Are you saying you don't love us?"

"No, I do love both of you. That's why it has bothered me so much over the years."

"Benny, there's nothing I can do to change that."

"No, but I can. I have always feared marriage, but now I'm over that. And now that I'm married, I can use what I've learned to be a good parent."

"I think you'll be a great parent."

"Mother, great parents don't exist, at least not in their children's eyes. But I realize that now. And that is the first step to being a good parent."

"Well, I wish we could have been better parents, but we did the best we could with what we had."

"I know that, Mother. I'm not blaming you for anything. In a way, it helped me mature faster and depend on myself more. And who knows? Maybe that was the way it was supposed to be."

"That sounds like predestination, Benny."

"It is."

"Baptists don't believe in that."

"Who said I was a Baptist?"

"You were saved and baptized in a Baptist church, thereby making—"

"Mother, I accepted Jesus as my savior, but I did not accept the church or the Bible as divine law. Both are flawed."

"I don't want to talk about this now."

"Good! Then let's go eat."

"Let me finish up my makeup."

"All right. We'll be upstairs." I walk back up the steps.

Walking upstairs, I realize that both my parents really did do the best they could. I also realize I could try to do even better. I really do love my mother although I don't always see eye to eye with her. But both my parents were there for me when I needed them most. And while it's hard to understand relationships like theirs, I think it helped me understand myself better. And I really understand Donna. I know there'll never be any verbal fights in front of our child. That I can promise. And any disagreements we have will be handled in private.

I walk back in to see Donna with the dogs.

"How did it go, Ben?"

"It went well."

"And?"

I smile and think., *There she goes answering with a question again.* "And I love you. Thank you for twisting my arm."

"So you'll be nice to your mother from now on."

"Yes, dear!"

"You're placating me again."

"You're absolutely correct, and I always will."

"What is that supposed to mean?"

"It simply means I'm pussy whipped, dear, and you're stuck with me."

"I don't know if that's a good or bad thing."

"Well, from your orgasm standpoint, I'd say good. From having to put up with me and my shit for the next forty-plus years, I'd say bad."

"You plan on being around forty more years?"

"If I'm lucky. I will probably die before that."

"From what?"

"From fucking myself to death."

"Really?"

"Yeah, either from fucking you or a watermelon."

"A watermelon?"

"Sorry, you haven't read that story yet. I just put that in the book."

"Ben, you really are weird."

"No shit, Sherlock."

My mother walks in. "Is everybody ready? Let's eat."

We decide to eat at the Cracker Barrel. Even though Donna and I have eaten there recently, it's nearby and Mother can eat country cooking. Plus, it's near Donna's old house. We can take her by to see where the yard sale will be. God, I'm glad I don't have to deal with that shit.

The drive to the restaurant was uneventful. Mother was too preoccupied talking to Donna to critique my driving. Now I'm thinking about asking Donna to go with me to take Mother home Sunday for that very reason.

We get seated at the table and place our drink order. I realize I'm like the invisible man and have to smile. The two of them talk nonstop, and since I can't get a word in edgewise, I sit and listen. Well, sort of.

I drift into a daze, remembering my childhood. I really did have fun as a child. I spent the summers swimming at the public pool across the street. My father took me fishing sometimes, mostly at the cabin. And my mother even bought me a minibike when I was eight. I had skateboards, bicycles, and even an aquarium. For a kid, I had a lot of stuff.

By the time I was ten, all my brothers and sisters had gotten married and left home. First was Jackie; she was the oldest. She got married when I was about five. Then Joanne got married. I was about seven. Kenny and Carol followed soon after that. I was the only child left.

That wasn't bad because from the age of six, I started becoming independent. I had my own alarm clock, and I would get up each morning and get ready for school. My parents had already left for work when I would awake. Of course, at that time, my mother had a beauty shop in the basement, so she was still in the house. But I still did everything for myself from getting dressed to fixing my breakfast. Then I would catch the bus.

It's funny the things we remember when we reflect. I was about six when I first saw a girl's private parts. She was five. It was just innocent curiosity—you know, the "I'll show you mine if you show me yours." But

I was shocked to see that she had an innie while I had an outie. I couldn't understand what happened to her wiener.

That's what my father called a penis, so I went to ask him. I remember asking something like "Daddy, Sally doesn't have a wiener, so how does she pee?" That was our first father-and-son chat. He took me to an outdoor faucet and turned the water on. He explained that a boy had a hose and we can hold it and direct its flow and that's why we can stand up and pee. He then removed the hose from the faucet and turned it back on. He then said, "A girl doesn't have a hose to hold on to, so she has to sit to pee." Well, that made sense since I had just seen an innie, but I had to ask why they didn't have a wiener. I think he said something like "God was tired when he made girls and didn't give them a wiener or a brain." Of course, I asked him that question after he and my mother had finished an argument.

Of course, knowing now that little girls didn't have a wiener, I had to show mine off to all the little girls in the neighborhood. Heck, some of the girls even touched it. Of course, one of the little girls told her parents, who promptly called my parents to complain, which led to our second father-and-son chat, which was "Keep your wiener in your pants or I'll spank your ass." As you can tell, that was a one-sided conversation. My father was good at putting things into perspective and also into words. So for the next ten years, no girl got to see my wiener until I was fifteen and lost my virginity.

By that time, my little wiener had become a bona fide dick. Actually, I was eleven when puberty hit. It seems like it was overnight though. I remember I awoke one morning with hair down there. Then one morning, I awoke with sticky sheets.

Then a miracle happened: I learned to masturbate. Talk about divine intervention. I was a quick study too. Some days I would spank the monkey four or five times. Yeah, I know I talk about masturbation a lot. But I guarantee that every one of you reading this book has played with yourself at some point in your life. And if you haven't, then you may need some professional help.

"Ben! Ben! Are you ready to order?"

"Yeah, I'll have the chef salad."

We place our food order.

"Where have you been, Ben ?"

"I was just daydreaming while you ladies were talking."

The food arrives, and we begin to eat. After eating, we stop by Donna's old house to arrange things for the big day tomorrow. I volunteer to bring some tables over when we get back home. It's a good excuse to get out of the house.

Donna also has some old clothes she wants to get rid of, so I'll bring those over as well. Donna informs me some of the girls from the real estate office are going to bring some of their things over tomorrow, and so are Julie and Denise. Looks like they'll have one hell of a junk sale—I mean, yard sell. I'm just glad we have a tournament now. I get to miss out on all this crap. Guys, you know where I'm coming from. If a man is around, you and I both know we get the shit detail, because we realize if we help out, we would be stuck doing all the shit work, like helping load stuff up. So I'm simply not going to do it. And I will make damn sure Donna doesn't help load anything up, because all I need is for her to go into premature labor.

Women just love yard sales. To them, it's like a fucking homecoming. They get to get together with all their girlfriends and gossip. Now if the girls talked about sex like guys do when they get together, I might be interested in helping out. But you'll never hear women talk about sex if a guy is around. We're kept in the dark where their secret society is concerned. Damn, I wish I could place a bug and tape what the ladies say just to hear what they really say.

We get back to the house, and Donna and my mother turn on the television. Mother wants to watch today's episode of *her soap opera*. She missed it since we were driving down when it was on. So she can catch the repeat airing on the soap channel. I go with Donna to the bedroom as she starts pulling out clothes for the yard sell.

"Ben, you want to get rid of any old clothes."

"Donna, I just gave a lot of old shirts to the Salvation Army. And my pants are in a state of flux. But once I get to my desired weight, I'll have a lot of pants to get rid of."

She gives me her "you're not being very helpful" look, and I take that as my cue to go load up the office tables. I pull the truck out to the barn when Whatley calls on my cell.

"Ben, I've got the beer iced down. Anything else I need to bring tomorrow?"

"No, if you've got beer, that's all you need."

"Denise is going to be at the yard sell tomorrow with Donna."

"Damn, it sounds like that's going to be the social event of the year."

"Well, it does get her out of my hair."

"True!"

"The reason I'm calling is, I have a truck full of shit I need to take over to Donna's old house and unload. Is there any way you can meet me there so I can do it tonight? I don't want to fuck with this shit in the morning."

"Actually, Whatley, I'm going to be heading over there in a few minutes myself for that same reason."

"Damn, Ben, great minds!"

"I'll bring a six-pack so we can get a jump start on tomorrow."

"Cool! Is Meat going to be there?"

"No, I think he is taking Julie to a movie."

"Do you know what they're going to see?"

"No, but I'd bet it's some chick flick."

"Yeah, he does stand a better chance getting some if they go to see a love story."

"Damn, Whatley, I'm impressed you knew that."

"Ben, even a blind squirrel can find a nut once in a while."

"True, but they also have been known to fuck a knothole in a tree."

"Only you would have thought that up."

"Thanks. I'll see you there in a few minutes."

With that, we hang up, and I load up the office tables. I pull back over to the house, and Donna is finished going through her clothes and is watching the soap opera with my mother.

"Donna, Whatley called and is going to meet me over at the old house. He has some of Denise's things that he wants to bring over tonight."

"Okay, honey. I'll see you when you get back."

I walk out the door. Damn, that was easy.

I pull into the drive and wait for Whatley. I have to say I love my satellite radio. I have it on the seventies station. I hear one of my favorite songs of all time: "New Orleans Ladies" by Le Roux. If you've never heard it, you should. It's a great song. After the song is finished, I open the garage door and head inside. I start setting up the tables and bringing in Donna's clothes. About that time, Whatley drives up. I help him unload five boxes of shit. I didn't ask what was in them, but I'm sure one was books because it was heavy as hell. Of course, I left it for him to unload. I only moved the light ones. Hey, I'm not stupid! We finish up and open up a beer.

"Ben, I heard your mother is visiting."

"Yeah, she'll be here through Sunday."

"How is she and Donna getting along?"

"Great, I think."

"Damn, that sucks."

"Yeah, it does. But it would be worse if they hated each other."

"Yeah, I guess. But you know now you'll be double-teamed if you fuck up and piss one of them off."

"Yeah, Donna has already scolded me for not being nice to my mother."

"You're fucked."

"Yep!"

"Well, at least she lives in Atlanta."

"Good point."

"But she is just a phone call away."

"Whatley, shut up. Jeez, you and Meat sure know how to cheer someone up."

"That's what we're here for."

"Are you ready for tomorrow?"

"Ben, I have beer!"

"True! That was a stupid question, wasn't it?"

We sit and finish off the beer and head back to our homes.

I get back to the house just as *All My Children* is ending. What timing. Okay, before you get your panties in a wad, I'm not busting on soap operas. Hell, my senior year in high school, I got hooked on them. I only had four classes, so I got out at noon. So when I got home, I started watching *All My Children*, *One Life to Live*, and *General Hospital*. That's when Luke and Laura were the big deal. Of course, I stopped watching them soon after that. Nothing ever happened. The story lines took forever to come to a conclusion. But I did start watching *Dynasty*, which was a prime-time soap. There must be something about seeing someone who has problems worse than yours that keep people watching them. My mother has always loved to watch them. Of course, I watched them for the hot women. Linda Evans, Joan Collins, and Emma Samms were smoking hot back in the day.

I look around and could tell everyone is tired. I'm sure my mother has worn Donna out. And I'm sure the drive down took its toll on my mother. So I suggest that everyone turn in early. Tomorrow is a going to be a busy day for all of us. No one put up an argument, not even the dogs. I walk Mother downstairs and come back up and kiss Donna good night. Once the house is quiet, I turn on the television in my bedroom. It's time for the *UFO Files*. Yeah, I'm hooked.

Rise and shine; it's Saturday morning. Today it's ball with the boys. I actually awake before Donna. So I go in to wake her up. I know she has a full day ahead of her and needs to get started. But I wish she really wouldn't do this. With her being pregnant, I have to admit I worry about her and the baby. I always think she is doing too much. But the doctor assures me it's okay as long as she doesn't strain. I put on my softball uniform, kiss Donna goodbye, and it's off to the complex.

I pull up and see Coy, Mark, and the rest of the gang talking. I get out of the truck.

"What's up, motherfuckers?"

Mark walks toward me with a package.

"Ben, we got you a little postwedding present."

I think, *How nice of them.* I open it up. "What the hell is this?" It looks like pink satin.

"Go ahead and pull it out. Rusti made it for you," Mark says.

I pull it out, and it's a pink cape with a big PW embroidered on it. "I suppose the PW stands for *pussy whipped*?"

"You got it, big guy."

"Well, tell Rusti when I wear it, I'll be thinking about her."

"Hey!"

"Just kidding. I'll wear it home tonight."

I put the cape back into my truck under some shirts. God, I hope no one else sees it. With that, we make our way down to the fields.

I can't help but think that Donna was just getting started preparing for the yard sale. I wonder what she and my mother will talk about. This is Donna's story told by Ben:

"Georgia, are you ready to go?"

"Yes, dear."

They lock up, and it's off to the yard sell. They get there and start pricing items for the sale. Soon Denise and Julie arrive. Then just as they finish up with the pricing, their first customer arrives. It's a couple in their fifties. The man looks like a janitor, and his wife is a chain-smoker with green teeth. They look at the sofa, love seat, and coffee table.

"How much is this?"

Donna looks at the man with dismay. "The prices are on them, sir. Both individually and as a set."

"I see that. I'm not blind! I mean, what will you take? Not what you're asking."

Donna starts to realize that I was correct for once. Really! She told me that later. She had 250 dollars marked as a set.

"I'll take two hundred, but you'll have to load it yourself."

"Sold. I would have given you the full 250."

"Well then, sir, you got a deal then."

The man and his wife load up their truck.

Donna walks away, shaking her head.

Georgia speaks up. "Looks like you made a sell."

"Yeah, but that guy scared me, Georgia. Ben may be right about yard sales."

"Well, honey, don't let him know that. It'll be our little secret."

"Good idea. Besides, he'd just dance around, saying 'I told you so.' Georgia, what was Ben like growing up?"

"Honestly? He was a typical little boy. He roughhoused and played with his friends a lot."

"I was just curious. I guess I'm trying to figure out what our son may be like."

"Donna, Benny was a sweet child. But he did get sick a lot. I think most of that was related to me smoking around him. He had terrible sinus problems. Then after he fell out of the tree house, he changed, he became introverted."

"Georgia, what happened with the tree house? Ben won't talk about it much."

"Well, his father built him a tree house. It wasn't very high, maybe ten feet off the ground. One day, he and his friends decided to tie a rope on a limb above it so they could slide down it like Batman. Well, they used an old rope, and it broke just as Benny grabbed a hold of it. He fell flat on his back and hit his head on a rock. It cracked his skull like you would an egg. There was blood everywhere. I thought he would die. In fact, he did stop breathing for a while. He was in a coma for a couple of weeks. When he did come to, he had vertigo so bad he couldn't get out of bed without throwing up. The doctor said he had a severe concussion. He also suffered some brain damage."

"I didn't know that."

"Donna, few people do. He doesn't like to talk about it. When he tried to speak, he stuttered, actually pretty severely."

"Wow!"

"He had problems reading and even doing simple math. The kids at school, when he started back, would make fun of him. I cried myself to sleep many nights because I didn't think he would overcome the accident."

"What changed him?"

"Hard work and being stubborn. He started to fight the kids that made fun of him. And we hired him a good speech therapist and several tutors. After a year or so, he got so he could talk without a noticeable impediment. But from time to time, if you listen closely, you'll still hear him stammer a little."

"I didn't know that."

"Yeah, he had a tough time with it. And he told me today that the marital problems that Larry and I had during that time also added to his problems."

"I'm sorry to hear that. I don't think he meant it like it sounded."

"Yes, he did. And he was right. I blamed Larry for Benny's accident. I didn't want the tree house. But the two of them insisted, so I went along with it. And it almost cost Benny his life."

"Why didn't you tell Ben that?"

"He has enough to deal with. And I denied it even existed."

"Well, Georgia, he did turn out great."

"Well, he got over the accident, but there's still some pain there. As extroverted as he appears, he still lives in a protected fort. He doesn't allow too many people to enter."

"Well, he has let me in. And I will tell you that he lets out a lot of emotion in his book."

"I'm glad he has you, Donna. I really am. He needs to be loved."

"Well, I really do love him. He is a great man and will be a great father."

"Yes, he will, but you will always need to understand he hides his emotions."

"Georgia, he has changed a lot lately."

"I hope so. One thing you'll learn by being a mother is that you never stop worrying about your children, no matter how old they are."

"That's what my mother says too."

"It's true, dear."

"Well, Mom, I'm glad we both have you."

"Donna, I'm glad Benny has you too."

"I'm glad I have him too!"

257

Their business suddenly picks up. I guess when passersby see several cars at a yard sale, they become more interested in it. Sort of like people slowing down for an automobile accident. Curiosity? Yes! We all feel the need to know what is going on. If people see lots of cars at a yard sell, they think there's some good shit there and that they're missing out. I guess that's a natural thing to do or think. But when you really think about it, it is stupid.

It's the same thing with the tabloids, magazines. They sell like crazy because we are so interested in what the celebrities are doing. I admit I buy one from time to time. Usually, it's something weird like alien abduction or some doomsday prediction. No, I don't believe them, but they do make for interesting reading when you're taking a dump. That said, I do feel sorry for celebrities. They really catch hell. They can't shop, shit, or go out to eat without someone reporting it. Princess Diana even died trying to escape from photographers. I realize it's a business and a celebrity story sells papers. But they are human too. They have lives. While I'm interested in the weird off the wall stuff, celebrities' personal lives don't interest me in the least.

I'm just glad you don't see too many stories about writers, especially bad ones. So I don't have anything to be concerned about. If I had to deal with being harassed by reporters, I'd be photographed beating someone's ass. I remember when Sean Penn beat the ass of someone who was harassing him. Hell, I thought it was justified. Now I don't agree with all his politics, but he got big fucking kudos from me for that. I can't imagine being stalked by photographers all the time trying to get a shot that they can sell to the tabloids. I can't imagine someone taking a photo of me pissing on a tree outside or skinny-dipping in my pool. The future governor of Alabama, Charles Barkley, is another example. He kicked ass several times. I have to say that anyone who would mess with him is probably crazy. He is one big bad dude. My point is simple. People shouldn't have to put up with that. Just because you're an actor, singer, or sports star doesn't mean you can be harassed all the time. America, get a life and stop living through other people's. If we all put the effort into our own lives (and by that I mean making ourselves better human beings), we wouldn't have time to worry about what goes on in Hollywood.

Our softball tournament went pretty good. We finished second. Considering we're still trying to jell as a team, that's not bad.

With all the new guys, things are starting to look up. Bryan is starting to fit back in, although some guys still resent him. I can feel the tension sometimes in the dugout. I'll give them another tournament or two to get over it before I talk to them. I'd hate to have to cut someone from the team, but if they can't respect my decision, then I'll have no other option.

On a positive note, Donna's yard sale also went better than I thought it would. She made nine hundred dollars. So I guess now I'll let her pay for dinner tonight. I called her a couple of times between games. And she sounded like they were having fun. She told me she enjoyed being with my mother. And believe it or not, that made me happy. I guess my greatest fear was them not liking each other. If I've learned anything today, it is that things do have a way of working out if you let them. I've also learned that I should not overreact to certain things. Whether or not I follow that rule is another story. Stay tuned.

After taking a shower from my day with the boys, Donna takes us out to eat. Since my mother doesn't eat Mexican food, Chinese food, or seafood, we settle on LongHorn Steakhouse. They have good food, and they're nearby. And considering we all are pretty pooped from our busy day, that is a good thing. After we're seated, I get to hear every single detail of their day, from the story of the green-teeth woman to the cutest little girl they've ever seen. Did they ask me about the ball game? You've got to be kidding. Of course not, they're women. If they had, I could have told them Todd made a great diving catch to end a game or Meat forced us all out of the dugout with a fart, something that's interesting. But no! So I sit there and pretend I'm interested in their boring day. Actually, I am glad they had a good time. Of course, I wonder what they talked about that they're not telling me.

We finish up eating and go back home. Since I want my mother and Donna to bond, I decide to go check out the softball websites, just to see what everyone is saying about the tournament. But before I do, I suggest to the girls they watch a movie. So I go get *Secondhand Lions*. Donna has seen it before, but my mother hasn't. It's a great movie, and it's fairly clean, so it shouldn't offend my mother. I know you readers are probably snickering. But I don't want to be responsible for giving my mother a heart attack. No way could she handle *The Libertine*, much less something like *Kill Bill*. I set the movie up and click on the computer.

It may sound strange, but I can't remember much about life before the internet. I know it's only been around about fifteen years or so. I've had it since '97. But it has changed the way we live. I get most of my news from it. I haven't watched a newscast from start to finish since 9/11. But what I really like is, I can read the news, as opposed to hearing some talking head with an agenda slanted toward their own beliefs. And I can select what I want to. I click on AlabamaSoftball.com. That's the site of my friend McCray. I think I've mentioned it before. It's the best site for softball news from Alabama.

From the message boards, I've met a lot of fellow players on there. You talk to them through the message boards, then at tournaments, sometimes you get to meet them. Most are just average guys living everyday lives. But the common denominator is, we love the game. I click on a report from our tournament. No one is bashing us. That's a good sign. Maybe we are starting to get some respect.

Respect is important to me if you haven't noticed—not just where softball is concerned, but in everyday life. I realize I repeat some things in this book, so please bear with me. Respect is something that is usually gained. I know we have respect for titles, such as president or minister. But as people, we are judged by our actions. And from those actions comes respect. I've never really cared if people liked me or not. But I do hope they respect me.

While I haven't lived a perfect life, I have always tried to be respectful of others—well, except a few teachers that I gave hell to. But they were full of themselves and looked down at all of us. By that I mean the students. But after I went to work for Phil, I gained a whole new perspective on respect. It's not what you have or who you know. It's who you are and how you treat others. That sounds kind of funny coming from a beer-drinking, foulmouthed Southern boy, doesn't it? Wait! Don't answer that.

I go back in to see the last few minutes of the movie. After the movie finishes, I suggest everyone turn in. Tomorrow will be a long day. They agree as well. I walk Mother downstairs. I'd hate for her to fall and break something on her last day with us. I then turn around and come back up to talk to Donna. My hopes are, she'll ride up to Atlanta with me to take Mother home.

"Darling, thanks for being such a nice host to my mother. I know she's a handful."

"Ben, I loved to finally get to meet your mom. She was delightful. She told me stories about you all day."

"Damn, that's scary."

"There were nice stories and some sad ones."

"Did she tell you I insisted on burying by pet goldfish when it died?"

"No, but I'm sure it's a good story."

"Well?"

"Well what?"

"What did you talk about then?"

"You know, girl talk."

"Oh no, sweet cheeks, you're not getting away that easy. What did she tell you?"

"Ben, they were just little things, nothing bad."

"Donna, I'm invoking my husbandly rights. I demand to know."

"You demand?" I could tell her voice is becoming harsh.

"Uh, I'd really like to know, darling."

"That's better! She told me about the tree house accident. Okay, are you satisfied now?"

"I told you about that."

"No, you didn't. Not in detail."

"Yes, I did. I fell out when a rope broke and got knocked out."

"You left out the parts about almost dying and having a speech impediment."

"That wasn't important. I got over it."

"Ben, it's a great story. You overcame a great deal of adversity. You should put that in your book."

"Sorry, dear, it was no big deal, and it's a downer. Besides, I do touch on it in the book."

"You don't get it, do you, Ben?"

"Get what, Donna? Kids get hurt every day. It was no big deal."

"Yes, Ben, it was a big deal. I just don't see what's wrong about talking about it in your book. It could be an inspiration to others trying to get over a problem."

"Donna, it's a downer. I'm trying to be cute and funny in the book, not dwell on sad shit."

"Ben, you wrote about Phil and the impact he had on your life."

"That's different."

"How is it different? He got Alzheimer's. Isn't that a downer?"

"Yes! I mean no. I learned a great deal from him. He deserved to be mentioned. He helped me mature into a man."

"Didn't you learn anything from your fall?"

"Yeah, never tie rotten rope to a tree limb."

"You're starting to piss me off now, Ben."

"Sorry!"

"No, you're not. What would you do if you read in the paper about a local boy falling from a tree and suffering the same injury?"

"Donna, that's not fair."

"Oh, but it is. Wouldn't you try to talk to the child and tell him you suffered the same injury and you got over it? To cheer him up? To give him hope?"

"That's a hypothetical question."

"Ben, hypothetical happens sometimes. And since I know you, I know you would be there for the boy and his parents."

"You think so?"

"Ben, I know so."

"Donna, the ages of eight to eleven were horrible for me. I don't really want to rehash them."

"Then just write down this discussion we're having."

"This is bullshit! You know that, don't you?"

"Call it whatever you like, but it's a story that needs to be told."

"Will it get you off my ass?"

"Yes!"

"Okay then, but I hope an editor cuts it from the final draft."

"You won't be that lucky."

"Well, lady, I do love you even though you can be a bitch at times."

"I love you too even though you can be such a pain in the ass."

"Thanks! You want to have makeup sex then?"

"We didn't have a fight."

"How about just making love then?"

"Your mother's here."

"Hell, she's downstairs. Plus, she caught me fucking a bologna sandwich once. You would be an improvement in her eyes."

"You say the sweetest but most juvenile things, Ben."

"Hey, I work hard at it. You know what else is hard?"

"Come here, big boy!"

Well, as you can tell, I had to put in the gory story of falling out of the tree house. But hey, I got great sex out of the deal, so I think I won this battle. Okay, I lost again. Damn, I knew I should have written a murder mystery.

Sunday morning, and I feel refreshed, renewed like a million dollars. Okay, so much for positive thinking. I'm still sleepy as hell even though I slept like a log. The problem is, this log still wants to lie on the ground in the forest, because sex makes me sleep like a baby. And if you show me an insomniac, I'll show you someone who isn't having enough sex. And if they are having enough sex and can't sleep, well then, they should see a doctor because something is fucking wrong with them.

I am dreading the drive to Atlanta. But at least Donna will be going up with me. Hopefully, she'll keep Mother from telling me how to drive.

I wake Donna and my mother. Since I can be ready in five minutes, I'll get the dogs squared away. We can grab a bite to eat somewhere on the road. The important thing is to get started back from Atlanta before the traffic gets heavy from all the locals returning home.

I have to admit my weekend went better than I thought it would. My mother was on her best behavior, and Donna played the gracious host to perfection. However, I am still against putting the whole tree house accident in the book. But Donna insisted, so like the pussy-whipped bastard I am, I did. Now I just hope they edit it out. If you've read it already, then the editor must have agreed with Donna.

I have to admit this whole book thing is getting crazy. I sit down now and just let my fingers go. I have no clue from day to day what's going to be written. And you're probably saying to yourself "No shit. You said that already" While I must admit I'm having fun, I'm also preparing for the rejections that will be forthcoming. I do know one thing though, and that is, I will have the book published even if I have to self-publish.

My friends are hounding me to death. They may be scared that I'm putting their secrets in it. Sorry I'm not. Their personal lives and reputations will be spared. Friends mean more to me than book sales. However, you could have a hit television show based on my friends and family. I even e-mailed a couple of networks about either a possible reality show or even a sitcom based on softball. Of course, I never heard from any of them, and to be honest, I never expected to. They must be swamped with proposals from would-be producers.

All things considered, my life is going great, and to be honest, that scares the shit out of me. I'm not used to all this contentment. Of course, the contractors will be starting soon, and that never goes as planned. I always hope for the best and plan for the worst.

"Ben, we're ready to go."

Sorry, I've got to go; the queen speaks, and it's time to leave for Atlanta.

The drive up is uneventful, which is a good thing. Maybe it is all the state troopers parked in the median and the few cars that they had pulled over, I assume, for speeding or reckless driving. Maybe it is Donna and Mother chatting all the way up. Whatever the reason, it is nice not to have any near-death experiences.

When we get to Mother's, we take time enough for a pit stop, and she insists on making some sandwiches for the drive back. Donna hugs Mother goodbye, and we're back on the road. Our only stop will be for gas and lottery tickets. Yeah, we decide to buy ten dollars' worth. Hell, the big game is worth eighty million. I know we'll never win, but what the hell. We start our drive home.

"Whew!"

"What's that for, Ben?"

"I'm just glad this weekend is over."

"Well, it was a bit strenuous, wasn't it?"

"Yeah, but maybe now we can settle back down into our mundane existence, at least till the baby is born."

"I should tell you, Ben, I invited your mother back down after the baby is born."

"That's fine with me."

"It is?"

"Yeah, I've come to grips about my childhood."

"I'm glad to hear that. What are your conclusions?"

"That my life wasn't much different from most, that no childhood is perfect, that life is what we make it."

"Well, I wasn't expecting that."

"What were you expecting, dear?"

"Something like 'I'm glad this weekend is fucking over.'"

"Donna, I'm shocked at that trashy mouth of yours. Where did you learn such vile language?"

"From the best husband in the world."

"Oh! I wasn't expecting that either."

"What else would I say?"

"Something like "For a redneck sack of poop, you're really not that bad."

"You want me to say that?"

"No, I liked yours better."

We take our time driving home. I just want to make sure we get there in one piece. We do have another conversation about relationships, specifically men. Donna has been harping on the subject ever since she saw *The Mind of the Married Man* on HBO—you know, those "Why do men think about sex so much? Can men be monogamous?" So she has plenty of questions, and I have plenty of time.

I tell Donna—and you ladies listen up too—that while you can't judge a book by its cover, you can tell a lot about a man by what kind of automobile he drives and how often he gets a new car. Now this is just a theory of mine, and I have no scientific proof to back it up, but it does seem to be accurate. I'll take the easy one first.

If a man changes cars every year or so, he is probably restless and will be more apt to cheat. He will always be looking for something better looking, faster with sleek lines. Those guys are hard to please. So unless a guy leases a car and has to turn it in every two years, stay away from those men. Guys who trade cars every year will dump you when a sporty newer model comes out. I have had many friends that fit this type of guy. And no, I won't mention names.

Now I'm just the opposite. No, I'm not tooting my own horn. I've had two trucks the last fifteen years. The truck I'm driving now is seven years old. It still looks good, and it still runs great, so I see no reason to change. When I start having mechanical problems, then I'll look for a new one. I hate to compare Donna to my truck, but she runs well and takes care of all my needs. So unless she trades me in for a new model, we'll be together for life. And that's my hope.

Now to what types of automobiles guys drive. If a guy drives a truck, SUV, or sedan, he is probably settled down and secure in himself. He has nothing to prove to anyone, so he has no need to impress. Those are usually good guys for women to choose. And if he drives a BMW, Lexus, or Mercedes, he's secure and has money. Of course, if he's rich, he may tend to cheat, so watch him carefully. If he drives a sports car and is over twenty-five, leave him alone. He still has wild hair and probably has a roving eye. The car says "Look at me," so don't look at him. He'll break your heart. And if you're married and your husband suddenly wants a sports car, hire a PI; he's probably having an affair. And most importantly, remember, this is just my theory. And I could be wrong.

Donna is shocked when I told her about guys and the cars they drive. She never really puts it all together, but she eventually agrees it had some merit to it. Now I'm not saying all guys driving sports cars will cheat. But that should tell you they have some wild oats left to sow in them. I also want you all to know this is not an exact fact, just merely a theory I have. I don't want to get sued or blamed for a failed marriage.

My theory doesn't apply to women very well, however. The best way to judge a woman is by her appearance. The way she dresses and her makeup tell me a lot. Again, this is not scientifically proven. But it's also pretty accurate. If a woman wears a lot of makeup, she either is insecure about her looks or has no taste at all. If I want a geisha girl, I'd get one. But too much makeup makes a woman look like a prostitute. And god, women who bathe in perfume make me sick as well. Women should only use light makeup to enhance their natural beauty, not look like a clown.

The women that I avoid are those who dress like sluts. They wear those low-cut jeans and often wear tube tops. They think they have something impressive to show. Now there's nothing wrong of being proud of your body. But you can show it off by wearing nice jeans or a dress. If you dress like a whore, you probably are one.

And before you ladies get pissed off, men can be whores as well. Guys who wear a Speedo on the beach should be horsewhipped. Children go to the beach as well as adults. And if a man is walking around with his dick bulging out of a little bathing suit, he is probably full of himself and has a problem with premature ejaculation. He should also be avoided like the plague.

I mentioned tattoos earlier, but while I'm on the subject of appearance, I'll mention it again. Tattoos look like shit on both men and women. I would never go out with a woman with tattoos. If a woman has a tattoo, the first thing that enters my mind is, she'll fuck anything, right or wrong; that's my first thought.

And the color of hair and hairstyle tell a lot about people. Anyone who has green or pink hair has a few screws loose in my book. The same holds true for haircuts like Mohawks. If someone needs pink hair, Mohawks, or tattoos to draw attention to themselves, then they have some serious personal issues and need help.

I think I can speak for most men on this issue. We want our wives to look like ladies with a flair and elegance that makes us proud to be seen with them. The same holds true for men. Dress nice and make an impression.

Most women don't want a man in cutoff jeans wearing a white undershirt. And while I'm pissing people off, I'll add this: fat/obese people should never wear a tank top or shorts in public. My god, that makes me sick. If you're overweight, do us all a favor and cover it up. Nothing looks as bad as a beer belly wearing a tank top or a fat ass hanging out of shorts. That applies to both men and women.

And finally, body piercing. If you think having your tongue, lips, eyebrow, or nose pierced makes you appealing, you are fucking stupid. The whole body-piercing thing seems to be mostly younger men and women. If my child came home with something pierced, I'd lock them in the basement for the rest of their life. That is truly disgusting.

If anything I've said has pissed you off, then you're the ones I'm talking about. If you agree with me, then you're ahead of the game. Learn to love yourself, not mutilate yourself. And, parents, if your child fits any of these characterizations, then put your foot down. Or if need be, put your foot up their ass. That has a way of grabbing their attention.

I think the drive home with Donna helps me appreciate her even more. I know we share some of the same values. But I get to see a side of her that she keeps hidden away most of the time. She really is pretty conservative. The longer we're together, the more I learn about her. The old saying "You don't know someone until you live with them" is true. And maybe even then, you may not truly know them. How many serial killers or rapists, when they're caught, are remembered by friends and relatives as great guys or wonderful women? You see the relatives go on the news programs defending them. Then boom, the DNA proves they were guilty. Now I know that Donna isn't a serial killer or rapist.

I'd bet my life on it. My point is merely that it takes a while to really know someone. I kept parts of my past from Donna because I thought some parts may be tough to explain, and honestly, some weren't important, at least to me. The tree house accident I didn't think was important. I only put it in the book at her insistence. In fact, I've had to go back and rewrite parts because she thought it was important. But if I put every detail of my life in this book, it would be two thousand pages long. So most of this book takes place after I've moved to Olive Grove. Actually, most of it is the past few months.

I'm sure I'll catch hell from my friends in Atlanta or even my brother and sisters for not saying more about that part of my life. I have a great relationship with all my family members, and I do love them. So to cover my ass, I'll tell their names. My brother's name is Kenny. My sisters are Jackie, Joan, and Carol. My nieces are Dena, Mindy, Mary, Lina, and Sharron. My nephews are named Ronny, Davis, Joe, and Charles. I love all of them. I have many good friends that I don't see or hear from much who are still in the Atlanta area. They are Donald, Danny, Saul, Freddy, etc. Too many to name. That's why I took the time to include them here. Maybe if I write another book, I'll start with the beginning or Georgia years. But this book is about my life in Alabama, so I won't mention them much anymore.

I hate books that give you five hundred names for you to try to remember all the characters. Damn, I'm lost again. Where was I? Sorry, I actually had to go back and reread to find out what the hell I was talking about. If I can get lost writing this stuff, I'm sure you're having a hell of a time following along. Sorry! Back to my subject.

It does take time to know someone because we all have things we try to hide, to keep buried. Maybe there are things we're ashamed of. I can honestly say I don't because I've learned from my mistakes.

I knew Donna is intelligent and independent before we married. I didn't know she was as determined as she is. If she thinks a principle is involved, she will fight tooth and nail to get you to see things her way. I admit I caved in and let her have her way on several things in the book. But to me, they weren't as important as they were to her. Maybe it was out of love, because love is strange thing. I don't know what it was that made me love her and not the other woman I dated. I dated strong, independent women before. Hell, that's the type of woman I was always attracted to. But there was something about her that captured my heart. And the longer we're together, the more I love her. And that scares me, but it also excites me. I guess that's why I believe marriage gets better the longer you're together. Trust, respect, and love grow the longer you're together.

However, I do have one concern, and that is whether Donna's sexual appetite will slow after the baby is born. I know that being a mother is a tough job, and she may lose some interest in sex. I just hope having the nanny will help her out. Okay, I admit I'm a horny, self-centered, pussy-whipped, one-woman man. Are you ladies satisfied now? Jeez! I thought so. However, I bet you would like to have a man just like me. Yeah, I thought so. You gals are digging the Ben kind of man now. Self-centered you say? You bet your cute little ass I am. And you ladies love it. You'll admit it sooner or later. Donna is going to kill me now.

Pulling into the carport is a welcome relief. I always love to hear the greeting party that's barking behind the door. But what awaits inside is always a mystery. With two old dogs, five hours alone is tough. Sometimes the dogs will piss or shit in the kitchen. I have forgotten to put papers down, so we may be walking into a mess. I let the dogs out, while Donna watches them. I go in and inspect the damage. Just as I thought, there is a puddle in the kitchen. I get the mop and clean it up. I'm sure it was probably Skipper. He is on blood pressure medicine and also takes a diuretic. I can't blame him; it is my fault for not putting the papers down. Hell, I can't go five hours without taking a whiz. So I certainly can't blame him.

Donna and the crew walk in. Home sweet home. I call my mother to let her know that we've made it home safely. She always insists I do that because she worries about me and the drive, which is what a mother is supposed to do, I guess. I pick up the phone.

"Hi, Mother, we made it home."

"Thanks, Benny. Tell Donna I loved being with her and if she needs me, just call."

I smile to myself, thinking, *I'm sure she will.* "I'll tell her. I love you, Mother."

"Love you too, dear."

I hang up the phone.

"Tell me what, Ben?"

"If you need her to call."

"That's so sweet. She really is nice, you know."

"Yeah, I know."

I also know I'm so fucked now. I have to play nice the rest of my life or have two women giving me hell.

"Ben, have you given any thought about supper?"

"No! But what would you like, Your Majesty?"

"I would like to have a Ben burger and a salad."

"Your wish is my command, my lady."

"Ben, stop with all the royal bullshit."

"Donna, you really are getting a trashy mouth these days."

"And your point is?"

"No point, but it does turn me on."

"Ben, a watermelon turns you on."

"Only the red ones, dear. Remember that."

Donna shakes her head and turns and walks out of the room.

"Where are you going?"

"If you must know, to change clothes and sit on my throne."

"Donna, you need to watch that."

"Watch what?"

"You're starting to develop a sense of humor."

"Well, you need to start cooking or this queen will have you beheaded."

"Which head?"

"The one that houses your brain that you keep in your pants."

"Ouch!"

I start making the hamburgers and explain to Mr. Happy she was just joking.

Donna comes back a few minutes later in her pink sweat suit.

"Donna, will you feed the boys? I'm tired of them staring at me."

Donna starts to fix the dogs their supper, while I'm tossing the salad. Donna puts down the four plates of food for the dogs. I catch a look at her and grin. She catches me.

"What are you smiling about?"

"You remind me of a bologna sandwich I once had."

"Our son has no chance!"

"I disagree, dear. He'll be ahead of the sexual learning curve."

"But what happens when we catch him screwing a T-bone steak?"

"I'll sit him down and tell him to use a cheaper cut of meat."

"You would, wouldn't you?"

"No, I'd actually give him the inflatable doll to practice on."

"Oh my god! I hope your mother didn't see that. You put that away, didn't you, Ben?"

"No, I left it out in the middle of the floor. Of course, I put that away. Do I look like a pervert to you? Wait, don't answer that."

"Ben, you really are funny."

"I hope you mean funny good and not funny strange."

"Ben, you have to admit you're a little weird."

"Well, just a little, but in a good way, right?"

"Yes, in a good way."

"Donna, that's what I love about you. You say the sweetest things. Are you ready to eat?"

"Yes, I'll eat my burger now and have a hot dog later."

"Does that mean what I think it does?"

"Yes, it does, my little burger boy."

We finish dinner and turn on the television.

Donna likes to channel surf, while I like to read the guide. Like a lot of couples, we disagree on what to watch, so you know what happens. She watches *Bridget Jones's Diary* in the den, while I go to the bedroom to watch a special on Area 51. Hey, I love to stretch out on the bed and watch television anyway. Skipper and Dusty come with me, and Sparky and Scruffy stay with her. I have to tell you, I think Sparky and Scruffy are having a gay relationship. I've seen them licking each other's balls. There's nothing wrong with that, though; I'd lick mine if I could. God knows I've just about broken my neck trying when I was younger. Okay, I know that's an old joke. But maybe somewhere out there, someone hasn't heard it yet.

The show on Area 51 is a repeat. But I watch it anyway. I've probably seen it as much as Donna has seen *Bridget Jones's Diary*. But it is interesting. And of course, you know I'm semi-obsessed with aliens and UFOs. When the show is over, Donna walks in.

"I'm fixing to grab a shower. You want to join me?"

"Are you inviting me or the burger boy?"

"Whichever one has the most meat."

"Is this enough?" I drop my pants.

"I think that will do nicely."

We go to her bedroom to undress.

"Donna, the next time we go grocery shopping, I'm going to watch your ass when we get to the meat department."

"You don't have to wait. You can watch my ass now."

She bends over, spreading her legs, giving me a clear view of paradise and then some.

I smile, knowing what lies ahead. "You are such a naughty girl, Donna Thompson."

"You don't know the half of it," she whispers something in my ear.

"Really! Are you sure? We've never done that before!"

"Yes, I am."

"Well, okay, we can try."

Sorry to leave you hanging, but I have to leave the rest up to your imagination. But we had a wonderful night.

Monday morning, and I'm awakened by the phone. It's the contractor. He is going to pick up the plans and get started on the addition. I am happy to hear that he is so gung ho about it. I realize most of the early part will be all the prep work. It will be a week or two before the logs get in. But at least it's a start. I just dread listening to all the sawing and hammering. But the sooner they get started, the sooner they finish, so there's a light at the end of the tunnel. The problem is, I haven't found the tunnel yet.

I hear a truck coming down the drive.

It must be the contractor, I think.

Sure enough, Homer is leading the parade of trucks. It looks like they have some heavy equipment too. Damn, I think he means business, which I am happy to see. Today, trying to find a good contractor is like finding a bar in Salt Lake City—in other words, not easy.

Homer gets out of the truck.

"Howdy, Mr. Ben! Nice morning we're having."

I smile and say, "Yes, it is, Mr. Wilkinson. And it looks like you've got half the county with you today."

"Ah, you can call me Homer. Heck, everyone else does."

"All right, Homer it is. I'll get out of your hair, Homer, and let you and your men get started. I'll be in my office downstairs if you need me. Do you guys need anything now?"

"You could point out where we can get power from."

"Sorry, Homer, there's a plug on the porch and also one on the pool deck near the table. And if any of you need to go to the bathroom, the bathhouse has a toilet, and also there's a bathroom downstairs you can use."

"The pool house will do just fine. These boys can sure smell up a bathroom when the mood hits 'em."

I think, *Probably not as bad as Meat.*

I turn and walk toward the basement, realizing I just made my first mistake. You should never get too chummy with people who are doing work for you. They can use their friendship to take advantage of you or do poor work. I guess my saving grace is that Homer comes highly recommended, and also I know, growing up in the South, all about good ole boys. And honestly, most work their asses off. My father was like that. He spent his entire life working in sheet metal. He chewed tobacco, drove a beat-up old truck, and drank beer—tons of it! But he also worked his ass off. So I have faith in Homer.

I go inside to my office to work on my book. Yeah, this one. I keep telling myself to hurry up and finish the damn thing. My friends tell me to hurry up with it as well. I want it to be over with; they just want to make sure they're not going to have to get a divorce lawyer. Okay, I admit it. I tell them I'm spilling the beans on them. They're all scared shitless. I know it's mean, but I enjoy yanking their chain. Plus, they deserve to be tormented a little.

Besides, I think a little fear can be a good thing. Donna once asked me if I had any fears. I told her I didn't, but that wasn't true. I think we all have fears. At the moment, my biggest one is the fear I'll be a bad father. Some mistakes you can correct, but if you raise a child wrong, you can't correct that. There are no second chances. I worry that I may do or say something that may impact him his whole life. That's frightening. I realize wanting to be a good father and actually being one are two different things.

Death is another fear. While I don't fear death, I do fear a long, drawn-out, painful one. I have a fear the world will implode. When I listen to the news, it's always bad. There are so many nutjobs either running countries or seeking nuclear weapons. Sooner or later, they'll wind up in terrorists' hands, and either Israel or the United States will have one go off inside its country. If that happens, it would make 9/11 look like a minor scuffle. I ask myself every day if it's fair to bring a child into this fucked-up world.

You can't fight against hate. While I supported it, along with the war on terror, it is going badly. Pulling out might not be the worst thing to do now. Let them have a civil war. Maybe we should let them kill one another. It's better than killing us! I'm sure the next president will be elected before this book gets published, if it ever does. It's funny thinking about the future since there's little we can do to change it. Maybe if we knew what was in store, we could alter it, but maybe not. Maybe everything is predetermined. Personally, I like to think we can change our future; if not, we're fucked!

Donna pops her head in the door.

"Ben, I'm off to work!"

"Drive carefully, dear!"

"Aren't you forgetting something, Ben?"

"Oh... I love you, dear!"

"When you say it like that, Ben, I almost believe you!" she says sarcastically.

"Sorry, dear, I'm trying to finish up this thing!"

"Well, have fun then. And, Ben, play nice with the contractor."

"Will do, sweetie, and call me if you need anything!"

With that, she leaves.

Okay, I can do some work now, I think. It's funny that I suddenly feel like a married man. Maybe it's that little piece of jewelry on my finger; maybe it's what I feel in my heart. Hell, maybe I've become that man Phil always thought I could be. I just know I'm happy, really fucking happy! Okay, I admit I still should stop saying *fuck* so much. Hey, I didn't say I am fucking perfect—yet! You readers are so nitpicky!

It's funny how time flies when you're having fun or, in my case, not watching the ticking clock! You folks happy now since I didn't say "fucking clock"? Sorry! I had to throw that in since you folks are a big part of the book now.

Hell, Homer has even stayed out of my hair, and that's a lot, considering he's a contractor. Yeah, the hammering is driving not only me but the dogs nuts as well, but at least I know they're working.

The phone rings; I see it's Donna.

"Hi, dear! How's your day going?"

"I'm fine, Ben! How are the contractors doing?"

"Good, I think. They're hammering up a storm and driving me nuts!"

"Well, Ben, you could use earplugs, you know."

"I like the pain! It's my form of penance for being perfect!"

"Oh, I see. I'm not talking to my husband Ben. I'm talking to the book Ben!"

"You got that right, Donna! Are you up for a Ben-and-Ben ménage à trois?"

Donna starts to laugh hysterically. "I'd be surprised you know how to say the word, and I'd love to see how you spelled it in the book!"

"Well, dear, I did spell it like you would spell 'manage a twa,' only I crammed the words together and found that was wrong. So I did the best I could do. An editor can correct it if need be."

"I'm sure that won't be all they correct!"

"Very funny, dear! Barbara Walters should hire you for *The View*! You do realize, Donna, you're wrecking my mojo, don't you?"

"Mojo? I thought you just wrote down whatever pops in your head."

"Hold on a minute!" I begin typing "Donna is a pain in the ass—at times!"

"Sorry, dear. I'm back! Where were we?"

"Ben, what did you just type?"

"Something that just popped in my head, like the way you said I wrote."

"And that was?"

"How much I love you, dear, of course. What else would I write?"

"Maybe 'Donna is a bitch'?"

"Hey, you said that, not me! I would never call you a bitch." *At least not to your face or in the book. I know better! You've got werewolf nails!*

"Have you ever thought it, Ben?"

"All men think it from time to time, except for me. I'm pure at heart!"

"You're full of shit, Ben! You do know that, don't you?"

"Actually, I took a dump this morning, so again, you're wrong!"

"Ben, your bowels could be empty, and you'd still be full of shit!"

"I love you too, dear! Now what is the reason for the call? Phone sex?"

"No, I called to see what you wanted for supper. How does KFC sound?"

"Sounds good too, Donna. You want me to pick it up?"

"No, I'll do it. I'm showing a house near there late this afternoon, so there's no reason on you making a special trip, Ben."

"Okay then! Well, I'll let you go then since I need to go check on Homer. Love you, Donna!"

"Love you too, Ben!"

Back to the book. I'm sure, since I've read books from best-selling authors, as I'm sure all of you have as well, that this book has surprised you. It is different, and truthfully, I wanted it to be. You see, I can only write what I feel. I can make things up, and yes, some things have been embellished. But a lot of it is my truth and my thoughts on topics. To sit down and write a fictional novel or even a biographical one, I cannot do. Those who do this for a living or make money from it, I salute. I know from talking to authors that the truly hard part will be getting it published. However, that doesn't concern me. I didn't write this to make money. I wrote this because I enjoyed the process, so if it doesn't get published, then it won't hurt my feelings. If you are reading it, I hope you look past some things to get to the main focus or lesson (I... preach, for lack of a better word)—that is, love yourself, help those in need, and try to be an example for others. If you do that, your life will have made a difference!

Hurry, Ben, hurry! That's all I could think about. How can life be so good one moment and hang in the balance the next? "I love you, Donna. Please don't die. Please, God, don't let anything happen to her or the baby."

I don't remember anything about the drive to the hospital, except it seemed like it took forever. I park the car and rush into the hospital.

"Can I help you?"

"Yes, my wife, Donna Thompson, was brought in a few minutes ago. She was in an automobile accident."

"Yes, sir. She's in surgery. There's a waiting room on the second floor. You can wait there. The doctors will come out and talk to you after the surgery. The elevator is around the corner."

I run around the corner and rush up the stairs. *Forget the elevator*, I think. I get to the top of the stairs and rush out the door to come up to a nurses' station. "Where's the waiting room for the family of patients in the operating room?"

"Through those double doors on the left."

I run to the waiting room; inside are her parents.

"Ben." Clair, still in tears, throws her arms around me. "Ben, Donna is in bad shape. She has internal injuries. They're going to induce labor. That's all we know now."

"Wayne, what happened?"

"All we know is, someone ran a red light and hit her in the side of her car."

Helpless—that one word describes how I feel. I've felt that way more times than I care to remember: when Jimmy died in high school, when Phil told me he had Alzheimer's, and when my father had his last stroke.

God, I wanted to hit something, to break something, to fucking scream. But what could I do? Nothing but sit, hope, and wait.

Some may think, like Wayne and Clair, that prayers help. I have prayed far too many times only to have them fall on deaf ears. So all I can do is just sit here in the quiet chaos, wait, and hope.

About that time, the door opens. It's a police officer.

"Are you the husband?"

"Yes, I am."

"I'm Officer Bruce."

"What the hell happened? Donna is the safest driver I've ever known."

"Mr. Thompson, your wife was hit by a man driving under the influence of alcohol. He ran a red light and hit her car in the back driver's side quarter panel."

"How is he?"

"We brought him in to be checked out and to have a blood alcohol test, which he failed. Now he's on his way to the police station to get booked."

"So he's okay?"

"Yes, sir."

"That son of a bitch is okay, and my wife and child are fighting for their lives. That's just fucking great."

"I'm really sorry, sir. We'll be in touch. I hope everything works out for you and your family, Mr. Thompson."

"Thanks, Officer Bruce."

With that, he leaves.

"Ben, God hears prayers. Come pray with us."

"I'm sorry, Wayne. I know you believe in God, but he has let me down so many times over the year I just don't have faith anymore. I don't think he'd like to hear what I would have to say now anyway."

I sit back down and think back to high school. My best friend Jimmy and I grew up in the same church and played baseball together; we were like brothers. At that time, he had thoughts about becoming a preacher himself. We were both sophomores at that time. He was several months older and already had his driver's license. He was in love with a sweet girl and had his whole life planned. Jimmy was also always doing something for others. He loved doing little things for the church, whether it was mowing the grass or replacing the screens on the doors. He loved God and was a far better Christian than anyone I have ever met. Then one rainy Tuesday night in the spring of 1978, he was taken away suddenly. His car drove underneath a tractor trailer that had missed his exit and was turning around on our exit. He didn't see it till it was too late. Why him? I asked that question so many times, yet I never found an answer.

The preacher gave the traditional answer they always give: "It was God's will." I've always thought that was a bullshit answer and still do. The truth is, he didn't know. Jimmy was such a great guy with so much to give, so much to live for. Yet God chose to take him from us. Why? Can anyone answer that? After Jimmy's death, I decided I would live for today, live for myself. If God would take a faithful servant like him, then he must not give a shit about the rest of us, how we feel, how I feel.

Some religions teach that everything happens for a reason. Some teach that everything we do and the date of our death are predetermined. I'm sorry, but I don't buy either one. Yes, I believe in God. After all, I have been saved. I'm not sure from what, but I've been saved. I remember the night I accepted Jesus as my savior. I felt my eyes open and this weight being lifted from my shoulders.

However, that didn't last long though. When Jimmy died, the walls came crashing in. Some might say I had lost my faith. And who knows? They may be right. Maybe I never had it to begin with. All I did know is that in a world filled with evil, my best friend was gone, a great friend.

Thinking about Jimmy makes me realize I need to call my best friend David to let him know what had happened. Actually, I just need someone to talk to. I call his number.

"David, Donna's been in a terrible automobile accident."

"What!" After a long pause, he says, "Which hospital is she in?"

"In town," I say.

"We'll be there in about an hour. We're in Roanoke."

Where would we be without friends to lean on in times of need?

I decide I need to take a walk, to get my head cleared. I guess mostly I just need to move around.

"Clair, Wayne, I'm going to see if I can find a soft drink machine. Do you want anything?"

"No, Ben."

"Call my cell if the doctor comes in."

With that, I leave. I hope they don't think I'm insensitive for not being able to sit and wait with them. I just can't sit and do nothing. I just don't do that well. When I'm upset, I've always felt the need to be alone. Not knowing which way to go and not really caring, I start walking down the hallways. With so much adrenaline flowing, my heart is racing. *My blood pressure must be sky-high*, I think, but I don't care. I continue down the hall and make a right turn and see the sign for the chapel. Like walking up to a rattlesnake in the woods, I freeze. *Do I dare go in? Would it really do any good anyway? Well, it can't do any harm*, I think. I walk in. The last time I was in a chapel was at my father's funeral. But this is different. It is a small room, and I am the only one there. There is a quiet peace about it, maybe because it is so dimly lit, I really don't know. I walk up to the altar and kneel.

"God, if you're listening, I need your help. I have failed you so much in life that I couldn't blame you if you didn't listen, except this is not about me. Well, I guess maybe it is. Wayne said we have to leave it up to you. We have to accept your will. I can't accept that. I know I'm a lousy Christian, and if I go to hell, well then, I have no one to blame but myself.

"But, God, Donna is a wonderful woman, and she's carrying our child. She has never harmed anyone, never wronged anyone in her life. If you need to take someone, take me, not her, because I'm the one who has failed you, not her. I admit I don't have any right to ask you to do anything for me. And I know I've only called on you in my times of need.

"But, Lord, I don't have anyone else to turn to. But with Donna and my son, I have a chance to change that. Please give me that chance. I don't think I could ever live without them. I don't want to live without them.

"God, if you spare them, I will never ask for anything else. I know I have to leave them in your hands, Lord. But please, God, let them live. In Jesus's name, I pray. Amen."

I lay my head on the altar and begin to cry. I must have dozed off, because I had a dream of a lifetime.

"Benny." It is the voice of Phil. "I've been sent here to comfort you. You haven't failed God. God places everyone here on earth for a reason—to grow spiritually so you can better serve him in the afterlife. He expects you to fail, to sin. Life is one big test for us on earth. And you know that. He does this so you and everyone else can learn from their mistakes to grow, to learn, and yes, to accept. So in the end, you can better serve not only him but your fellow man."

"But, Phil, you suffered so long. My... my father suffered so long. I don't understand. What can you learn from pain, and how does that help your fellow man?"

"Benny, I wasn't in pain. When I lost touch with reality, I was comforted by a far greater power. While my body was no use to me anymore, it served to help bring my family closer together. Everything does happen for a reason."

"But, Phil, I still don't understand."

"Yes, you do. You just don't want to accept certain things, things that you can't control. You are still the butt-headed kid I first met in some ways. You think you have control, you don't. God crossed our paths for a reason, so I could have a better understanding of my children, and you helped me do that. You needed someone to give you guidance. We grew together. Benny, I loved you as if you were my son, and I still do. God loves you too and always has. That's why I'm here. You need to have faith in yourself, in others, and in God. To do so, you have to realize that faith is just that. You have to truly believe it for it to come true. And you must accept that whatever happens, happens for a reason.

"Remember the day I found out I had Alzheimer's, how you came to my house to cheer me up? You lifted my spirits. We laughed, and we cried together, but you gave me hope. You showed a maturity far beyond your years. Benny, you always wanted to know what your role in life is. The truth is, you've always known. But you're afraid of failure, to feel pain or show your emotions. You've spent your life being what everyone wanted you to be, not who you really are."

"Phil, I don't know who I am."

"Yes, you do. You're a leader, you've always been one. People respect you, look up to you, ask for your opinion. I knew you were different from most of the guys that worked for me from day 1. That's why I pushed you so hard, to bring that out. Benny, you have been blessed more than most men could ever possibly dream of."

"Why then do I have all this tragedy in my life?"

"You have no more tragedy than anyone else. We live, we die. Your problem is accepting things out of your control. That's what you have to get over. Benny, God has blessed you with many gifts. You have insight, you know how to relate to people and their problems, you have compassion, you'll stop on the highway to pick up a stray animal. Remember when the minister at your father's funeral told you he saw a gold aura around you from the pulpit?"

"I forgot about that. How do you know about that?"

"I know, God knows."

"I just thought he said that to me because he wanted me to come to church more often."

"No, it's because he realized that you have been blessed. And you have, but now you must accept that blessing."

"Phil, what's going to happen to Donna and my son?"

"Benny, that's not for me to say. Some things are out of my hands, but not out of yours. Benny, I have to go."

"Wait, Phil, one more question."

"No, Benny, you don't have to be a minister to be a leader."

"How did you know what I was going to ask?"

"I know you remember. Use your gifts to help others in need. What you gain will be more precious, more gratifying than anything you've ever done. And the reward will be greater than anything you can imagine."

My cell phone rings.

I wake up.

"Ben, the doctor is on his way in."

"I'll be right there." I rush back to the waiting room.

"Ben, where have you been?" Clair says.

"I got lost in something. I'm sorry."

In walks a doctor still in his surgical garb. "Are you Ben?"

"Yes, I am!"

"I'm Doctor Hampton. I'm the neurosurgeon that operated on your wife. She has suffered a lot of serious injuries—a lacerated liver, broken ribs, and the most severe injury is a fractured skull. She has a lot of fluid that has built up on the brain. We had to insert a tube to relieve the pressure."

She's still alive. That is enough for me. "Doctor Hampton, what's the prognosis on her? How's the baby?"

"I'm sorry, I should have told you the baby is fine, just a few weeks premature. The fact that the baby escaped injury is a miracle in itself."

"What about Donna?"

"Ben, I'm going to be honest, it doesn't look good. The next forty-eight hours are going to be critical. Right now she is in a coma, and there's no way to know for certain how much, if any, brain damage was done. If she survives the next two days, there's a fifty-fifty chance of survival."

"Can I see her and the baby?"

"Yes, the nurse will take you back."

"Thanks, Doc." I swallow hard and try to pull myself together. *I must be strong*, I tell myself. *I must*.

The nurse asks me, as we walk down the hall toward the back of the hospital, to take the elevator to the fourth floor.

"Who do you want to see first?"

"I want to see our son so I can tell her about him."

We walk quietly to the nursery and through the sliding glass door.

"That's him." She points over to an incubator.

I walk over quietly. I feel a tear running down my cheek. "God, he's beautiful," I say aloud.

The nurse walks over and says, "Yes, he is! Have you named him yet?"

"No, but I think I'll name him right now. His name is William Philip, but we'll call him Phil." I start to cry as I stare down at him. "Can I touch him?"

"Yeah, let me get you some gloves and a gown."

I put on the gloves, and she opens the incubator. I reach my hand in and touch his. His little hand wraps around and clutches my finger. I can tell he's frightened. His life has changed as much as mine has the last few hours. I can only imagine what he is feeling at this very moment. My guess is, the same as mine—to hold and be held by his mother.

"Phil, it's going to be all right, son. I promise. I'll always be here for you, and so will Momma." I realize right then and there I am going to will Donna back to health. She would not die. Dammit! She just couldn't.

"Okay, Nurse, I'm ready to see Donna."

We walk down the hall to the ICU. I notice how white the walls are. It's like the tunnel of white light that people who have near-death experiences talk about going through. No pictures hang on the walls either. It's just two blank walls that lead to the most important thing in my life.

We arrive at the intensive care unit. I try to prepare myself for what lies ahead. I clinch my hands into a fist, trying to regain my composure. We walk through the double doors inside. The nurse walks over to the nurses' station to find out which cubicle she is in.

It's cold inside the ICU. It almost feels like death. There's a sickly aura to it, almost surreal. With the hum of running machines, I begin to realize then that these machines are keeping these people alive, including Donna.

The nurse comes over to me. "She's over here."

We walk to a cubicle in the corner. There's a clear plastic drape used for a door. It reminds me of the movie *The Boy in the Plastic Bubble*. I swallow hard and walk inside.

I see her lying on a bed. I really couldn't tell it was her. For a moment, I hope they had made a mistake. But I know. I know in my heart it is her. She has so many tubes running in and out of her body. Her face is swollen and bruised. She has cuts on her arms. But she is alive.

I walk over to the bed and stroke her hand gently to not disturb the IV going into it.

"Ben," the nurse says, "some people believe that people in a coma hear us, so go ahead and talk to her. I'll leave you alone." With that, she walks out of the cubicle.

"Donna, I just saw our son. He's... he's almost as beautiful as his mother is. God, I can't wait for you to see him. His hands are so tiny yet still perfect. His eyes are filled with the same pure, unconditional love like yours is. The doctor said it was a miracle he wasn't hurt at all in the accident. Donna, when I saw him, I knew what we had to name him. I hope you won't be mad, but I want to name him Philip and call him Phil. I know you'll understand when I tell you the reason why.

"Donna, the nurse said that you may be able to hear me. If you can, darling, you have to fight through this. You just have to fight—for me, for our son, and for our life together. I can't raise our son alone. I need you! I need you there with me, for me, to help me. Donna, you may not know this, but I think you do. You are my rock. I have never admitted this to you, but I'm not afraid to now. I need your love, I need your strength. I can't go through this life alone without it, without you."

I begin to feel the tears running down my cheek then dripping onto my arm. For someone who always controlled his emotions, I am a wreck. And I don't give a shit.

"God, please, please let her hear me. Donna, the doctor said you're hurt badly and there's a chance you could die. I can't... I won't let that happen. You have to fight this, you can't give in. I need you, Phil needs you. We're a family now.

"Donna, I love you more than life itself. Please don't give up. Don't ever give up!"

About that time, one of her fingers moves. I don't know if it is involuntary or if she has heard me. I believe she has heard and understood. Maybe this is my sign that everything is going to be okay.

The nurse walks in. "Mr. Thompson, we need to leave now."

With that, we walk back to the waiting room. Inside are David and Julie. They come over and give me a hug. Sometimes a hug says a lot more than words ever can.

"Have you eaten anything?"

"No, I haven't."

"Well, let's go eat. You'll need to keep your strength up."

Even though I am not hungry, I realize David is right. I've got to remain strong for Donna and Phil.

"All right, as long as it isn't sushi."

"You got it, bro!"

Sometimes I think back to my times at the islands, about all the stupid things I did, like jumping off bridges, how I could have easily gotten killed or paralyzed. I guess we can learn from our mistakes, if we live through them. I realize in my life, I've made my share. Would I jump off a bridge now? No way.

It's also ironic that Donna has been injured by someone driving under the influence of alcohol. Too many times I've driven home after having too many drinks. I guess someone is looking out for me and the other drivers on the road. I've never been stopped, much less arrested, for DUI. How would I feel if I hurt or killed someone while driving drunk? I would never be able to forgive myself. I wonder, How does the driver that injured Donna feel? What's going through his mind? Does he have any remorse?

I guess I need to know. I call and leave a message for Officer Bruce to call me.

After eating, David and Julie take me back to the hospital. They offer to stay with me, but I tell them to go home. I'll let them know if anything happens.

In the waiting room, my cell phone rings.

"Mr. Thompson, this is Officer Bruce. I'm returning your call."

"Yes, sir. I'm sorry to bother you, but there's something eating at me. The man that hit Donna, who is he? I guess I need to know something about him."

"Well, his name is Jonathan Smith. He's thirty-eight. He works at the mill in town. It's all in the report."

"Is this his first DUI?"

"No, actually it's his third, his second accident under the influence."

I wish now I hadn't called; I can feel the anger coming back. "How? How can a man have two DUIs and still have a license to drive?"

"He pleaded no contest on the first offense. The second one with the accident, he lost his license for six months."

"Six months?"

"Mr. Thompson, I know you don't want to hear this, but that's how the system works. Judges don't want to put whom they feel are productive people in jail for what they consider minor offenses."

"Minor offenses?"

"Yes, but if it's any consolation to you, Mr. Smith will probably get jail time with this offense."

"How much time are we talking about?"

"I don't know. I'm not the DA, but it's usually based on the severity."

"You mean, if someone dies, they'll get more time than if someone lives."

"Yes, it's not a perfect system, but that's the way it works."

"Thank you, Officer Bruce." With that, I hang up.

Sitting in the waiting room has given me time to think back about my life. Growing up, I was a pretty normal boy. I loved sports, played army, and caught fireflies in the summer, although I had my share of accidents—like a bicycle wreck that required stitches (I still carry a scar above my left eyebrow as a reminder) and falling out of the tree house at the age of nine (that one almost killed me). Somehow I always knew that I was different from the other kids. I wasn't the best student or the best-looking guy in class or even the best athlete. But I was different—different in a good way. I didn't need or want to be accepted by the in crowd. I always knew I was in. In what was a different story.

I've also had a number of psychic experiences along the way that I've passed off as mere coincidences. Some have saved me from harm. Others are more like a déjà vu experience. Could it be that Phil was right? I mean, I'm the leader of the softball team. Granted, that isn't much. I don't bitch when things don't go our way. I try not to get emotional when times get rough. That would show weakness. Sure, at times I'm tough on the guys; I may even yell, but I never lose hope.

Maybe that's why the deaths of Jimmy, Phil, and my father took the toll on me. I can't accept the finality of death because in death, all hope is gone. It is true I can't accept things I can't control. Maybe it's because I think we somehow control our own destinies. It may be that deep in our souls, we decide when to call it quits. Maybe that's why I know Donna won't die. I just have the sense that as long as I fight, she will too. And this feeling gives me hope like I've never experienced before.

Since I've started writing this book, so many things in my life have changed. Maybe it's because I've changed. Maybe the book has helped open my eyes for the first time to really see inside of myself. Hopefully, some of you may have even taken a closer look at yourselves as well.

I've come to realize what's truly important in life, at least in mine. It's not being wealthy or having great power. It's being loved and giving love. That's why Donna has to survive. While I've known a lot of women in my life, I've never known their souls. And Donna and I have this connection that transcends life. I know that may sound funny, but it's true. It's a bond that I've never known before or ever will again.

I decide to go home. I have a number of calls to make. And to be honest, I need to get my shit in order.

"Wayne, why don't you and Clair go home? I'm going to. The nurse will call if there's any change."

"Ben, we can't leave her."

"Clair, I'm telling you, Donna is going to come through this, I just know it. Besides, you're going to need some rest. You already look exhausted. We have to be prepared for the long haul."

"You're right, Ben. Call us if there's any news."

"I will! Just drive carefully!"

I drive slowly home. I pull over at the intersection where she had her accident. Some glass still glimmers on the side of the road as the light reflects off it. I can almost relive the accident in my mind. I can picture the truck running the red light and slamming into her car. I reach down to pick up a piece of glass to keep as a reminder—a reminder that I don't ever want to forget: I will never drink and drive again. After Donna gets over this, I want to remember this night. I start to think back to our wedding vows: "For better or for worse, in sickness and in health." I push the "Till death do us part" out of my mind. If anything, this experience has only made my love for her stronger than ever. So I get back in my car and take a deep breath then drive home.

Pulling into the garage, I hear the barks and the pitter-patter of sixteen little puppy dog feet. At least I won't be alone tonight.

I turn on the television to CNN to catch up on the news. Actually, it's just to hear someone talk. There's been another suicide bombing in Israel. I'll never understand why someone takes innocent lives and then kills themselves, all in the name of God. I don't know if I'm right when it comes to my religious beliefs, but I believe there is only one God. I don't think God is Baptist, Catholic, Jewish, Muslim, Hindu, or any other religion. God is God, pure and simple. It doesn't matter what name you call him—Buddha, Allah, Jehovah, or Bob. You can worship God however you choose, but you should never kill in his name. I guess I'm disturbed that while two people I love fight for life, some brainwashed idiot takes his own plus eleven innocent lives with him. So much for television. I'll try to get some sleep.

Lying in bed, I realize my nerves are supersensitive. I can hear the ticktock of the grandfather clock in the living room. I hear the ice maker kick on then off. I even notice Sparky's snoring. I spend most of the night watching the minutes change on the digital alarm clock, realizing that each minute that passes is a minute that's lost forever and that in a lifetime filled with years, days, and hours, every minute is precious and can never be replaced. In one sense, I have never felt so alone in my life. Yet I've never had more to live for, to look forward to. While I feel helpless in my fear, I don't feel hopeless. And I know I have to be strong, yet I'm not sure where to draw the strength.

I decide that since I can't go to sleep, I'll try to put my feelings on paper. I came up with this. It has no title.

> There've been times in my life
> when I've felt so alone.
> But when you became my wife,
> your love made me strong.
> From the first day we met,
> I knew you were meant for me.
> And, Donna, I can never forget
> how your love set me free.
> You've given me hope
> with your unconditional love.
> You're my lifesaver, my rope,
> sent from heaven above.
> You've given so much, with so much left to give.
> So, Donna, for me, for Phil, you just have to live.

With that, I am able to sleep. I awake the next morning at eight o'clock. I let the dogs out to do their business and walk out to pick up the paper. I decide to have a light breakfast before heading back down to the hospital. I read the paper over a bowl of cereal. There on page 8 is a small article (actually, it is more of a note) about the accident. I am happy to see that her name wasn't mentioned. It did, however, say Mr. Smith's blood alcohol was 0.22, nearly three times the legal limit.

After putting food down for the dogs, I make my way for the hospital. For some reason, I feel like I'm in a daze; maybe the shock hasn't worn off yet. Either way, I realize it's going to be a long day, so I stop for some reading material. As I start to get out of my car at the bookstore, my cell phone rings. It's a hospital phone number.

"Hello."

"Mr. Thompson, this is Nurse Franklin. Dr. Hampton asked me to call to see if you could come to the hospital. There's been some change in your wife's condition."

Change? That could either be good or bad, I think. "I'm on my way."

287

I haven't thought about asking the nurse for details, but that could take too long. And if it's bad news, I don't want to know anyway. I forgot to ask if they had called Wayne and Clair, so I call them.

"Wayne, the nurse called and said the doctor wanted to see us at the hospital. There's been some kind of change in Donna's condition."

"Did she say what?"

"No, I didn't ask."

"We'll be there in ten minutes."

I am only two or three minutes away myself.

I manage to find a parking space right away and run inside. I make my way to the fourth-floor ICU. Nurse Franklin greets me and walks back to the ICU with me. We walk past the nursery. The curtains are open, and I glance inside to spot my son. God, I still can't believe I'm a father. Inside the ICU, I see that Dr. Hampton is talking to one of the nurses at the nurses' station.

"I'll tell Dr. Hampton you're here," Nurse Franklin says.

"Thank you." I look to the corner where Donna is to see if I could tell anything. But I couldn't.

Dr. Hampton walks over. "Ben, thanks for coming. Donna's condition seems to have stabilized somewhat. I'm not saying she's out of the woods, but she is in a lot better shape than last night. We were lucky the accident happened so close to the hospital. Had she been farther away, she probably wouldn't be alive now."

"Doc, what are we looking at long term?"

"Ben, that's hard to say. She could have complications from the surgery."

"Such as?"

"Well, blood clots are always a concern, of course."

"We really won't know anything unless she comes out of the coma."

When Dr. Hampton said that, I remember reading about people who survived accidents only to live the rest of their lives in a coma.

"Doc, is there anything we can do to help bring her out?"

"Comas are a strange thing. Some people come right out, others may come out months or even years later. And some, unfortunately, never come out."

"Can I see her?"

"Sure, I was going to look in on her anyway."

We walk over to the cubicle and push aside the plastic drape. I couldn't help but notice her eyes are open.

"Donna," I say, hoping to get a response.

She just continues to stare blankly at the ceiling. I know that stare; my father, in the last few months he was alive, had that same look.

Dr. Hampton walks over and shines a light into her eyes.

I notice all the machines. My eyes become fixed on the machine that monitors the blood pressure and pulse. Its numbers are red, like the numbers I watched last night on the clock.

Dr. Hampton is looking at some kind of printout. "Ben," he says, "she has good brain activity." His words bring me out of my self-induced trance.

"What did you say, Doc?"

"She has brain activity."

About that time, Wayne and Clair walk in.

"How is she, Ben?" Wayne asks.

"Well, she's stabilized somewhat, and she has brain activity. Right, Doc?"

"That's right. We're just waiting for her to come out of the coma. We'll know more then. Ben, I have to make my rounds. Here's my pager number if you need to reach me." With that, he hands me a card with his number on it.

Clair walks over to Donna's bed. "My baby," she says as she strokes the side of her face. Tears are rolling down her cheeks. I guess no love transcends that of a mother for her child.

"Clair, I think we should all take turns sitting with Donna around the clock."

"Like a vigil?" she says.

"Yeah, like a vigil."

For some reason, I couldn't remember what it was called.

"I'll call some of her friends to also help out." Since Clair and Wayne had driven farther, I would leave and come back later. "Call me if there's any news."

I walk to the nursery. I decide to knock on the door. A nurse walks over and opens the door.

"Can I help you?"

She is a different nurse from the one before. Her last name is Jacobs.

"I just wanted to know if I could see my son. I'm Ben Thompson. That's him over there." I point him out.

"Sure, you can. That little guy has been through a rough time," she says.

289

"Yes, he has."

"How is your wife doing?"

"Well, she's still fighting."

"That's good. You can hold him if you like."

When she said that, I almost pass out. You see, I have a fear of babies. I'm afraid I'll drop them or squeeze them too tight.

"I, uh, am not sure about that. I, um, have never held an infant, Nurse Jacobs."

"Honey, if you can make 'em, there's no reason not to hold 'em. Sit over in the rocker. I'll bring him over."

I walk over and take a seat. My hands are already sweaty. She walks over with Phil. The moment is at hand.

"Put your arm under his head like this. There you go. You're a natural."

I can't believe it. My fear is washed away from the adrenaline rush of him being in my arms. This little guy is my son, so small, so fragile. I start to cry. I'm not a man who is used to showing emotion. But I just couldn't help it.

I take his tiny, little hand in mine. I imagine taking him fishing or just tossing a baseball around, teaching him to ride a bike, drive a car. I think back to when my father taught me how to ride a bike. I can imagine watching him run downstairs on Christmas to open his presents. But what I imagine, what I want most is the three of us being a family. I mean, most fairy tales end happily ever after, right? Phil begins to cry. "Nurse."

She comes over to take him. "I think he's hungry," she says.

I think, *Well, he is like his old man after all.* I get cranky as hell when I'm hungry.

She takes him over and begins to feed him from a bottle. I can't help but think about Donna feeding him. She so much wanted to breastfeed him. She had read books about the importance of breastfeeding in the first few months of the baby's life. I guess that's not going to happen now with all the medications that she's given. But the most important thing she can give him is her love. And when she wakes up from this ordeal, he will be showered with it.

I start making my calls. Money can buy a lot of things in life, but one thing it can't buy is friendship. I know that's been said many times before, but it's true. Since last night, my phone has been ringing off the hook with friends wanting to help. The women at the real estate office have been especially thoughtful. Some will take part with the bedside vigil; all have Donna in their prayers. You can't ask for more than that.

I drive home. I'll make all my calls except to my mother. It's the one I dread most. I know she's going to get emotional. And with lupus, I don't want to cause her to get ill. I decide to wait to see how things work out first. You may think it's a cop-out on my part, and maybe it is, but I'm just trying to protect her. And I have enough on my plate without worrying about her health. A few more days won't make a big difference anyway.

I have a couple more hours till it's time to go back to the hospital. Might as well check out the message board. My eyes light up when I see all the messages from the guys on the team. In a way, I knew there would be some from well-wishers, but I never expected to see some from players on other teams. I realize I'm fairly well-known, but there has to be fifty messages from players outside my team. When we play in a tournament, I talk to a lot of guys. I don't know a lot of their names, but it's always friendly. I mean, when someone walks up and says "How's it going, Ben?" you have to take the time to respond. Plus, I think a lot of them know me from the message board or from my trashy poems. Either way, it is a thoughtful gesture. I decide to post a thank-you. I title it "Thanks."

> Guys, I know you have heard about Donna's accident. While it's been a tough time for me, I've come to realize how often we take little things for granted. Health is one. If you have that, you can overcome any adversity there is. But the thing I've taken for granted most is friendship. Guys, I can't put into words what your friendship means. And I must not forget the ladies either; you have given me so much support the last thirty-six hours. Your friendship means more to me than you'll ever know or I can ever say. So I'll end this before I get mushy with a simple *thank you*.
>
> Ben.

Well, it's time to go back to the hospital. On the way, I think about what I should say to Donna. If she really can hear me, surely there's something I can say that might snap her out of it. But what? Upon arriving, I decide a positive, upbeat approach might work.

I make my way through the maze of hallways, trying a different route. Yeah, I get slightly off course. But I get to see a different part of the hospital. I find the restaurant. I knew there was one here; now I know where it is. Now if I could find the damn elevator. I run into a man I knew from my days at the gym. He's a retired military man, a super nice guy.

"Ray? Ray, how are you doing? Remember me? I'm Ben from the health club." I notice he is wearing a hospital badge with his name on it.

"Yeah, Ben, I remember you. I'm not senile—yet," he says with a grin.

"Ray, do you work here? I'm trying to find the elevator."

"I don't work here. I volunteer twice a week, four hours a day."

"Volunteer? What do you do?"

"I usually take patients who come in for outpatient surgery to check in and from recovery."

"That's great."

"Well, the hospital was good to me when my wife was ill. After her death, I realized I needed to stay active, and I wanted to do something for the hospital, to give something back. Plus, since I need to walk every day anyway, I can do it all at once."

"Well, you look good. Can you tell me how to get to the elevator?"

"Go down to the next hallway, take a left, go down to where it dead-ends, take a right. It's about thirty feet on the right. Why didn't you just go straight when you came into the hospital?"

"Been there, done that. I wanted to take the scenic route. Thanks, Ray."

I was sorry to hear about Ray's wife. I never met her, but he would always talk about her biscuits when we were in the steam room at the same time. And at close to eighty, he is in great shape—not just for eighty, but for any age.

I find my way to the elevator. One thing this experience has done is, it has opened my eyes to everything around me. Here I am, at a hospital, where life begins and ends, where families face both joy and tragedy. I've never really given much thought about that. I guess, like everyone else, I'm too caught up in my own life. I know now that I won't ever take anything else for granted.

As I walk into the ICU, I'm greeted by Clair.

"Ben, the nurses are giving Donna a bath. I'm leaving for a while. Call me if you need me."

"Will do." I stand back and let them finish their work. When they finish, I enter the cubicle and pull a chair over to the bed. The problem with the ICU is, they have no television, no magazines, nothing.

I start my conversation. "Donna, you know all this rest your getting is killing me. If you wake up, I promise from now on, I won't give you a hard time about peeling grapes. Hell, I'll even peel them for you. How about that? Okay, just lie there and let me suffer. You're probably dreaming about lying on the beach somewhere, sipping champagne, having some good-looking muscle head rub suntan oil on you. Jealous, you say? Ha! Not hardly. He's probably gay."

About that time, I hear "Ben, I forgot my keys. See if they're on the table."

"Here they are, Clair."

"Take care of my baby. She's all I have."

"Will do."

As Clair walks away, a little light goes on in my head. Damn, why didn't I think about that before? "Take care of my baby." *My baby.* Of course, that's it.

I walk to the nurses' station. "Nurse, can I ask you to do me a favor?"

"What is it?"

"I want to bring our son in here to meet his mother. She's in a coma, and it may just be what she needs to bring her out."

"I'll have to call and get permission."

"Do whatever you have to. Call Dr. Hampton. Hell, call Dr. Ruth. Just get it done."

I know I may have been tough on her, but this just may work. I go back to Donna's bedside. After what seems like hours, I hear the voice of Nurse Jacobs.

"Mr. Thompson, here is your son."

I look up, and there he is, wrapped in a light-blue blanket. I take him in my arms and walk over to Donna.

"Donna, I want to introduce you to someone. This is our son, Phil." I take his tiny hand and touch hers. Phil begins to cry.

"Mr. Thompson, look." The nurse spots Donna's fingers move as if trying to touch him.

I hand Phil back to the nurse and grab Donna's hand. "Donna, can you hear me? Blink if you understand me."

She does. Sleeping Beauty is awake. Thank you, God, thank you!

"Call Dr. Hampton! Someone call Dr. Hampton!"

Donna makes a curling motion with her finger, and her eyes look toward Phil.

"You want to see your son?" I ask.

She blinks again.

I sit in the chair by the bed, holding Phil. I take her hand and brush it against his face.

A tear begins to form in her eye. I watch mesmerized as it slowly runs down her face. "I love you, Donna, and Phil loves you too."

She tries to speak but could only move her lips. But I could tell she said "I love you too."

Dr. Hampton walks in. "What's all the commotion in here?" he says with a grin.

I guess the nurse that called told him the news.

He walks over to Donna's bed. He shines a light into her eyes.

Her pupils dart as the light shines in.

"Donna, I want you to try to move a finger on your left hand and then your right hand."

She does.

"OK, Donna, I want you to try to move your toes."

I watch in amazement as she obeys the commands.

"Donna, I'm going to hold your hand. I want you to tap the number of the fingers I hold up, OK?"

She blinks in agreement.

First, he holds up one finger. She lightly taps his hand once. Next, he holds up three. Again, she taps him three times on his hand.

"Donna, my name is Dr. Hampton. You were in an automobile accident. I performed your surgery. I'm going to send Ben and the baby out so I can run some tests on you. They'll be in the waiting room, okay?"

Again she blinks.

I walk out of the ICU with the nurse. I have so many more calls to make, happy calls at that.

First, I must call Clair. "Clair, Donna is awake. She moved her fingers, toes, how many everything."

"Ben, slow down. Say it again."

"Clair, Donna came to. She saw and touched Phil for the first time. Then Dr. Hampton came in and got her to move her fingers and toes. Then he held up fingers, and she knew how many he held up."

"Thank you, God! Praise the Lord! Ben, I'm on my way. I'll call Wayne at work."

"Okay!"

That was just the first of many calls I would make and receive the next few hours. I know she still has a long way to go and that she's not completely out of the woods yet. But now I have something I'm not sure I really had before: I have hope.

The next couple of days come and go. With each day, she seems to get a little bit stronger. The doctors now have taken some of the tubes out, but not all of them. When she tries to talk, her voice is still weak. All you hear is a soft whisper, but it's enough for me, although I can tell she's in pain. She tries to cover it up when there are people around. She still winces when she takes a deep breath. And the nurse says she complains of a headache and dizziness when no one's around. All this, Dr. Hampton says, is to be expected and is a good sign.

Well, today makes a week since her accident. Today the doctor wants her to get out of bed and walk. The last remaining tube is removed from her bladder. I arrive at the hospital, not knowing what to expect. I know that I'm nervous as hell, but I can't imagine how she feels, what she's going through. But one thing I do know is, I have to be strong for her.

I get to the ICU. Donna is sitting up in bed. As I approach, I try to be funny.

"Hey there, sexy lady. If you're ever looking to do the nasty, give me a call."

"Sorry, I'm a married woman."

"Damn, your husband is a lucky man. He must be great in bed."

"No, actually he's not. Maybe you can leave me your phone number. I'll call you when he is away." She smiles for the first time in over a week.

"Donna, I can hear you. Your voice is back." Granted, it is still a little raspy. But I could hear her.

"That's not all that's back," says the nurse who walks in behind me. "She ate some breakfast this morning after her walk this morning. She will probably go into a private room."

"Damn, that's great news," I say.

"Ben, you can help me lift her into the wheelchair if you like. I've got to take her to rehab."

"Can I go with her?"

"No. If you went, she might try to do too much."

I guess what the nurse said made sense. I put my arms underneath hers and help her stand. She winces a little from the pain in her ribs.

"How long do you think it'll take, Nurse?"

"Oh, give her an hour or two. I think they'll move her into a private room afterwards."

With that, I decide to leave. When I get outside the hospital, my cell phone rings.

"Ben, this is Mark. Robby called and wanted to know if we were playing in the ISA State Tournament this weekend. He didn't want to bother you."

"Of course, we are."

"Well, with Donna and all, I wasn't sure. I told him we would let him know today."

"Mark, if you would call him, I'd appreciate it. I'm covered up."

"Will do, big guy. How's Donna doing?"

"Well, they're going to get her to walk today."

"Damn, that's good news for a change."

"Yes, it is. I'll talk to you later."

I have forgotten about the softball tournament this weekend. This is what we all play for, the state championship. It will be good for me to get my mind off things. There's still one thing I need to do: find a live-in nanny. When Donna comes home from the hospital, she won't be able to take care of the baby. We had even talked about it before her accident. Now we will need one more than ever. I have no idea where to find one.

It's not like there are nannies around the corner. I decide to check with my lawyer; I know he has one. I'll call his office.

I dial his number.

"Eli Brand's office. This is Jackie. How may I direct your call?"

"Jackie, this is Ben Thompson. How are you doing?"

"I'm good," she says in a sexy voice.

"I bet you are."

We have known each other for years and always flirt with each other.

"Ben, I'm sorry to hear about Donna. I just want you to know she's in our prayers. What can I do for you?"

Any other time, I would say something like "A back rub," but since I need information, instead of an ego massage, I say, "Jackie, I need to find out where Eli found his nanny. When Donna comes home, she's going to need some help with the baby."

"Ben, Eli's in court, but when he comes in, I'll ask him to give you a call."

"Thanks. I owe you one, Jackie."

I couldn't help but smile as I hang up. It seems like years since I've felt like smiling. It seems like my life is finally getting back in order.

So I'm actually looking forward to the softball tournament. As much as I love softball, it has started to wear on me the last couple of years. Just about every weekend from March 1 till the end of September, we're playing ball. And depending on where we're playing, we have to get up earlier to leave for the tournament that most guys have to get up for work. So there's no sleeping in on the weekends. So about this time each year, I start dreading it, except for the state tournaments. That is what we play for. But this tournament is special—not just because it's a state tournament, but because it's my first as a father.

Maybe having a family has given me a different perspective on life. Maybe there is something more important than just winning. I guess when I think about it, maybe I've already won. Think about it. I work at my leisure. I have a nice income. I have a woman who loves me. And who would have ever thought that? Not me. And I have a son who's healthy.

I do have one fear though. What if, when Phil grows up, he doesn't want to play sports? What if he wants to play in the band? Is that scary or what? Before some of you tuba-playing guys get offended, I'm just pointing out my fear. I'm sure your parents are happy you can read music. I'd just rather my son is able to read a defense. But if he wants to play in the band, so be it.

Having a son has started me thinking about so many things. I guess I'll have to tell him about the birds and bees when he's old enough. Can someone tell me why a father-and-son sex talk is referred to as the birds and the bees? That's really bothered me for some time. I have no clue. And how do birds and bees have sex? I've seen dogs and cats. After all, isn't that where doggy style got its name? I guess I'll have to watch *Wild Kingdom* or something to find out. See? I really don't know it all. Damn, I'm starting to feel like my old self again.

I do hope that Phil grows up to enjoy fishing. There's nothing that a father and son can enjoy doing together more. I can't wait to see him bait his own hook, catch his first fish, and tell his first fishing story, about the big one that got away. After all, I'm a master of this, so I'm sure it'll come naturally for him as well. I want him to grow up enjoying all the things nature has to offer but to respect all that lives in it.

However, I hope he doesn't want to be a hunter. Killing animals may be sport for some but not me. Besides, guns are dangerous. While I want him to be able to fire a gun correctly (and I do support the NRA safety is paramount), hunting accidents happen every year, killing and injuring far too many people. Yeah, I know I sound like an overprotective father. And I probably will be. But he is my son. And I will watch out for him.

It's time to check on Donna. She should be finished by now. I go back into the hospital and up to the nurses' station. I see my new friend nurse, Jacobs.

"Is Donna finished with her rehab?"

"Yes, she did very well. She's been moved to a private room. Wait, and I'll get the number for you." She goes back to the nurses' station and looks on the computer.

I have a newfound respect for hospitals, especially for nurses. They don't get paid nearly enough. They have to put up with cranky doctors, angry patients, and their families. But they always seem so pleasant and willing to help. I think we all should make a point to try to treat them better. I really do.

"Mr. Thompson, she's in room 2469."

"Thanks, Nurse," I say, laughing.

"What's so funny?"

"Just the room number. Two, four, sixty-nine. Get it?"

She smile and says, "It's been a while, hasn't it?"

"Yes, it has, but it's worth waiting for."

"Nurse Jacobs, one more thing."

"What's that?"

"Thanks for being so nice to me and taking care of Donna."

"That's my job."

With that, I walk toward the elevator. The Disney song "Zip-A-Dee-Doo-Dah" pops into my head. And as the song says, "My, oh my, what a wonderful day."

I get to the room. On the door, there's a sign Bath in Progress.

Damn, they give a lot of baths in the hospital, I think. So I wait outside the door.

After about ten minutes, a male nurse walks out. I admit the first thought was, I didn't like another guy giving my wife a bath. Then I realize I was being jealous. Me jealous? That's a first. I open up the door, and she's lying on the bed in a bathrobe, watching *All My Children*. I walk in.

"Aha, don't think I don't know."

"Know what?" she says.

"I saw that beefy male nurse leaving your room with a smile on his face."

"Well, I guess there's no need lying to you then. I didn't want you to find out this way. But since you have, I guess I should be honest with you. Damn, he's got skills. What he can do with a washcloth is pure heaven." She throws her head back. "Got a cigarette?"

"Okay, that's enough, Julia Roberts."

She smiles. God, I love to see her smile.

"How did rehab go?"

"It was hard, but I walked around some and did some small exercises."

"Good. Is there anything I can do?"

"No, they're going to bring Phil down in a little while. I just want to hold him."

Damn, now I wish my cell phone had a camara. "Donna, I'll be right back." I leave the room and run down to the gift shop. I want to buy a disposable camera. I want a picture of her holding the baby. I walk in, pick up the camera, and head for the checkout.

"Anything else, sir?"

I look around and see they sell flowers. "Yes, send a dozen red roses to room 2469 and a nice flower arrangement up to the ICU nurses' station."

"Anything on the cards?"

"Yeah, just write 'Thank you for all the work you've done' on the one to the nurses' station. And on the roses for 2469, write 'I love you with all my being.' Sign it 'Your lifelong grape peeler.'"

"Grape? Like the fruit?"

"Yes, she'll understand." I rush back up to the room. Good. Phil isn't here yet. My cell phone rings. It's Eli. I step outside the room. "Hello."

"Ben, it's Eli. I hear you need a nanny?"

"Yeah, it's going to be a while till Donna gets back on her feet. And I know Rosa has done a great job with Ian and Katy. I just wanted to know what agency you used."

"Ben, ol boy, I can do you one better."

"How's that?"

"Take Rosa. The kids are in school now. We really only use her as a housekeeper now anyway."

"You think she'll come?"

"I'll ask her and let you know."

"Thanks, Eli."

"No problem. I'll send you a bill," he says with a laugh.

"I bet you will."

I walk back into the room.

"Donna, I need to run something by you. Since you're going to need some help for a while, at least till you get over the injuries, I want to hire a nanny to help out."

"Ben, didn't you read about the nanny who shook the baby until he died?"

"Well, Rosa has worked out well for Eli."

"There are not many Rosas out there."

"Well—"

There's a knock at the door. "I have a delivery." It's the roses.

"Put them over there by the window," I say.

"Ben, see who sent them."

I walk over and pick up the card. "Well, it says..." I have to think fast.

> Giving you a bath was a lot of fun,
> from washing your breasts to those tight little buns.
> When you get rid of the hubby, just give me a call.
> I forgot to tell you, my name is Paul.

"Well, Ben, they're beautiful, but his name was Stan, as in the Man."

"Ouch, that hurt. Anyway, Donna, if I could get Rosa, would you consider it?"

"Of course, but I don't think Eli would be dumb enough to let her go."

"Well, remember he is a lawyer."

"You have a point there."

I'm glad Donna feels the same way about lawyers as I do. The door opens up. It's Clair and Wayne; they also have flowers. It's carnations and daisies.

"Put them by the roses, Mom!"

Clair does so. "These must be from Ben," Clair says. She reads the card, "From your lifelong grape peeler."

Donna says, "That's the sweetest thing you've ever said to me."

"Well, I didn't mean it."

"Well, I think this card can be viewed as a written contract, and I will sue."

We all laugh. About that time, a nurse walks in with Phil. The room gets quiet. The nurse starts to hand Phil to Donna.

"Wait." I grab the camera. "Go ahead." I start snapping pictures. I get pictures of everyone with the baby, but mostly just Donna and Phil. I never, in my wildest dreams, thought this day would come. And what lies ahead is anyone's guess. I just know now, I'm ready to accept whatever life throws at me.

I remember years ago reading books by Norman Vincent Peale and Robert Schuller. They were books about the power of positive thinking— you know, the "if life hands you lemons, make lemonade" type. Well, I guess they just take a few years to sink in. Funny how sometimes we make things tougher than they actually are.

But since I'm in a reflective mode, I guess I've found the answer to the song by Foreigner. The song is titled "I Want to Know What Love Is." Now I know. Love is giving it all, without fear, even your life, if necessary. You can love many things—your wife or lover, your country. But with love comes risk. How many soldiers have died out of love for their country? Their love cannot even be measured for they paid the ultimate price for it, for which we should all be eternally grateful to them. My love for Donna and Phil took only me removing the fortress that I had built around my heart—to let someone in, to allow someone to love me. That and that alone allowed me to understand the true meaning of love. And yes, I would die for them or for my country.

I spend the rest of the day watching my son with his mother, listening to Wayne and Clair tell their "when Donna was a baby" stories. I didn't know that Donna would only go to sleep when Wayne would dance with her. I can hear Luther Vandross's "Dance with My Father" playing in my head as he speaks. I can imagine Donna dancing with my son. This may sound funny, and I don't know if I can put it into words, but I feel like what Jimmy Stewart's character in *A Wonderful Life* must have felt—renewed, reborn, awake—or like the old Johnny Nash song "I Can See Clearly Now." But for once in my life, I can see the big picture.

The nurse comes back in to take Phil back to the nursery, and it's time for me leave. I walk out with Clair and Wayne. Donna needs her rest. Outside the room, Wayne begins to speak.

"Ben, when I first met you, well, I didn't like you. I thought you were cocky and that you would use and then hurt Donna."

He sounded like someone else I know, I think.

"Well, Wayne, if it's any consolation, I thought you were a stuffy, religious nut."

"And now?"

"I don't know, maybe a 'not quite as stuffy as I thought,' religious nut. But at least I've always tried to like you," I say with a smile.

"Well, I like you too, especially now that I realize you're perfect for Donna. But I also wish you'd start going to church with Donna when she's back on her feet."

"Wayne, I'll think about it."

"Ben, I know how you feel about churches. I know there is a lot of political stuff that goes on there. That's between them and God. The reason to go is for God. After what has happened with Donna surviving, it has renewed my faith. It may renew yours. The church is, after all, the Lord's house. Ben, you could do so much good there and would be a great help."

"Wayne, honestly, I'm afraid."

"Of what?"

"I really don't know. I wish I did." *Maybe*, I think, *all the barriers aren't down.*

"Ben, will you do me a favor?"

"What's that?"

"Ride with me over to the church."

"Now?"

"Well, first, we'll drop Clair off at the house."

"Not today, Wayne. But I promise once Donna is able, I'll come at least one Sunday."

With that, we say our goodbyes. It's hard for me to try to explain my religious beliefs to others. I'm not even sure I understand them myself. I enjoy the serene feeling of being in a church alone. I guess in a selfish way, I don't want to share my God. It's like being a kid and having an imaginary friend. You can talk to him whenever you're alone, but you don't dare do it around anyone. Some people may think you're crazy. But the main reason is, I don't want to be scrutinized by people who don't understand my views. Religion is a mystery, at least to me.

People are told to believe in a supernatural force that no one has ever seen. What do we really know about God? Where did he come from? Is there just one? Is God of alien origin? The Bible was written by men—probably well-intended men but with an agenda nonetheless. It was not written by God. Sure, Jesus is quoted in the New Testament, but again it's not firsthand. We're pushed to accept whatever the Bible says as divine fact without ever questioning it. That's where I have a problem. Too many stories simply don't make sense. So yes, I have questions. I look at the Bible as more of a how-to guide, how to live your life. I've said this before, so bear with me, but the Ten Commandments are wonderful, moral laws to live by. And Jesus spoke many wonderful truths. But to accept the Bible as the Word of God without questioning it, I simply can't do. It was men from the church who chose what books were allowed in the Bible. We have knowledge of some of the books omitted but not a lot.

About thirty years of the life of Jesus is missing. Why leave that out? The pseudo Christian leaders today want to dictate to you how and what to believe. I don't know if Jesus and Mary Magdalene were married and had a child or not. But it's not hard to believe that Jesus could love a woman. And the truth is, it wouldn't change how most people feel about him. It wouldn't change my view anyway. Just like George Washington was the father of our country, Jesus is the father of our faith. Whether he was married or not should not matter.

My belief is, the Catholic church wanted to keep their priests from marrying and having sex, so they removed any mention of that possibility. Did Jesus have a wife? I don't know, and neither do the leaders bashing *The Da Vinci Code*, both the book and the movie. I mean, if Jesus had a wife, it would piss off the priests and nuns who took the oath of celibacy. And if you ask me, that's foolish anyway. I'm not sure how not having sex can help you better serve God anyway. But *The Da Vinci Code* sent some religious leaders in a state of panic. The ironic thing to me is, they're both books and, in my view, are fiction, at least in parts. It's not hard for me to believe that the authors of the books in the Bible didn't embellish or even make up parts of their stories.

My beliefs are simply this: Does God exist? Yes! Did Jesus die for the sins of mankind? Yes! Do I accept Jesus as my savior? Yes, he is the basis for my faith, and I have accepted that. Is the Bible the Word of God? No! I think it's man's version of the Word of God. I can accept some things as divine wisdom and words to live by but not as divine truth. For the truth about God, I think you have to ask him. If you do and search your heart, you'll find the answer.

To me, being a Christian isn't just going to church or giving money to the church. Your acts make you a Christian. How you treat others and how you live your life are what's important. If hell does exist, then a lot of so-called Christians will end up there. Because some people view church as a social commitment, they think it'll help their image in the community or business affairs, just the way being a member of a country club does. Well, I have news for you. It doesn't work that way. All true Christians carry their church with them at all times. It's called your heart. If you follow it, it will show you the way. The bigger church or temple is only a meeting place for like-minded people. The minister is merely the leader.

You probably wonder how someone with my history can say all this? Well, I've never said I was perfect. And I believe everything I have experienced happened for a reason. Phil is right. You can't learn from what you don't experience. The Bible talks about false prophets, false gods who come in thy name. I like to call them pseudo Christians. They are men and women who use God for their own personal gain. They live in the mansions they bought with money from selling God. I'm not saying it's wrong for a man of God to have money. I'm saying it's wrong to sit in a television studio and ask people to send in money for missions or to keep a television ministry going when you're worth millions or get on a political show and criticize governmental policy. Their egos are the size of the Grand Canyon, and I've seen too many of them fall from grace and out of favor in scandals. There are, however, some men I have the utmost respect for, with Billy Graham being one of them, but they are few and far between.

I realize what I've just said may upset some of you. And I'm sorry if that's the case. But I've tried to be honest with you all through this journey of a book. I have admitted embellishing it somewhat. But I haven't embellished what I truly believe. There is one verse in the Bible that rings true and is fitting to end my tirade on this subject, and this is it: "Seek and ye shall find." But that's up to you.

Watching Donna with Phil has made me realize how much mothers play a part in our lives. A father can love his children with all his heart and be willing to die for them, but a mother's bond is far greater. As men, we can't imagine carrying a child inside us for nine months. We may think we can, but since we can't experience it firsthand, we have to leave it up to our imagination. A woman experiences the child growing inside her. She is one with it. I've said before it is a bond unlike any other.

I realize I have been critical of my mother at times in the book, maybe more often than I should have. But it's not because I don't love her. It's just the opposite. It's just that now at this point in my life, I feel the need to take care of her. I can see the multilevel people taking her money in a scam. But she can't. I can see her health declining. We're almost at a point in our relationship where the roles reverse, when the children have to care for their parents. And my mother is very independent and doesn't want anyone taking care of her. I can't blame her for that because I don't want Phil to have to take care of me either. But sometimes we have to give in. She was and is a loving mother. Maybe she was afraid I would get a girl pregnant in high school and didn't want to see me waste my life. I can accept that. But she was always there whenever I got hurt to comfort me. And I know she has always loved me. And I have always loved her.

Watching Donna with Phil, I realize that she will be the driving force in his life. While I'll have an active role, I could never take the place of his mother. Had she died, not only would I have been devastated, but Phil would have been shortchanged. A child needs his mother. I also know that I will now have to share Donna. That may sound strange on the surface, but it's true. I know some men who are jealous of their children and feel like their wives don't give them enough attention. It's even been the reason some men give for having affairs or even divorce. A man should never ask his wife to choose between him and his children, because given the choice, most women would choose their children, and justifiably so.

When I started out writing this book, it was going to be about men's softball. What it's become now, I don't really know. Maybe a reflection into my soul. I do know that I've grown from the time I first started writing it. I've thought about and said things that I never had before. My intention for writing this book was merely for laughs, but the joke turns out to be on me.

I thought the climax would be winning a state championship and acting like a fool. But so much has changed its start to near finish. With the state tournament knocking at the door, it means very little to me now. Yes, I still want to win it. What a way to close out the book. But the truth is, I've already won. And if I don't get another chance to thank you, I want to do it now. This whole experience, I'm sure, has been bumpy and is maybe not what you expected. But it really is a season in my life.

A couple of days have passed, and now it's time to get ready for the state tournament. Tomorrow is the big day. Usually at this time, I'm starting to get butterflies, but not now. I guess I've been through so much this isn't that big a deal. I still want to win it, mind you. It just doesn't have the same degree of importance that it once did. I haven't told anyone, but this is my last hurrah, that I'm going to give it up, well, until Phil starts Little League—that is, if he wants to play. If he does play, I will probably coach.

In a way, it's a relief; in another, it's a realization that I am getting older. Do I dread getting older? No. I've worked hard to get where I am. I realize I will have to work harder to keep myself in shape and that I can't do all the things I did in high school. But that's the trade-off. I can honestly say that I have no regrets.

I guess this book and my life have been about growth—growth in every sense of the word: mentally, physically, and spiritually. You may or may not like what I've said or how I've said it, but it's who I am. Those who can accept it, then it's great. Those who don't, I won't waste my time on.

I've also decided to submit this book for publication. It may not ever get published, but at least I will have tried. And honestly, I can live with that.

Saturday morning arrives. And today is the day. We're playing for the state championship. David calls me early Saturday morning.

"Ben, I'm going to drive down to the complex. Julie and Lacy are coming with me."

"Okay, I'll see you there."

I didn't know it, but the guys decided to get there early for a team meeting. They wanted to dedicate the tournament to me and wanted everyone to be on the same page.

When I show up forty-five minutes early, everyone is already there warming up. I look at my watch. Damn, I was sure some of the late-night partiers would show up at game time.

"Coach Ben, you're late." I'm not sure who said it; I believe it was Kroy.

"So fine me. I'm going to check in." I see the complex director, Luke Parker, and walk over.

"What's up, dude? Ready to win a championship?" he says. "What's up, dude?" is sort of his catchphrase.

"Yeah, it would be nice for a change. Hell, we've been the bridesmaid too many times."

"Speaking of brides, how's Donna?"

"She's doing a lot better. In fact, she and Phil will be coming home soon."

"Good luck today, Ben. I hope you win it!"

"Thanks. If you get a chance, we've got beer in the coolers." With that, I walk off and start to do the lineup. I get back to the dugout and start to make out the lineup. The guys walk up.

"Coach Ben," Bryan says, "we're sorry about Donna. We want to dedicate this tournament to you and Donna."

"Thanks, Bryan. I just want all you guys to have fun and nothing more. Win it for yourselves and as a team."

That day was a blur in some ways. Maybe it was simply that I was in a daze. I've never seen guys play so hard, running, diving for balls. Every play of every game, they gave everything they had and then some. They bled, they sweat, and they busted their asses till they had nothing left to give. Did we win the tournament? No, we lost in the finals to the Bigtime Ballers. They were just the better team on the field. After we lost and were packing up to leave, I notice guys had their heads hanging down.

Bryan said, "Coach Ben, I'm sorry we let you down. We wanted you to take home the little man."

I smile and say, "Guys, I appreciate the hustle and, truthfully, the sentiment. But I'll be taking the little man home soon enough, and this is just a game! No one here has let me down. Just the opposite. You've been here for me in a time of need. You're all winners, and truthfully, I love you guys!" I could tell my voice is starting to crack. I guess Meat could tell too.

"Let's all go have a beer. I don't need to have a *Brian's Song* moment," he says.

With that, we walk up the hill to the coolers.

The following week, Phil comes home. Three days later, Donna comes home too. I realize my life has changed forever. But it's changed for the better. I no longer have the fear of failing as a father. Failure can only exist if you quit trying. And I will never quit. I will dedicate my life to my family and, yes, to God, to helping those who need it. I will try to learn to make sense out of senseless acts so when I see my dear friends Phil, Jimmy, and others again on the other side, they'll be proud.

"Wake up, Ben. You need to get dressed."

"What the? What time is it, Donna?"

"Time for you to get your butt out of bed and get dressed for church!"

I look up at Donna, and the sunlight surrounds her like she's in an angelic painting. I smile knowing how lucky we both are, but me especially. My only rebuttal? "Yes, dear!"

I realize this ending isn't the cliff-hanger you may have expected or even what I expected. This book simply takes place during a season in my life, and seasons don't truly end; they only change! And this has been my biggest season of change! I've learned much about myself and learned to let go of bottled up emotions I've kept suppressed.

I truly hope I haven't offended anyone with content or language. I tried to stay true to the characters. I need to thank those who rode out the storm with me in this book.

Understand I had a different ending for this book but fate struck and I changed it only because I have to write a second part. Yes I said had to! Until then I have to say…

To Be Continued

CPSIA information can be obtained
at www.ICGtesting.com
Printed in the USA
LVOW12*1843060218
565496LV00005B/59/P